mitudak

BREAD

BY THE SAME AUTHOR

SALT

> OR THE EDUCATION OF GRIFFITH ADAMS

"Ye are the salt of the earth; but if the salt have lost his savour, wherewith shall it be salted?"

—*Matthew* V:13

BRASS

> A NOVEL OF MARRIAGE

"Annul a marriage? 'Tis impossible!
Though ring about your neck be brass not
    gold,
Needs must it clasp, gangrene you all the
    same!"

—*Robert Browning*

E. P. DUTTON & COMPANY

BREAD

BY
CHARLES G. NORRIS
AUTHOR OF "BRASS," "SALT," ETC.

NEW YORK
E. P. DUTTON & COMPANY
681 FIFTH AVENUE

First—twelfth printing ....July, 1923
Thirteenth—sixteenth printing ....Aug., 1923

DEDICATED TO

THE WORKING WOMEN OF AMERICA

CONTENTS

BOOK I

BOOK I

BREAD

CHAPTER I

§ 1

"*One* and two and three and four and—*one* and two and three and four and . . ."

Mrs. Sturgis had a way of tapping the ivory keys of the piano with her pencil when she was counting the beat during a music lesson. It made her little pupils nervous and sometimes upset them completely. Now she abruptly interrupted herself and rapped the keys sharply.

"Mildred, dearie—it doesn't go that way at all; the quarter note is on 'three.' It's one and two and *three* and . . . You see?"

"Mama." A tall dark girl stood in the doorway of the room.

Mrs. Sturgis affected not to hear and drew a firm circle with her pencil about the troublesome quarter note. There was another insistent demand from the door. Mrs. Sturgis twisted about and leaned back on the piano bench so that Mildred's thin little figure might not obstruct the view of her daughter. Her air was one of martyred resignation but she smiled indulgently. Very sweetly she said:

"Yes, dearie?" Jeannette recognized the tone as one her mother used to disguise annoyance.

"It's quarter to six . . ." Jeannette left the sentence unfinished. She hoped her mother would guess the rest, but Mrs. Sturgis only smiled more sweetly and looked expectant.

"There's no bread," Jeannette then said bluntly.

Mrs. Sturgis' expression did not change nor did she ease her constrained position.

"Well, dearie . . . the delicatessen shop is open. Perhaps you or Alice can run down to Kratzmer's and get a loaf."

"But we can't do that, Mama." There was a note of exasperation in the girl's voice; she looked hard at her mother and frowned.

"Ah . . ." Mrs. Sturgis gave a short gasp of understanding. Kratzmer had been owed a little account for some time and the fat German had suggested that his bills be settled more promptly.

"My purse is there, dearie"; she indicated the shabby imitation leather bag on the table. Then with a renewal of her alert smile she returned to the lesson.

"One and two and three and four and—*one* and two and——"

"Mama, I'm sorry to interrupt . . ."

Mrs. Sturgis now turned a glassy eye upon her older child, and the patient smile she tried to assume was hardly more than a grimace. It was eloquent of martyrdom.

"I'm sorry to have to interrupt," Jeannette repeated, "but there isn't any money in your purse; it's empty."

The expression on her mother's face did not alter

but the light died in her eyes. Jeannette realized she
had grasped the situation at last.

"Well . . . dearie . . ." Mrs. Sturgis began.

Jeannette stood uncompromisingly before her. She
had no suggestion to offer; her mother might have
foreseen they would need bread for dinner.

The little music-teacher continued to study her
daughter, but presently her gaze drifted to Mildred
beside her perched on a pile of music albums.

"You haven't a dime or a nickel with you, dearie?"
she asked the child. "I could give you credit on your
bill and your papa, you see, could pay ten cents less
next time he sends me a check . . ."

"I think I got thome money," lisped Mildred,
wriggling down from her seat and investigating the
pocket of her jacket which lay near on a chair.
"Mother alwath givth me money when I goeth out."
She drew forth a small plush purse and dumped the
contents into her hand. "I got twenty thenth," she
announced.

"Well, I'll just help myself to ten of it," said Mrs.
Sturgis, bending forward and lifting one of the small
coins with delicate finger-tips. "You tell your papa
I'll give him credit on this bill."

She turned to Jeannette and held out the coin.

"Here, lovie; get a little Graham, too."

There was color in the girl's face as she accepted
the money; she drew up her shoulders slightly, but
without comment, turned upon her heel and left the
room.

Mrs. Sturgis brought her attention once more cheerfully back to the lesson.

"Now then, Mildred dearie: *one* and two and three

and four and —*one* and two and *three* and four and
. . . Now you have it; see how easy that is?"

§ 2

Jeannette passed through the dark intervening
rooms of the apartment, catching up her shabby velvet
hat from her bed, and came upon her sister Alice in
the kitchen.

There was a marked contrast between the two girls.
Jeannette, who was several months past her eighteenth
birthday, was a tall, willowy girl with a smooth olive-
tinted skin, dark eyes, brows and lashes, and straight,
lustreless braids of hair almost dead black. She gave
promise of beauty in a year or two,—of austere stateliness,—but now she appeared rather angular and ungainly with her thin shoulders and shapeless ankles.
She was too tall and too old to be still dressed like a
schoolgirl. Alice was only a year her junior, but Alice
looked younger. She was softer, rounder, gentler.
She had brown hair, brown eyes and a brown skin.
"My little brown bird," her mother had called her as
a child. She was busy now at the stove, dumping and
scraping out a can of tomatoes into a saucepan. Dinner was in process of preparation. Steam poured from
the nozzle of the kettle on the gas range and evaporated in a thin cloud.

"Mama makes me so mad!" Jeannette burst out
indignantly. "I *wish* she wouldn't be borrowing money
from the pupils! She just got ten cents out of Mildred
Carpenter."

She displayed the diminutive coin in her palm.
Alice regarded it with a troubled frown.

"It makes me so sick," went on Jeannette, "wheedling a dime out of a baby like that! I don't believe it's necessary, at least Mama ought to manage better. Just think of it! Borrowing money to buy a loaf of bread! . . . We've come to a pretty state of things."

"Aw—don't, Janny," Alice remonstrated; "you know how hard Mama tries and how people won't pay their bills. . . . The Cheneys have owed eighty-six dollars for six months and it never occurs to them we need it so badly."

"I'd go and get it, if I was Mama," Jeannette said with determination, putting on her hat and bending her tall figure awkwardly to catch her reflection in a lower pane of the kitchen door. "I wouldn't stand it. I'd call on old Paul G. Cheney at his office and tell him he'd have to pay up or find someone else to teach his children!"

"Oh, no, you wouldn't, Janny!—You know that'd never do. Paul and Dorothy have been taking lessons off Mama for nearly three years. Mama'd lose all her pupils if she did things like that."

"Well—" Jeannette drawled, suddenly weary of the discussion and opening the kitchen door into the hall, "I'm going down to Kratzmer's."

§ 3

In the delicatessen store she was obliged to wait her turn. The shop was well filled with late customers, and the women especially seemed maddeningly dilatory to the impatient girl.

"An' fifteen cents' worth of ham . . . an' some of that chow-chow . . . and a box of crackers. . . ."

Jeannette studied the rows of salads, pots of baked beans, the pickled pig's-feet, and sausages. Everything looked appetizing to her, and the place smelled fragrantly of fresh cold meat and creamy cheeses. Most of the edibles Kratzmer offered so invitingly, she had never tasted. She would have liked to begin at one end of the marble counter and sample everything that was on it. She looked curiously at the woman near her who had just purchased some weird-looking, pickled things called "mangoes," and gone on selecting imported cheeses and little oval round cans with French and Italian labels upon them. Jeannette wondered if she, herself, would ever come to know a time when she could order of Kratzmer so prodigally. She was sick of the everlasting struggle at home of what they should get for lunch or dinner. It was always determined by the number of cents involved.

"Well, dearie," her mother invariably remonstrated at some suggestion of her own, "that would cost thirty cents and perhaps it would be wiser to wait until next week."

A swift, vague vision arose of the vital years that were close at hand,—the vital years in which she must marry and decide the course of her whole future life. Was her preparation for this all-important time ever to be beset by a consideration of pennies and makeshifts?

"Vell, Miss Sturgis, vat iss it to-night?"

Fat Mrs. Kratzmer smiled blandly at her over the glass shelf above the marble counter. Jeannette watched her as she deftly crackled thin paper about the two loaves, tied and snapped the pink string. Kratz-

mer and his wife were fat with big stomachs and round,
double chins; even Elsa Kratzmer, their daughter, who
went to the High School with Jeannette and Alice, was
fat and had a double chin. The family had probably
all they wanted to eat and a great deal more; there
must be an enormous amount of food left on the plat-
ters and dishes and in the pans at the end of each day
that would spoil before morning. Kratzmer, his wife
and daughter must gormandize, stuff themselves night
after night, Jeannette reflected as she began to climb
the four long flights of stairs to her own apartment.
It was disgusting, of course, to think of eating that
way,—but oh, what a feast she and Alice would have
if they might change places with the trio for a night
or two!

As she reached the second landing, a thick smell of
highly seasoned frying food assailed her. This was
the floor on which the Armenians lived, and a pungent
odor from their cooking frequently permeated the
entire building. The front door of their apartment
was open and as Jeannette was passing it, Dikron
Najarian came out. He was a tall young man of
twenty-three or -four, of extraordinary swarthy
beauty, with black wavy masses of hair, and enormous
dark eyes. He and his sister, Rosa,—she was a few
years older and equally handsome,—often met the
young Sturgis girls on the stairs or fumbling with the
key to the mail-box in the entrance-way below. Jeannette and Alice used to giggle sillily after they had
encountered Dikron, and would exchange ridiculous
confidences concerning him. They regarded the young
man as far too old to be interested in either of them-

selves and therefore took his unusual beauty and odd, foreign manner as proper targets for their laughter.

Jeannette now instinctively straightened herself as she encountered her neighbor. Upon the instant a feminine challenge emanated from her.

"Hello," Dikron said, taken unawares and obviously embarrassed. "Been out?"

For some obscure reason Jeannette did not understand, she elected at that moment to coquet. She had never given the young Armenian a serious thought before, but now she became aware of the effect their sudden encounter had had upon him. She paused on the lower step of the next flight and hung for a moment over the balustrade. Airily, she explained her errand to Kratzmer's.

"What smells so good?" she asked presently.

She thought the odor abominable, but it did not suit her mood to say so.

"Mother's cooking mussels to-night; they're wonderful, stuffed with rice and peppers. . . . Have you ever tasted them? Could I send some upstairs?"

Jeannette laughed hastily, and shook her head.

"No—no,—thanks very much. . . . I'm afraid we wouldn't . . ." She was going to say "appreciate them" but left the sentence unfinished. "I must go on up; Mother's waiting for the bread."

But she made no immediate move, and the young man continued to lean against the wall below her. Their conversation, however, died dismally at this point, and after a moment's uncomfortable silence, the girl began nimbly to mount the stairs, flinging over her shoulder a somewhat abrupt "Good-night."

§ 4

"Get your bread, dearie?" Mrs. Sturgis asked cheerfully as Jeannette came panting into the kitchen and flung her package down upon the table. Her daughter did not answer but dropped into a chair to catch her breath.

Mrs. Sturgis was bustling about, pottering over the gas stove, stirring a sauce-pan of stewing kidneys, banging shut the oven door after a brief inspection of a browning custard. Alice had just finished setting the table in the dining-room, and now came in, to break the string about the bread and begin to slice it vigorously. Jeannette interestedly observed what they were to have for dinner. It was one of the same old combinations with which she was familiar, and a feeling of weary distaste welled up within her, but a glimpse of her mother's face checked it.

Mrs. Sturgis invariably wore lace jabots during the day. These were high-collared affairs, reinforced with wires or whalebones, and they fastened firmly around the throat, the lace falling in rich, frothy cascades at the front. They were the only extravagance the hardworking little woman allowed herself, and she justified them on the ground that they were becoming and she must be presentable at the fashionable girls' school where she was a teacher, and also at Signor Bellini's studio where she was the paid accompanist. Jeannette and Alice were always mending or ironing these frills, and had become extremely expert at the work. There was a drawer in their mother's bureau devoted exclusively to her jabots, and her daughters made it their business to see that one of these lacy adornments was

always there, dainty and fresh, ready to be put on.
Beneath the brave show of lace about her neck and
over the round swell of her small compact bosom, there
was only her "little old black" or "the Macy blue."
Mrs. Sturgis had no other garments and these two
dresses were unrelievedly plain affairs with plain
V-shaped necks and plain, untrimmed skirts. The
jabots gave the effect of elegance she loved, and she
had a habit of flicking the lacy ruffles as she talked,
straightening them or tossing them with a careless
finger. The final touch of adornment she allowed
herself was two fine gold chains about her neck. From
the longer was suspended her watch which she carried
tucked into the waist-band of her skirt; while the other
held her eye-glasses which, when not in use, hung on a
hook at her shoulder.

The tight lace collars creased and wrinkled her
throat, and made her cheeks bulge slightly over them,
giving her face a round full expression. When she was
excited and wagged her head, or when she laughed, her
fat little cheeks shook like cups of jelly. But as soon
as her last pupil had departed for the day, off came the
gold chains and the jabot. She was more comfortable
without the confining band about her neck though her
real reason for laying her lacy ruffles aside was to
keep them fresh and unrumpled. Stripped of her
frills, her daughters were accustomed to see her in
the early mornings, and evenings, with the homely
V-shaped garment about her withered neck, her cheeks,
lacking the support of the tight collar, sagging loosely.
Habit was strong with Mrs. Sturgis. Jeannette and
Alice were often amused at seeing their mother still

flicking and tossing with an unconscious finger an imaginary frill long after it had been laid aside.

Now as the little woman bent over the stove, her older daughter noted the pendant cheeks criss-crossed with tiny purplish veins, the blue-white wrinkled neck, and the vivid red spots beneath the ears left by the sharp points of wire in the high collar she had just unfastened. There were puffy pockets below her eyes, and even the eyelids were creased with a multitude of tiny wrinkles. Jeannette realized her mother was tired —unusually tired. She remembered, too, that it was Saturday, and on Saturday there were pupils all day long. The girl jumped to her feet, snatched the stirring spoon out of her mother's hand and pushed her away from the range.

"Get out of here, Mama," she directed vigorously. "Go in to the table and sit down. Alice and I will put dinner on. . . . Alice, make Mama go in there and sit down."

Mrs. Sturgis laughingly protested but she allowed her younger daughter to lead her into the adjoining room where she sank down gratefully in her place at the table.

"Well, lovies, your old mother *is* pretty tired. . . ." She drew a long breath of contentment and closed her eyes.

The girls poured the kidney stew into an oval dish and carried it and the scalloped tomatoes to the table. There was a hurried running back and forth for a few minutes, and then Jeannette and Alice sat down, hunching their chairs up to the table, and began hungrily to eat. It was the most felicitous, unhurried hour of their day usually, for mother and daughters unconsciously relaxed, their spirits rising with the warm food, and the agreeable companionship which to each was and always had been exquisitely dear.

The dining-room in the daytime was the pleasantest room in the apartment. It and the kitchen overlooked a shabby back-yard, adjoining other shabby back-yards far below, in the midst of which, during summer, a giant locust tree was magnificently in leaf. There were floods of sunshine all afternoon from September to April, and a brief but pleasing view of the Hudson River could be seen between the wall of the house next door and an encroaching cornice of a building on Columbus Avenue. At night there was little in the room to recommend it. The wall-paper was a hideous yellow with acanthus leaves of a more hideous and darker yellow flourishing symmetrically upon it. There was a marble mantelpiece over a fireplace, and in the aperture for the grate a black lacquered iron grilling. Over the table hung a gaselier from the center of which four arms radiated at right angles, supporting globes of milky glass.

Mrs. Sturgis' bedroom adjoined the dining-room and was separated from it by bumping folding-doors, only opened on occasions when Jeannette and Alice decided their mother's room needed a thorough cleaning and airing. The latter seemed necessary much oftener than the former for the room had only one small window which, tucked into the corner, gave upon a narrow light-well. It was from this well, which extended clear down to the basement, that the evil smells arose when the Najarians, two flights below, began cooking one of their Armenian feasts.

In the center of the apartment were two dark little chambers occupied by the girls. Neither possessed a window, but the wall separating them was pierced by an opening, fitted with a hinged light of frosted glass which, when hooked back to the ceiling, permitted the necessary ventilation. These boxlike little rooms had to be used as a passageway. The only hall was the public one outside, at one end of which was a back door giving access to the kitchen and the dining-room, and, opposite this, a front one, opening into the large, commodious sitting-room, or studio—as it was dignified by the family—in which Mrs. Sturgis gave her music lessons.

It was this generous front room, with its high ceiling, its big bay window, its alcove ideally proportioned to hold the old grand piano, which had intrigued the little music-teacher twelve years before, when she had moved into the neighborhood after her husband's death and begun her struggle for a home and livelihood. Whether or not the prospective pupils would be willing to climb the four long flights of stairs necessary to reach this thoroughly satisfactory environment for the dissemination of musical instruction was a question which only time would answer. Mrs. Sturgis had confidently expected that they would and her expectations had been realized. The dollar an hour, which was all she charged, had appealed to the more calculating of their parents; moreover Henrietta Spaulding Sturgis was a pianist of no mean distinction. She was a graduate of the Boston Conservatory, was in charge of the music at Miss Loughborough's Concentration School for Little Girls on Central Park West, and was the accompanist for Tomaso Bellini, a well-known in-

structor in voice culture who had a studio in Carnegie
Hall. These facts the neighborhood inevitably learned,
and that lessons at such a price could be had from a
teacher so well equipped was confided by one shrewd
mother to another. The stairs were ignored; a little
climbing, if taken slowly, never hurt *any* child!

But while year after year it became more and more
advertised that bustling, round-faced, cheerful Mrs.
Sturgis *did* have charge of the music at Miss Loughborough's school on Tuesdays and Fridays of each
week, and *did* play the accompaniments for the pupils
of Signor Bellini at his Carnegie Hall studio on Mon-
days and Thursdays, no one suspected that sharp Miss
Loughborough handed Mrs. Sturgis a check for only
twenty-five dollars twice a month and that thrifty
Signor Bellini paid but five dollars a day to his accompanist. Wednesdays and Saturdays were left for
private lessons at a dollar an hour, and although Mrs.
Sturgis could have filled other days of the week with
pupils, Miss Loughborough and Signor Bellini represented an income that was certain, while nothing was
more uncertain than the little pupils whose parents
sent them regularly for a few months and then moved
away or summarily discontinued the instruction often
without explanation. Jeannette and Alice had urged
their mother repeatedly to drop one or the other of her
close-handed employers and take on more pupils, but
to these entreaties Mrs. Sturgis had shaken her head
with firm determination until her round little cheeks
trembled.

"No—no, lovies; that may be all very well,—they
may be underpaying me,—perhaps they are, but the
money's *sure* and that's the comfort. It's worth much

more to me to know *that* than to earn twice the amount.''

It was the dreary hot summers that Mrs. Sturgis and her daughters dreaded when Miss Loughborough's school closed its doors and Signor Bellini made his annual pilgrimage to Italy, and the little pupils who had filled the Wednesday and Saturday lesson hours drifted away to the beaches or the mountains. July and August were empty, barren months and against their profitlessness some provision had to be made; a little must be put by during the year to take care of this lean and trying period. But somehow, although Mrs. Sturgis firmly determined at the beginning of each season that never again would she subject her girls to the self-denials, even privations, they had endured during the summer, every year it became harder and harder to save, while each summer brought fresh humiliations and a slimmer purse. Even in the most prosperous seasons the small family was in debt, always a little behind, never wholly caught up, and as time went on, it became evident that each year found them further and further in arrears. They were always harassed by annoying petty accounts. Miss Loughborough's and Signor Bellini's money paid the rent and the actual daily food, and when a parent took it into his or her head to send a check for a child's music, the amount had to be proportioned here and there: so much to the druggist, the dentist and doctor; so much to the steam laundry; so much to the ice company and dairy; so much for gas and fuel.

Emerging from the chrysalis of girlhood, Jeannette and Alice were rapidly becoming young women, with a healthy, normal appetite for pretty clothes and amusement. These were simple enough and might so easily have been gratified, Mrs. Sturgis often sadly thought, if her income would keep but a lagging pace with modestly expanding needs. It required a few extra dollars only each year, but where could she lay her hands on them? When a business expanded and its earnings grew proportionately, an employee's salary was sure to be raised after a time of faithful service. Mrs. Sturgis did not dare increase the rates she charged for her lessons. She felt she was facing a blank wall; she could conceive of no way whereby she might earn more. Skimping what went on the table was an old recourse to which she and her children were now thoroughly accustomed. She did not see how she could possibly cut down further and still keep her girls properly nourished.

§ 5

She watched them affectionately now as they finished their dinner, observing her older daughter's fastidious manipulation of her fork, the younger one's birdlike way of twisting her small head as she ate. A fleeting wonder of what the future held in store for each passed through her mind. Jeannette was the more impetuous, and daring, was shrewd-minded, clear-thinking, efficient, was headstrong, and actuated ever by a suffering pride; she would undoubtedly grow into a tall, beautiful woman. Alice,—her mother's "brown bird,"—seemed overshadowed by comparison and yet Mrs. Sturgis sometimes felt that Alice, with her simpler, unexacting, contented nature, her gentle faith, her meditative mind, was the more fortunate of the two. She, herself, turned to Jeannette for advice, for discussion of ways and means, and to Alice for sympathetic understanding and uncritical loyalty. They were both splendid girls, she mused fondly, who would make admirable wives. They must marry, of course; she had brought them up since they were tiny girls to consider a successful, happy marriage as their outstanding aim in life; she had trained them in the duties of wives, even of mothers, but she shuddered and her heart grew sick within her as she began dimly to perceive the time approaching when she must surrender their bloom and innocence and her complete proprietorship in them to some confident, ignorant young male who would unhesitatingly set up his half-baked judgment for his wife's welfare against her hard-won knowledge of life. Yet both girls must marry; her heart was set on that. Marriage meant everything to a girl, and to the right husbands, her daughters would make ideal wives.

With the speed of long practice, the remains of the dinner were swept away and the kitchen set to rights. Both girls attempted to dissuade their mother from performing her customary dish-washing task, urging her that to-night she must rest. But Mrs. Sturgis would not listen; she was quite rested, she declared, and there was nothing to washing up the few dishes they had used; why, it wasn't ten minutes' work! She invariably insisted upon performing this dirtier, more vigorous task; Alice's part was to wipe; Jeannette's to clear the table, brush the cloth, put away the china and napkins, and replace the old square piece of chenille curtaining which had for years done duty as a table cover. Then there was the gas drop-light to

set in its center, and connect with the gaselier above
by a long tube ending in a curved brass nozzle that
fitted over one of the burners. Where this joining occurred, there was always a slight escape of gas, and
it frequently gave Mrs. Sturgis or her daughters a
headache, but beyond an impatient comment from one
of them, such as "Mercy me! the gas smells horribly
to-night!" or "Open the window a little, dearie,—
the gas is beginning to make my head ache," nothing
was ever done about it. It was one of those things
in their lives to which they had grown accustomed and
accepted along with the rest of the ills and goods of
their days.

Mother and girls used the dining-room as the place
to congregate, sew, read or idle. They rarely sat
down or attempted to make themselves comfortable in
the spacious front room. It was not nearly so agreeably intimate, and they felt it must always be kept in
order for music lessons and for rare occasions when
company came. "Company" usually turned out to be
a pupil's mother or a housemaid who came to explain that little Edna or Gracie had the mumps or
was going to the dentist's on Saturday and therefore
would not be able to take her lesson, or a messenger
from Signor Bellini to inquire if Mrs. Sturgis could
play for one of his pupils the following evening. Such
was the character of the callers, but the fiction of
"company" was maintained.

The group Mrs. Sturgis and her daughters made
about the dining-room table in the warm yellow radiance of the drop-light was intimately familiar and
dear to each of them. There was always a certain
amount of sewing going on,—mending or darning,—

and hardly an evening passed without one or another industriously bending over her needle. Usually they were all three at it, for they made most of their own clothes. Each had her own particular side of the table and her own particular chair. They were extremely circumspect in the observance of one another's preferences, and would apologize profusely if one happened to be found on the wrong side of the table or incorrectly seated. Mrs. Sturgis, on the rare occasions when she found herself with nothing particular to do, spread out a pack of cards before her and indulged in a meditative solitaire; Alice had always a novel in which she was absorbed. Generally three or four books were saved up in her room, and she considered herself dreadfully behind in her reading unless she had disposed of one of them as soon as she acquired another. Jeannette studied the fashions in the dress magazines and sometimes amused herself by drawing costume designs of her own.

But dressmaking occupied most of the evenings. There was usually a garment of some kind in process of manufacture, or a dress to be ripped to pieces and its materials used in new ways. Alice acted as model no matter for whom the work was intended. She had infinite patience and could stand indefinitely, sometimes with a bit of sewing in her hands, sometimes with a book propped before her on the mantel, indifferent and unconcerned, while her mother and sister crawled around her on the floor, pinning, pulling and draping the material about her young figure, or else sitting back on their heels and arguing with each other, while they eyed her with heads first on one side, then on the other.

§ 6

To-night Jeannette was making herself a corset cover, Alice was struggling over a school essay on "Home Life of the Greeks in the Age of Pericles," and Mrs. Sturgis was darning. They had not been more than half-an-hour at their work, when there was the sound of masculine feet mounting the stairs, a hesitating step in the hall, and a brief ring of the doorbell. They glanced at one another questioningly and Alice rose. Alice always answered the bell.

"If it's old Bellini wanting you to-night . . ." Jeannette began in annoyance. But the man's voice that reached them was no messenger's; it was polite and friendly, and it was for Alice's sister he inquired. Jeannette found Dikron Najarian in the front room. The young man was all bashful breathlessness.

"There's an Armenian society here in New York, Miss Sturgis. My father was one of its organizers, has been a member for years. We're having a dance to-night at Weidermann's Hall on Amsterdam Avenue, and my cousin, Louisa, who was going with me, is ill; she has a bad toothache. I have her ticket and . . . will you come in her place? Rosa's going, of course, and . . . tell your mother I'll bring you home at twelve o'clock."

It was said in an anxious rush, with hopeful eagerness. Jeannette, bewildered, went to consult her mother. Mrs. Sturgis hastily pinned one of her jabots around her neck and appeared to confront young Najarian in the studio. She listened to the invitation thoughtfully, her head cocked upon one side, her lips pursed in judicial fashion. Janny was still very young,

she explained; she had never attended anything quite
—quite so grown-up, she was used only to the parties
her school friends sometimes asked her to, and Mrs.
Sturgis was afraid. . . .

Suddenly Jeannette wanted to go. She pinched her
mother's arm, and an impatient protest escaped her
lips.

"Oh, please, Mrs. Sturgis . . ." pleaded the young
man.

A rich contralto voice sounded from the hallway of
the floor below. The door to the apartment had been
left open and now they could see big handsome Rosa
Najarian's face through the banisters as she stood
halfway up the stairs.

"Do let your daughter come, Mrs. Sturgis. They
are all nice boys and girls. I will keep a sharp eye
on her and bring her home to you safely."

"Well," said Mrs. Sturgis, "I just wanted to feel
satisfied that everything was right and proper."

There were some further words. Jeannette left her
mother talking with Dikron and flew to the dining-
room, to her sister.

"Quick, Alice dearie! Dikron Najarian's asked me
to a dance. I must fly! Help me get ready. He's
waiting."

Instantly there was a scurry, a jerking open of
bureau drawers, a general diving into crowded closets.
The question immediately arose, what was Jeannette
to wear? In a mad burst of extravagance, she had
sent her dotted Swiss muslin to the laundry. There
remained only her old "party" dress, which had been
done over and over, lengthened and lengthened, until
now the velvet was worn and shiny, the covering of

some of the buttons was gone and showed the bright
metal beneath, the ribbon about the waist was split in
several places. Yet there was nothing else, and while
the girl was hooking herself into it, Alice daubed the
metal buttons with ink, and sewed folds of the ribbon
over where it had begun to split. Jeannette borrowed
stockings from her sister and wedged her feet into a
pair of her mother's pumps which were too small for
her. Her black lusterless locks were happily becom-
ingly arranged, and excitement brought a warm dull
red to her olive-tinted cheeks. She was in gay spirits
when Najarian called for her some fifteen minutes
later, and went off with him chattering vivaciously.

Mrs. Sturgis stood for a moment in the open doorway of her apartment and listened to the descending
feet upon the stairs, to the lessening sound of gay
young voices. She assured herself she caught Rosa
Najarian's warmer accents as the older girl met her
brother and Jeannette two flights below; she still bent
her ear for the last sounds of the little party as it made
its way down the final flight of stairs, paused for an
interval in the lowest hallway, and banged the front
door behind it with a dull reverberation and a shiver
of glass. As the house grew still she waited a minute
or two longer with compressed lips and a troubled
frown, then shook her round little cheeks firmly,
turned back into her own apartment, and without comment began to help Alice hang up Jeannette's discarded clothing and set the disordered room to rights.

§ 7

Jeannette found her mother sitting up for her when
she returned a little after twelve. Mrs. Sturgis was

engaged in writing out bills for her lessons which she would mail on the last day of the month. The old canvas-covered ledger with its criss-crossed pages, its erasures and torn edges in which she kept her accounts was a familiar sight in her hands. She was forever turning its thumbed and ink-stained leaves, studying old and new entries, making half-finished calculations in the margins or blank spaces. She sat now in the unbecoming flannelette gown she wore at night, her thin hair in two skimpy pig-tails on either side of her neck, a tattered knitted shawl of a murderous red about her shoulders, and a comforter across her knees. In the yellow light of the hissing gas above her head, she appeared haggard and old, with dark pockets underneath her scant eyebrows and even gaunt hollows in the little cheeks that bulged plumply and bravely during the day above her tight lace collars.

"Well,—*dear*-ie!" Bright animation struggled into the mother's face, and her voice at once was all eagerness and interest. "Did you have a good time? . . . Tell me about it."

Immediately she detected something was amiss. There was none of the gay exhilaration and youthful exuberance in her daughter's manner, she had confidently expected. One searching glance into the glittering dark eyes, as the girl stooped to kiss her, told her Jeannette was fighting tears, struggling to control a burst of pent-up feeling.

"Why, dearie! What's the matter? . . . Tell me."

"Oh——!" There was young fury in the exclamation. Jeannette flung herself into a chair and buried her face in her hands, plunging her finger-tips deep into her thick coils of black hair. For several minutes she would not answer her mother's anxious inquiries.

"Wasn't Mr. Najarian nice to you? Didn't he look after you? Didn't you have a good time? Tell Mama," Mrs. Sturgis persisted.

"Oh, yes,—he was very nice, . . . yes, he took good care of me,—and Rosa did, too."

"Then what is it, dearie? What happened? Mama wants to know."

Jeannette drew a long breath and got brusquely to her feet.

"Oh, it's this!" she burst out, striking the gown she wore with contemptuous fingers. "It's these miserable things I have to wear! There wasn't a girl there, to-night,—not even one,—that wasn't better dressed. I was a laughing-stock among them! . . . Oh, I know I was, I know I was! . . . They all felt sorry for me: a poor little neighbor of Dikron Najarian's on whom he had taken pity and whom he had asked to a dance! . . . Oh! I can't and *won't* stand it, Mama."

Tears suddenly choked her but she fought them down and stilled her mother's rush of expostulations.

"No—no, Mama! . . . It's *nobody's* fault. You work your fingers to the bone for Allie and me; you work from daylight till dark to keep us in school and in idleness. I'm not going to let you do it any longer. . . . No, Mama, I'm not going to let things go on as they are. I needed some experience like to-night's to make me wake up."

"What experience? Don't talk so wild, baby."

"Finding out for myself I was the shabbiest dressed girl in the room! There were a lot of other girls there,

—really nice girls. I didn't expect it. I suppose I thought I wouldn't find any American girls like myself at an Armenian dance. I don't know *what* I thought! . . . But there were only a few like Rosa and Dikron, and all the other girls were beautifully dressed.''

Jeannette broke off and began to blink hard for self-control. Her mother, her face twisted with sympathy and distress, could only pat her hand and murmur soothingly over and over: "Dearie—my poor dearie—my dearie-girl——"

"I saw one old lady sizing me up," Jeannette went on presently. "I could see right into her brain and I knew every thought she was thinking. She looked me over from my feet to my hair and from my hair to my feet. There wasn't a thing wrong or right with me that that old cat missed! She didn't mean it unkindly; she was merely interested in noting how shabby I was. . . . And Mama,—it was a revelation to me! I could just see ahead into the years that are coming, and I could see that that was to be my fate always wherever I went: to be shabbily dressed and be pitied."

"Now—now, dearie,—don't take on so. Mama will work hard; we'll save——"

"But that's just what I won't have!" Jeannette interrupted passionately. "I'm not going to let you go on slaving for Allie and me, making yourself a drudge. . . . What's it all for? Just so Allie and I can marry suitable rich young men! Isn't that it? Ever since I can remember, I've heard you talk about our future husbands and what kind of men they are to be. You've been describing to us for years the time when we'll be going to dances and theatres. Going, yes, but how?

Dressed like this? Worn, shabby old clothes? To be pitied by other women? . . . No, Mama, I won't do it. I'd rather stay home with you for the rest of my life and grow up to be an old maid!''

"Oh, Janny, don't talk so reckless. You take things so seriously, and you're always imagining the worst side of everything. There are thousands of girls a great deal worse off than you. There are thousands of mothers and fathers and daughters in this city right this minute who are facing just this problem. It's as old as the hills. But there's always a way out,— a way that's right and proper. Don't let it trouble you, dearie; leave it to Mama; Mama'll manage.''

"No, Mama, I *won't* leave it to you! I've got eyes in my head and I see how hard you have to struggle. We're always behind as it is,—pestered by bills and the tradespeople. Why, this very afternoon we didn't have a cent in the house,—not even a copper,—and you had to borrow a dime from Mildred Carpenter to buy bread! Just think of it! *We didn't have money enough for bread!*''

"But, dearie, I've got Miss Loughborough's check in my purse.''

"Yes, and we owe ten times its amount! . . . We're running steadily behind. I don't see anything better ahead. It's going to be this way year after year, always falling a little more and a little more behind, until—until, well—until people won't trust us any more.''

"Perhaps we could cut down a bit somewheres, Janny.''

"Oh, Mama, don't talk nonsense! I'm going to work,—that's all there is about it.''

"Jeannette! . . . You can't! . . . You mustn't!"

"Well, I am just the same. Rosa Najarian is a stenographer with the Singer Sewing Machine Company, and she gets eighteen dollars a week! . . . Think of it, Mama! Eighteen dollars a week! She took a ten weeks' course at the Gerard Commercial School and at the end of that time they got her a job. She didn't have to wait a week! . . . No, I'm not going to High School another day. To-morrow I'm going down to that Commercial School."

"But, dearie—dearie! You don't want to be a working girl!"

"You're a working woman, aren't you?"

"But, my dear, I had no other choice. I had my girls to bring up, and I've grubbed and slaved, as you say, just so my daughters would never have to take positions. I've worked hard to make ladies of you, dearie,—and no lady's a shop-girl. . . . Oh, I couldn't bear it! You and Allie shop-girls! . . . Janny,—it would *finish* me."

"Well, Mama, you don't feel so awfully about Rosa Najarian—do you? You consider Rosa a lady, don't you?"

"She's an Armenian, Jeannette, and I know nothing about Armenians. Besides she is not *my* daughter. The kind of men I want for husbands to my girls will not be looking for their wives behind shop counters!"

"But, Mama, stenographers don't work behind counters."

"Oh, yes, they do. . . . Anyway it's the same thing."

Jeannette felt suddenly too tired to continue the discussion. Her mind began turning over the changes

the step she contemplated would occasion. Mrs.
Sturgis' fingers played a nervous tattoo upon her
tremulous lips. She glanced apprehensively at her
daughter and in that moment realized the girl would
have her way.

"Oh, dearie, dearie!" she burst out. "I can't *have*
you go to work!"

Jeannette knew that no opposition from her mother
would alter her purpose. Where her mind was made
up, her mother invariably capitulated. It had been so
for a long time, and Jeannette, at least, was aware
of it. As she foresaw the full measure of her mother's
distress when she put her decision into effect, she came
and knelt beside her chair, gathered the tired figure
in its absurd flannelette nightgown in her arms and
kissed the thin silky hair where it parted and showed
the papery white skin of her scalp. Mrs. Sturgis bent
her head against her daughter's shoulder, while the
tears trickled down her nose and fell upon the girl's
bare arm. Jeannette murmured consolingly but her
mother refused to be comforted, indicating her disapproval by firm little shakes of her head which she
managed now and then between watery sniffles.

There were finally many kisses between them and
many loving assurances. The girl promised to do
nothing without careful consideration, and they would
all three discuss the proposition from every angle in
the morning. When they had said a last good-night
and the girl had gone to her room, Mrs. Sturgis still
sat on under the hissing gas jet with the red, torn
shawl about her shoulders, the comforter across her
knees. The tears dried on her face, and for a long

time she stared fixedly before her, her lips moving unconsciously with her thoughts.

The little suite of rooms she had known so intimately for twelve long years grew still; the chill of the dead of night crept in; Jeannette's light went out. Mrs. Sturgis reached for the canvas-covered ledger on the table beside her and began a rapid calculation of figures on its last page. For a long time she stared at the result, then rose deliberately, and went into her room. There she cautiously pulled an old trunk from the wall, unlocked its lid, raised a dilapidated tray, and knelt down. In the bottom was an old *papier-maché* box, battered and scratched, with rubbed corners. She opened this and began carefully to examine its contents. There was the old brooch pin Ralph had given her after the first concert they attended together, and there were her mother's coral earrings and necklace, and the little silver buckles Jeannette had worn on her first baby shoes. There were some other trinkets: a stud, Ralph's collapsible gold pencil, a French five-franc piece, a scarf-pin from whose setting the stone was missing. Tucked into a faded leather photograph case was a sheaf of folded pawn tickets. That was the way her rings had gone, and the diamond pin, Ralph's jeweled cuff-links and the gold head of her father's ebony cane. She picked up the pair of silver buckles and examined them in the palm of her hand; presently she added the gold brooch and the collapsible pencil before she put back the contents of the trunk and locked it. For some moments she stood in the center of her room gently jingling these ornaments together. Then her eye travelled to her bureau; slowly she approached it, and one after another lifted the gold chains she wore during the day. These she disengaged from her eye-glasses and watch, and wrapped them with the buckles and the brooch in a bit of tissue paper pulled from a lower drawer. But still she did not seem satisfied. With the tissue-paper package in her hand, she sat on the edge of her bed, frowning thoughtfully, her fingers slowly tapping her lips. Presently a light came into her eyes. She lit a candle and stole softly through the girls' rooms, into the great gaunt chamber that was the studio. In one corner was a bookcase, overflowing with old novels, magazines, and battered school-books. It was a higgledy-piggledy collection of years, a library without value save for five substantial volumes of Grove's Musical Dictionary on a lower shelf. Mrs. Sturgis knelt before these, drew them out one by one, and laid them beside her on the floor. She opened the first volume and read the inscription: "To my ever patient, gentle Henrietta, for five trying years my devoted wife, true friend, and loving companion, from her grateful and affectionate husband, Ralph." There was the date,—twelve years ago,—and he had died within six months after he had written those words. Her fingers moved to her trembling lips and she frowned darkly.

She closed the book, carried the five volumes to a shelf in a closet near at hand, and tucked them out of sight in a far corner. There was one last business to be performed: the books in the bookcase must be rearranged to fill the vacant place where the dictionary had stood. Mrs. Sturgis was not satisfied until her efforts seemed convincing. At last she picked up her wavering candle and made her way back to her own room. As she got into bed the old onyx clock on the mantel in the dining-room struck three blurred notes upon its tiny harsh gong. Only when darkness had shut down and the night was silent, did tears come to the tired eyes. There was then a blinding rush, and a few quick, strangling sobs. Mrs. Sturgis stifled these and wiped her eyes hardily upon a fold of the rough sheet. She steadied a trembling lip with a firm hand and resolutely turned upon her side to compose herself for sleep.

CHAPTER II

§ 1

It took all Jeannette's young vigorous determination to carry into effect the plan she had conceived the night of the Armenian dance. She met with an unexpected degree of opposition from her mother, and even from Alice, who was as a rule indecisive, and the vaguest of persons in expressing opinions. It was too grave a step; Janny might come to regret it bitterly some day, and it might be too late then to go back; Alice thought perhaps it would be wiser to wait awhile. But Jeannette did not want to wait. The more she thought about being a wage-earner, and her own mistress, free to do as she pleased and spend her money as she chose, the more eager she was to be done with school and the supervision of teachers. She felt suddenly grown up, and looked enviously at the young women she met hurrying to the elevated station at Ninety-third Street in the early mornings on their way downtown to business. She noted how they dressed and critically observed those who carried their lunches. She thought about what she should wear, the kind of hat and shoes she would select, when she was one of them. If it meant skipping her noonday meal entirely, she decided, she would never be guilty of carrying lunch with her. Alice and her intimates at school on a sudden became drearily young to her; she was irritated by their giggling silliness. She chose to treat them all with a certain aloofness, and began to regard herself already as a highly-paid, valued secretary of the president of a large corporation. In the evenings she found excuses for visiting Rosa Najarian and eagerly listened to the older girl's account of the business routine of her days.

The tuition at the Gerard Commercial School for ten weeks' instruction in shorthand and typing was fifty dollars payable in advance, and it was her inability to get this sum that prevented Jeannette from putting her plan immediately into effect. She made herself unhappy and her mother and sister unhappy by worrying about it. Mrs. Sturgis fretted uncomfortably. She alone was aware of an easy way by which the money could be obtained, but since she did not approve of her daughter's purpose, she had no inclination to divulge it.

A five thousand dollar paid-up insurance policy from a benevolent society had become hers at the time of her husband's death. It represented a nest-egg, the thought of which had always been the greatest comfort to her. In sickness or in case of her death, the girls would have something; they would not be left absolutely destitute. She had never mentioned this policy to her daughters, always being afraid she might borrow on it, and many a time she had been sorely tempted to do so. With the knowledge of its existence unshared with anyone, Mrs. Sturgis felt herself equal to temptation; but once taking her children into her confidence, she feared she would soon weakly make inroads upon it.

Now as Jeannette became restive and impatient for

want of fifty dollars, her mother grew correspondingly
depressed. It was to protect herself against just such
wild-goose schemes as this, she told herself over and
over, that she had refrained from telling her darlings
anything about the money.

But events, unforeseen, and from her point of view,
calamitous, robbed her of her fortitude, and forced
her to play into her daughter's hands. Scarlet fever
broke out in the neighborhood; an epidemic swept the
upper West Side; the Wednesday and Saturday lessons,—all of them,—had to be discontinued; Miss
Loughborough's school closed its doors. Mrs. Sturgis
found some music to copy, but the money she earned
in this way was far short of the meager income upon
which she and her daughters had depended. The days
stretched into weeks and still new cases were reported
in the district. The time came when there was actual
want in the little household, literally no money with
which to buy food, and no further credit to be had
among the tradespeople.

Jeannette applied for and secured the promise of a
job in a small upholsterer's shop in the neighborhood
at six dollars a week, and in the face of her firm resolution to accept the offer and go to work on the following Monday morning, Mrs. Sturgis confessed her
secret. As she had foreseen, Jeannette had little difficulty in persuading her,—since now she would be compelled to borrow on her store,—to make the amount of
her loan fifty dollars additional.

"Why, Mama, I'll be earning that much a month in
ten weeks, and I can pay it back to you in no time."

"I know—I know, dearie. But I just hate to do it."

Eventually, she gave way before her daughter's

flood of arguments. It was what she had feared ever
since Ralph died; there would be no stopping now the
inroads upon her little capital; she saw the beginning
of the end.

But Jeannette went triumphantly to school.

§ 2

After the first few days while she felt herself conspicuous as a new pupil, she began to enjoy herself
immensely. The studies fascinated her. Hers was an
alert mind and she was unusually intelligent. She
had always been regarded as an exceptionally bright
student, but she had achieved this reputation with little
application. Her school work heretofore had represented merely "lessons" to her; it had never carried
any significance. But now she threw herself with
all the intensity of her nature upon what seemed to
her a vital business. She realized she had only ten
weeks in which to master shorthand and typing, and
at the end of that time would come the test of her
ability to fill a position as stenographer. She dared
not risk the humiliation of failure; her pride,—the
strongest element in her make-up,—would not permit
it. She must work, work, work; she must utilize every
hour, every minute of these precious weeks of
instruction!

The girl knew in her heart that she had many of
the qualifications of a good secretary. She was pretty,
she was well-mannered, intelligent, and could speak
and write good English. To find ample justification
for this estimate, she had but to compare herself with
other girls in the school. These for the most part

were foreign-born. A large percentage were Jewesses, thick-lipped and large-nosed, with heavy black coils of hair worn over ill-disguised "rats." Jeannette detected a finer type, but even to these exceptions she felt herself superior. They chewed gum a great deal, and shrieked over their confidences as they ate their lunches out of cardboard boxes at the noon hour. She could not bring herself to associate with such girls, and forestalled any approach to friendliness on their part by choosing a remote corner to devote the leisure minutes to study. In consequence she became the butt of much of their silly laughter, and though she winced at these whisperings and jibes, she never betrayed annoyance. There was a sprinkling of men and boys throughout the school, but the male element was made up of middle-aged dullards and pimply-necked raw youths, none of whom interested her.

The weeks fled by, and Jeannette was carried along on an undiminished wave of excitement. Everything she coveted most in the world depended upon her winning a diploma from the school at the end of the ten weeks' instruction. She discovered soon after her enrollment, that while this might be physically possible, it was rarely accomplished, and most of her fellow students had been attending the school for months. A diploma represented to her the measure of success, and as the time grew shorter before she was to take the final examinations, she could hardly sleep from the intensity of her emotions.

At home, matters had materially improved. The epidemic was over; Miss Loughborough's school had reopened its doors, and Mrs. Sturgis was again beginning to fill her Wednesdays and Saturdays with lessons. But the problem of finances was still unsolved. There was a loan of five hundred dollars now on the insurance policy, and Jeannette foresaw her mother would not cease to fret and worry over that until it had somehow been paid back. Everything, it seemed to her, depended on her success at school. There was no hope for the little family otherwise. Alice—trusting, complacent little Alice—was not the type who could shoulder any of the burden; her mother was perceptibly not as strong as she had been. There would always be debts, there would always be worry, there would always be skimping and self-denial, unless she, Jeannette, got a job and went to work.

Weary with fatigue, she would drive herself at her practice on the rented typewriter in the studio every evening until her back flamed with fire and her finger-tips grew sore. She made Alice read aloud to her while she filled page after page in her notebook with her hooks and dashes, until her sister drooped with sleep. Mrs. Sturgis protested, actually cried a little. The child was killing herself to no purpose! There wasn't any sense in working so hard! She was wasting her time and it would end by their having a doctor!

Jeannette shook her head and held her peace, but when the reward came and old Roger Mason, who had been principal of the school for nearly twenty years, sent for her and told her he wanted to congratulate her on the excellent showing she had made, she felt amply compensated. But none of those who eagerly congratulated her,—not even her mother nor Alice,—suspected how infinitely harder than mastering her lessons had been what she had endured from the

jeering, mimicking girls who had made fun of her
through the dreadful ten weeks.

But that was all behind her now. She could forget
it. She had justified herself, and stood ready to prove
to her mother and sister that she could now fill a position as a regular stenographer, could hold it, and moreover bring them material help. She was all eagerness
to begin,—frightened at the prospect, yet confident of
success.

§ 3

Graduates of the Gerard Commercial School ordi-
narily did not have to wait long for a job. The demand
for stenographers was usually in excess of the supply.
Little Miss Ingram, down at the school, who had in
hand the matter of finding positions for Gerard graduates, was interested in obtaining the best that was
available for Miss Sturgis who had made such an
excellent record, and Jeannette was thrilled one morning at receiving a note asking her to report at the
school without delay if she wished employment.

Miss Ingram handed her an address on Fourth
Avenue.

"It's a publishing house. They publish subscription
books, I think,—something of that sort. I don't urge
you to take it,—something better may come along,—
but you can look them over and see how you think
you'd like it. They'll pay fifteen."

"Fifteen a week?" Jeanette raised delighted eyes.
"Oh, Miss Ingram, do you think I can please them?
Do you think they'll give me a chance?"

Miss Ingram smiled and squeezed Jeannette's arm
reassuringly.

"Of course, my dear, and they'll be delighted with you. You're a great deal better equipped than most of our girls."

The Soulé Publishing Company occupied a spacious floor of a tall building on Fourth Avenue. Jeannette was deafened by the clatter of typewriters as she stepped out of the elevator.

The loft was filled with long lines of girls seated at typewriting machines and at great broad-topped tables piled high with folded circulars. Figures, silhouetted against the distant windows, moved to and fro between the aisles. It was a turmoil of noise and confusion.

As she stood before the low wooden railing that separated her from it all, trying to adjust her eyes to the kaleidoscopic effect of movement and light, a pert young voice addressed her:

"Who did chou want t' see, ple-ease?"

A little Jewess of some fourteen or fifteen years with an elaborate coiffure surmounting her peaked pale face was eyeing her inquiringly.

"I called to see about—about a position as stenographer."

Jeannette's voice all but failed her; the words fogged in her throat.

"Typist or regular steno?"

"Stenographer, I think; shorthand and transcription,—wasn't that what was wanted?"

"See Miss Gibson; first desk over there, end of third aisle." The little girl swung back a gate in the railing, screwed up the corners of her mouth, tucked a stray hair into place at the nape of her neck, and with an assumed expression of elaborate boredom waited for Jeannette to pass through.

It took courage to invade that region of bustle and
clamor. Jeannette advanced with faltering step, felt
the waters close over her head, and herself engulfed in
the whirling tide. Once of it, it did not seem so terrifying. Already her ears were becoming attuned to the
rat-ti-tat-tating that hummed in a roar about her, and
her eyes accustomed to the flying fingers, the flashing
paper, the bobbing heads, and hurrying figures.

Miss Gibson was a placid, gray-haired woman, large-
busted and severely dressed in an immaculate shirtwaist that was tucked trimly into a snug belt about her
firm, round person.

She smiled perfunctorily at the girl as she indicated
the chair beside her desk. Jeannette felt her eyes
swiftly taking inventory of her. Her interrogations
were of the briefest. She made a note of Jeannette's
age, name and address, and schooling. She then
launched into a description of the work.

The Soulé Publishing Company sold a great many
books by subscription: *Secret Memoirs, The Favorites
of Great Kings, A Compendium of Mortal Knowledge.*
Their most recent publication was a twenty-five volume
work entitled *A Universal History of the World.* This
set of books was supposed to contain a complete historical record of events from the beginning of time,
and was composed of excerpts from the writings
of great historians, all deftly welded together to make
a comprehensive narrative. A tremendous advertising
campaign was in progress; all magazines carried full-
page advertisements, and a coupon clipped from a
corner of them brought a sample volume by mail for
inspection. When these volumes were returned, they
were accompanied by an order or a letter giving the

reason why none was enclosed. To the latter, a personal reply was immediately written by Mr. Beardsley,—Miss Gibson indicated a young man seated by a window some few desks away. He dictated to a corps of stenographers, and followed up his first letters with others, each containing an argument in favor of the books.

Miss Gibson enunciated this information with a glibness that suggested many previous recitations. When she had finished, with disconcerting abruptness, she asked Jeannette if she thought she could do the work. The girl, taken aback, could only stare blankly; she had no idea whether she could do it or not; she shook her head aimlessly. Miss Gibson frowned.

"Well,—we'll see what you can do," she declared. "Miss Rosen," she called, and as a young Jewess came toward them, she directed: "Take Miss—Miss"—she glanced at her notes,—"Sturgis to the cloak room, and bring her back here."

Jeannette's mind was a confused jumble. "They won't kill me,—they won't eat me," she found herself thinking.

Presently she stood before Miss Gibson once more. The woman glanced at her, and rose.

"Come this way." They walked toward the young man she had previously indicated.

"Mr. Beardsley, try this girl out. She comes from the Gerard School, but she's had no practical experience."

Jeannette looked into a pleasant boy's face. He had an even row of glittering white teeth, a small, quaint mouth that stretched tightly across them when he smiled, blue eyes, and rather unruly stuck-up hair.

She wanted to please him—she could please him—he seemed nice.

"Miss—Miss—I beg pardon,—Miss Gibson did not mention the name."

"Sturgis."

"There's a vacant table over there. You can have a Remington or an Underwood—anything you are accustomed to; we have all styles. . . . Miss Flannigan, take charge of Miss Sturgis, will you?"

A big-boned Irish girl came toward him. She was a slovenly type but apparently disposed to be friendly.

"I'll lend you a note-book and pencils till you can draw your own from the stock clerk. You have to make out a requisition for everything you want, here. You'll find paper in that drawer, and that's a Remington if you use one."

Jeannette slipped into the straight-back chair and settled with a sense of relief before the flimsy little table on which the typewriter stood. She was eager for a moment's inconspicuousness.

"This is the kind of stuff he gives you."

Miss Flannigan leaned over from behind and offered her several yellow sheets of typewriting.

Jeannette took them with a murmured thanks, and began to read.

". . . deferred payment plan. Five dollars will immediately secure this handsome twenty-five volume set. . . . On the first of May, the price of these books, as advertised, must advance, but by subscribing now . . ."

She wet her dry lips and glanced at another page.

"The authenticity of these sources of historical information cannot be doubted. . . . Eliminating the traditions which can hardly be accepted as dependable chronicles, we turn to the Egyptian records which are still extant in graven symbols."

She couldn't do it! It was harder than anything she had ever had in practice! She saw failure confronting her. The sting of tears pricked her eyes, and she pressed her lips tightly together.

Blindly she picked up a stiff bristle brush and began to clean the type of her machine. She slipped in a sheet of paper, and, to distract herself, rattled off briskly some of her school exercises. Those other girls could do it! She saw them glancing at their notes, and busily clicking at their machines. They did not seem to be having difficulty. Miss Flannigan,—that raw-boned Irish girl with no breeding, no education, no brains!— how was it that *she* managed it?

She frowned savagely and her fingers flew.

"Miss Sturgis."

Young Mr. Beardsley was smiling at her invitingly. She rose, gathering up her pencils and notebook.

"Sit down, Miss Sturgis. This work may seem a little difficult to you at first but you'll soon get on to it. Most of these letters are very much alike. There's no particular accuracy required. The idea is to get in closer touch with these people who have written in or inquired about the books, and we write them personal letters for the effect the direct message . . ."

He went on explaining, amiably, reassuringly. Jeannette thawed under his pleasant manner; confidence came surging back. She made up her mind she liked this young man; he was considerate, he was kind, he was a gentleman.

"The idea, of course, is always to have your letters

intelligible. If you don't understand what you have
written, the person to whom it is addressed, won't
either. I don't care whether you get my actual words
or not. You're always at liberty to phrase a sentence
any way you choose as long as it makes sense. . . .
Now let's see; we'll try one. Frank Curry, R.F.D. 1,
Topeka, Kansas. . . . I'll go slow at first, but if I
forget and get going too rapidly, don't hesitate to
stop me.''

Jeannette, with her note-book balanced on her knee,
bent to her work. Beardsley spoke slowly and distinctly. After the first moments of agonizing despair,
she began to catch her breath and concentrate on the
formation of her notes. More than once she was
tempted to write a word out long-hand; she hesitated
over "historical," "consummation," "inaccurate."
She had been told at school never to permit herself
to do this. Better to fail at first, they had said, than
to grow to depend on slipshod ways.

The ordeal lasted half-an-hour.

"Suppose you try that much, Miss Sturgis, and see
how you get along.''

She rose and gathered up the bundle of letters.
Beardsley gave her a friendly, encouraging smile as
she turned away.

"How pleasant and kind everyone is!'' Jeannette
thought as she made her way back to her little table.

But her heart died within her as she began to decipher her notes. Again and again they seemed utterly
meaningless,—a whole page of them when the curli-
cues, hooks and dashes looked to her like so many
aimless pencil marks. She frowned and bent over her
book despairingly, squeezing hard the fingers of her

clasped hands together. What had he said? How had
he begun that paragraph? . . . Oh, she hadn't had
enough training yet, not enough experience! She
couldn't do it! She'd have to go to him and tell him
she couldn't do the work! And he had been so kind
to her! And she would have to tell capable, friendly
Miss Gibson that a month or two more in school perhaps would be wiser before she could attempt to do
the work of a regular stenographer! And there were
her mother and sister, too! She would have to confess
to them as well that she had failed! The thought
strangled her. Tears brimmed her eyes.

"Perhaps you're in trouble? Can I help?" A
gentle voice from across the narrow aisle addressed
her. Jeannette through blurred vision saw a round,
white face with kindly sympathetic eyes looking
at her.

"What system do you use? The Munson? . . .
That's good. Let me see your notes. Just read as far
as you can; his letters are so much alike, I think I
can help you."

Jeannette winked away the wetness in her eyes, and
read what she was able.

"Oh, yes, I know," interrupted this new friend;
"it goes this way." She flashed a paper into her
machine and clicked out with twinkling fingers a dozen
lines.

"See if that isn't it," said the girl handing her the
paper.

Jeannette read the typewritten lines and referred to
her notes.

"Yes, it's just the same." Her eyes shone. "I'm
so much obliged."

"It seemed to me awfully hard at first. I thought I never could do it."

"Did you?" Jeannette smiled gratefully.

"Oh, yes; we all had an awful time. He uses such outlandish words."

§ 4

The morning was gone before she knew it. She went out at lunch-time, walked a few blocks up Fourth Avenue and then turned back to the office. She did not eat; she did not want any lunch; her mind was absorbed in her work; she had hardly left the building before she wanted to get back to her desk, to recopy a letter or two in which she had made some erasures. The afternoon fled like the morning.

A whirl of confused impressions spun about in her brain as she shut her eyes and tried to go to sleep that night. Although she ached with fatigue, she was too excited to lose consciousness at once. The day's events, like a merry-go-round, wheeled around and around her. On the whole she was satisfied. She had finished all of the letters Mr. Beardsley had given her; he had beckoned her to come to him after he had read them, had commended her, and given her back but one to correct in which the punctuation was faulty.

"I'm sure you'll do all right, Miss Sturgis," he told her. "You'll find it much easier as soon as you get used to the work."

And Jeannette felt she had made a real friend in Miss Alexander, the girl across the aisle who had so generously, so wonderfully helped her. Among the riff-raff of girls that surged in and out of the office, cheaply dressed, loud-laughing, common little chits,

Beatrice Alexander was easily recognizable as belonging to Jeannette's own class. Each had discerned in the other a similarity of thought, of taste and refinement that drew them immediately together.

A wonderful, tremendous feeling of importance and self-respect came to Jeannette as she had made her way across crowded Twenty-third Street and encountered a great tide of other workers homeward bound; as she climbed the steep elevated station steps, and with the pushing, jostling crowd wedged her way on board a train; as she hung to a strap in the swaying car and squeezed herself through the jam of people about the doorway when Ninety-third Street was reached, and as she walked the brief block and a half that remained before she was at last at home. Every instant of the way she hugged the soul-satisfying thought that she had proven herself; now she was truly a full-fledged wage-earner, a working girl. She had achieved, she felt, economic value.

§ 5

Life began to take on a new flavor. The future held hidden golden promises. Jeannette had always had a protecting, proprietary attitude toward her mother and Alice, but now she was acutely aware of it, and the thought was sweet to her; she revelled in the prospect of the rôle she must inevitably assume. All her world was centered in her eager, hard-working, ever-cheerful, fussy little mother, and her gentle brown-eyed sister who looked up to her with such adoration and implicit faith. Jeannette felt she had forever established their confidence in her by this successful step into the business world. Her mother had been completely won by her good fortune, and her stout little bosom swelled with pride in her daughter's achievement. Eagerly she told her pupils about it, and even regaled with the news fat good-natured Signor Bellini and politely indifferent Miss Loughborough.

To Jeannette, the Soulé Publishing Company became at once a concern of tremendous importance. Before little Miss Ingram had mentioned its name to her, she was not sure she had ever heard it. Now she seemed to see it wherever she turned, heard about it in chance conversations at least once a day; it leaped at her from advertisements in the newspapers and from the pages of magazines. Books, she casually picked up, bore its imprint. A great pride in the big company that employed her came to her: it was the largest and most enterprising of all publishing houses; it was spending a million dollars advertising *The Universal History of the World;* it had hundreds of employees on its pay-roll!

If there were less roseate aspects of the concern that paid her fifteen dollars every Saturday, Jeannette did not see them. She never stopped to examine critically the history she was helping to sell, nor to glance into the pages of the *Secret Memoirs,* nor to open the leaves of the set of books labelled *Favorites of Great Kings.* She never thought it curious that the firm employed so many cheaply dressed, vulgar-tongued little Jewesses, and sallow-skinned, covert-eyed girls. Nor did she wonder that she never observed any important-looking individuals who might be officials of the company, walking about or up and down the aisles of the racketting, bustling loft. There was only Mr. Kent. The

others, whoever they might be, confined their activities,
she came to understand, to the main offices of the Company on West Thirty-second Street. This great loft
with its sea of life was only a temporary arrangement,
—part of the great selling campaign by which a hundred thousand sets of the History were to be sold before May first. Something of tremendous import was
to happen on this fateful date,—an upheaval in trade
conditions, a great change in the publishing world.
Jeannette was not sure what it was all to be about, but
she was convinced that after May first, the public
would no longer have this wonderful chance to buy the
twenty-five volumes of the History at such a ridiculously low price.

Behind glass partitions in one corner of the exten-
sive floor were the inner offices,—the "holy of holies"
Jeannette thought of them,—where Mr. Edmund Kent
existed, pulled wires, touched bells, and gave orders
that generalled the activities of the hundreds of human
beings who clicked away at their typewriters, or deftly
folded thousands and thousands of circulars, to tuck
into waiting envelopes that were later dragged away
in grimy, striped-canvas mail sacks. Mr. Edmund
Kent was the Napoleon, the great King, the Far-seeing
Master who in his awesome, mysterious glass-parti-
tioned office, ruled them with arbitrary and benevolent
power. All day long, Jeannette heard Mr. Kent's
name mentioned. Miss Gibson quoted him; Mr.
Beardsley decided this or that important matter must
be referred to him. What Mr. Kent thought, said,
did, was final. The girl used to catch a glimpse of the
great man, now and then, as he came in, in the morning, or went out to a late lunch: a square-shouldered,

firm-stepping man with a derby hat, a straight, trim mustache, and an overcoat whose corners flapped about his knees. He seemed wonderful to her.

"Shhhh . . ." a whisper would come from one of the girls near by; "there's Mr. Kent"; and all would watch him out of the corners of their eyes as they pretended to bend over their work.

"Mr. Kent is President of the Company?" Jeannette one day ventured to ask Mr. Beardsley.

"Oh, no, just the selling agent," he replied. This was perplexing, but it did not make Jeannette regard with any less veneration the stocky figure in derby hat and flapping coat corners which strode in and out of the office.

There were other mysterious persons who had desks in the "holy of holies," but Jeannette was never able to make out who these were, nor what might be their duties. Miss Gibson was in charge of the girls on the floor; Mr. Beardsley was her immediate "boss." There was a cashier who made up the pay-roll and whose assistants handed out the little manila envelopes on Saturday morning containing the neatly folded bills. She had no occasion to be concerned about anyone else.

Her "boss's" full name was Roy Beardsley. *Roy!* She smiled when she heard it. He was young,— twenty-three or -four; he was a recent Princeton graduate, was unmarried and lived in a boarding-house somewhere on Madison Avenue. She found out so much from the girls her second day at the office; they were glib with information concerning any one of the force.

Jeannette liked her young boss, principally because

it soon became apparent that he treated her with a
courtesy he did not accord the other girls. She was,
after all, a "lady," she told herself, straightening her
shoulders a trifle, and he was sufficiently well-bred himself to recognize that fact. He must see, of course,
the difference between herself and such girls as—well
—as Miss Flannigan, for instance. But more than this,
Jeannette grew daily more and more convinced that
he was beginning to take a personal interest in her for
which none of these considerations accounted. Nothing definite between them gave this justification.
There was no word, no inflection of voice that had any
significance, but she saw it in a quick glimpse of his
blue eyes watching her as she sat beside his desk, in
the smile of his strange little mouth that stretched
itself tightly across his small teeth when he first
greeted her in the day and wished her "good-morning." Some strange thrilling of her pulses beset her
as she sat near him. It irritated her; she struggled
against it, even rose to her feet and went to her desk
upon a manufactured excuse to check the subtle influence that began to steal upon her when she was near
him. All her instincts battled against this upsetting
something, whatever it was,— she could not identify
it by a name—which began more and more to trouble
her.

Jeannette was a normal, healthy girl budding into
womanhood, with broadening horizons and rapidly increasing intimate associations with the world. She
was growing daily more mature, more impressive in
her bearing, and notably more beautiful. She was
fully conscious of this. Her mirror told her so, the
glances of men on the street contributed their evidence,

the covert inspection of her own sex both in and out of the office confirmed it. She was becoming aware, too, of a growing self-confidence, of poise and power in herself that she had never suspected.

With what constituted "crushes," "cases," with what was implied in saying one was "smitten," she was thoroughly familiar. To a confidant she would now have frankly described Roy Beardsley as having a "crush" on her. He was not the first youth of whom she could have truthfully said as much. Various boys at one time or another, during her school days, had slipped notes to her as they passed her desk, or shamblingly trailed her home after school, carrying her books for her, and had hung around the doorstep of the apartment house, loitering over their leave-taking, digging the toe of a shoe into the pavement, grinning foolishly. Some of them had confided to her that they "loved" her and asked her to promise to be their "girl." She, herself, had had a "terrible case" on a vaudeville dancer named Maurice Monteagle, and on a youth of Greek extraction who worked in Bannerman's Drug Store on the corner near her home, tended the soda-water counter there and whose name she never learned.

But in none of these affairs of her young heart had there been anything like this. She began by being somewhat flattered by Beardsley's attention, and was guilty of provoking him a little at first with a smile and glance. Like all girls of her age, she had been willing, even anxious, to whip his interest into flame. But she soon grew frightened. There was now something in the air, something in herself she could not quite control; she could not still the sudden throbbing

of her heart, the swimming of her senses. The moment
came when she actually dreaded meeting him in the
mornings, when the minutes she was obliged to sit
beside his desk and listen to the peculiar little twang
in his voice were an ordeal. She dared not lift her
eyes to meet his, but she could see his long white
fingers moving about on the desk, playing with pencil
and pen, and she could feel him looking at her when
his voice fell silent. These were the moments that
disturbed her most, when she could not—not for the
life of her—control the mounting color that began
somewhere deep down within her, and swept up into
her cheeks, over her temples, to the roots of her hair.
She had to rest her hand against her note-book, to keep
it from trembling. During these silences when she
felt him studying her she sometimes thought she must
scream or do something mad, unless he turned his eyes
elsewhere. She seriously considered resigning and
seeking another position.

§ 6

Jeannette drank deeply of satisfaction in being a
wage-earner. She walked the streets of the city with
a buoyant tread; she gazed with pride and affection
into the eyes of other working girls she passed; she
was self-supporting like them; she had something in
common with each and every one of them; there was
a great bond that drew them all together.

But while she felt thus affectionately sympathetic
to these girls in the mass, no one of them drew the line
of social distinction more rigidly, even more cruelly
than did she, herself. She felt she was the superior
of the vast majority of them, and the equal of the best.

She might not be earning the salary perhaps some of them did who were private secretaries, but she was confident that she would. Her experience with stenography confirmed this self-confidence. With three weeks of actual practice the trick, the knack, the knowledge,—whatever it was,—had come to her of a sudden. Now she could sweep her pencil across the page of her note-book, leaving in its wake an easy string of curves, dots and dashes, setting them down automatically, keeping pace with even the swiftest of young Beardsley's sentences. Nothing could stop her progress in the business world; she loved being of it, revelled in its atmosphere, realizing that she was cleverer than most men, shrewder, quicker, with the additional advantage of unerring intuition.

This new-born ambition told her to keep herself aloof from other working girls. Not that she had any inclination to associate with them; they offended her, —not only those in the office but the giggling, simpering girls she saw on the street, who were obviously of the same class, teetering along on ridiculously high heels, wearing imitation furs, and building their hair into enormous bulging pompadours. They were the kind who did not leave the offices where they worked at the noon hour but gathered in groups to eat their lunches out of cardboard boxes and left a litter of crumbs on the floor; they were the kind who crowded Childs' restaurant, adding their shrill voices and shrieks to the deafening clatter of banging crockery.

Jeannette, feeling that it was a working girl's privilege to become an habitué of Childs', eagerly entered one of these restaurants at a noon hour during the early days of her employment. Accustomed as she had become to the din of an office, the noise in the eating place did not distress her. But she shrank from rubbing elbows with neighbors whose manner of feeding themselves horrified her. A study of the price card and an estimate of what she could buy for fifteen cents, the amount she decided she might properly allow herself for lunches, completed her dissatisfaction with the restaurant and similar places. She decided to go without lunch and to spend the leisure time of her noon-hour wandering up and down Fifth Avenue and Broadway, looking into shop windows,—Lord & Taylor's, Arnold Constable's and even Tiffany's on Union Square,—and in making tours of inspection through the aisles of Siegel-Cooper's mammoth establishment on Sixth Avenue.

It was in the rotunda of this gigantic store, where stood a great golden symbolic figure of a laurel-crowned woman, that there was a large circular candy counter and soda fountain, and here the girl discovered one might get coffee, creamed and sugared, and served in a neat little flowered china cup, and two saltine crackers on the edge of the saucer, for a nickel. In time, this came to constitute her daily lunch. She could stand at the counter, sipping her drink, and nibbling the crackers at her ease, feeling inconspicuous and comfortable, presenting, she realized, merely the appearance of a lady shopper, who had taken a moment from her purchasing for a bit of refreshment.

The nourishment, slight as it was, proved sufficient. On the days she had gone lunchless, she had developed headaches late in the afternoon, but the coffee and crackers, she found, were enough to sustain her from a seven o'clock breakfast to dinner at six-thirty. A nickel for lunch, a dime for carfare—sometimes she walked downtown—took less than a dollar out of her weekly wage. That left fourteen dollars to spend as she liked. She gave her mother nine and kept five for clothes. Five dollars a week for new clothes! Her heart never failed to leap with joy at the thought. Five dollars a week to save or to spend for whatever she fancied! Oh, life was too wonderful! Just to exist these days and to plan how she would dress herself, and what else she would do with her earnings, filled her cup of joy to the brim.

Her little mother protested vehemently when she put nine dollars in crisp bills into her hand at the end of the first week of work.

"Oh—dearie! What's this? . . . What's all this money for?"

"It's what I'm going to give you every week, Mama."

Mrs. Sturgis for a moment was speechless, gazing with wide eyes into her daughter's smiling face. She wouldn't accept it. She wouldn't hear of such a thing. It was the child's own money that she had earned herself and not one cent of it should go for any old stupid bills or household expenses. She shook her head until her round fat cheeks trembled like cupped jelly.

But Jeannette had her way, as she knew, and her mother knew, and admiring, exclaiming Alice knew she would from the first. That same evening, after the pots and pans and the supper dishes had been washed, Mrs. Sturgis established herself under the light at the dining-room table with the canvas-covered ledger before her and began to figure. Thirty-six dollars a month! Thirty-six dollars a month! Six times six? That was . . .? Why, they'd almost be out of debt in six months! And they wouldn't need to fall behind a cent during summer! It was wonderful! It was too—too wonderful! Tears filmed Mrs. Sturgis' bright blue eyes; her glasses fogged so that she had to take them off and wipe them. She didn't deserve such daughters! No woman ever had better girls!

They got laughing happily, excitedly over this, an hysterical sob threatening each. They kissed each other, the girls kneeling by their mother's chair, their arms around one another, and clung together. And then Alice said she had half a mind to go to work, too, and do her share.

But there was an immediate outcry at this from both her mother and sister. What nonsense! What a foolish idea! She musn't *think* of such a thing! Just because Jeannette had given up her schooling and gone out into the world was no reason why both sisters should do it. There was not the slightest necessity. Alice's place was at school and at home. Some one had to run the house; that was her contribution. She was fitted for it in every way: she was domestic, she liked to cook and she liked to clean.

A still more convincing argument that persuaded apologetic Alice that indeed she was quite wrong, and her mother and sister were entirely right, was voiced by Jeannette. Alice had much too retiring a nature to be a success in business. Assurance, self-assertiveness, even boldness were required, and Alice had none of these qualities. This was undeniably true; they all agreed to it. It seemed to be the last word on the matter; the topic was dismissed. Mrs. Sturgis went back to figuring on her bills; Jeannette to speculating about

Roy Beardsley as she darned a tear in an old shirtwaist.

"I've often wondered," ventured Alice after a considerable pause, "just what I should do,—how I could support myself if both of you happened to die. I mean —well, if Jeannette should go off somewhere,—to Europe, maybe,—and Mother should get sick, and I should have to . . ."

Her voice trailed off into silence before the astonished looks turned upon her.

"Well, upon my word . . ." began Jeannette.

"Why, Alice dearie, what's got into you?"

"You're going to kill us both off,—is that it? I'm to run away and leave Mother sick on your hands?"

"I mean—well, I meant——" struggled the confused Alice.

"Dearie," said her mother, "you won't have to worry about the future. Mama'll take care of you until some nice worthy young man comes along to claim you for his own."

"You'll be married, Allie dear, long before I will. You're just the kind rich men fall madly in love with."

"Oh, hush, Janny! . . . please."

But her sister's thoughts were already upon a more engaging matter. She was busy once again with Roy Beardsley.

CHAPTER III

§ 1

SPRING burst upon New York with a warm breath
and a rush of green. The gentle season folded the
city lovingly in its arms. Everywhere were the evidences of its magic presence. The trees shimmered
with green, shrubbery that peeped through iron fence
grillings vigorously put forth new leaves, patches of
grass in the areaways of brownstone houses turned
freshly verdant, hotels upon the Avenue took on a
brave and festal aspect with blooming flower-boxes in
their windows, florist shops exhaled delicate perfumes
of field flowers and turned gay the sidewalks before
their doors with rows of potted loveliness, the Park
became an elysian field of soft invitingness, with
emerald glades and vistas of enchantment like tapes-
tries of Fontainebleau. Spring was evident in
women's hats, in shop windows, in the crowded tops
of lumbering three-horse buses, in the reappearance
of hansom cabs, in open automobiles, in the smiling
faces of men and women, in the elastic step of pedestrians. Spring had come to New York; the very walls
of houses and pavements of the streets flashed back
joyously the golden caressing radiance of the sun.

Walking downtown to her office on an early morning
through all this exhilarating loveliness, stepping along
with almost a skip in her gait and a heart that danced

to her brisk strides, Jeannette felt rather than saw a
man's shadow at her elbow and turned to find Roy
Beardsley beside her, lifting his hat, and smiling
at her with his tight little mouth, his blue eyes twinkling.

"Oh!" she exclaimed, her fingers pressed hard
against her heart. She had been thinking of him almost from the moment she had left home.

"Morning. . . . You don't mind if I walk along?
. . . It's a wonderful morning; isn't it glorious?"

"Oh, my, yes,—it's glorious." She had herself in
hand by another moment and could return his smile.
They had never stood near one another before, and
the girl noticed he was half-a-head shorter than herself.
There were other things the matter with him, seen thus
upon the street while other men were passing, and with
his hat on! Jeannette could not determine just what
they were. Glancing at him furtively as they walked
together down the Avenue, she was conscious of a
vague disappointment.

"Do you walk downtown every morning?" he asked.

"Oh, sometimes. How did you happen to be up this
way so early?"

"I take a stroll through the Park occasionally. It's
wonderful now."

"Yes, it's very beautiful."

"I think New York's the loveliest place in the world
in spring."

"Well, I guess it is," she agreed.

"And you have to go through a long wet winter like
this last one to appreciate it."

"Yes, I think you do."

"I thought we'd never get rid of the snow."

"They clean the streets up awfully quickly though;
—don't you think so?"

"Yes, they have a great system here."

"The poor horses have a terrible time when it's
slippery."

"There was a big electric hansom cab stuck in the
snow for four days in front of the place where I live.
They had to dig it out," he said.

"It makes the spring all the more enjoyable when
the change comes."

"Yes, the people seem to take a personal pride in
the weather."

"It's as though they had something to do with it
themselves."

"That's right. I noticed it the first year I was
here."

"You're not a New Yorker, then?"

"Oh, no; my home's in San Francisco. I only came
East three years ago to go to college."

"I thought you were . . . one of the girls at the
office mentioned you were a Princeton man."

"I was, but I . . . well, I flunked out at Christmas.
I was tired of college, anyway. I wanted to go into
newspaper work, but I couldn't get a job with any of
the metropolitan dailies, so temporarily I am trying
to help sell the *Universal History of the World*."

They talked at random, the man inclined to give
more of his personal history; the girl, pretending indifference, commented on the steady encroachment of
stores upon these sacred fastnesses, the homes of
the rich. She interrupted him with an exclamation
every now and then, to point out some object of interest
on the street, or something in a shop window.

It was thrilling to be walking together down the brilliant Avenue in the soft, morning sunshine. They paused at Madison Square before beginning to weave their way through the traffic of the street, and striking across the Park, gay with beds of yellow tulips, trees budding into leaf, and fountains playing. Roy put his hand under the girl's forearm to guide her. The touch of his fingers burnt, and set her pulses thrilling. She pointedly disengaged herself, withdrawing her arm, when they reached the farther side of the Avenue.

Crossing the Square, she glanced at him critically once more. He seemed absurdly young,—a mere college boy with his cloth hat at a youthful angle, his slim young shoulders sharply outlined in the belted jacket. It was possible he was a few years her senior, but she felt vastly older.

He was commenting on the portentous date, May first, when the price of the History was to advance. The company had somehow succeeded in postponing the fateful day for two weeks, and the public was to have a fortnight longer in which to take advantage of the low prices.

". . . and after that, no one knows what will happen. Perhaps we'll all lose our jobs."

"Oh,—do you really think so?" Jeannette was aghast.

"Well, some of us will go; they can't continue to keep *that* mob on the pay-roll. I don't think they'll let you go, though, you're such a dandy stenographer. I shall certainly recommend them to keep you, but I doubt if they'll have any further use for me. They'll let me out, all right."

He smiled whimsically. It was this whimsical smile the girl found so appealing and só—so disconcerting.

"I shall be sorry if that happens," she said slowly.

"Will you?"

"Why, of course."

"But will you be really sorry if—if I'm no longer there?"

"We-ll,—it will be hard getting used to someone else's dictation; I'm accustomed to yours now."

"Yes,—I'll be sorry to go," he said after a moment. "I like the work, after a fashion, . . . but, of course, it isn't getting me anywhere. I want to write; I've always been interested in that. If I could get any kind of work on a newspaper or a magazine, it would suit me fine. My father's awfully sore at me for being dropped at Princeton. He's a minister, you know,"—Beardsley laughed deprecatingly with a glance at his companion's face,—"and he didn't like it a little bit. I didn't want to go back home like—well—like the prodigal son, so I wrote him I'd get a job in New York, and see what I could do for myself."

"I see," the girl said with another swift survey of his clean features and tight, quaint smile. There was an extraordinary quality about him; he was pathetic somehow; she felt oddly sorry for him.

"I'd like to make good for my father's sake. . . . He's only got his salary."

"I see," she repeated.

"But summer's the deuce of a time to get a job on a newspaper or magazine in New York, everybody tells me. . . . I don't know what I'll do if I don't get something."

Jeannette wondered what she would do herself. She had begun to enjoy so thoroughly her daily routine, and to take such pride in herself! . . . Well, it would be too bad. . . .

They had reached the intersection of Fourth Avenue and Twenty-third Street where the ground was torn up in all four directions, and hardly passable.

"I'll say a prayer of thankfulness when they get this subway finished, and stop tearing up the streets," Jeannette remarked.

Once again Roy caught her elbow to help her over the pile of débris, across the skeleton framework of exposed tracks, and again the girl felt the touch of his young fingers like points of flame upon her arm. She caught a shining look in his eyes. Love leaped at her from their blueness. A moment's giddiness seized her, and there came a terrifying feeling that something dreadful was about to happen, that she and this boy at her side were trembling on the brink of some dreadful catastrophe. Instinct rose in her, strong, combative. She turned abruptly into the open door of a candy shop and steadied herself as she bought a dime's worth of peppermints.

Emotions, burning, chilling, conflicting, took possession of her the rest of the day. From her typewriter table she covertly studied Beardsley, as he leaned back in his armed swivel-chair before his flat-topped desk, his fingers loosely linked together across his chest, his eyes unseeing, fixed on some distant point through the window's vista, dictating to the stenographer who bent over her note-book, as she scribbled beside him. What was it about him that moved her so strangely? What was it in his twinkling blue eyes,

his quaint mouth with its whimsical smile that stirred
her, and set her senses swimming? He was in love
with her. Perhaps it was just because he cared so
much that she was thus deeply stirred. There had
been others, she reminded herself, who had been in
love with her, but they had awakened no such emotion.

Had she come to care herself?

She asked the question with a beating heart. Was
this love,—the feeling about which she had speculated
so long? Love,—the *great* love? Was she to meet
her fate so soon? Was her adventure among men to
be so soon over? Was this all there was to it? The
first man she met? She and Roy Beardsley?

She denied it vehemently. No, it was nonsense,—
it was ridiculous! Roy Beardsley was a boy,—a mere
youth who had been dropped from college. She would
not permit herself to become interested in him. It was
preposterous,—absurd!

She assured herself she would have no difficulty in
controlling her emotion in future, but the emotion
itself continued to puzzle her. What was it, she felt
for this man? Was she in love,—*really* in love,—in
love at last? She looked at him a long time. She
wondered.

§ 2

That he would meet her on the Avenue next morning she felt was almost certain. She said to herself
a hundred times it would be much wiser for her to take
the elevated train, or at least to walk down another
street and avoid the possibility of such an encounter.
If she were not to permit herself to become further
interested, it was obvious she must see him as little

as possible. But when morning came it was into Fifth Avenue she turned. . . . She felt so sure of herself; she wanted to see if he would really be there.

Once or twice she thought she recognized his distant figure coming toward her. Each time her heart came into her throat. She stopped and made a pretense of studying a milliner's window, while she wrestled with herself. She was mad, she was a fool, she had no business to let herself play with fire this way! At the next corner she would turn eastward, and go down Fourth Avenue. But when she reached the cross street she decided to walk just one more block, and in that interval he stepped from a doorway where he had been watching for her, and joined her.

"Good-morning."

"Oh—hello!"

The sudden sight of him, the sound of his voice affected her like fright. She hurried on, trying to still the pounding in her breast, turning her face toward the traffic in the street to hide her confusion.

"What's the hurry?" he laughed. "It isn't half past eight yet."

"I have a personal letter to type before office hours," Jeannette said abstractedly, but she lessened her pace.

"I love these early walks on the Avenue," he said.

"I always walk down if I have time," she replied. "I wouldn't miss it for anything." She gave him a quick inspection. He was insignificant,—he had a weak, effeminate expression,—his features were small and lacked resolution. And yet it was the same face with its blue eyes, always brightly alight, its twisted mouth and thin lips stretched tightly over his small,

glittering, even teeth when he smiled, that haunted her
through the day, pursued her to her home, gleamed at
her from the blackness of her room after she had gone
to bed, visited her in her dreams, and greeted her with
its irresistible charm when she awoke in the mornings.
She loved that irresolute face, with all its weakness,
its curious eccentricities; she loved the grace of that
slight boyish figure with its square, bony shoulders,
its tapering, slim waist; she loved those thin, almost
emaciated white wrists, and those long chalk-hued
hands and attenuated fingers. She loved the way he
bore himself, the poise of his figure, the lithesomeness
and suppleness of his young body. And she despised
herself for loving, and hated him for the emotion he
stirred in her. She wanted to kiss him, she wanted to
kill him, she wanted him in her arms, she wanted never
to see him again; she wanted him to be madly, desperately in love with her, and she wanted herself to
be coldly indifferent.

The spring sunlight flooded the Avenue gloriously;
the green omnibuses, dragged by three horses harnessed abreast, rumbled up and down; cabs teetered
on their high wheels, and weaved their way through
the traffic at a smart clip-clap; hurrying women, with
the trimming of their flowered hats nodding to their
energetic gait bustled upon their early morning
errands; stores were being opened, shirt-sleeved por-
ters were noisily folding the iron gates before the
doors back into their daytime positions; shop-girls,
and stenographers, briskly on their way to their offices,
half smiled at one another as they passed.

It was impossible not to respond to the infectious
quality that was in the air. Jeannette laughed happily

into her companion's face, and he gazed at her eagerly, his eyes shining, his mouth twisted into its whimsical smile. They were exhilarated, they were enthralled, they were oblivious to everything in the world except themselves.

He stopped her abruptly, a block from the office.

"I think perhaps . . . I believe you would prefer it, Miss Sturgis, if—if you and I . . . if you were not seen entering the building, with—with an escort. It might be easier, pleasanter for you, if I . . ."

He hesitated, floundering helplessly. They stood still a moment facing one another, each thinking of impossible things to say. Then Beardsley murmured: "Well . . . " lifted his hat, and she put her hand in his. He held it tightly in the firm grip of his thin white fingers, until she had to free it. She laughed shakily, as she turned away.

"That was really very nice of him," she thought as she hurried on. "That was really very nice. I shan't mind walking with him occasionally, if it doesn't set the office gossiping."

§ 3

Love swept them tumultuously onward. There was no time to pause, to consider, no time to calculate, none to take stock of one's self. In a week Jeannette Sturgis and Roy Beardsley were friends, in ten days they were lovers. Every morning he met her on the Avenue and walked with her to within a block of the office, and in the evening he joined her for the tramp homeward. He begged her again and again to lunch with him but to this she would not agree. They knew they loved each other now, but dared not speak of it.

He was diffident, eager to ingratiate himself with her, fearful of her displeasure; and she,—while she confessed her love to herself,—passionately resolved he should never guess it nor persuade her to acknowledge it. She had an unreasonable primitive dread of what might follow if Roy should speak. Their love was all too sweet as it was. She did not want to risk spoiling it, and trembled at the thought of its avowal.

Yet in her heart she knew what must inevitably happen. Their attraction for one another was stronger than either; it was rushing them both headlong down the swift current of its precipitous course.

On the very day the words were trembling on her lover's lips came the staggering announcement that on the fifteenth day of May the activities of the Soulé Publishing Company in selling the *Universal History of the World* would cease, and the services of all employees would terminate on that date.

The girls told Jeannette the news the moment she arrived at the office, and she found it confirmed on a slip of paper in an envelope on her typewriting table.

"All? Every one?" she asked blankly. She had confidently expected that she would be kept on,—for a month at least.

"Well, that's what they say; Mr. Beardsley, Miss Gibson,—everybody."

"Oh," murmured Jeannette, betraying her disappointment.

"Did you think they'd keep you on the pay-roll after the rest of us were fired?" asked Miss Flannigan airily.

Jeannette perceptibly straightened herself and levelled a cool glance at the girl.

"Perhaps," she admitted.

"Oh-h,—is that so?" mimicked Miss Flannigan
"Well, you got another think coming,—didn't you?"

Jeannette drowned the words by attacking her ma
chine, her fingers flying, the warning ping of the tiny
bell sounding at half-minute intervals. But her hear
was lead within her, and her throat tightened con
vulsively. She was going to lose her job! She was
going to be thrown out of work! She was going to
be among the unemployed again! Her mother! . . .
And Alice! . . . That precious five dollars a week that
was all her own!

The rest of the day was dreary, interminable.
Demoralization was in the air. The girls whispered
openly among themselves, and filtered by twos and
threes to the dressing-room, where they congregated
and gossiped. The spring sunshine grew stale, and
poured brazenly through the west windows. Miss
Flannigan chewed gum incessantly as she giggled
noisily over confidences with a neighbor. Even
Beardsley seemed to have lost interest for Jeannette.

Yet when she came to his desk later in the day for
the usual dictation, he handed her a paper on which
he had written:

"You mustn't be downhearted. There is always a
demand for good stenographers. You won't have the
slightest difficulty in getting another job. I wish I was
as sure of one myself. May I walk home with you
this evening?"

She gave him no definite answer but she liked him
for his encouragement and sympathy. Whenever she
sat near his desk, note-book in hand, waiting for him
to dictate to her, he was to her a superior being, one

whose judgment and perception were above her own; he was her "boss." It was different when she met him outside the office; he was just a boy then,—a boy who had flunked out of college. Now he, too, had lost his job. Like her, he would soon be unemployed. No longer need she fear his possible censure of her work, or take pleasure in his praise of it. She realized he had lost weight with her.

After office hours that evening, he met her outside the building and as he walked home with her was full of philosophical counsel.

"Why, Miss Sturgis, it's never hard for a girl to get a job,—a girl who's got a profession, and who's shown herself to be a first-rate stenographer. The offices downtown are just crazy to get hold of girls like you. You won't have the slightest difficulty in finding another position. . . . If you were me, you'd have something to worry about. I've got to get a job that will land me somewhere,—a job in which I can rise to something better."

"But so have I," said Jeannette.

"Well, yes, I know. . . . But girls're different. They only want a job for a little while,—a year, two or three years perhaps, and then they get married. Working for girls is only a sort of stop-gap."

"No, it isn't; not always. There's many a girl who perhaps doesn't regard matrimony with such awful importance as you men think. I mean girls who aren't thinking about marriage at all, and who really want to become smart, capable business women."

Roy smiled deprecatingly. "But I'm talking about the average girl," he said.

"And so am I. Girls have a right to be economically

independent, and I can't see why they have to stop working just because they marry,—any more than men do.''

"Girls have to stay home and run the house."

"Oh, what nonsense!" cried Jeanette. "It's no more her home than it is the man's.''

Roy shrugged his slight shoulders. He had no desire to argue with her. He was more concerned with the thought that in the future there would be no office to bring them together daily.

"There are only two days more. Saturday we get our last pay envelope.''

They walked on in silence.

"I hope you'll let me come to see you. We've become such good friends. I'd hate to . . ."

He left the sentence awkwardly unfinished.

"Oh,—I'd like to have you call some evening," she said with apparent indifference. "I'd like to have you meet my mother and sister.''

"I'd love to. . . . I want to know them both."

"Well, come Sunday,—to—to dinner. We have it at one o'clock. I suppose it's really lunch, but we're awfully old-fashioned and we always have our Sunday dinner in the middle of the day. . . . You mustn't expect much; we live very simply.''

"Thanks, awfully. . . ."

"We don't keep any servant, you know."

"I quite understand. You're very good to invite me.''

"I'm sure my mother and sister will be glad to meet you.''

"I'm awfully anxious to know *them*."

"Well, come Sunday."

"You bet I will."

"Of course, they've heard about 'Mr. Beardsley.'"

"Have they? . . . Do you talk about me sometimes to them?"

"Why, of course! . . . Naturally. . . . What do you expect?"

"I hope you've given me a good character."

"I daresay they think you're an old bald-headed man with a thick curly beard."

"Oh, no! . . . They'll be terribly disappointed!"

"I'm going to tell them you're a gruff old codger with a perpetual grouch."

"Miss Sturgis,—please!"

They were both laughing hilariously.

"Here's your home. I had no idea we had walked so far. . . . Shall I see you to-morrow? I'll be waiting at the Seventy-second Street entrance to the Park."

"All right."

"At eight o'clock?"

She nodded, waved her hand to him, and ran up the stone steps. He waited until she had fitted her key into the lock, and the heavy glass-panelled door had closed behind her.

§ 4

Saturday was their first intimate little meal by a window in a café. It had been their last morning at the office, and by noon the activities of the Soulé Publishing Company in selling the *Universal History of the World* had ceased. Pay envelopes had been distributed shortly after eleven, and an hour later all the little Jewesses with their absurd pompadours and high heels, the Misses Rosens and Flannigans, the office clerks and office boys had packed the great elevators for the last time, laughing and squeezing together, and swarmed out of the building not to return. And Roy and Jeannette were among them.

"You will go to lunch with me?" he had written on a sheet of paper and pushed toward her as she sat at his elbow. "I've got a lot of things to talk to you about, and it's our last day here together."

She had tried to consider the matter dispassionately, but a glimpse of his bright, eager eyes fixed on her had sent the blood flooding her neck and cheeks, and before she quite knew what she had done she had nodded.

He joined her at the street entrance and together they made a happy progress toward Broadway.

A great felicity descended upon them. Their senses thrilled to the beauty of the warm day and their being thus together. Roy piloted her through the hurrying noontime throng, his hand about her arm. She tingled again at the touch of his fingers, and loved it. Then they entered the café of a hotel, and found a cozy table for two by the window where, dazzled and enthralled by their great happiness, they smiled into one another's eyes across the white cloth, glittering with cutlery and glasses.

Love was wonderful! He loved her; she loved him. They both knew it; they were drunk with the thought. This was their adventure,—theirs and theirs alone!

"I may have to go home this summer," Roy said with a troubled air after he had given their order to the waiter. He stared at the winding crowd that surged back and forth beneath their window. "But I'm coming back right away. In August."

"You mean to San Francisco?"

"My father wants me to come West for a month or two. He sent me my ticket. . . . I guess he expects me to settle down out there. Of course he wants me to. The ticket is only a one-way one. But he's in for a disappointment. I can't be happy in San Francisco; I want to come back to New York."

They both fell silent, thinking their own thoughts. Jeannette was conscious of the dreariness and drabness of life once more; it was disheartening and depressing to be unemployed. All these people hurrying past the window, she reflected, were intent upon some particular errand; each one had a job; the whole world had jobs but herself. There would be nothing for her to do but "apply for employment."

"Please can you give me a position? . . . Excuse me, sir, I'm looking for work. . . . Could you use a stenographer?"

Oh, it was detestable, it was intolerable! It dragged her pride in the dust! . . . And there would be no one to sympathize, to advise her,—or help her! She would be alone all summer in New York with no one interested!

Roy, watching her, guessed her thoughts.

"I'm coming back . . ."

She flushed warmly.

"Would you like me to come back? Would it make any difference to you, if I did? If you'll just say you'd like me to come back, I will; . . . I'll promise! . . . Will you?"

The girl bent over her plate, hiding her face with the brim of her hat. The giddiness she had experienced that day in the street threatened her.

"Would you want me to come back?" Roy insisted.

She raised her eyes and met his gaze; he held them with the burning intentness of his own, and for a long, long moment they stared at one another.

"You know I love you," he said tensely.

His lip quivered; his face was aglow.

"I love you with every fibre of my being! I'll come back to you,—I'll come back from the ends of the earth. Only just say you love me, too, Jeannette. . . . You *do* love me, don't you? . . . You're the most wonderful girl I've ever known, Jeannette! . . . God, Jeannette, you're just wonderful!"

Why was it that in the supreme moment of his great avowal he seemed a little ridiculous to her? She felt suddenly like laughing. He was so absurdly young, so juvenile, so school-boyish, leaning toward her across the table in his youthful Norfolk jacket, with his unruly hair sticking up on top his head!

§ 5

He kissed her when they parted from one another late that afternoon. They had been absorbed in talk, and the hours slipped by until before they were aware it was five o'clock. He walked home with her and just inside the heavy glass doors of the old-fashioned apartment house where she lived he put his arms about her, their faces came close together, and for the briefest of moments their lips met. It was a shy kiss, hardly more than a touch of mouth to mouth. For another moment they stood raptly gazing into each other's eyes, their fingers interlocked. Then Jeannette fled, running up the stairs, nor did she grant him

another look, even when she reached the landing above
and had to turn. But on the third flight of stairs she
paused, held her breath to still the noise of her panting,
and listened. There was nothing. A cautious glance
over the balustrade down through the narrow well of
the stairs revealed his shadow on the stone flagging
below. She sank to the step, and waited to catch her
breath, her ears strained for a sound. Presently she
heard him moving; there was a crisp clip of his shoes;
she guessed he was searching the gloom of the stair-
well for a glimpse of her. But she would not look, and
sat motionless with tightly clasped hands. After a
long interval she heard his hesitating step again. The
half-opened door swung slowly back, brightening the
hallway below a moment with yellow daylight from the
street, then closed with a dull jangle of heavy glass.
She sat for a moment more, then a tiny choking sound
burst from between her close-shut lips, and she buried
her glowing face in her hot hands, pressing her finger-
tips hard against her eyeballs until the force of them
hurt her.

§ 6

That night Jeannette experienced all the exquisite
joy and fierce agony of young love. It was an exhaust-
ing ordeal; she lived over and over the thrilling hours
of the day that had terminated in that glorious, intoxicating second when the boy's thin lips were against
her own, and she had felt their warm, tingling pressure. The recollection brought to her wave upon wave
of hot flushes that began somewhere deep down inside
her being and flooded her with ecstasy. She strove
against it, yet had no wish to control her thoughts.

Shame,—some curious sense of wrong,—distressed her.
It was not right;—it was all wrong! Instinct grappled
with desire. She wept deliciously, convulsively, burying her head in her pillow and pressing its smothering
softness against her mouth to stifle her sobbing breath
that neither her mother nor Alice might hear it. Past
midnight she rose and went noiselessly to the bathroom where she washed her face, carefully brushed
and re-braided her hair. Her head ached and her
swollen eyes were hot and painful. But she felt calmer.
She studied her face for a long moment in the battered
mirror that hung above the wash-stand, and as she
looked a great quivering breath was wrung from her.

"Roy . . . I can't . . . it can never be . . . never,
never be," she whispered despairingly to her image.

For the moment she felt triumphant. She had conquered something, she did not know what. She
dimmed the gaslight and found her way back to bed.
Sleep came mercifully, and she did not wake until her
mother kissed her the next morning.

§ 7

It was Sunday, the day he had promised to come to
dinner. Dinner, with the Sturgises on Sunday, was
always the noontime meal. Cold meat or a levy on
Kratzmer's delicatessen counters, with weak hot tea,
constituted Sunday supper. Dinner, however, invariably involved roast chicken and ice cream which was
secured at the last moment from O'Day's Candy
Parlor, and carried home by one of the girls, packed
in a thin pasteboard box. There was seldom ice in
the leaky ice-box, and Sunday dinner was therefore

usually a hurried affair, as mother and the girls were always acutely conscious during every minute of its duration of the melting cream in the kitchen.

For this Mrs. Sturgis was responsible. Her frugality would not allow her leisurely to enjoy her meal at the sacrifice of the ice cream. The fear of its becoming soft and mushy pressed relentlessly upon her consciousness.

"Now, dearie,—don't talk! Eat your dinner. It's much more digestible if it's eaten while it's hot," she would urge her daughters almost with every mouthful.

No one ever spoke of the ice cream itself. The reason for such close application to the business of eating was never voiced. It was part of the ritual of Sunday dinner that it should not be mentioned. Not until Alice had piled and crowded the aluminum tray with the soiled dishes, carried these away, and returned with the mound of cream sagging upon its platter, could Mrs. Sturgis and her daughters allow themselves to relax. No matter how well the rest of the dinner might be cooked, it must be gulped down and its enjoyment wasted for the sake of a quarter's worth of frozen cream.

It was upon these circumstances that Jeannette's rebellious thoughts centered on the morning of Roy Beardsley's visit. She was worn out after her troubled night, and the prospect of seeing him so soon after the tremendous occurrences of the previous afternoon and her stormy reflections upon them made her nervous, apprehensive. She wanted time to think things out, to consider matters. . . . Anyhow—what would her mother and sister think of him? What would he think of them?

"Dearie—dearie!" Mrs. Sturgis expostulated more than once. "Whatever makes my lovie so cross this morning? . . . You'll get another position, dearie,— if that's what's troubling you."

"Oh, you make me tired!" thought her daughter, angrily, though the words were unsaid.

"Well, I *do* hope we can at least have some other kind of dessert," she said aloud. "We always have to rush so infernally through dinner; it makes me sick! . . . Or, I'll tell you what," she went on hopefully, "we can get in a little ice."

"It will leak all over the floor," Alice objected. "The old thing is full of holes."

"There's nothing better than O'Day's strawberry cream," Mrs. Sturgis declared; "and there isn't a thing in the house, so I can't make a pudding."

Jeannette said nothing further but gloomed in silence. She elected to be furiously energetic, and undertook a thorough cleaning of the studio, strewing strips of damp newspaper over the floor, sweeping vigorously, her head tied up in a towel. The broom shed its straw, and she discovered little triangles of dirt in obscure corners which Alice had evidently deliberately neglected. The white curtains were dingy, the front windows needed washing, and in the midst of her cleaning, Dikron Najarian came in upon her to ask her to walk with him in the afternoon. In a fury she attempted to move the piano to pull loose a rug, and in the effort, which was far beyond her strength, she hurt herself badly. Her mother found her lying on the floor, crying weakly.

"Dearie—*dearie!* What happened to you! My

darling! You shouldn't work so hard; there's no necessity for your being so thorough."

The girl had really injured herself. Mrs. Sturgis called wildly for Alice, and between them they carried her to her room and laid her on her bed. She had wrenched her back, but she refused to admit it. She wouldn't be put to bed. She was all right, she told them; just a few moments' rest, and she would be herself again. It was twelve o'clock and Roy would be there at one!

She lay on her bed, and gazed blindly up at the old familiar discolored ceiling; presently her eyes closed and two large tears stole from under her lashes and rolled down her cheeks. She knew she had hurt herself far more seriously than she would let her mother or sister suspect. Something had given way in the small of her back; she made an effort to sit up, and the pain all but tore a cry from her. But she was determined they should not know; she would get up, and meet Roy, and go through with dinner as though nothing was the matter!

Struggling, with tiny explosions of pent-up breath and smothered groans, her hand at every free moment pressed to her side, she managed to dress herself. The effort exhausted her; a film of perspiration covered her forehead, her upper lip and the backs of her hands. She steadied herself now and then by leaning against the dresser, until her strength came back to her. She did not care, now, whether Roy Beardsley found the studio clean or not, whether or not he was hustled through dinner, thought her home cheap and poor, her mother and sister commonplace and fussily solicitous.

He was ahead of time. She met him with careful step and a fixed smile of welcome. He was glowing with eagerness; his hands trembled a little as he held them out to her. At sight of him, a moment's wave of yesterday's emotion swept over her, but immediately there came a sharp stab of pain, and she caught a quick breath from between the lips that held her smile. His anxious questions were cut short by the bustling entrance of Mrs. Sturgis and Alice.

Jeannette's mother was at once flutteringly hospitable, inviting the guest to sit down and make himself comfortable, while she established herself with an elegant spread of skirts on the davenport, and began to toss the lacy ruffles of her best jabot with a careless finger.

Were Mr. Beardsley's parents living? Ah, yes,—in San Francisco. They had fogs out there a great deal, she'd heard. And he had lost his mother. Consumption? Ah, that was indeed a pity! . . . And his father was a clergyman? Eminently laudable profession. . . . And he had wanted to come East to college? Quite right and proper. Princeton was a fine college; nice boys went there. . . . And he had spent some time in New York? Wonderful city,—but a very expensive place to live,—probably the most expensive in the world. . . .

Jeannette recognized a favorite theme and broke in with an inquiry about dinner. She was suffering miserably; she wondered if she would have the strength to get to the dining-room. Alice already had disappeared; the slam of the back door some moments before had announced her departure for O'Day's Candy Parlor. Mrs. Sturgis excused herself with many profuse explanations, and departed kitchenward, whence presently there came the bang of pots in the sink and the hiss of running water.

Left together, Roy turned eagerly to Jeannette where she stood beside the mantel, a white hand gripping its edge.

"Dearest, I've been so crazy to see you! . . . Is anything wrong? You're not angry with me after yesterday?"

Her eyes softened, but, as if to check for that day any moment's tenderness, there was again a sharp twinge. Involuntarily she winced.

"Jeannette! You're not well! What's the matter?"

She laid her hand on his arm to reassure him and steady herself.

"Nothing," she breathed. "I hurt my back this morning. I must have wrenched it. It's really nothing. Now and then it gets me."

She managed a disarming smile.

"Mother and Allie mustn't know a thing about it. I don't want to alarm them; they're so excitable. Tomorrow, I'll be quite all right again. . . . You must help me."

"Why, surely; you know I will. . . . But, dearest——"

"Oh, please! Don't make a fuss." Her tone was sharp, and at once he fell silent, watching her face anxiously.

"Do you love me?" he queried in a low voice.

She did not answer; she was in no mood for lovemaking. In a moment, she moved with difficulty to the window, and stood there, fighting her pain, and looking down vacantly into the street. Provokingly, tears rose to her eyes. She was afraid she was going to cry. She could see Allie returning with the square paper box held with a finger by its thin wire handle, and presently the great front door of the house shut with a jangle.

Roy's arm stole about her waist, but its touch hurt her.

"Oh, please!" she begged crossly.

"I'm sorry,—awfully sorry. I forgot. . . . You're in terrible pain, aren't you? . . . Shall I get a doctor? . . . Don't you want to lie down? . . . Would you like me to go?"

She wanted to slap him.

"Just leave me alone!"

Mrs. Sturgis' eager step was approaching, and in a moment she presented at the doorway a face reddened from the heat of the stove, and moist with perspiration.

"Dinner's ready, dearie," she announced. "Won't you come this way, Mr. Beardsley? We use our bedrooms for a passage-way, although the hall outside, I suppose, is really better, but, you see, it's much more convenient . . ."

Jeannette motioned him to precede her, and followed, holding on by the furniture as she made her way. Her mother was in the kitchen and Alice's back was turned as in anguish she got into her chair.

Dinner was endless. The soup had curdled; the potatoes were scant; the salt-cellar in front of Roy had a greenish mold about its top; Roy, himself, kept fiddling with his silverware,—rattling knife and fork, and fork and spoon; her mother and sister had never, in Jeannette's opinion, jumped up from the table so incessantly for errands to kitchen or sideboard. The pain in her back every now and then became excruciating. She sat through the dragging meal with a set smile upon her lips, turning her head with assumed brightness from face to face as each one spoke. Her mother did most of the talking, keeping up a continual flow of chatter to fill the silences. Alice rarely volunteered an observation when there was company, and Jeannette's misery made her dumb. Mrs. Sturgis rose to the occasion and supplied conversation for all three. Jeannette, watching Roy's face, resented his polite show of interest. Her mother had what her daughters described as a "company" manner. When it was upon her she interrupted herself every little while with nervous giggles and to-day, Jeannette decided, she had never indulged in them so often. She was eloquent during the meal with reminiscences of her childhood's escapades and early cuteness, and Jeannette watched the animated face with its jogging, pendent cheeks in an agony of spirit that matched her physical misery.

". . . Nettie,—we always called Janny, 'Nettie,' when she was little,—was only six then, and she was awfully pretty and cute. We were having dinner at a restaurant downtown,—her papa had a friend to entertain. Allie . . .? I don't remember where Allie was . . ."; Mrs. Sturgis gazed in sudden perplexity at her younger daughter. "I guess you were at home with Nora, lovie. . . . At any rate, we were at this restaurant and a waiter was serving us nicely, and nobody was paying any attention, when all of a sudden Nettie says loud and pertly to the waiter: 'Now that you're up, will you please get me a glass of milk?'" Mrs. Sturgis shut her eyes and laughed until her little round

cheeks shook. "Imagine," she finished, " 'Now that
you're *up!*' . . . To the *waiter!*" She went off into
gales of mirth.

Roy laughed too, a thin, polite laugh, without a trace
of spontaneity. Jeannette hated him. She hated her
sister, too, for her smug complacency. Alice sat there
encouraging her mother with responsive twitterings
every time Mrs. Sturgis threw her head back to chuckle.
Jeannette felt she was suffocating; the pain dug itself
steadily and cruelly into the small of her back; she
could not draw one adequate breath.

The platter and remains of the hacked and dismem-
bered chicken, and the soiled dishes eventually were
removed; Alice brushed the table-cloth with a folded
napkin, sweeping crumbs and litter, ineffectually, as
Jeannette noted in utter desolation, into the palm of
her hand, carrying the refuse handful by handful to
the kitchen, until the operation was complete. The
ice cream was borne in in mushy disintegration, and
her mother commented on its melted condition and
the various responsible reasons, until the girl thought
she would scream in protest.

She could not eat; she could not drink; lifting her
hand to her lips was misery. Roy's solicitous glance
was more and more intently fixed upon her; Alice,
also, was beginning to send concerned looks in her
direction. She felt her strength rapidly ebbing from
her. She could endure but little more—but little, little
more. Her will power was deserting her, resolution
forsaking her, she felt it going—going; it was slipping
away . . . she was going to fall! . . . Ah, she *WAS*
falling . . . !

"Janny, dearie!" Her mother's alarmed cry faintly
reached her dimming consciousness.

CHAPTER IV

§ 1

THE following summer was one of the hottest on record in New York City. The thermometer persistently hung around ninety, and the newspapers gave daily accounts of deaths and prostrations. Thousands of East-siders sought Coney Island and the cool beaches to spend their nights upon the sands. Thunderstorms brought but temporary relief. Jeannette, slowly regaining strength and energy, declared she had never known so many violent thunderstorms in the space of one short summer. She hated the vivid, blinding darts and the cracking ear-splitting detonations. She could reason convincingly with herself that there was but the minutest atom of danger, yet the menacing crashes never failed to bring her heart into her mouth and make her wince.

She had been in bed four weeks since the Sunday Roy had dined with the family, and she had fainted at the table. The doctor, when he arrived, had declared, after careful examination, that several ligaments had been torn from the bone, and the muscles of her back had been badly strained. She had been tightly bandaged with long strips of adhesive tape, and put to bed in her mother's room, where she had lain for a month, rebellious and raging, at the mercy of a horde of disturbing thoughts.

Roy sent flowers, a box of candy, magazines. He wrote her long letters in a boyish hand in which he boyishly expressed his concern for her condition, his earnest hope of her speedy recovery, his tremendous devotion. It was for the last that she eagerly looked when she unfolded his scrawled pages. But his words never seemed to satisfy her wholly; they were never vehement enough. She longed for something more vigorous, aggressive, violent.

At the end of ten days he begged to be allowed to come to see her. There was no reason why he shouldn't, Jeannette reflected, but she could not bring herself to the point of asking her mother to arrange for the visit. She did manage to say, with a light air of ridicule, one morning, when Mrs. Sturgis brought her breakfast tray to her bedside:

"Roy's got the nerve to want to come to see me."

"Why don't you let him, dearie,—if you'd like it? He seems a right nice young fellow, and you could put on your dressing sacque, and Alice could do your hair. . . . I'll be home to-morrow,—all day, you know. It would be quite right and proper."

But the girl only made a grimace.

"That kid! That rah-rah boy! . . . He thinks he's got an awful case."

"Why do you treat Mr. Beardsley so mean, Janny?" Alice asked her a few days later, closely studying her face. "You know," she continued slowly, "sometimes I think you're really in love with him."

"Love!" cried her sister. "Hah! with *that* kid?"

"I think he's terribly attractive, Janny."

"Half baked!" Jeannette said scornfully.

"Well, I think he's *charming*."

"You can have him!"

"Oh, Janny! . . . You're *dreadful!*"

But in the dark nights Jeannette would kiss the
scrawled writing, press the stiff note-paper to her
cheek, and let her thoughts carry her back to their
first meeting, their first encounter on the Avenue,
their first kiss in the hallway downstairs, their memorable lunch together. . . .

Ah, it was beautiful? It was all so very beautiful,
—so infinitely beautiful! Every glance, every word,
every moment! She loved him! She could not deny
it. Oh,—she loved him, she loved him!

He wrote he was obliged to go to San Francisco.
It was impossible to find a position in New York during midsummer, and his father had telegraphed him to
come home. He would have to go, but he longed to
see Jeannette just once before he went. He *must* see
her, if only to say "good-bye." He was coming back
the first of September, and then he would . . . But
they must talk everything over. Wouldn't she please
let him come?

Jeannette still hesitated. She wanted to see him
again; yet she was afraid,—afraid of disappointment,
of what her mother and sister might think, of herself
and Roy. In the end, with what seemed to her a weakness she despised, she wrote him, and named an afternoon. Although the doctor had said she was to remain
in bed for another week, she prevailed upon her mother
and sister to move her into the studio, where with
pillows about her and a comforter across her knees,
and her hair arranged in the pretty fashion Alice
sometimes liked to dress it, she received her lover.

It was as unsatisfactory an interview as she had

feared. Constraint held them both. Jeannette was intent upon not betraying the delicious madness into which her thoughts of Roy had led her during the empty hours of her long illness, and she sat up stiffly, unbendingly. Roy did not understand. He thought the change in her was due to her illness, but there was something about her that troubled him. They made their promises to one another, they held each other's hands, they kissed good-bye, but there was nothing fervid about any of it. At the door, however, when he turned, hat in hand, for a final, searching look, she saw a glitter in his eyes, his queer little mouth was straight and drawn harshly, unsmilingly across his teeth. It was that last look of him, that wet gleam in his eyes which took her courage and brought her own tears in a rush. But by then he was gone. The dull boom of the hall-door closing downstairs announced his departure with stern finality.

§ 2

The summer bore on, hot, unalleviated. The apartment smelled of strange odors, was close, airless in spite of open windows. The Najarians, with much banging and clattering, left with their trunks and boxes for several weeks at the seashore, and on the first of the month old Mrs. Porter, who had occupied the first floor since the building was erected thirty years before, moved away. Only the two trained nurses, one flight down, who were rarely at home, remained in the city during the burning weeks of July and August.

With the Sturgises, life became dreary and grew

drearier. Miss Loughborough's school closed, Signor
Bellini departed for his beloved Italy, the Wednesday
and Saturday pupils became fewer and fewer and by
mid-July had evaporated entirely. Mrs. Sturgis, fret-
ting over the trivial expenses each day inevitably
brought, wore a worried, harassed air. She found
some work to do, copying music, but this had to be
given up, as her teeth commenced to give her trouble.
How long she was able to disguise her discomfort
from her daughters, they never guessed, but her
misery eventually was discovered, and she was summarily driven to a dentist. It developed that her teeth
were in such a decayed condition they would all have
to be pulled, and replaced by an artificial set.

Poor Mrs. Sturgis wept and protested. She objected
strenuously to anything so drastic. It wasn't *in the
least necessary!* She couldn't *possibly* afford it! Her
daughters urged her and argued with her until they lost
their tempers and there was almost a quarrel in the
little household. The dentist declined to modify his
advice. Pain—cruel, persistent pain, that robbed her
of her sleep, and sapped her strength—finally compelled her to give way.

"I'll do it,—but my girlies haven't the faintest idea
what they are letting me in for! It will be the death
of me!" wailed Mrs. Sturgis.

Jeannette, able to sit up now and hobble from one
room to another, regarded her mother with frank
impatience as she rocked vigorously back and forth,
weeping abjectly into a drenched little handkerchief.
She felt sorry for her, she would have made any sacrifice to alleviate her pain to make matters easier for
her, and yet it was obvious there was no other course

for her, and the sooner the teeth were out and a false
set in their place, the better it would be for them all.
The girl gazed gloomily out of the window.

"And my daughter's no comfort to me," continued
Mrs. Sturgis, piteously, conscious of Jeannette's un-
voiced criticism. "The child that I've raised through
sorrow and tribulation, through hunger and self-denial,—the daughter for whom I've worked and sac-
rificed my life. . . ."

Jeannette continued to stare stonily into space,
locked her fingers more tightly together, but said
nothing.

Eventually there came the terrible day when Mrs.
Sturgis and Alice went forth to the dental surgeon,
and when the young girl brought her spent and broken
mother home in a cab. The four flights of stairs for
the exhausted woman were a dreadful ordeal. Jeannette, catching a glimpse of the labored progress, as
she gazed over the balustrade from the top landing,
forgot her own weakened condition, the doctor's cau-
tion, and hurried to her mother's assistance. She ran
down the stairs and grasped the little woman's almost
fainting figure in her young arms. Together the sisters
dragged and pushed her up the remaining steps, but
the older girl knew before she reached the top, that
she had put too great a strain upon her own partially
regained strength.

She paid for the imprudence by another three weeks
in bed. It was the longest three weeks of her life.
Her mother roamed about from room to room, toothless and inarticulate, unable to eat solid food, waiting
for her lacerated gums to heal. She complained and
mumbled almost incessantly, harassed by the thought

of doctor's and dentist's bills which she declared over
and over she saw no way of ever paying. Jeannette,
chained to her bed, had to listen unhappily. Mrs.
Sturgis gave her no respite. She refused to leave
the house for fear of meeting a friend in the street
who would discover her toothlessness. Alice went to
market and ran the errands, while Mrs. Sturgis rocked
back and forth, back and forth, beside Jeannette's bed,
picked at her darning, and complained of life. It was
not like her mother, thought the daughter wearily; she
of indomitable spirit, who had never been afraid of
hardships, but rejoiced in overcoming them.

Letters from Roy brought the only alleviating spots
in these long, tiring days. He wrote almost every day
and there were numerous picture post-cards. His
letters were full of assurances and young hopes.
Jeannette loved his endearments, his underscored pro-
testations, but the plans which he elaborately unfolded
seemed so uncertain, their realization so improbable
that they left her cold. She read the scrawled words
in the immature script, and tried to conjure up a picture of him penning them. It eluded her. The boy
in the Norfolk jacket with the stuck-up hair, blue eyes,
and whimsical smile, that had so strangely fired her
heart, had already become hazy and remote. Her own
weak back and helplessness, her mother's trembling
cheeks and mumbled complaints were harsh realities,
very close at hand. The summer sun blazed on un-
sparingly, and perspiration covered her arms and neck
and trickled down between her breasts. Spring and
young love, the glittering Avenue, walks and talks and
murmured confidences that whipped the blood and
caught the breath, were of a far distant yesterday.

Was there ever a time when thoughts of this boy had kept her awake at nights, a time when at the memory of his kiss her tears had blinded her? It was some other Jeannette,—not the one who sighed wearily and wished Alice would keep the door shut, and not let in the flies to bother her.

§ 3

Slowly Nature reasserted herself. Strength returned, old hopes revived, youth throbbed again in the veins, life once more took on a pleasing aspect. The late August day, that found Jeannette making a cautious way toward the Park on her first venture from the house, was brilliant with warm but not too hot sunshine, and the foliage of trees and shrubbery in the Park vistas never appeared greener or more inviting.

Mrs. Sturgis' false teeth had made a great improvement in her appearance, had rounded out her face, given strength to her jaw, and made her seem ten years younger. The little woman was delighted with the effect, and was now evincing a gratified interest in her appearance. Signor Bellini had returned earlier than he expected, had already started his Monday and Thursday classes, while Miss Loughborough's Concentration School for Young Ladies was about to open its doors, and pupils were flocking back from their vacations. And lastly, and to the girl, most important of all, Roy was returning to New York.

He would arrive in the city in a few days, and she wondered how she would feel toward him when they met. As she sat upon a Park bench, enjoying the sun and the toddling children playing in the soft gravel of the pathway near by, she asked herself if she cared. She could not tell. Of far more interest to her was the prospect of work again. She had been stifled all summer by illness and heat, but now she wanted to get back to the business world and win her independence anew. Her ambition was afire; she was all eagerness to have a job once more. . . . Roy? . . . Well, it would be pleasant to have him making love to her again, to watch him tremble at her nearness.

But she found herself thrilling on the afternoon he was to see her. He had telephoned in the morning from the station, and his voice had sounded wonderfully sweet and eager. When his ring at the door announced him, her heart raced madly. Delicious tremors, one after another, coursed through her.

He came hurrying up the stairs and she met him in the studio. Their hands instantly found one another's, and they stood so a moment, smiling happily and ardently into each other's eyes; then she drifted into his arms, and it seemed the peace of the world had come.

Ah, she had forgotten how dear he was, how lovable, how sweet! It was good to have him take her to himself that way, and feel his thin arms about her, and have him hold her close against his young hard breast.

Plans—plans,—they were full of them. They were engaged now; Mrs. Sturgis and Alice must be told, the father wired, and Roy must immediately set about finding a job. He had some corking letters, he told her eagerly, and he was on the trail of a splendid position already. Jeannette was going to find work, too; they would both save, buy all the clothes they would

need, and be married,—oh, some time in the spring!
Roy, holding both her hands, gazed at her with shining eyes, his whole face glowing with excitement.

"Oh, God, Jeannette—oh, God! Just think! You
and me! Married!"

It *was* a wonderful prospect.

§ 4

In less than a week, he had obtained a promising
position with the Chandler B. Corey Company, publishers of high-class fiction and the best of standard
books. It was a new but flourishing organization with
offices on Union Square. In addition to its book business, there were two monthly magazines, *The Wheel
of Fortune* and *Corey's Commentary*, and Roy was
made part of the staff that secured advertisements for
the pages of these periodicals. He was full of enthusiasm for his new work. Mr. Featherstone, the advertising manager, who was also a member of the firm,
was the jolliest kind of a man, and the other fellows in
the department, Humphrey Stubbs and Walt Chase,
were "awfully nice" chaps. He was to receive from
the start, twenty dollars a week, and Mr. Featherstone promised him a raise of five dollars at the end
of three months, if he made good. The gods were with
them. Jeannette and he could be married early in
the spring.

The girl listened and pretended to rejoice, but her
heart was sick within her. Roy, getting twenty dollars
a week!—back in a job!—independent and secure once
more!—a bright future and rapid advancement ahead
of him! She was bitterly envious. She longed for the

old life of business hours, of office excitement, for her neatly managed if frugal lunches, for the early hours in the mornings and the tired hours at night, for the heart-warming touch of the firm, plump little manila envelope on Saturday mornings, and, above all, she longed for the satisfaction of being a wage-earner again, of being financially her own mistress, and being able to contribute something toward the household bills each week.

The next day she started out to find work. She knew it would be a humiliating business, but she found it worse than she feared. The advertisements for stenographers in the newspapers which she answered, all turned out to be disappointing. The most she was offered was ten dollars a week, and in the majority of cases only six or eight. She had made up her mind to accept nothing less than what she had earned before. She would walk out of an office into the glaring street with the prick of tears smarting her eyes, with lips that trembled, but she would vigorously shake her head, and renew her determination.

She went to interview Miss Ingram of the Gerard Commercial School, but Miss Ingram had no vacant positions on her list.

"I've never seen anything like it," the little teacher said with a forlorn air; "I've got three girls now just waiting for something to turn up, but all they want downtown are boys—boys—boys!"

Twice Jeannette had the unpleasant experience of having men to whom she applied for work lay their hands on her. One slipped his arm about her, and tried to kiss her, pressing a bushy wet mustache against her face; the other placed his fat fingers

caressingly over hers and, leering at her, promised
he would find her a good job, if she'd come back later
in the day. She was equal to these occasions but there
was always a sickening reaction that left her weak
and trembling with a salt taste in her mouth. She
said nothing about them at home.

Her mother and Alice, even Roy, had urged her not
to go to work again. Mrs. Sturgis reiterated her
original objection; Alice thought it was not necessary,
that Janny had better take things easy and devote her
time to wedding preparations. Roy did not like the
idea, he frankly admitted, of her associating so intimately with a lot of men in an office, and, besides, it
distracted her, made her nervous.

"In three months, sweetheart, I'll be getting twenty-
five dollars a week and we can get married. A hundred
a month is enough for a while. You ought to run the
table on ten dollars a week,—your mother does that
for the three of you!—and out of the remaining sixty,
we surely will have enough for rent, and a lot left over
for clothes and theatres."

"Oh, yes," Jeannette sighed wearily, "it's plenty,—
only I want—I want to earn some money myself. I
need clothes, and I ought to have everything for a
year, at least!"

September passed, and October came with a tingle
of autumn, and an early touch of yellow, drifting
leaves. Jeannette missed the chance of an excellent
position in the manager's office of a large suit and
cloak manufacturer by no more than a minute or two.
She saw the other applicant enter the office just ahead
of her, and was presently told the place was filled.
The girl who had preceded her was Miss Flannigan!

There was another position in a lawyer's office for which she eagerly applied. She heard the salary was twenty-five dollars a week, but when she was interviewed, and it was discovered she had no knowledge of legal phraseology, she was rejected.

Desperate and discouraged, she was obliged to listen in the evenings to Roy's glowing praise of his new associates, to detailed accounts of small happenings in the office, and gossip between desks. She learned all about Mr. Featherstone, his devoted and adoring wife, his small, crippled son, his own good nature, and hearty joviality. She heard a great deal about Humphrey Stubbs and Walt Chase. Stubbs, she gathered, was already Roy's enemy. He had made several efforts to discredit the newcomer, and was on the lookout for things about which to criticize him to his chief. Walt Chase, on the contrary, was amiable and inclined to be very friendly. Walt had been married less than a year, lived in Hackensack, and his wife had just had a baby.

Jeannette listened enviously, with despair in her heart, when she heard about Miss Anastasia Reubens, the editor of *The Wheel of Fortune*. That Miss Reubens was forty-five and had spent all the working years of her life on the editorial staff of one magazine or another made little difference to Jeannette. She hated to inquire about her, but her curiosity was too great.

"What do you suppose she gets?" she asked Roy with a casual air.

"Oh, I don't know; perhaps fifty or sixty a week. I'm sure I haven't an idea. None of the folks down there get high salaries; everyone is underpaid. Mr. Corey hasn't more than got the business started. He only began it five years ago. He tells us, we've got to wait with him, until the money begins to come in, and then we'll all share in the profits.''

"Fifty or sixty a week?" sniffed Jeannette. "Did she tell you she got that? . . . She's lucky, if she gets twenty-five!"

Roy shrugged his shoulders. He had an irritating way of avoiding arguments, Jeannette noticed, by lapsing silent. She considered the matter for a moment further, but decided it was not worth pressing.

"What kind of a man is Mr. Corey?" she asked.

"Oh, Corey? Corey's a peach. He's a dynamo of energy, and has all sorts of enthusiasm. He's got the most magnetic personality I've ever seen in my life. He's going to make a whale of a big business out of that concern. Every Wednesday we all lunch together,— that is, the men in the editorial and book departments, —and we go to the Brevoort; we've got a private room down there, and Mr. Corey always comes and talks to us about the business and we try to offer suggestions that will help each other. We call it 'The Get Together Club.' It's great."

Jeannette studied her lover's face and for a moment felt actual dislike for him. What did *he* know? Why should *he* be so fortunate? Why should everything go so smoothly for *him?* Why shouldn't *she* have a chance like that?

"Mr. Featherstone may send me to Boston Friday to see the Advertising Manager of Jordan & Marsh about some copy. He said something about it last night. I'd hate to go, but, gee! it would be a great trip!"

Jeannette rose to her feet abruptly and lowered a

hissing gas-jet. Oh, she was unreasonable, silly, un-
generous! But she couldn't listen any longer. It
made her sick.

§ 5

Mr. Abrahms, of Abrahms & Frank,—fur dealers and
repairers of fur garments,—would pay twelve dollars
a week for a first-class "stenog," who "vood vork
from eight till sigs." He was very anxious that Jeannette should accept his offer.

"I need a goil chust lige you, who c'n tage letters
vot I digtate an' put 'em into nice English, and be
polide to der customers vot come in ven I am busy,"
he explained.

It was a cheap little establishment, crowded into the
first floor and basement of an old private dwelling,
now devoted to similar small enterprises. A dress-
maker occupied the second floor, an electrician the
next, and a sign-painter the last and topmost. It was
far from being the kind of employment Jeannette
wanted, but it was the best that had been offered, and
she promised to report on Monday.

She went dismally home on the "L," deriving a
bitter satisfaction in picturing to herself what her days
would be like, cooped up in an ill-ventilated back office
with the swarthy, none-too-clean Mr. Abrahms, inter-
viewing the none-too-clean customers who would be
likely to patronize such a place. Still it was a job and
she was a wage-earner again. There would be some
comfort in announcing the news to Roy and to her
mother and sister.

She found a message from Roy when she reached
home. It had been brought by the clerk in Banner-

man's Drug Store. He had said, Alice repeated for
the hundredth time, that Mr. Beardsley had 'phoned
and asked him to tell Miss Jeannette Sturgis to come
down at once to his office; he had said it was important.
Alice didn't know anything more than that; there
wasn't any use asking her questions; the clerk had
just said that, and that was all.

"Perhaps he's got a job for me!" Jeannette exclaimed with a wild hope. "He knows how badly I
want one!"

"I'm sure I haven't the faintest idea." Her sister
turned back to the soapy water in the wash-tub where
she was carefully washing some of her mother's jabots.

"Well, I'll fly."

Jeannette hurried to her room, and jerked the tissue
paper out of her best shirtwaist. Her fingers trembled
as she re-dressed herself; the tiny loops that connected
with small pearl buttons on her cuffs eluded her again
and again until she was almost ready to cry with fury.
She felt sure that Roy had a job for her; he would
have telephoned for no other reason. In thirty minutes she was aboard the "L" again, rushing downtown.

As she crossed Union Square the gold sign of the
Chandler B. Corey Company spreading itself impos-
ingly across the façade of an ancient office building
made her heart beat faster, and her rapid, breathless
walk doubled with her excitement into almost a skip
as she hurried along. Oh, there was good news awaiting her! She felt it!

The wheezy elevator bumped and rumbled as it
leisurely ascended. At the fourth floor she stepped
out into a reception room whose walls were covered

with large framed drawings and paintings. There were some magazines arranged on a center table. The place smelt of ink and wet paste. A smiling girl rose from a desk and came toward her.

"I'll see if he's in," she said in reply to Jeannette's query and disappeared.

Upon an upholstered wicker seat in one corner of the room an odd-looking woman wearing a huge cartwheel hat was talking animatedly to another who listened with a twisted, sour smile. They were discussing photographs, and the woman in the cart-wheel hat was handing them out one by one from a great pile in her lap. Jeannette was forced to listen.

"This one is of some monks in a village monastery in Korea, and this shows some of the Buddhist prayers for sale in a Japanese shop,—did you ever see such a number?—and here is a group of our Bible students at Tientsin,—could you ask for more intelligent faces? . . . Wonderful work. . . . these men are sacrificing their lives . . . twelve thousand dollars . . ." The words trailed off into an impressive whisper.

Down in the Square the trees were a mass of lovely golden brown and golden yellow shades. Tiffany's windows across the way sparkled with dull silver.

Roy's quick step sounded behind her, and Jeannette turned to meet his grinning, eager face, his smile stretched to its tightest across his small and even white teeth.

"Gee, I'm glad you've come, Janny!" he exclaimed boyishly. "Say, you look dandy!—you look out-of-sight!" He eyed her delightedly. The woman with the sour, twisted smile glanced toward them casually. Jeannette was all cool dignity.

"What was it, Roy? . . . Why did you send for me?"

He continued to smile at her, but at last her serious, expectant look sobered him.

"I think I've got a job for you!" he said quickly, dropping his voice. "I only heard about it this morning. I couldn't telephone until I went out to lunch. One of our regular stenographers is sick; she's very sick and is not coming back. Mr. Kipps, the business manager, was explaining why they were short-handed upstairs and I was right there, so of course I heard about it. I spoke to Mr. Featherstone about you, and he sent me to Kipps, and Kipps told me to tell you to come down, so he could talk to you. I told him what a wizard you were, and he seemed awfully interested. I didn't lose a minute; I telephoned as soon as I went out to lunch. I had a deuce of a time making that drug clerk understand. . . . Gee, you look dandy! . . . Gee, you look swell! . . . Gee, I love you!"

He piloted her a few minutes later into the inner offices. Jeannette gained a confused impression of crowded desks and clerks, the iron grilling of a cashier's cage, an open safe, a litter of paper, wire baskets of letters, and stacks of bills. Before she knew it, she found herself confronting Mr. Kipps, and Roy had abandoned her. She was aware of a nervous, fidgety personality, with a thin, hawklike face and long, thin fingers. He had unkempt hair and mustache, and wore round, black tortoise-shell glasses through which he darted quick little glances of appraisement at the girl who had seated herself at his invitation beside his desk.

He fitted his finger-tips neatly together as he ques-

tioned her, lolled back in his swivel armchair, and
swung himself slowly from side to side, kicking the
desk gently with his feet. He asked her to spell
"privilege" and "acknowledgment," and to tell him
how many degrees there were in a circle. He nodded
with her replies.

He would give her a trial; she could report in the
morning. He dismissed her with no mention of what
salary she would receive.

But Jeannette did not care. She was delighted and
in high spirits. This was just the kind of a job she
wanted, just the sort of an atmosphere she longed for;
she felt certain that, whatever they paid her at first,
she would soon make them give her what she was
worth.

When Roy arrived that evening there was great
hilarity in the Sturgis household. He had never seen
Jeannette in such wild spirits, or found her so affectionate with him. The coldness he sometimes met in
her, the reserve, the unyieldingness, were all absent
now. He pulled the shabby davenport up before the
fire, and they sat holding hands, watching the dying
fire flicker and flicker and finally flicker out, and when
the light was gone she lay close against him, his arms
about her, and every now and then, as he bent his head
over her, she raised hers to his, and their lips met.

§ 6

Her desk, with those of the five other stenographers
employed by the publishing company, was located on
the floor above the editorial offices. Here were also
the circulation and mail order departments. Light en-

tered from three broad front windows but it was far
from sufficient and thirty electric bulbs under green
tin cones suspended by long wire cords burned
throughout the day over the rows of desks and tables
that filled the congested loft. At these were some
hundred girls and women, and half a dozen men. In
the rear, where the daylight failed almost completely
to penetrate, the cones of electric radiance flooded the
dark recesses brilliantly. Old Hodgson, who was in
charge of the outgoing mail, there had his domain, and
it was in this quarter that the lumbering freight elevator occasionally made its appearance with a bang
and crash of opening iron doors. Toward the front,
near the windows, and separated from the rest by low
railings, were located the desks of Miss Holland and
Mr. Max Oppenheim. The former was a tall, thin-
faced woman with iron-gray hair and a distinguished
voice and manner. Just what her duties were Jeannette could not guess. She had her own stenographer
and was forever dictating, or going downstairs with
sheaves of letters in her hands for conferences with
Mr. Kipps. Oppenheim was the Circulation Manager.
He was a Jew, intelligent and shrewd, with a pallor so
pronounced it seemed unhealthy, further emphasized
by a thick mop of coal-black glistening hair that swept
straight back without a parting from his smooth white
forehead. Jeannette thought she recognized in him a
type to be avoided; but she never saw anything either
in his manner toward her or the other girls at which
to take exception.

There was one other individual in the room who had
a department to herself. This was a chubby, bespec-
tacled lady with an unpronounceable German name who

presided over a huddle of desks and conducted the mail order department. No one ever seemed to have anything to say to her, nor did she in her turn appear to have anything to say to anyone. She plodded on with her work, unmolested, lost sight of. Sometimes Jeannette suspected that Mr. Corey and Mr. Kipps and the other men downstairs had forgotten the woman's existence.

The stenographers with whom she was immediately and intimately thrown were distinctly of a better class than the girls who had been her associates in the Soulé Publishing Company. Miss Foster was red-headed and given to shouts of infectious mirth, Miss Lopez was Spanish, pretty and charming, Miss Bixby was a trifle hoidenish but good-natured, and Miss Pratt was frankly an old maid for whom life had been obviously a hard and devastating struggle; there remained Miss La Farge, who, Jeannette suspected, was not of the world of decent women; her be-ribboned *lingerie* was clearly discernible through her sheer and transparent shirtwaists, and she was given to rouge, lavish powdering, and strong scent.

The first day in her new position was as difficult as Jeannette anticipated. She knew she gave the impression of being cold and condescending, but her shyness would not permit her to unbend. The girls were politely distant with her at first, but Jeannette was fully aware that each and every one of them was alive to her presence, and everything they did and said was for her benefit.

She made an early friend of Miss Holland. The tall woman stopped at her desk in passing, smiled pleasantly at her and asked if everything was going all right. Something of quality, of good breeding in the older woman's face brought the girl to her feet, and it was this trifling act of courtesy that won Miss Holland's approval and favor, which Jeannette never was to lose.

There were plenty of girls scattered among the tables where the business of folding circulars, addressing envelopes, and writing cards went on, who were of the high-heeled, pompadoured, sallow-skinned variety with which Jeannette was already familiar, but these persons came and went with the work; few of them were regular employees.

When a stenographer was needed in the editorial department a buzzer sounded upstairs and the girl next in order answered the summons. Miss Foster usually took Mr. Corey's dictation and also that of his secretary, Mr. Smith, but the other girls went from Mr. Featherstone to Mr. Kipps to Miss Reubens and to the rest as they were required.

Mr. Kipps sent especially for Jeannette on her first morning. She was nervous and her pencil trembled a little as she scribbled down her notes. She found his dictation extremely difficult to take; he hesitated, paused a long time to think of the word he wanted, corrected himself, asked her to repeat what he had said, or to scratch out what she had written and to go back and read her notes to a point where he could recommence. But he seemed pleased when she brought him the finished letters.

"Very good, Miss Sturgis,—very good indeed," he said without enthusiasm, tapping his pursed lips with the tip of his penholder as he scanned her work.

She was jubilant. She looked for Roy; she was

eager to tell him what Mr. Kipps had said. But he was not at his desk as she passed through the advertising department, nor was he waiting for her—as she hoped—when five o'clock came and she started home.

Well, she was satisfied,—she had gotten just what she wanted,—she would soon make herself indispensable. . . . Mr. Kipps was really a lovely man, although one would never suspect it from his nervous manner. She felt a sudden assurance she was going to be very happy.

Roy found her again in her sweetest, kindest mood that evening. They began at once to discuss everyone in the entire organization of the company from the President, himself, down to Bertram, the little Jew office boy, who was inclined to be fresh. The publishing house had suddenly become their entire world and everyone in it was either friend or foe.

"I hope I make good," sighed Jeannette.

"Make good?" repeated her lover indignantly. "Of course, you'll make good. Don't *I* know how good you are? Why, *say*, Janny dear, you've got that bunch of girls skinned a mile!"

It was soon evident to Jeannette that Roy was right. The next day she made a point of glancing at some of Miss Foster's and Miss Lopez's letters; she noted two errors in the former's, and the latter's were rubbed and full of erasures; the letters, themselves, were poorly spaced and the sheets in several instances were far from being clean. She was genuinely shocked at such slovenliness. They would not have tolerated it at the school for a minute! The girls who had been with her under Beardsley had done better work than

that! . . . She paused over the thought and smiled.
It was funny now to think of dear old Roy as the Mr.
Beardsley who had once filled her with such awe and
in fear of whose displeasure she had actually trembled.

§ 7

Her satisfaction with her new position found utter
completeness when on her first Saturday morning her
pay envelope reached her, and she discovered she was
to receive fifteen dollars a week. It was the last drop
in her felicity. She flung herself into her work with
all the eagerness of an intense young nature. In turn
she took dictation from Mr. Featherstone, Miss
Reubens, Mr. Olmstead, the auditor, and young Mr.
Cavendish, who edited *Corey's Commentary*. Everyone seemed to like her. Miss Reubens, having tried the
new stenographer, thereafter invariably asked for her,
and while this was gratifying in its way, Jeannette
would have willingly foregone the distinction. Miss
Reubens was not a pleasing personality for whom to
work; she referred to Jeannette as "the new girl,"
treated her like a machine, and kept her sitting idly
beside her desk while she sorted papers or carried on
long conversations at the telephone. She was a high-
strung, perpetually agitated person, given to complaining a great deal, undoubtedly overworked, but
finding consolation in pitying herself and in bemoaning
her hard lot. Jeannette recognized in her the lady
with the twisted, sour mouth who had been inspecting
photographs the day she first came to the office.

Mr. Olmstead, the auditor, was a tiresome old man,
who teetered on his toes when he talked and tapped his

thumb-nail with the rim of his eye-glasses to emphasize his words. He took a tedious time over his dictation, and Jeannette had to shut her lips tightly to keep from prompting him.

Mr. Cavendish, on the other hand, was charming. He was about thirty-three or -four, Jeannette judged, handsome, with thick, very dark red hair, and a thick, dark red mustache. He was always very courteous, and had an ever-ready stock of pleasantries. She was aware that he admired her, and she could not help feeling self-conscious in his company. They joked together mildly and their eyes frequently held one another's in amused glances. Of all the people in the office she liked best to take dictation from him; he never repeated himself, his sentences were neatly phrased and to the point, and his choice of words, she considered, beautiful. That he was unmarried did not detract from her interest in him. She read some of the recent back numbers of *Corey's Commentary* and particularly the editorials, and told Roy she admired them enormously.

She was far happier in the environment of the editorial rooms than upstairs where she worked with the other stenographers in the midst of the bustle, racket and confusion of the circulation and mail order departments. She soon discovered she had little in common with Miss Foster or Miss Bixby; Miss Lopez was a pretty nonentity; Miss Pratt, an elderly incompetent, and Miss La Farge, a vulgar-lipped grisette. The girls realized she looked down on them and clannishly hung together, to talk about her among themselves. They were not openly rude, but Jeannette was aware she was not popular with them.

Miss Holland alone on the first floor attracted her. They smiled at one another whenever their eyes met, and Jeannette enjoyed the feeling that this faded, kindly gentlewoman recognized in her a girl of her own class.

§ 8

There were a dozen other personalities in the company that the new stenographer learned to know and with whom she came more or less into contact. Important among these was Mr. Corey's secretary, Mr. Smith, whom nobody liked. He was suspected of being a tale-bearer, an informant who tattled inconsequences to his chief. He was obviously a toady, and treated everyone in the office, not a member of the firm, with an air of great condescension. Mrs. Charlotte Inness of the book department was a regal, gray-haired personage, with many floating draperies that were ever trailing magnificently behind her as she came and went. Miss Travers, who was cooped up all day behind the wire grilling of the Cashier's cage, was a waspish, merry individual, and although sometimes common, even vulgar, was both friendly and amusing. Francis Holme and Van Alstyne spent most of their time on the road visiting book dealers. Van Alstyne was English and inclined to be patronizing, but Holme was large-toothed, large-mouthed and big-eared, bluff and frank, noisy and good-hearted. And there was also Mr. Cavendish's assistant, Horatio Stephens, a tall, rangy young man, with rather a dreamy, detached air, with whom Roy shared a room at his boarding-house. Jeannette found him vaguely repellent; there was something about his long skinny hands and droop-

ing eyelids that made her creepy. And then there was
Mr. Corey himself.

Chandler B. Corey was, as Roy had described him,
a man of vivid personality. Although not yet in his
fifties, he had a full head of silky white hair. In sharp
contrast to this were his black bushy eyebrows and his
black mustache which curled gracefully at the ends
and which he had a habit of pulling whenever he was
thinking hard. His skin was pink and clear as a boy's,
but there was nothing effeminate in his face with its
heavy square jaw. There was a dynamic quality about
him that communicated itself to everyone who came in
contact with him, and yet with all his energy and fire,
Jeannette noted there was an extraordinary gentleness
about him, somewhat suggesting sadness.

On a day toward the end of her third week, she took
a long and important letter from him. Miss Foster
was struggling with a pile of other work he had already
given her, and Mr. Smith sent Bertram upstairs with
a request for Miss Sturgis to come down.

She had never been in Mr. Corey's office before. At
once she was struck with its quality. Compared with
the noisy ruggedness and bare floors outside, it was
quiet, luxurious. Sectional bookcases, filled to overflowing, and many autographed framed photographs
lined walls that were covered with burlap. There were
one or two large leather armchairs and in the center a
great flat-topped desk heaped with manuscripts and
stacks of clipped papers. A film of dust lay over many
of these, and the scent of cigar smoke was in the air.
Mr. Corey's silvery head beyond the desk appeared as
a startling blot of white against the background of
warm brown.

She was surprised to discover how tersely he dictated. There was nothing of a literary quality about his sentences, nothing savoring of the polish of Mr. Cavendish. He was all business and dispatch. She felt oddly sorry for him; more than once during the brief quarter of an hour that she was with him a great sympathy for him came over her. He seemed weighed down with responsibilities. A paper mill was pressing him for money; no funds would be available for another three months; his letter offered them his note for ninety days. While he dictated, the telephone interrupted him; something had gone wrong with the linotype machines, and the delay would result in *The Wheel of Fortune* being two or three days late on the news-stands. In the midst of this conversation Mr. Featherstone came in to report that Shreve & Baker had cancelled their advertisement and had definitely refused to renew it. An army of annoyances pressed around on every side.

She told Roy about it when he came to see her that night.

"Oh, C. B.'s a wonder," he agreed; "he carries that whole concern on his shoulders, and you can rest assured there's nothing goes on down there that he doesn't know. They all depend on him."

"He seems so over-burdened, and so—so harassed," Jeannette said.

"I guess he's all of that. You know he's had an awful hard time getting a start; the business is just about able to stand on its own feet now."

"I don't think Mr. Smith is much help to him. He could save him a whole lot if he would."

"Oh, *that* fish! He's no good. He told C. B. a most

outrageous lie about Mr. Featherstone; there was an awful row.''

"Then why doesn't Mr. Featherstone have him discharged?''

"Nobody's got anything to say down there except Mr. Corey. He owns fifty-one per cent of the stock, I understand, and if he likes Smith, Smith is going to stay.''

"I can't see how Mr. Corey can put up with him.''

"How did C. B. like your work?''

"I don't know. Mr. Smith took it when I brought it downstairs, and carried it in to him. I didn't hear a word; but he didn't send it back to me for anything.''

"He was pleased all right. You've made a hit with everyone. They're all crazy about you; Miss Reubens always wants you; and Cavendish, I notice, seems to take a special interest in his dictation now.''

The last was said with an amused scrutiny of her face.

"Oh, don't be silly, Roy!''

"I'm not," he declared sensibly. "I don't care if he admires you. Men are always going to do that. Holme asked me the other day who the new queen was, and I was mighty proud to tell him you were my fiancée. I guess I appreciate the fact that the smartest, loveliest girl in the world is going to be my wife!''

"Oh,—don't!'' Jeannette repeated. There was trouble in her face.

§ 9

Her days were packed full of interest now. She enjoyed every moment of the time spent within the shabby portals of the publishing house. The rest of the twenty-four hours were given to happy anticipation of new experiences awaiting her, or in pleasant retrospect of happenings that marked her advancement. For it was clear to her she was progressing, daily tightening her hold upon her job, making the "big" people like her, bringing herself nearer and nearer the goal she some day eagerly hoped to reach: of being indispensable to these delightful, new employers. To what end this tended, how far it would carry her, under what circumstances she would achieve final success she could not surmise. She was conscious these days only of an intense satisfaction, a delight in knowing she was steadily, though blindly, attaining her ambition.

Often she wished during these early weeks she had a dozen pairs of hands that she might take everyone's dictation and type all the letters that left the office. She became interested in the subject and purpose of these letters. Cavendish wrote an urgent note to a Mr. David Russell Purington, who was a regular contributor to *Corey's Commentary* from Washington, telling him how extremely important it was, in connection with a certain article shortly to appear in the magazine, for him to obtain an exclusive interview on the subject with the Japanese plenipotentiary at that time visiting the capital. Miss Reubens fretted and murmured complainingly as she worded a communication to Lester Short, the author, explaining that it was impossible for *The Wheel of Fortune* to pay the price he asked for his story, *The Broken Jade*. Mr. Kipps, through her, informed the Typographical Union, Number 63, that under no conditions would the Chandler B. Corey Company reëmploy Timothy Conboy and that if the union persisted, the Publishing Company was prepared to declare for an open shop. Mrs. Inness confided to her hand an enthusiastic memorandum to Mr. Corey urging him to accept and publish at once a novel called *The Honorable Estate* by a new writer, Homer Deering, which she declared was of the most sensational nature.

But after typing these letters and memorandums Jeannette heard nothing more of them. She wanted to know whether or not Mr. David Russell Purington succeeded in obtaining the much desired interview, what Lester Short decided to do about the seventy-five dollars Miss Reubens offered, how the Typographical Union, Number 63, replied to Mr. Kipp's ultimatum, and if Mr. Corey accepted Homer Deering's significant manuscript. Her curiosity was seldom gratified; she hardly ever saw the replies to the letters she had typed with such interest. Miss Foster, Miss Lopez, Miss Pratt, Miss Bixby or Miss La Farge continued the correspondence. Often she would see a letter unwinding itself from a neighboring machine at the top of which she would recognize a familiar name, but she had no time to read further, and there was a certain restraint observed among the girls about overlooking one another's work. Jeannette realized she was merely a small cog in a machine and that her prejudices, enthusiasms, her interest and opinion were of small consequence to anyone.

She rose early in the morning, sometimes at five, and her mother would hear her thumping and pounding with an iron in the kitchen as she pressed a shirtwaist to wear fresh to the office, or clitter-clattering in the bathroom as she polished her shoes or washed stock-

ings. Her costume was invariably neat and smart,
but she dressed soberly, with knowing effectiveness
for her working day. Her mother, yawning sleepily or
frowning in mild distress, would find her getting her
own breakfast at seven.

"Why, dearie," she would plaintively remonstrate,
"whatever do you want to bother with the stove for?
I'm going to get your breakfast; you leave that to
me. . . . I don't see," she might add querulously,
"why you have to get up at such unearthly hours."

Alice would shortly make her appearance, and with
wrappers trailing, slippers clapping and shuffling about
the kitchen, her mother and sister would complete the
simple preparations for her morning meal, and set
about getting their own. About the time they had
borne in the smoking granite coffee-pot again to the
dining-room, and had hunched up their chairs to the
table, Jeannette would be ready to leave the house.
When she came to kiss them good-bye, she would always find them there, her mother's cheek soft and
warm, Alice's firm, hard face, cool and smelling faintly
of soap. She would seem so vigorously alive as she
left them, so confident and capable. There was always
a tremendous satisfaction in feeling well-dressed, well-
prepared and early-started for her day's work. As she
left the house, and filled her lungs with the first breath
of sharp morning air, there would come a tug of
excitement at the prospect of the hours ahead. She
loved the trip downtown on the bumping, whirring
elevated; she loved the close contact with fellow-
passengers, wage-earners like herself; she loved the
brisk walk along Seventeenth Street and across the
leaf-strewn square, where she faced the tide of clerks

and office workers that poured steadily out of the Ghetto and lower East Side, and set itself toward the great tall buildings of lower Fifth Avenue and Broadway, and she loved the first glimpse of the gold sign of the Chandler B. Corey Company, with the feeling that she belonged there and was one of its employees.

She would be at her desk half to three-quarters of an hour ahead of the other girls. There would usually be work left over from the previous day. She liked settling herself for the busy hours to come when no one was around and she could do so with comfort.

She would hardly be conscious of the other girls' arrival, and would often greet them with a smiling good-morning, or answer their questions with no recollection afterwards of having done so.

The whirlwind of office demands and the tide of work would soon be about her. Miss Reubens wanted her, Mr. Kipps rang for a stenographer, Mr. Featherstone had an important letter to get off before he went out. Would Miss Sturgis look up that letter to the Glenarsdale Agency? Would Miss Sturgis come down when she was free? Mr. Cavendish had an article he wanted copied as soon as possible. Miss Bixby was busy, Miss Foster was busy, Miss Lopez, Miss Pratt, Miss La Farge were busy; Miss Sturgis was busiest of all. She thrilled to the rush and fury of her days. There was never a let-up, never a lull; there was always more and more work piling up.

At noon, at twelve-thirty, at one,—whenever she was free for a moment about that time,—she would slip out for her lunch. She had learned she must eat,— eat something, no matter how little, in the middle of the day. She still patronized the soda and candy counter in the big rotunda of Siegel-Cooper's mammoth department store for her china cup of coffee and two saltine crackers. Sometimes she spent another nickel for a bag of peanut brittle. Somewhere she had read that the sugar in the candy and the starch in the peanuts contained a high percentage of nutritious value. She nibbled out of the bag on her way back to the office.

She would be gone hardly more than half the hour she was allowed for luncheon. Between one and three in the afternoon was the time she was least interrupted, and in this interval her fingers flew, and letter after letter,—slipped beneath its properly addressed envelope,—would steadily augment the pile in the wire basket that stood beside her machine. She rejoiced when it grew so tall, the stack was in danger of falling out.

In the late afternoon came the rush and the most exacting demands. Miss Reubens had a letter that must go off that night without fail; Mr. Featherstone had just returned from a conference with a big advertiser and wanted a record of the agreement typed at once; Mr. Kipps had a communication to be instantly dispatched; Mr. Corey needed a stenographer. The girls were all busy; they had too much to do already; they could not finish half the letters that had been given them. Well, how about Miss Sturgis? Could Miss Sturgis manage to get out just one more? It was *so* important. Yes, Miss Sturgis could,—of course she could; it might be late, but if the writer would remain to sign it, she'd manage to finish it somehow.

"You're a fool," Miss Bixby said to her one day sourly. "Nobody's going to thank you for it; you

don't get paid a cent more; I don't see why you want
to make a beast-of-burden out of yourself. They just
use you like a sponge in this office; squeeze every ounce
of strength out of you, and then throw you away.
Look at Linda Harris!"

Linda Harris was the girl who had sickened, and
whose place Jeannette now filled.

Perhaps Miss Bixby was right, Jeannette would say
to herself, riding home after six and sometimes after
seven o'clock on the lurching train, tired to the point
where her muscles ached and her sight was blurred.
But there was something in her that rose vigorously
to this battle of work, that made her reach down and
ever deeper down inside herself for new strength and
new capacity.

§ 10

Wearily, her hand dragging on the stair rail, she
would pull herself step by step up the long flights to
the top floor. Tired though she might be, her mind
would still be buzzing with the events of the day: Mr.
Cavendish's letter to Senator Slocum,—had she remembered the enclosures? Mr. Kipps had been short
with her, or so he had seemed; perhaps he had been
only vexed at the end of a long day of worry. Mr.
Corey's smile at a comment she had ventured was consoling. Then there was that friction between Miss
Reubens and Mrs. Inness; they had had some sharp
words; she wondered which one of them eventually
would triumph. Mrs. Inness, of course. . . . And
little Miss Maria Lopez had confided to her in the
wash-room she was going to be married!

"Hello, dearie! . . . Home again?" Jeannette's

mother would call to her cheerfully as she pushed open the door. Alice would turn her head with a " 'Lo, Sis''; she would kiss them dutifully, perfunctorily. The kitchen would be hot and steamy; the smell of food would make her feel giddy, perhaps faint. She would be ravenously hungry. She would go to her dark little bedroom, light the gas, remove her hat, blouse, and skirt and stretch herself gratefully on her bed. . . . Would Mrs. Inness go to Mr. Corey about her difference with Miss Reubens? . . . Miss Holland had had a conference with Mr. Kipps all afternoon; what could it be about? . . . Would Bertram be discharged for losing that manuscript? . . . Mr. Van Alstyne had certainly been unnecessarily curt; she cordially disliked him. . . . And Mr. Smith had most assuredly not given her Mr. Corey's message; why, she remembered distinctly . . .

"Dinner, dearie.'' She would drag herself to her feet, rub her face briskly with a wet wash-rag, and in her wrapper join her mother and sister at table.

"Well, tell us how everything went to-day,'' Mrs. Sturgis would say, busy with plates and serving spoon.

"Oh,—'bout the same as usual,'' Jeannette would sigh. "Bertram, the office boy, lost a manuscript to-day. It was terribly important. We were awfully busy upstairs, and Mrs. Inness sent the book out to be typed, and he left the package somewheres,—on the street car, he thinks. Mr. Kipps will probably fire him; he deserves it; he's awfully fresh.''

"You don't say,'' Mrs. Sturgis would murmur abstractedly. "Drink your tea, dearie, before it gets cold.''

Jeannette dutifully sipping the hot brew would consider how to tell them of the trouble between Mrs. Inness and Miss Reubens.

"Miss Reubens,—you know, Mother,—is the editor of *The Wheel of Fortune,* and Mrs. Charlotte Inness runs our book department. They dislike each other cordially and I just know some day there's going to be a dreadful row——"

"Alice, dearie,—get Mother another tea-cup," Mrs. Sturgis might interrupt, her eye on her older daughter's face to show she was attending. "And while you're up, you might glance in the oven. . . . Yes, dearie?" she would say encouragingly to Jeannette.

The girl would recommence her story, but she could see it was impossible to arouse their interest. Their attention wandered; they knew none of the people in the office; it was no concern of theirs what happened to them.

"Kratzmer had the effrontery to charge me thirty cents for a can of peaches to-day," Mrs. Sturgis would remark. "I just told him they were selling for twenty-five on the next block and I wouldn't pay it, and he said to me I could take my trade anywhere I chose, and I told him that that was no way to conduct his business, and he as much as told me that it was *his* business and he intended to run it the way he liked! I wouldn't stand for such impudence, and I just gave him a piece of my mind." An indignant finger tossing an imaginary ruffle at her throat suggested what had been the little woman's agitated manner.

"Kratzmer's awfully obliging," Alice commented mildly.

"Well, perhaps,—but the idea!"

"Mr. Corey was unusually nice to me to-day," Jeannette remarked.

Her mother would smile and nod encouragingly, but her eyes would be inspecting her daughters' plates, considering another helping or whether it was time for dessert.

"I couldn't match my braid," Alice would murmur in a disconsolate tone. "I went to the Woman's Bazaar and to Miss Blake's and they had nothing like it. I suppose I'll have to go downtown to Macy's. Do you remember, Mother, where you got the first piece?"

"No, I don't, dearie," her mother would reply slowly. "Perhaps it was O'Neill & Adams. . . . How much do you need?"

"About three yards. I could manage with two. Do you suppose you'd have time to-morrow, Janny, to try at Macy's?"

"Maybe; I can't promise. You have no idea how rushed we are sometimes."

"You know I've a good mind to try Meyer's place over on Amsterdam; it always seems so clean. Kratzmer's getting too independent."

"Kratzmer knows us, Mama, and sometimes it's awfully convenient to charge."

"I know. That's perfectly true. But the *idea* of his talking to me that way!"

"They might have it at Siegel-Cooper's. You could ask there to-morrow. It would only take you five minutes. I hate to go all the way downtown, and there's the carfare."

"I've traded with Kratzmer ever since he moved into the block. I guess he forgets I've been a resident in this neighborhood for nearly thirteen years. He shouldn't treat me like a casual customer; it's not right and proper."

"It would be the greatest help if I could get it to-morrow. I'm absolutely at a standstill on that dress until I have it. Siegel's sure to keep a big stock. I'll give you a sample."

"I've always liked the look of things at Meyer's. All the Jewesses go there and they always know where to get the best things to eat,—but I suppose he *is* more expensive."

"It oughtn't to cost more than twenty cents a yard. Do you remember what you paid for it, Mama?"

"Dearie,—it's so long ago; I'm sorry. . . . I'd rather hate to break with Kratzmer after all these years. You can't help but make friends with the trades-people. Do you think Meyer's would really be more high-priced, Janny?"

Jeannette would shrug her shoulders and carefully fold her napkin. They were dears,—she loved them best of all the world,—but they seemed so small and petty with their trifling concerns: matching braids and disagreeing with trades-people.

The dinner dishes would be cleared away. Jeannette would brush the cloth, put away the salt and pepper shakers, the napkins, and unused cutlery; then she would carefully fold the tablecloth in its original creases, replace it with the square of chenille curtaining, and climb on a chair to fit the brass hook of the drop-light over the gas-jet above.

Roy would arrive at eight,—he was always there promptly,—and she would have a bare twenty minutes to get ready. She would hear her mother and sister scraping and rattling in the kitchen as she dressed, water hissing into the sink, the bang of the tin dishpan, their voices murmuring.

She would be glad when her lover came. A flood of questions, surmises, hazarded opinions about office affairs, poured from her then. She was free at last to talk as she liked about what absorbed her so much; she had an audience that would listen eagerly and attentively to everything. What *would* Mr. Kipps do about Bertram, and if the manuscript was really lost, what *would* Mrs. Inness do about it? . . . Did he hear anything about the row between Mrs. Inness and Miss Reubens? Well,—she'd tell him, only she wanted first to ask his advice about whether she should go to Mr. Corey and simply tell him that Smith had certainly *never* given her his message?

Roy would meet this eager gossip with news of his own. Mr. Featherstone had given Walt Chase an awful call-down for promising a preferred position he had no right to, and Stubbs was starting on a trip to Chicago and St. Louis. There was talk of putting Francis Holme in charge of the Book Sales Department, and Roy hoped he'd get it instead of Van Alstyne. And what did Jeannette think the chances would be of Horatio Stephens getting Miss Reuben's job if Miss Reubens quit on account of Mrs. Inness?

Roy would tire eventually of this shop talk. He longed to reach the love-making stage of the evening; he was eager to tell her how much he adored her, and to have her confess she cared for him in return; he liked to have her nestle close against him, his arms about her, to hold her to him and have her raise her lips to his each time he bent over her. But Jeannette

grew less and less inclined these days to surrender herself to these embraces. Each time Roy mentioned love,
she would tell him not to be silly, and would speak of
another office affair. It distressed her lover; he would
fidget unhappily, not quite understanding how she
eluded him. Again and again he would return to the
question of their marriage. Did Jeannette think
March would be a good month? It was three months
off. Yes, March would be all right, but did he suppose
Miss Reubens was really overworked? Roy didn't
know whether she was or not; she complained a good
deal, he admitted. But now about where they were to
live; he had heard of a little house in Flatbush that
could be rented for twenty dollars a month. How did
she feel about living in Brooklyn?

But marriage did not interest her for the present;
she was too much absorbed in the affairs of the publishing company. Weddings could wait; hers could,
anyhow. Just now she wanted Roy to help her guess
the salaries of everyone in the office.

And when, as ten and ten-thirty and eleven o'clock
approached, Roy, conscious of the passing minutes,
would press his love-making to a point where Jeannette could no longer divert him, she would send him
home. She would suddenly remember she had her
stockings to wash out, or gloves to clean before she
went to bed. She would realize at the moment, how
dreadfully tired she was, and the morrow always
presented a difficult day.

"You must go now, Roy," she would say. "You
simply *must* go. I'm dead and I've got to get some
sleep. Please say good-night."

"Not until you kiss me," he would insist.

". . . There. Now go."

"But tell me first you love me?"

"Oh, *Roy!*"

"No,—you must tell me."

"Why, of course; you know I do."

"Lots?"

"Yes—yes."

"And you'll marry me?"

"Surely."

"When?"

"Now, Roy, you *must* go. I tell you I'm dropping, I'm so tired."

"But tell me when you'll marry me?"

"Well,—whenever we're ready."

"You darling! Kiss me again."

"Roy!"

"Kiss me. . . . Oh, kiss me *good.*"

"Good-night!"

"Good-night. . . . You darling!"

CHAPTER V

§ 1

Roy wanted to be married; he wanted Jeannette to set the date; he wanted her to make up her mind where she preferred to live, and to start making plans accordingly. Just before Christmas his salary was raised five dollars a week and the last barrier—for him—to the wedding was removed. There was nothing to prevent their being married at once. Everyone agreed, even Jeannette herself, that a hundred dollars a month would be sufficient for their needs the first year. With a mysterious air, Mrs. Sturgis hinted at responsibilities that might come to them, but Roy's salary would undoubtedly be raised more than once by that time. She liked her daughter's promised husband; he had such an honest, clean face, his eyes were so clear and blue. He made her think of her Ralph. She felt she could with safety entrust Jeannette's happiness to him. Alice was frankly a warm admirer of her prospective brother-in-law. She agreed with everything he said and always sided with him in an argument. Mother, sister and future husband shared the opinion that the marriage must soon take place; there was no sense in Jeannette's wearing herself to death down there at that office; she took it all too seriously; she was undermining her health.

Jeannette, with vague misgivings, agreed. It was too bad; she liked the business life so much. But marriage was the thing; she must make up her mind to be married and settle down in a little house with Roy over in Brooklyn,—presumably. She thought of the dish-washing, bed-making, carpet-sweeping, cooking, and shuddered. She hated domesticity. Alice would have loved it; but she was different from Alice.

Roy? . . . Oh, she loved Roy, she guessed, but not with the fluttering pulse and quickened breath he had once occasioned. She liked him; he was sweet and companionable. Sometimes she felt very motherly toward him, liked to brush his stuck-up hair and rest her cheek against his. She could see herself happy with him, knowing she would always dominate him and he was disarmingly amiable. Sometimes she thought about babies. She wouldn't mind having them. She had always imagined she would like one some day, to dandle about and cuddle close to her. Roy was sure to be a sweet-tempered father. But she sighed when she thought of the office, the progress she was making there, her popularity, and particularly the five dollars a week that was her own to spend just as she pleased. She loved that five dollars; once she touched the soft greenback to her lips.

She agreed to be married on the second of April.

§ 2

It was shortly after the beginning of the new year that the news went around the office that Mr. Smith was going;—fired, everyone decided. No one knew how the rumor got about, but there was universal and secret rejoicing. It was whispered that, as Mr. Corey's secretary, he had been indiscreet.

There were to be other changes in the office. Miss Travers was to take Smith's place, Mr. Holme was to be put in complete charge of the Book Sales department, Van Alstyne was leaving, and Miss Holland was to go downstairs to assist Mr. Kipps.

Jeannette, excited by these readjustments, surmised that her own news of resignation would create its particular stir. How interested everyone would be to learn that she and Roy Beardsley of the Advertising Department were to be married! There would be a lot of rejoicing and good wishes. The office would consider it a happy match. Her going would be regretted, —she knew that she was valued,—but all would be glad nevertheless that she and young Beardsley were going to be man and wife. An ideal couple!—Happy romance!—Miss Sturgis and Mr. Beardsley! How delightful! Well—well!

If everyone was sure to think so well of her marriage, why should she have any doubts about it?

She was pondering on this, one day, while mechanically folding her letters and putting them into their proper envelopes, when there came a summons from Mr. Corey. She found him idly thumbing the pages of an advance dummy of one of the magazines. When she had seated herself and flapped back her note-book for his dictation, he asked her without preamble how she would like the idea of being his secretary. He elaborated upon what he should expect of her: there would be plenty of hard work, long hours sometimes, she might have to come back occasionally in the evenings, and there must be no gossiping with other employees of the company or outside of the office.

"What goes on in here, what you learn from my letters or see from my correspondence, what you come to know of my business or private life, must be kept strictly to yourself. Nothing must be repeated,—not even what may seem to you a trivial, insignificant fact. I wish to have no secrets from my secretary, and I do not wish my affairs discussed with anyone, not even with members of the firm, such as Mr. Kipps, or Mr. Featherstone. Understand? Miss Holland thinks you're qualified to fill the position,—recommends you warmly,—and Mr. Kipps has a good word for you. Personally I have a feeling you will do very well, and that I can trust you. If you think you can do the work, we will start you at twenty-five a week. . . . What do you say?''

Jeannette's throat went dry, her temples throbbed, her face burned. Visions swift, tormenting, rose before her: she saw Roy, her mother, sister!—she saw herself a bride, a wife, with hair hanging about her face, bending over a steaming pan full of dirty dishes; she saw herself sitting where Mr. Smith had sat, moving about the office, respected, looked up to, feared and conciliated. She thought of the number of times she had said that Smith was of small help to his chief, and the number of times, in her secret soul, she had pictured herself in some such post as his, helping, protecting, serving as she knew she could help, protect and serve. She gazed at the kind face with its crown of silvery white, and into the dark eyes studying her, as she felt rising up strong within her the consciousness of how she could work for this man, and be to him all he could ever expect in a secretary. The sadness that surrounded him, the big fight he was waging to make his business a success touched her imagination. She sensed his need of her,—his great need of her,—and she saw in the dim future how dependent he would grow to be on her. She would have a part in his struggle; she could help him achieve his ambition as he could help her achieve hers. Suddenly Roy's stricken face interposed again. Rebellion rose passionately! . . . But it was too late. She was going to be married; she was going to be Roy's wife. . . . Yet how desperately she longed to be this big man's secretary! She thought of the sensation the promotion would cause, how it would stagger Miss Foster, Miss Bixby, the other girls,—how it would impress her mother, Alice, —*Roy!*

Her strained, hard expression brought a puzzled look to her employer's face. She tried to speak; her lips only moved soundlessly.

"Well, well,—you don't have to make up your mind at once," Mr. Corey said. "Suppose you try it for a month or two. I don't think you'll find it as hard as you anticipate. I am away for some months every year,—I go abroad in the spring,—and while that does not mean a vacation for you, the work is naturally easier. I would greatly appreciate loyalty and conscientiousness. I think you have just the qualities. Try it, as I suggest, until, say the first of March, and then we'll see how we get along together and whether you think the work too hard."

She could not bring herself to tell him she was going to be married, that she was thinking of resigning in a few weeks; she could not dash from his hand the cup, brimming with all her ambitions realized, which he held out to her so persuasively. No,—not just yet. He suggested she try the position until the first of

March. There was nothing to hinder her from doing that! The glory would be hers, even if she were to enjoy it but for six weeks. She would be "Mr. Corey's secretary" before the office; everyone would know of it, her mother, Alice, Roy,—all of them would see how she had succeeded. On the first of March,— went her swift mind,—she could talk it over with Mr. Corey, tell him the work was beyond her strength, that she didn't like it,—or that she was going to be married! It wouldn't matter then.

"Well,—what do you say?" Mr. Corey leaned forward slightly, his shrewd eyes watching her.

She swallowed hard, and met his steady gaze.

"Yes,—I'll try it. I—I think I can do it."

"Good. Then we'll start in to-morrow. Mr. Smith leaves us Saturday. He can show you about my private filing system and some of the ropes before he goes."

§ 3

Quietly she told the news to her mother and sister that evening. At once there was a hubbub; they were lavish with kisses, hugs and congratulations. Alice, clapping palms, exclaimed:

"That will give you seventy-five—ninety dollars more to spend on your trousseau! . . . Oh, what will you *do* with it, Janny?"

"It's more than Roy gets," Mrs. Sturgis commented proudly with an elegant gesture of her hand.

"No, he was raised just before Christmas."

"Well, it's as much anyway. Think of it: twenty-five dollars a week! . . . For a *girl!* . . . Why, your father never earned much more!"

Roy was delighted, too.

"By golly!" he exclaimed enthusiastically. "I told you, didn't I? I guess I can tell a good stenographer when I see one. You were worrying—remember?—when you first went down there whether you were going to make good or not. . . . Well,—*say,*—isn't that great! . . . I guess I've got a pretty smart girl picked out for a wife; hey, old darling? You're just a wonder, Janny! You can do anything. I wish I was good enough for you, that's all. . . . Poor old C. B.! He'll be disappointed as the deuce when you quit!"

Nevertheless, within the next few days Roy wondered if he altogether liked the change in Jeannette's status. Her manner towards him became different. She no longer would gossip about office matters, and during business hours she treated him with cold formality. There had always been a pleased light in her eyes at a chance encounter with him and sometimes he would find a little note on his desk she had left there. But now she held him at a distance rather pompously, he thought. She answered "I don't know," or "Mr. Corey didn't say," when he asked some casual question about business. She had become close-mouthed, and gave herself an air as she went about her work.

"I can't act differently towards you than I do towards anybody else," she said in her defence when he complained. "Don't you see, Roy, I've got to be a kind of machine now. I've got to treat everybody alike. Mr. Corey wouldn't like it if he thought I was intimate with you."

"But we're *engaged to be married!*"

"Yes, of course,—but he doesn't know it. And I

want to make good, even if it's only for a few weeks.
You understand, don't you, Roy?''

Perhaps he did, perhaps he didn't. Jeannette did
not concern herself. She was absorbed in adequately
filling this coveted job which satisfied her heart and
soul and brain.

The hour of triumph when the news went abroad of
her promotion was as gratifying as she could possibly
have wished. The girls crowded about her, congratu-
lating her, wringing her hands; Miss Foster impulsively kissed her. Jeannette knew they envied her; she
knew that, for the time being, they even hated her; but
their assumed pleasure in her good fortune was none-
the-less agreeable. Miss Reubens complained sourly
that the general office had lost its only efficient stenographer; Mr. Cavendish charmingly expressed his personal satisfaction in her advancement and gave her
hand a warm pressure of friendliness; Mr. Kipps and
Mr. Featherstone both complimented her with hearty
enthusiasm. Jeannette was not cynical but she believed
she put a proper value on these felicitations,—particularly those of these last two gentlemen. Mr. Corey
was indeed the dominant power behind them all; their
destinies lay largely in his hands, and she was now
the go-between, the avenue of approach between the
underlings and leader. As they had feared and disliked Smith, so they would fear and perhaps dislike her.
She hoped they would learn to like her in time, but it
was natural they should feel a great respect for President Corey's secretary, and be anxious to gain her
favor, hoping that to each of them she might prove a
"friend at court." Still they were not wholly insin-
cere. Miss Holland, Jeannette felt, was genuinely

pleased. The older woman held both her hands and told her how happy the news had made her; her eyes shone with the light of real pleasure. The girl felt her to be indeed a friend.

Jeannette took her new work with the utmost seriousness. She determined at the outset to treat everyone in the office with absolute impartiality, to carry whatever anybody entrusted to her to the President's attention with an equal measure of fidelity, to see to it that Mr. Kipps or Horatio Stephens would fare the same at her hands. She planned to execute her secretarial duties automatically, disinterestedly, with the impersonal functioning of a machine.

But she discovered the futility of this scheme of conduct within the first few days. Miss Reubens wished to speak to Mr. Corey. Was Mr. Corey busy? Would Miss Sturgis be so good as to tell her when she might see him for a few minutes? Jeannette knew, as it happened, what Miss Reubens wished to interview Mr. Corey about; Miss Reubens had already discussed it with him, and he had already advised her. It would be merely adding to his troubled day to go over the matter again; nothing more would be accomplished. Besides, Jeannette knew Miss Reubens bored Mr. Corey just as she bored everybody else. The interview did not take place.

Again, Mr. Cavendish had promised a check to a distinguished contributor to *Corey's Commentary;* he had assured the author-statesman it would be in the mail that afternoon without fail; would Miss Sturgis manage to get Mr. Corey to sign it at once? Miss Sturgis could and did, but a check to an engraving company, which Mr. Olmstead wished to be sent the same day, waited until next morning for the hour which Mr. Corey set apart for check-signing.

Her first concern was for Mr. Corey himself. She had guessed he was harassed and harried, but had no idea how greatly harassed and harried until she came to work at close quarters with him. He had tremendous capacity, was an indefatigable worker, but she had not observed his methods a week before she noted he did far too much that was unnecessary. Insignificant things engaged and held his attention; he frittered away his time upon trivialities. She set herself to save him what she could and began by keeping the office force from troubling him. Mr. Corey had a delightful personality, was a charming and stimulating talker, a most pleasing companion; his secretary understood quite clearly why every member of the staff liked to sit in an easy chair in his office and spend half-an-hour with him, chatting about details. He was too ready to squander his precious moments on anyone who came to him. It was difficult to sidetrack these time-wasters but in some measure she succeeded. Memorandums that came addressed to him, she dared answer herself; she even went so far as to lift papers from his desk and return them whence they came with a typed note attached: "Mr. Corey thinks you had better handle this. J. S." Her daring frightened her sometimes. It was inevitable she should run into difficulties.

One afternoon the "buzzer" at her desk summoned her; it sounded more peremptory than usual.

"Miss Sturgis," Mr. Corey addressed her, "Mr. Kipps left some information about our insurance on my desk a day or two ago; have you seen it?"

"Yes, sir, I returned it to him early this morning and suggested that he take care of the matter for you." As she spoke she felt the color rushing to her face.

Corey's black brows came together in an annoyed frown. He cleared his throat with a little impatient cough, and jerked at his mustache.

"I wish, Miss Sturgis,—I wish you would not be quite so officious."

Jeannette squared herself to the criticism, and stood very erect, returning his look.

"I thought Mr. Kipps could take care of the matter, without bothering you further," she said, beginning to tremble.

There was silence in the room. The girl's defiant figure, tall and straight, confronted the man at the desk, and the dark frown that bore down upon her. She was very beautiful as she stood there, with the warm color tinging her olive-hued cheeks, her eyes clear and unwavering, her head flung back, her small hands shut, resolute, unflinching. Perhaps Corey saw it, perhaps it occurred to him that she showed a fine courage, bearding him in this fashion, facing him with such spirit, acknowledging her high-handedness yet defending it. As he considered the matter, it came to him that she was right. Kipps was perfectly capable of taking care of this insurance business himself.

What was passing in the man's mind the girl never knew. Slowly she saw the scowl drift away, the stern face relax. He swung his chair toward the window and contemplated the horizon. The sun was setting over the Jersey shore, and the glow of a red sky was reflected on his face.

"Very well," he said at last. It was ungracious, it was curt, but there was nothing more. There was no dismissal. The girl waited a few minutes longer, then turned and quitted the room.

There were errors—serious errors—for which she was accountable. She incorrectly addressed envelopes in the hurry of dispatching them, she mixed letters and sent them to the wrong people, she mislaid certain correspondence that upset the whole office, and she kept the great Zeit Heitmüller, painter and sculptor,—of whom she had never heard,—waiting for more than an hour in the reception room, though Mr. Corey had begged him to call. Mr. Featherstone criticized her sharply when she neglected sending off some advertising copy after Mr. Corey had O.K.'d it, and she was aware that Mr. Olmstead complained of her in great annoyance when she returned to him an inventory he had prepared after it had lain four days on Mr. Corey's desk. At times she felt herself an absolute failure, and at others knew she was steadily gaining ground in the confidence and regard of the man she served. There were hard days, days when everything went wrong, when everybody was cross, when it was close and suffocating in the office, and whatever one touched felt gritty with the grime of the dusty wind that swept the streets. There were days when Corey was short and critical, when whatever Jeannette did, seemed to irritate him. A dozen times during a morning or afternoon she might be near to tears and would rehearse in her mind the words in which she would tell him that since she could not do the work to satisfy him, he had better find someone else to take her place. There were other days when he chatted with her

in the merriest of moods, asked how she was getting
along, inquired about herself and her family, looked up
smilingly when she stood before his desk to interrupt
him, and thanked her for having protected him from
some trifling annoyance.

Her heart swelled with pride and satisfaction the
first Saturday she tore off a narrow strip from the
neat, fat little envelope Miss Travers handed her, and
found folded therein two ten- and one five-dollar bills.
Twenty-five dollars a week! She rolled the words
under her tongue; she liked to hear herself whisper it.
"Twenty-five dollars a week!" There were hundreds
and hundreds of men who didn't earn so much, and a
vastly larger number of women!

Her mother, warmly seconded by Alice, refused to
allow her to contribute more than ten dollars toward
the household expenses. She had her trousseau to
buy, they argued, and this was Jeannette's own money
and she ought to spend it just as she chose and for
what she chose. Finances at the moment were much
less of a problem than they had been for the little
household. A wealthy pupil of Signor Bellini with a
fine contralto voice had engaged Mrs. Sturgis as her
regular accompanist, and paid her ten dollars every
time she played for her at an evening concert.

Jeannette allowed herself to be persuaded, and Saturday afternoons became for her orgies of shopping.
She priced everything; she ransacked the department
stores. She knew what was being asked for a certain
type and finish of tailor suit on Fifth Avenue, and
what "identically the same thing" could be bought for
on Fourteenth Street. She got the tailor suit, and a
new hat, a pair of smart, low walking pumps, some

half-silk stockings, be-ribboned underwear, a taffeta
petticoat, everything she wanted. She lunched at the
St. Denis in what she felt to be regal luxury, and
indulged herself in a bag of chocolate caramels afterwards. The joy of having money to spend intoxicated
her; she revelled in the glory of it; it was exciting,
wonderful, marvellous. Not one of the things she
bought would she allow herself to wear; everything
was to be saved until she was married, and became
Mrs. Roy Beardsley.

Her future husband took her one Sunday to inspect
the small brick house in Flatbush which could be rented
for twenty dollars a month. The weather was unduly
warm,—an exquisite day with a golden sun,—one of
those foretastes of spring that are so beguilingly de-
ceptive. From the janitor, who showed them over it,
they learned that the house would cost them twenty-
two dollars a month. It was one of a solid, unrelieved
row of fourteen others exactly like it, all warmed by a
central heating system, and supplied similarly with
water and gas. It was dark, the floors were worn and
splintery, the windows dingy; the whole place smelled
of old carpets and damp plaster. Still it had three bedrooms upstairs, and a living-room, a really pleasant
dining-room, and a kitchen on the ground floor. Roy
watched Jeannette's face eagerly as they stepped from
room to room, but he failed to detect any sign of
enthusiasm. It impressed the girl as anything but
cheerful. She saw herself day after day alone in this
place, sweeping, dusting, making beds, washing dishes,
getting herself a plate of pick-up lunch and eating it at
the end of the kitchen table, trying to read, trying to

sew, trying to amuse herself during the empty afternoons until it was time to start dinner and wait for
her husband to come home. After the bustle and excitement of the office, it would be insufferably dull.

As they waited a moment on the front steps for the
janitor to lock up after them, Jeannette noticed a
large, fat woman in a shabby negligée, watching them
from the upper window of the adjoining house, her
plump, pink elbows resting on a pillow, as she leaned
out upon the sill, enjoying the mellowness of the afternoon. On the ground floor behind the looped lace curtains of a front window, her husband was asleep in a
large upholstered armchair, Sunday newspapers scattered about him, the comic section across his round,
fat abdomen.

"These would be the kind of neighbors she would
have!" thought Jeannette. Oh, it wasn't what she
wanted! It wasn't her kind of a life—*at all!* She
would be lonely, lonely, lonely.

Roy was getting twenty-five dollars a week; she was
getting twenty-five dollars a week. Why couldn't they
go on working together in the same office and have a
joint income of fifty dollars a week,—two hundred
dollars a month! The idea fired her.

But she found no one to share her enthusiasm.
Alice pressed a dubious finger-tip against her lips;
Roy frowned and said frankly he didn't think it was
the right way for a couple to start in when they
got married; her mother indulged in firm little shakes
of her head that set her round cheeks quivering. When
the heated discussion of the evening was over and Roy
had taken himself home, Mrs. Sturgis came to sit on

the edge of Jeannette's bed after the girl had retired, and in the darkness discoursed upon certain delicate matters which evidently her dear daughter hadn't considered.

"I hope my girl won't have responsibilities come upon her too soon after she's married," she said, after a few gentle clearings of her throat, "but, dearie, you know about babies, and you'll want to have one, and it's right and proper that you should. But where would you be if a—if a—you found you were going to have one,—and you were working in an office? You must consider these things. Roy's perfectly right in not wanting his wife at a dirty old desk all day. . . . And then, dearie, there are certain decencies, certain proprieties. A bride cannot be too careful; she must always be modest. Suppose you actually tried this— this wild scheme of yours, and after your happy honeymoon, went back to the office among your old associates, the men and women with whom you've grown familiar; imagine how it would seem to them, and what dreadful thoughts they might think about you and Roy! One of the lovely things about marriage, Janny, is the dear little home waiting to shield the young bride."

"Oh, but Mama . . ." began Jeannette in weary protest. But she stopped there. What use was it to argue? None of them understood her; none of them was able to grasp her point of view.

Roy voiced the only argument that had weight with her.

"I don't think C. B. would like it; I don't think he would want to have a secretary who was married to somebody in the same office."

Jeannette felt that this would be a fact. No matter how well she might please Mr. Corey, a secretary who was married to another employee of the company would not be satisfactory. It was highly probable that in the event of her marriage he would be unwilling for her to continue with him.

No, it was plain that if she married Roy, she must resign, she must let go her ambition, her hopes for success in business, and she must accept Flatbush, and the dismal little brick house, the unprepossessing neighbors, and the lonely, lonely days.

Well — suppose — suppose — suppose she *didn't* marry!

The relief the idea brought was startling. But she couldn't bring herself to give up Roy,—she couldn't hurt him! She loved him,—she loved him dearly! Never in the last few months since he had come back to her from California had she been so sure she loved him as now. Those eager blue eyes of his, that unruly stuck-up hair, that quaint smile, that supple, boyish figure,—so sinuous and young and clean,—she couldn't give them up!

A battle began within her. It was the old struggle,— the struggle of ambition and independence, against love and drudgery, for marriage meant that to her; she could think of it in no other way.

Daily in her work at the office, she felt a steady progress; daily, she beheld herself becoming increasingly efficient; daily, more and more important matters were entrusted to her.

"Thank you very much, Miss Sturgis." "That's fine, Miss Sturgis." "Please arrange this, Miss Sturgis." "Miss Sturgis, will you kindly attend to this matter yourself?"

These from Mr. Corey, and in the office she overheard:

"Well,—get Miss Sturgis to do that." "Better ask Miss Sturgis." "Miss Sturgis will know." "If you want C. B.'s O.K., get Miss Sturgis to put it up to him."

It was wine to her. She felt herself growing ever more confident, established, secure.

§ 4

"Now, Janny,—what are you going to do about a house or an apartment or something where we can begin housekeeping? Gee, I hate the idea of boarding! We ought to have a place we can call our *home*. April second is only two weeks off, and I don't suppose it's possible to find anything now. We'll have to go to a hotel or a boarding-house for a while until we can look 'round. . . . Do you realize, Miss Sturgis, you're going to be Mrs. Roy Beardsley inside of a fortnight!"

"Roy—*dear!*" she exclaimed helplessly.

"But, my darling,—you've got to make up your mind."

Make up her mind? She could not. She listened dumbly, miserably while her mother and sister discussed, with the man she had promised to marry, the details of the wedding, and what the young couple had better do until they could find a suitable place in which to start housekeeping.

"We'll go over to the church on Eighty-ninth Street
about six o'clock, and Doctor Fitzgibbons will perform the ceremony and then we'll come back here for
a happy wedding supper," planned Mrs. Sturgis
confidently.

On what was she expected to live? asked Jeannette,
mutinously, of herself. Twenty-five dollars a week for
both of them? It had seemed ample when they first
discussed it. Her mother's income for herself and
two daughters had rarely been more and frequently
less. Mrs. Sturgis paid thirty dollars a month rent
for the apartment, and Alice was supposed to have ten
dollars a week on which to run the table; in reality
she provided the food that sustained the three of them
at an expenditure of one dollar a day. But at forty
dollars a month for food and twenty or twenty-five a
month for rent and at least five dollars a week for
Roy's lunches and carfare, what was she, Jeannette,
to have left to spend on clothes or amusement? She
would be a prisoner in that dismal little Flatbush
house, bound hand and foot to it for the lack of carfare across the river to indulge in a harmless inspection of shop windows! Now she was free,—now she
could get herself a gay petticoat if she wanted one, or
a new spring hat in time for Easter, or take Alice and
herself to a Saturday matinée and nibble chocolates
with her, hanging excitedly over the rail of the gallery
from front row seats! And she was to relinquish all
this liberty, which now was actually hers, actually her
own to enjoy and delight in rightfully and lawfully,
and manacle her hands, rivet chains about her ankles
and enter this prison, whose door her mother, her sis-

ter and Roy held open for her, and where they expected
her to remain contentedly and happily for the rest of
her life!

It was too much! It was preposterous! It was in-
human! She didn't love *any* man enough to make a
sacrifice so great. She was self-supporting, independent,—beholden to no one,—she could take care of herself for life if necessary, and after her room and
board were paid for, she would always have fifteen
dollars a week—sixty dollars a month!—to spend as
foolishly or as wisely as she chose with no one to call
her to account. She hugged her little Saturday envelopes to her breast; they were hers, she had earned
them, she would never give them up,—never—never—
never!

§ 5

She persuaded Roy to postpone the wedding. There
was no special need for hurry. It would require a lot
more saving before they could properly furnish a
little house or an apartment; it was much wiser for
them to start in right; in a few months they could have
two or three hundred dollars. She presented the matter to him in a rush of words one evening and, as she
had foreseen, he was overborne by her vehemence.
Roy was sweet-tempered, he was amiable, he was
always willing to give way in an argument. Often she
had felt impatient with him for this easy tractability.
He didn't have enough backbone! Even now his readi-
ness to concede what she asked disappointed her.
Something within her clamored for an indignant rejection of her proposal. She wanted him to insist
with an oath that their marriage must take place at

once, that she must make good her promise without
further to-do. He lost something very definite in her
regard at that moment; he never meant quite so much
to her again. It was the pivotal point in their
relationship.

Alice let her hands and sewing fall into her lap
when her sister told her the marriage was to be postponed, and said anxiously: "Oh, Janny,—I'm awfully
sorry," but her mother unexpectedly approved.

"There's no need of your rushing into all the troubles and worries of marriage, dearie,—until you're
quite, quite prepared. I think you're very wise to wait
a little while; it's right and proper; you and Roy are
showing a lot of real common sense. You'll have some
capital to start in with, and you can take your time
about finding just the right kind of a place to live in.
And then it means I'm going to have my darling all
summer. . . . Only," she added with a reproachful
glance at the girl and a pout of lips and cheeks, "I
wish you'd give up that horrid, old office and stay at
home with your mother and sister, and have a few
months to yourself before you fly away to be a bride."

What a relief to know she had escaped for a time
at least the net that had been spread for her! With
head held high, and a free heart, with eager step and
a pulse tuned to the joy of living, Jeannette plunged
on with her work.

CHAPTER VI

§ 1

THE cold of winter clung with a tenacious grip to the city that year until far into April. Jeannette had eagerly looked forward to the spectacular flower-vendors' sale of spring blooms in Union Square on the Saturday before Easter but a bitter wind began to assert itself early in the day and by ten o'clock had wrought pitiful havoc with the brave show of potted lilies and azaleas. The Square was littered with their battered petals and torn leaves. Three days before the first of May a flurry of snow clothed the city again in white, and then, without warning, summer breathed its hot, moist breath upon the town. The air was heavy with water; a mist, thick and enervating, spread itself like a miasma from a stagnant pool, through the streets. A tropical heat,—the wet clinging heat of a conservatory,—enveloped New York. And in June came the rain, an intermittent downpour that lasted for weeks.

It was a trying time for everyone. The office felt damp, and there was a constant smell all day of wet rubber and damp woolens. Black streams of water meandered over the floor from the tips of wet umbrellas, stacked in corners. On the fifth floor the roof leaked, and old Hodgson had to be moved elsewhere. In the midst of the general discomfort Mr. Corey fell sick.

It proved nothing more serious than a heavy bronchial cold, but his physician ordered him to bed, and he was warned he must not venture into the damp streets until the last vestige of the cold had disappeared. The doctor consented to let him see his secretary and to keep in touch with the office by telephone. It was thus that Jeannette came to visit her employer in his own home.

Mr. Corey lived in one of three cream-painted brick houses on Tenth Street, a hundred yards or so from the corner of Fifth Avenue. The houses were quaint affairs, only two stories in height, with square-paned glass in the shallow windows and wide, deep-panelled front doors ornamented in the center with heavy, shining brass knockers. They were old buildings, dating back to the early nineteenth century, and had somewhat of a colonial atmosphere about them. The Corey family consisted of Mrs. Corey and two children,—a boy of eighteen, Willis Corey, in his first year at Harvard, and a girl, Helen, a year younger, who lived at home and was called "Babs." Jeannette was disappointed, not to say disturbed, at meeting her employer's wife.

"I wasn't aware that I had a preconceived idea of her," she said to Alice in recounting her impressions. "Mr. Corey seems to be devoted to her, and has a large silver-framed photograph of her on his desk. I supposed from her picture and from the way he speaks about her that she was the same kind of earnest, hardheaded, clear-thinking person as himself. But she isn't that way at all. In the first place, she's very tall and stately; she's got lots of hair,—it's quite gray and very curly,—and she piles it up on top of her head and always wears a bandeau or a fillet to bind it. She's rather intense in her manner and a trifle theatrical. She's a handsome woman, faded of course now, but she has very large dark eyes, that she uses effectively, and really beautiful brows. She affects the weirdest of costumes, all lace and floating scarf, with lots of color. She had several rings on her fingers and bracelets dangling and jingling on her wrists. I thought her stupid; I mean *really* dense. When I got to the house she came out to the hall where I was waiting, led me into the parlor and made me sit down. She said she wanted to have a good talk with me. She was so glad Mr. Smith had gone, and she went on at once to say how she had urged 'Chandler!'—it was funny to hear Mr. Corey called by his first name!— how she had urged him to make a change for a long time. She said he said to her: 'Where do you think I could find anybody to replace him?' and she said: 'Well, how about that clever Miss Sturgis who's just come to you?' She told me she had begged him for weeks to give me a trial before he consented.

"You know, Allie, it rather puzzled me what her object could be in romancing that way, for, of course, I don't believe a word of it. She never heard of me until Mr. Corey happened to tell her he had a new secretary! And then she went on to talk about the business. My dear, it was pathetic! She wanted me to think that she knew about everything that went on at the office, that Mr. Corey kept nothing from her, and talked over every important decision with her before he made up his mind. I almost laughed in her face! She doesn't know one single thing about his affairs. She hasn't the faintest idea, for instance, that he's in debt, that the paper company could wind up his affairs to-morrow if it wanted to, nor what bank has helped to finance him from the start, nor where the money comes from that buys her food and clothing. She supposes, I presume, that it comes from profits. Profits are a negligible quantity with the Chandler B. Corey Company and have been ever since Mr. Corey launched it. It's getting in better shape all the time, and some day there *will* be profits.

"Mrs. Corey looked brightly at me with her large soulful eyes and said: 'Those two volumes of *The Life and Letters of Alexander Hamilton* are quite wonderful, aren't they? Such beautiful bookmaking!' and 'We were quite successful with *The Den,* weren't we?' Imagine, Alice! *'We!'* What she knows about the business is about as much as she can gather from the books Mr. Corey publishes and occasionally brings home to her! She talked a lot about the magazines, and asked me if I didn't think Miss Reubens was making a very wonderful periodical out of *The Wheel of Fortune.*

"I just nodded and agreed with her. She was trying to impress me how well-informed she was, and I let her think she succeeded. Toward the end she got started on Mr. Corey, and how hard he worked, and how keenly I ought to feel it my duty to save him from petty annoyances; I must consider myself a guard, a sentinel, stationed at the door of his tent to keep the rabble from disturbing the great man! I let her rave on, but it was all I could do to listen. I thought as I sat there that in all probability she was the noisiest and most disturbing of the lot. She wound up by telling me what the doctor had said to her about Mr.

Corey having caught cold, and she wanted to urge me particularly to guard him against draughts. Then she asked me if Mr. Corey ever took me to lunch! Now what do you think made her ask me a question like that? You don't suppose she's jealous? It seems too ridiculous even to think about. My goodness! When you see the kind of women some men get for wives you wonder how they put up with them!''

§ 2

All Mr. Corey's personal mail passed through Jeannette's hands; she opened and read most of it. He dictated to her his letters to his son at Cambridge, and even those to his wife and Babs when they went to Kennebunkport for the summer. Jeannette learned that Willis had been madly in love with a married woman who sang in the choir of a Fifth Avenue church, that he was given to midnight carousing, smoked far too many cigarettes, that his mother spoiled him, and his father was disgusted with him. With the aid of a ''cramming'' school, he had somehow wiggled himself into Harvard, but Mr. Corey had made him distinctly understand that at the first complaint concerning him he would have to withdraw and go to work. Jeannette came to know, too, that Babs was epileptic and that early in May she had had the first fit in two years, and that the day after her mother and herself had arrived in Kennebunkport, she had had another. Letters of a very agitated nature passed between the parents as to what should now be done. Nothing was decided. Likewise Jeannette learned that Mrs. Corey

was at times recklessly extravagant. Her husband repeatedly had to call her to account, and sometimes
they had violent quarrels about the matter. Just before Mrs. Corey departed for Maine she had bought
six hats for herself and Babs, and had charged over
three hundred dollars' worth of new clothing. Mr.
Corey had been exasperated, as only a few weeks before he had made a point of asking her to economize
in every way possible during the coming summer.
He himself, Jeannette knew, must shortly undergo a
more or less serious operation, of which his family
was totally ignorant, that he was worried because his
Life Insurance Company had declined after an examination to increase the amount of his insurance, and
that he had successfully engineered a loan to wipe off
his indebtedness to the big Pulp and Paper Company.

There was little that concerned him with which she
did not become acquainted. She knew that his house
on Tenth Street was heavily mortgaged and that on
the second loan carried by the property he was paying
an outrageous rate of interest; that on the tenth of
every month he never failed to send a check for sixty-
six dollars and sixty-seven cents to a man in Memphis,
Tennessee, that his dentist threatened to sue him unless he settled a bill that had been owing for two
years; that on the first of every month, Mr. Olmstead
deposited to his account in the Chemical National Bank
five hundred dollars; that no month ever passed without his chief sending for the old man and directing
him to deposit an additional hundred, or two hundred,
or sometimes three hundred to his account, and that
these sums appeared on the books of the company as

personal indebtedness. Frequently this levy upon the Company's bank balance upset Mr. Olmstead, and more than once Jeannette heard the old cashier emphatically assert as he rapped his eye-glasses in his agitated fashion upon his thumb-nail:

"All right, Mr. Corey,—you're the boss here, and I've got to do as you say, but I won't answer for it, Mr. Corey. I warn you, sir, we won't have enough for next week's pay-roll!"

"Oh, yes, yes, yes," Mr. Corey would soothe him. "We'll manage somehow; you pay the money in the bank for me and we'll talk about it afterwards."

There were even more intimate things about the man she served which became his secretary's knowledge. He sometimes took the sixtieth of a grain of strychnine when he was unusually tired, he dyed his mustache and eyebrows, and wore hygienic underwear for which he paid six dollars a garment. She had charge of his personal bank account. She drew the checks, put them before him for his signature, and sent them out in the mail. While Mrs. Corey was in Kennebunkport, she paid all the household expenses of the establishment on Tenth Street: electric light and milk bills, grocer's and butcher's accounts, the wages of the cook. She knew what were Mr. Corey's dues and expenses at the Lotus Club, what he paid for his clothes, what he owed at Brooks Bros., and at the Everett House where he had a charge account and signed checks for his lunches. There were no secrets in his life that were closed to her; he had less than most men to conceal; she considered him the most generous, the most upright, the most admirable man in the world.

§ 3

It was on a hot Saturday afternoon in July when no one but themselves were in the office, that Jeannette told Mr. Corey about Roy. She had not seen quite so much of Roy lately; he had been away on a business trip, and Horatio Stephens had asked him to spend his fortnight's vacation with himself and family at Asbury Park. He had written her letters full of endearments and underscored assertions of love, and had returned to plead eagerly that she set the day for the wedding and begin to plan with him how and where they should live. His earnestness made her realize she could temporize no longer.

"It isn't that I don't care for him," she said to Mr. Corey; "it's just that I don't want to get married, I guess."

The windows were open and a gentle hot wind stirred the loose papers on the desk. A lazy rumble of traffic rose from the street, punctuated now and then by the shrill voices of children in the Square, and the merry jingle of a hurdy-gurdy.

"You mustn't trifle with your happiness, Miss Sturgis," Corey said, pulling at his mustache thoughtfully. "You know this is all very well here for a time, but you must think of the future."

Jeannette stared out of the window and for some minutes there was silence; she spoke presently with knitted brows.

"Oh, I've gone over it and over it, again and again, and it seems more than I can do to give up my independence and the fun of living my own life just yet. I—I like Mr. Beardsley; I think we'd be happy to-

gether. He's devoted to me, and he's most amiable,''
—she glanced with a smile at her employer's face.
''My mother and my sister are eager to have me marry
him, but I just can't—can't bring myself to give up
my work and my life here to substitute matrimony.''

''No consideration for me, my dear girl, ought to
influence you. I'd be sorry to lose you, of course;
you're the best secretary I ever had, and I'd be hard
put to it to find anyone who could begin to fill your
place even remotely. But you mustn't think I couldn't
manage; I'd find somebody. Your duty is to yourself
and living your own life.''

''It isn't that, Mr. Corey. It's the work that I love;
I don't want to give it up,—the excitement and the
fun of it. It's a thousand times more exhilarating
than cooking and dish-washing. . . . And then there's
the question of finances, which, it seems to me, I'm
bound to consider. Mr. Beardsley's getting twenty-
five and I'm getting twenty-five; that's fifty dollars a
week we earn, but if I marry him, we both would have
to live on just his salary.''

''Yes,—that's very true,'' the man admitted.

The girl threw him a quick glance, and went on
hesitatingly:

''I don't suppose we could marry and each of us
go on holding our jobs?''

Mr. Corey considered, stroking his black mustache
with a thoughtful thumb and finger.

''Well,'' he said slowly, ''what do you gain? If you
went on working, you'd find it difficult to keep house;
you'd have to live in a boarding-house. And that isn't
homemaking. And then, Miss Sturgis, there's the
question of children. What would you do about them?

You wouldn't care to have a child as long as you came downtown to an office every day. . . . No, I wouldn't advise it. If you love your young man well enough, I would urge you to marry him."

"I *don't!*" Jeannette said to herself violently on her way home.

But did she? Almost with the denial, she began to wonder.

That night when Roy came to see her and asked her again for the thousandth time to name the day, she took his face between her hands and kissed him tenderly, folded his head against her breast, and with arms tight about him, pressed her lips again and again to his unruly hair.

Later, when he had gone and she was alone, she dropped upon her knees before the old davenport where they had been sitting, and wept.

It was the end of the struggle. She told no one for a long time, but in her mind she knew she would never marry him. Her work was too precious to her; her independence too dear; to give them up was demanding of her more than she had the strength to give.

END OF BOOK I

BOOK II

BREAD

CHAPTER I

§ 1

THE Chandler P. Corey Company was moving its
offices. A twenty-year lease had been taken on a building especially designed to fit its needs in the East
Thirties. The new home was a great cavernous concrete structure of eight spacious floors. On the ground
floor were to be the new presses destined to print the
magazines, and perhaps some of the books in the
future; the next two floors were to house the bindery,
the composing room and typesetting machines; the
editorial rooms were to be located on the fourth floor,
and above these would come in order the advertising,
circulation and pattern departments, each with a
stratum in the great concrete block to itself. The
eighth floor was to be given over to surplus stock, and
it would also serve as a store-room for paper and
supplies.

Both *Corey's Commentary* and *The Wheel of Fortune* had made money for their owners during the past
three years. It was the day of the "muck-raking"
magazine, and Cavendish had unearthed a Wall Street
scandal that sent the circulation of *Corey's Commentary* climbing by leaps and bounds. *The Wheel of*

Fortune had been rechristened *The Ladies' Fortune*, and its contents were now devoted to women's interests and fashions. The pattern business, that had been launched in connection with it, had proven from the outset immensely successful. Horatio Stephens was now its editor, and Miss Reubens conducted the special departments appearing among the advertising in its back pages, always referred to in the office as "contaminated matter." The circulation of both periodicals had increased so rapidly that Mr. Featherstone had been obliged to announce an advance in their advertising rates every three months.

Other branches of the business, too, had grown and shown a profit. Francis Holme, who was head of the Book Sales Department, and now a member of the firm, had developed the manufacture and sale of book premiums and school books. He sold large quantities of the former to the publishers of other magazines, for use in their subscription campaigns, and was even more successful with the latter among private schools and some public ones throughout the country. One or two recent novels had sold over the hundred thousand mark, and the general standing of the Chandler B. Corey publications had improved. It was conceded in the trade they had now a better "line." Something was being done, too, in the Mail Order Department, in charge of Walt Chase, and more and more sets of standard works were being sold by circularizing methods.

The installation and operation of their own presses had been a grave undertaking. Mr. Kipps had strenuously opposed it, arguing that the new building was enough of a responsibility, and that they should mark

time for awhile and see how they stood, rather than
incur a new loan of half a million dollars which the
new presses involved. Mr. Corey was convinced, however, that a tide had arrived in their affairs which de-
manded a rapid expansion of the business, and if he
and his partners were to make the most of the opportunity thus presented, they must rise to the occasion,
and show themselves able to expand with it.

"There's no use of our trying to crowd back into
our shells after we've outgrown them, is there, Miss
Sturgis?" he said to his secretary, with an amused
twinkle in his eye, after a heated conference with the
other members of the firm, during which Kipps in high
dudgeon had left the room.

Jeannette smiled wisely. She believed that her chief
was one of those few men who had far-seeing vision,
and could look with keen perception and unfaltering
eye into the future, and that he would carry Mr. Kipps,
Mr. Featherstone, the office, his family, herself, everybody who attached themselves to him, to fame and
fortune in spite of anything any one of them might do.
When he was right, he knew it, and knew it with conviction, and nothing could shake him.

He had only one weakness, his secretary felt, and
that was his attitude toward his son, Willis, who, two
years before, had been withdrawn from the intellectual
atmosphere of Cambridge, and put into the business,
presumably that his father might watch him. He was
one of the sub-editors of *Corey's Commentary* and
demoralized the office by his late hours, his disregard
of office rules against smoking, and his condescending
attitude toward everyone in his father's employ.

The three years that Jeannette Sturgis had been

Mr. Corey's secretary had seen many changes. Poor
Mrs. Inness had turned out to be a dipsomaniac.
Jeannette guessed her secret long before it was discovered by anyone else, and she had been full of pity
and sorrow when this gray-haired, regal woman had
to be dismissed. Van Alstyne was gone, and Humphrey Stubbs as well; Max Oppenheim likewise had
departed. The new Circulation Manager was a shrewd,
keen-eyed, spectacled young Scotchman, named Mac-
Gregor, whom everyone familiarly spoke to and of as
"Sandy." Miss Holland was still Mr. Kipps' assistant, and now most of the routine affairs of the business
were administered by her. Besides Mr. Holme, there
was another new member of the firm, Sidney Frank
Allister, who had come into the Chandler B. Corey
Company from a rival house, and was now entrusted
with the book-publishing end of the business. It was
usually his opinion that decided the fate of a manuscript. He had his assistants: a haughty Radcliffe
graduate, named Miss Peckenbaugh, whom Jeannette
heartily disliked, and old Major Ticknor, who had a
stiff leg since his Civil War days, and who stumped into
the office two or three times a week with his bundle of
manuscripts and stumped out again with a fresh supply. Very rarely Mr. Corey was consulted; he frankly
declared he hated to read a book, and would only do so
under the most vigorous pressure.

"Do I *have* to read this, Frank?" Jeannette would
often hear him ask Allister, when the latter brought
him a bulky manuscript and laid it on his desk. "You
know, I don't know anything about literature," he
would add, smilingly, with his favorite assumption of

being only a plain business man and lacking in appreciation of the arts.

"Well, Mr. Corey, this is really important," Allister would say. "We don't agree about it in my department."

"Has Holme read it? He can tell you whether it will sell or not."

"Mr. Holme doesn't think it will, but I believe this is a very important book, and one we most assuredly ought to have on our list."

Frequently Mr. Corey would hand the manuscript over to Jeannette after Mr. Allister had left the room, and beg her to take it home with her, read it, and give him a careful synopsis and her opinion. She used to smile to herself when she would hear him quoting her, and once when he repeated a phrase she had used in her report, he winked at her in a most undignified fashion.

"I'm nothing but a hard-headed business man, you know," he would say, justifying himself to his secretary when they were alone together. "I haven't any time to read books. I can hire men to do that,—men with much keener judgment about such things than I have. I'm watching the circulation of our magazines, the advertising revenues, our daily sales report, and seeing that our presses are being worked to their maximum capacity. I'm negotiating with a mill for a year's supply of paper, and buying fifty thousand pounds of ink, and at the same time arranging for a loan from the bank. I haven't got time for books. Anyhow I never went to college,"—this with a humorous twinkle as he had a general contempt for college men,—"and I don't know anything about 'liter-a-choor.'"

§2

Jeannette took a tremendous pride in the new building. She had an office to herself, now,—one adjoining Mr. Corey's. He left the details of equipping both to her. She took the greatest delight in doing so. She bought some very handsome furniture,—a great mahogany desk covered with a sheet of plate glass for Mr. Corey, some finely upholstered leather armchairs, a rich moquette rug, and she had the walls distempered, and lined on three sides with tall mahogany bookcases with diamond-paned glass doors. She had all the authors' autographed photographs reframed in a uniform narrow black molding, and hung them herself. She arranged to have some greens always on the bookcases, and a great bunch of feathery pine boughs in a large round earthenware jar on the floor in one corner.

There had come to exist a very warm and affectionate companionship between the president of the publishing house and his secretary. Jeannette thought him the finest man she knew. She admired him tremendously, admired his shrewdness, his cleverness, his extraordinary capacity for work. He was impatient beyond all reason, sometimes. She had often seen him jump up with a bang of a fist on his desk and an angry exclamation on his lips when an office boy had dallied over an errand, or had heard these things when it was she who was keeping him waiting, and he would come himself after the carbon of the letter, or the report, or the book he had asked for. He would stride through the aisles between the desks, or across the floor to somebody's office with great long steps, his fists swinging, his brows knit, intent upon putting his hands at once upon what he wanted. He could be brutally rude, when annoyed, and he gave small consideration to anyone else's opinion when he had a definite one of his own. But she could forgive these shortcomings. She saw the odds against which he contended, she saw the ultimate goal at which he aimed, and she saw the vigorous battle he was waging toward this end,—and her esteem for him knew no bounds.

She felt herself to be his only real ally though she did not overestimate her services. Among those who came close to him—his business associates and family —she was the only one not an actual drag upon him. Mr. Featherstone and Mr. Kipps were of no more assistance to him in conducting the affairs of the company than any two of the salaried clerks. Frequently they hampered him, rubbing their chins or hemming and hawing over one of his brilliant flashes of wisdom, to rob him of his enthusiasm. As the business increased, they were more and more inclined to demur at any new scheme he proposed. His family were so much dead weight about his neck. The boy had proved himself of small account, the daughter was epileptic, Mrs. Corey an exacting, extravagant, capricious wife.

Jeannette's surmise upon their first meeting that her employer's wife was already unaccountably jealous of her soon found ample confirmation. Mrs. Corey grew more and more resentful of Jeannette's intimate knowledge of her personal affairs, the complete confidence of her husband which she enjoyed, the close daily association with him. Jeannette was aware there had been several violent quarrels over her between husband and wife, Mrs. Corey demanding that she be dismissed, Mr. Corey firmly declining to agree. It did not make matters any too pleasant for the girl. Whenever Mrs. Corey encountered her, she was effusively sweet, but her manner suggested: "You and I, my dear, *we* know about him," or "We women,—his secretary and his wife,—must stand together for his protection." Jeannette was keenly conscious of the utter falseness and insincerity of this attitude. She knew that Mrs. Corey hated her, and would gladly see her summarily dismissed. She would smile with equally apparent sweetness in return, and fume in silence. She considered she was often doing for Mr. Corey what his wife should have been doing, that she filled the place of assistant, philosopher and friend only because Mrs. Corey was utterly incompetent to fill any of these rôles. If her relation to her employer had grown to be that of companion and helpmate, if she had been obliged to assume part of the province of a wife, none of the compensations were hers, she reflected indignantly. Mrs. Corey lived in luxury, came and went as she pleased, observed no hours, exercised no self-restraint, posed as her husband's partner in life, his guide and counsellor, spent his money extravagantly, and enjoyed the satisfaction of being the wife of the president of what had now become one of the big publishing houses in New York, while she, Jeannette, who worked beside him eight, nine, sometimes eleven or twelve hours out of every twenty-four, got thirty-five dollars a week!

But in moments of fairer judgment she realized she received much more than merely the contents of her

pay-envelope. She had an affection and a regard from
Mr. Corey that he never had given his wife. She was
closer to him than anyone else in the world; she was
what both wife and daughter should have meant to
him; he loved her with a warm paternal feeling, and
her love for him in return was equally sincere, deep
and devoted. She sometimes felt that she and this
man for whom she slaved and whom she served and
helped could conquer the world. There existed no sex
attraction between them; each recognized in the other
the half of an excellent team of indefatigable workers;
their relation was always that of father and daughter,
but their feelings could only be measured in terms of
love,—staunch, enduring, unswerving loyalty.

§ 3

There was nothing in Jeannette's life from which
she derived more satisfaction than the way in which
she had deflected Roy Beardsley's interest in herself
to her sister. There was a time after she had made
up her mind she could not marry him, when dark hours
and aching thoughts assailed her, when she felt she
was sacrificing all her happiness in life to a mere idea.
But she had fought against these disturbing reflections, resolutely banishing Roy from her mind, and
making herself think of ways in which their relationship could be put upon a platonic basis. She took
walks with him, made him read aloud to her when he
came in the evenings, persuaded him to take her to
lectures, and formed the habit of going with him once
a week to a vaudeville show in a neighboring theatre
on upper Broadway. Her policy was always to be

doing things with him, never to be idle or to sit alone
with him, for this always led to intimate talk and love-
making. She strove to keep the conversation impersonal. Roy was so easily managed, she sometimes
smiled over it. And yet there came times when it
was hard to deny herself the firm hold of his young
arms.

What proved an immediate and tremendous help in
conquering herself was a discovery she made from a
chance glimpse of her sister's earnest, brown eyes
fixed upon Roy's face. The three of them were in
the studio one evening, and happened to be discussing
religion. Roy delivered himself sententiously of a trite
truism, something like: "It should be part of everyone's religion to respect the religion of others." As
Jeannette was considering him rather than his words
at the moment, her gaze happened to light upon her
sister's face, and little Alice's secret stood revealed.
The girl sat with her mouth half-open, staring at Roy
with wide eyes, and an adoring look, eloquent of her
thoughts. Jeannette was staggered. She was instantly aware of a great pain in her own heart, a great
longing and hurt. It was clear Alice did not understand herself, had no suspicion that she was in love.

At once the elder sister began to readjust herself,
"clean house," as she expressed it. She marvelled
again and again about Alice; it was hard to accept the
idea that love had come to her little sister, yet the
look in the rapt face had been unmistakable, and as
the days went by Jeannette found plenty of evidence
to confirm her suspicions. It was surprising how much
the knowledge of her sister's secret helped her to
overcome any weakness for Roy that remained in her

own heart. She saw at once the suitableness of a match between them; Alice and Roy were ideally suited to each other, and their coming to care for one another would surely be the best possible solution to her own problem. She could not, would not, marry him; the next best thing, of course, would be for him to marry her sister.

She set about her schemes at once. The very next evening it had been arranged Roy was to go with her to the theatre. They usually sat in one of the back rows of the balcony. That afternoon she left a little note on his desk to say she wanted to see him when he came in, and when he appeared, told him she would be obliged to work with Mr. Corey that evening, and suggested he take her sister to the show in her place. When he came of an evening to see her at her home, she would send Alice out to talk to him, while she dallied over her dressing. Whenever Alice happened to join her and Roy, she found an excuse to leave them together. She persuaded the young man frequently to include her sister in their jaunts or walks, and in the evenings, more and more often she complained of a headache, took herself to bed, and left Alice to entertain him. Poor little Alice was blindly unconscious of the strings that were being pulled about her, but she came to a full and terrifying realization at last of where her heart was leading her. She began to mope and weep, to talk of going away. She spoke of wanting to be a trained nurse.

Roy was still placidly indifferent to her interest in him. His ardor for Jeannette had cooled, but he still fancied himself in love with her, and expected that some day they would be married. He no longer fretted

her, however, with demands or troubled her with love-
making. His days were full of interests: he had his
friends, his work at the office, his companionship with
the two Sturgis girls,—all of which was very agreeable
and entertaining. Jeannette and he would be married
some day before long; he was content to let matters
idrift until she was ready to name the day. . . . Alice?
Oh, Alice was a lovely girl,—a *deuce* of a lovely girl.
She was going to be his sister-in-law soon.

Before long Mrs. Sturgis came fluttering in great
agitation to her oldest daughter. By various circum-
locutions, she approached the subject which was
causing her so much distress. It was quite evident
that Alice was not well; she was run down and getting
terribly nervous. Had Jeannette noticed anything
wrong with her? Jeannette didn't suppose it could
be a *man*, did she? The little brown bird was still her
mother's baby after all, but you never could tell about
girls. Alice was,—well, Alice was nineteen! And if
it *was* a man,—the dear child acted exactly as if there
was one,—who could it possibly be? She didn't see
anybody but Roy; she didn't go any place with anybody else. Now her mother didn't want to say *one*
word to distress Jeannette, or to say anything that
would—would upset her. . . . Perhaps she was all
wrong about it anyway, but—but did Jeannette think
it was possible that Alice and Roy,—that Alice,—that
Alice . . .

Amused, Jeannette watched her anxious little
mother floundering on helplessly. Then she suddenly
took the plump and worried figure in her arms, hugged
her, and told her all about it.

Mrs. Sturgis could only stare in amazement and

interject breathless exclamations of "But, *dearie!*"
"Why, *dearie!*" "Well, I don't know what to make
of you!"

But the question now remaining was how to jog
Roy's consciousness awake, make him see the little
brown flower at his feet that looked up at him so ador-
ingly, only waiting to be plucked. Jeannette said
nothing to her mother, but she went to Roy direct.
She felt sure of her touch with him.

First she made him realize that she could never be
satisfied with being his wife. She explained carefully
and convincingly why it could never be, and then while
he gazed tragically at the ground, twisting his lean
white fingers, she spoke to him frankly of Alice.

As she talked it came over her with fresh conviction that, had she married him, she could have done
as she liked with Roy; he was putty in her hands. But
her husband must be a man who would mold *her,* make
her do what he wished, bend her to his will. Only such
a man would awaken her love and keep it. She despised Roy for his amiability.

He looked very boyish and silly to her now, as he
rumpled his stuck-up hair, and dubiously shook his
head. He was surprised to hear about Alice, and,—
Jeannette could see,—at once interested. She left the
thought with him and confidently waited for it to take
hold. Mr. Corey, she felt, would have handled the
situation in just some such fashion as she had,—
direct, cutting the Gordian knot, plunging straight to
the heart of the matter.

One night at dinner she casually told her mother
and sister that her engagement with Roy had been
broken by mutual consent. She explained they both

had begun to realize they did not really love one
another well enough to marry and had decided to call
it off. Roy was a sweet boy, she added, and would
make some girl a splendid husband. She glanced covertly at Alice. The girl was bending over her plate,
pretending an interest in her food, but her face was
deadly white. A rush of tenderest love flooded Jeannette's heart. At the moment she would have given
much to have been free to take her little sister in her
arms and tell her everything, assure her that the man
she loved was beginning to love her in return and
would some day make her his wife.

And that was how it turned out. A year later Roy
and Alice were married by the Reverend Doctor Fitzgibbons in the church on Eighty-ninth Street in just
the way the bride's mother had planned for her older
daughter, and now they were living in a small but
pretty four-room apartment out in the Bronx for which
they paid twenty-five dollars a month. Happy little
Mrs. Beardsley's mother and sister were aware that
very shortly those grave responsibilities at which Mrs.
Sturgis had often mysteriously hinted were to come
upon her. Alice was "expecting" in March.

Roy was no longer an employee of the Chandler B.
Corey Company. He had found another job just
before he married and was now with *The Sporting
Gazette,* a magazine devoted to athletic interests, gam-
ing, and fishing, where he was getting forty dollars a
week as sub-editor. He had always wanted to write
and this came nearer his ambition than soliciting
advertisements. Moreover there was the increase in
salary. Of course *The Sporting Gazette* was new and
had nothing like the circulation of the Corey publica-

tions, but Roy considered it a step ahead. He had given Mr. Featherstone a chance to keep him, but Mr. Featherstone had rubbed his chin and wagged his head dubiously when asked for a raise. No,—there mustn't be any more raises for awhile, no more increases in salary until the company was making larger profits; they were expanding; there was the new building with the larger rent, and all those new presses to be paid for. So Roy had gone in quest of another job, and had found it in one of three rough little rooms comprising the editorial offices of *The Sporting Gazette.* He considered himself extremely happy, extremely fortunate.

The attraction Jeannette had once felt for him was as dead as though it had never been.

§ 4

Mrs. Sturgis no longer had to work so hard. She had given up her position as instructor in music at Miss Loughborough's Concentration School for Little Girls and her work as accompanist for Signor Bellini's pupils. Jeannette had made her resign from both places. With Alice married and gone, it was better for her mother to stay at home and take charge of the housekeeping. Mrs. Sturgis gave private lessons, now, —a few hours only in the morning or afternoon,—and these, she asserted, were a "real delight." It left her plenty of time for marketing and for preparing the simple little dinners she and her daughter enjoyed at night. She took the keenest interest in these, and was always planning something new in the way of a surprise for her "darling daughter when she comes

home just dead beat out at the end of the day.''
Finances were no longer a problem. Jeannette contributed twenty dollars a week to the household expenses while her mother earned as much and sometimes
more. She often reminded her daughter she could
do even better than that, especially during the winter
months, but Jeannette would not hear of her working
harder.

"But what's the use, Mama?" she would ask.
"We've got everything we want. I can dress as I
like on what's left out of my salary, and there is no
sense in your teaching all day. I love the idea of your
being free to go to a concert now and then, and Alice's
going to need you a lot when the baby comes and
afterwards.''

"That may be all very true, dearie, but I don't just
feel right about having so much time to myself. I
could easily do more. There was a lady called this
afternoon and just *begged* me to take her little girl.
You know I have all Saturday morning.''

"No,'' said Jeannette decisively; "I won't consider it.''

They were really very comfortably situated, the
girl would reflect. Once a week, sometimes oftener,
Mrs. Sturgis would be asked to accompany a singer
at a recital. That meant five dollars, often ten,—ten
whenever Elsa Newman sang. Then there was the
twenty she, herself, contributed weekly, and the lessons
that brought in an equal amount. Between her mother's earnings and her own, their income was never less
than two hundred and fifty dollars a month. They
were rich; they lived in luxury; they need never worry
again. Jeannette knew she could remain with Mr.

Corey for life if she wanted to; there was no possible
danger of her ever losing her job. Her mother fussed
about the apartment, cooked delicious meals, took an
interest in arranging and managing their little home
in a way that previous demands upon her time had
never permitted. A new rug was bought for the studio,
and some big easy chairs, which they had talked about
purchasing for years. The piece of chenille curtaining
that had done duty as a table cover so long in the
dining-room was supplanted by a square of handsomer
material; the leaky drop-light vanished and was replaced by one more attractive and serviceable. More
particularly Jeannette had seen to it that her mother
got new clothes. Mrs. Sturgis had always favored
lavender as the shade most becoming to her, and her
daughter bought her a lovely lavender velvet afternoon
dress which had real lace down the front and was
trimmed with darker lavender velvet ribbon. Some
lavender silk waists followed, and a small lavender hat
upon which the lilac sprays nodded most ingratiatingly.
Mrs. Sturgis was radiant over her new apparel. Her
extravagant delight touched the daughter. It was pathetic that so little could give so much intense enjoyment.

Once or twice a month, Jeannette took her mother
to a matinée. She loved to go to the theatre herself,
and studied the advertisements, read all the daily theatrical notes and never missed a review. She would
secure seats for the play, weeks in advance, and always
took her mother to lunch downtown before the performance. These were wonderful and felicitous occasions for both of them. They had great arguments
each time as to where they should eat, what they should

select from the magnificent menus, and later about the play itself. Jeannette liked to startle her mother by selecting some extravagant item from the bill-of-fare, or surprise her by handing her a little present across the table. Sometimes as they came out of the theatre she would pilot her without preamble toward a hansom-cab and before the excited little woman knew what it was about, would help her in, and tell the cabby to drive them home slowly through the Park.

"Oh, dearie, you're not going to do this again!" Mrs. Sturgis would expostulate drawing back from the waiting vehicle. She really wished to protest against the needless extravagance. Jeannette would smile lovingly at her, and urge her in. Later as they were rumbling through the leafless Park and met a stream of automobiles and sumptuous equipages going in the opposite direction, Mrs. Sturgis would settle herself back with a sigh of contentment and say:

"Really, dearie, I don't think there is anything I enjoy quite as much as riding in a hansom. You're very good to your old mother. We may land in the poorhouse, but we're having a good time while the luck lasts."

On the occasion of the first performance of *Parsifal* at the Metropolitan, Jeannette, through Mr. Corey, was able to secure one ten-dollar seat for her mother. It was the greatest event in little Mrs. Sturgis' life. She longed for Ralph, and wept all through the Good Friday music.

Frequently on Sunday afternoons Jeannette's mother made her daughter accompany her to Carnegie Hall for a concert or a recital. Then, she declared, it was her turn to treat and she would not allow the

girl to pay for anything. Her entertainments were
never as "grand" as her daughter's, but she took a
keen delight in playing hostess, and after the music
always suggested tea. They were both exceedingly
fond of toasted crumpets, and Mrs. Sturgis was ever
on the lookout for new places where they were served.
But neither of her daughters inherited her love for
music. Jeannette went to the concerts dutifully, but
the satisfaction derived from these afternoons came
from giving her mother pleasure rather than from the
jumble of sound made by the wailing strings, tooting
wood-winds and blaring trumpets. She could make
nothing out of it all. When there was a soloist she
was interested, especially if it was a woman, of whose
costume she made careful notes.

Mother and daughter also went to church sometimes.
Doctor Fitzgibbons had made a deep impression upon
Mrs. Sturgis when he officiated at the marriage of Roy
and Alice. She had been "flattered out of her senses"
when the clergyman called upon her a few weeks after
the ceremony to inquire for the young couple. He had
talked to her about "parish work," and expressed the
hope that she would see her way clear "to join the
church" and become interested in his "guild." Mrs.
Sturgis had laughed violently at everything he said,
and had promised all he suggested. Thereafter she
referred to him as her "spiritual adviser," and Jeannette was aware she called occasionally at the rectory
to discuss what she termed her "spiritual problems."

Sunday evenings, Mrs. Sturgis and Jeannette usually
invited Alice and Roy to dinner, and sometimes they
were the guests of the young couple in the little Bronx
apartment. Roy and Alice were like two children

playing at keeping house, Mrs. Sturgis said with one
of her satisfied chuckles. Jeannette, too, thought of
them as children. Alice had always seemed younger
to her than she really was, and even when her own
thoughts had been filled with Roy, he had always impressed her as a "boy." She often wondered nowadays, when he and his happy, dimpling, brown-eyed
bride sat side by side on the sofa, their arms around
one another, their hands linked, exchanging kisses
every few minutes in accepted newly-wed fashion,
what she had ever seen in him that had made her own
senses swim and her heart pound. He was just a
sweet, amiable boy to her now, with a fresh, eager
manner, and rather an attractive face. She still liked
his quaint mouth, his whimsical smile, his quick flashing blue eyes, but they no longer stirred her. She
could kiss him in affectionate sisterly fashion without
a tremor.

Jeannette and Mrs. Sturgis took great delight in
observing the young couple together, in watching them
in their diminutive but pretty home, and in discussing
them afterwards. They were ideally happy,—laughing, romping, playing little jokes upon one another,
deriving vast amusement from words, signs and
phrases, the meaning of which were known to them
alone. Both were affectionately demonstrative, forever holding hands, caressing one another and kissing.
Jeannette said it made her sick, was disgusting, but
her mother scolded when she betrayed her distaste,
and reminded her it was "only right and proper."

Roy, against the prospect of his marriage to Jeannette, had saved money; Mrs. Sturgis, urged by her
older daughter, had once again placed a loan of five

hundred dollars upon the nest-egg in the savings bank;
Jeannette had contributed another hundred, and Roy's
father had shipped from San Francisco a half car-load
of family furniture which had been in storage for many
years. The wedding had awaited the arrival of this
freight, and as soon as it came the stuff had been un-
crated, and installed in the little Bronx apartment.
The ceremony then followed and Roy took his blushing,
laughing, excited bride from her mother's arms, from
the old-fashioned apartment where she had lived almost since she could remember, and from the wedding
supper, direct to the new home in the Bronx which
together they had furnished with such joy and hours
of planning and discussion.

They had nearly a thousand dollars to spend, but
Alice wisely decided, so her mother thought, that only
half of it should go into house-furnishing. The furniture shipped by the Reverend Dwight Beardsley was
designed in the style of an earlier day and much of
it was too large for the snug little rooms of the Bronx
flat. A large sideboard with a marble slab top and
huge mirror could not be brought into the apartment
at all, and was sold to a second-hand furniture dealer
on Third Avenue for fifteen dollars. But most of the
furniture from California was usable, and all of it good
and substantial. Alice made the curtains for the din-
ing and living rooms herself; she and Roy, on their
hands and knees, painted the floors a warm walnut
tone. They bought three or four rugs, a fine second-
hand sofa with a rich but not too gaudy brocaded
cover, bed and table linen, and everything needed for
the kitchen. Horatio Stephens and his family sent
them a colored glass art lamp, and Mr. Corey, con-

sulting Jeannette, presented a beautiful clock with silvery chimes.

No young husband and wife ever took greater delight in their first home. They were always "fixing" things, arranging and rearranging them, cleaning and dusting. Roy bought a Boston fern during an early week of the marriage, paid three dollars for a brass jardiniere at a Turkish vendor's to hold it, and the plant flourished on a small taboret in the front windows. They took the most assiduous care of this, watering it several times a day and digging about its roots with an old table knife whenever either of them had an idle moment. When one of the curling fronds began to turn brown, they had long discussions as to whether it should be trimmed off or not. They acquired a canary, too, which shared with the fern the young couple's devotion. Alice had bought the bird because she was so "miserably lonely" without Roy all day long that she would "go out of her senses wanting him" unless there was something alive 'round the house to keep her company. The fact that the canary never opened his throat to make a sound,—although Alice had been assured by the man in the bird-store that he would "sing his head off"—did not in any wise detract from her love for the little feathered creature that hopped about in his cage and made a great fuss over giving himself a bath in the mornings. They called him "Sonny-boy" and took turns at the pleasure of feeding him.

Alice was a good cook. She had a gift for the kitchen, and Jeannette and her mother would exclaim in admiration over the delicious meals she prepared

when they came to dinner. Roy would glance from
mother to sister-in-law when the roast appeared or
when a particularly appetizing-looking pudding was
brought in, and at their exclamations of delight, he
would say:

"Guess I've got a pretty smart wife,—hey? Guess
I know a good cook when I see one, huh? Why, Alice's
got most women I know skinned a mile! She's just
a wonder; she can do anything. I only wish I was
good enough for her. She's a wonder, all right—all
right."

Jeannette was deeply moved when her sister told
her she was going to have a baby. It tore at her heart
to think of little Alice, to herself so young, so immature, so tender and weak and inexperienced, bringing a child into the world. She worried about it, wondered if Alice would die, felt with terrifying conviction
that that would be the way of it. Her mother's pleasure and complacency about the matter reassured her
but little. Alice was having a child much too soon
after her wedding; she ought to have waited for a
year or so at least.

She watched the changes in her sister's face and
figure with growing wonder. Child-bearing was a
mystery. Jeannette had never known a woman intimately who had had a baby; now she was both curious
and concerned. After the early months of discomfort
had passed, a benign gentleness settled upon Alice;
her expression became placid, serene, beautiful. A
quality of goodness transfigured her. She moved
through the days toward her appointed time with
supreme tranquillity. Whenever Alice spoke of "my

baby," Jeannette winced, while her mother maddened
her each time with the remark that it was "only right
and proper."

One morning early in March, shortly after Jeannette had reached the office, her mother telephoned
her in a great state of excitement. She had just heard
from Roy; Alice's baby would arrive that day; they
were taking her right away to the hospital; she wasn't
in any pain yet, but the doctor thought it would be best
to have her there; he didn't say when the child was
likely to be born.

There was no more news. The morning stretched
itself out endlessly. Jeannette worried and suffered
in silence; at noon she telephoned the hospital and got
Roy; there was little change; Alice was miserable,
but there was no talk about when the baby would be
born; the doctor had promised to be in at three; Roy
would let her know if anything happened. All afternoon there was a meeting of the members of the firm in
Corey's office; the question of the move to the new
building was being discussed; it lasted until four, until
five, until quarter to six. Jeannette was beside herself.
Alice was dead and they were afraid to let her know!

At six o'clock her mother telephoned again. Alice
was having her pains with some regularity now; the
baby ought to be there about eight or nine o'clock, the
doctor said.

As soon as she was at liberty Jeannette left the
office. She did not want to eat, but took the elevated
direct to the hospital. Her mother and Roy met her
and they kissed one another again and again. Alice
was "upstairs" now. They sat with their elbows
touching on a hard leather-covered seat in the recep-

tion-room. Jeannette's head began to ache; she counted the sixty-three squares in the rug on the floor twenty-two times; the black on the Welsbach burner in the lamp looked exactly like two people kissing.

Towards midnight the baby was born.

When Jeannette first saw her niece, the upper part of the little head and forehead were carefully bandaged. Her mother whispered that it had been an "instrument case"; Roy was not to know for a while at any rate. The baby was perfect,—a fine, healthy, eight-pound girl, and Alice was doing nicely.

But Alice did not leave the hospital for six weeks and was six months in recovering her old strength and buoyancy.

CHAPTER II

§ 1

It was some three months after the publishing house had been established in its new offices, that Jeannette had the card of Martin Devlin brought to her. It was embossed and heavily engraved, with a small outline of the earth's two hemispheres in one corner and bisecting these, in tiny capitals, the words: THE GIBBS ENGRAVING COMPANY. Mr. Corey was out; Jeannette told the boy to inform the caller. In a minute or two the messenger returned to say that the gentleman would like to speak to Mr. Corey's secretary, but Jeannette had no time to waste on solicitors of engraving work, and sent word that she was occupied. The boy reappeared presently with another of Mr. Devlin's cards, on the back of which was pencilled:

"Dear Miss Sturgis,—I'd be grateful for two minutes' interview. Have a message from an old friend of yours.   M. DEVLIN."

Jeannette frowned in distaste, and looked up at the boy, annoyed. She was extremely busy, typing a speech for Mr. Corey which he was to read that night at a Publishers' Banquet at the Waldorf. It was twenty minutes past four; she expected him to return at any minute.

"Tell the gentleman to come again, will you, Jimmy? I'm really too busy to see him to-day."

The boy went out and she returned to her work, her fingers flying.

"The responsibility of molding public opinion," went her notes, "rests perhaps with our press, but to whom do the discriminating readers of the nation in confidence turn for the formation of their taste in literature, their acquaintance with the Arts, the dissemination of those inspiring idealistic thoughts and precepts of the fathers of our great——"

She estimated there were another three pages of it.

The door of her office opened and a young man of square build, with broad shoulders, and a grin on his face, filled the aperture.

"Beg pardon, Miss Sturgis," he began. "I hope you won't think I'm butting-in."

He had a strong handsome face, big flashing teeth, black hair and black eyebrows.

Jeannette looked at him, bewildered. She had never seen this man before; she did not know what he was doing in her office, nor what he wanted.

"I'm Martin Devlin," he announced, advancing into the room.

At once she froze; her breast rose on a quick angry intake, and her eyes assumed a cold level stare.

"I hope you're not going to be sore at me." He smiled down at her in easy good humor.

"Mr. Corey's not in," said the girl. She was staggered by this individual's effrontery.

"Well, that's too bad, but I really called to have a few minutes' chat with you," he returned nonchalantly. "We have a friend of yours down at our office: Miss

Alexander, Beatrice Alexander. 'Member her? She
says a lot of nice things about you.''

"Oh!" Jeannette elevated her eyebrows and surveyed the speaker's head and feet.

"I'm afraid you're sore at me," he said. He laughed
straight into her cold eyes, showing his big teeth.

Jeannette straightened herself and frowned. She
felt her anger rising.

"Er—you—a——" she began, deliberately clearing
her throat with a little annoyed cough. "I think
you've made a mistake. Mr. Corey is not in. As you
see, I am busy. Good-day."

She looked down at her notes and swung her chair
around to her machine.

"Whew!" whistled Mr. Devlin. He took a step
nearer, put his hand on her desk, bent down to catch a
glimpse of her face, and said with a pleading note in
his voice and with that same flashing smile:

"Aw—please don't be sore at me, Miss Sturgis!"

The man's sudden nearness brought Jeannette up
rigidly in her seat. Her eyes blazed a moment, but
there was something in this person's manner and in
the ingratiating quality of his smile that made her
hesitate. Her first thought had been to call the porter
or one of the men outside, and have him summarily
put out. Instead she said in her most frigid tone:

"Really, Mr. Devlin, you presume too far. You see
that I am busy and I've told you that Mr. Corey is
not in."

"Well that's all right, but what do you want me to
tell Miss Alexander? She'll be wanting to know if I
delivered her message."

"Miss Alexander, as I remember her, is a very

lovely girl. You can tell her that I've not forgotten her, and that I am sorry that . . . that in her office there are not more mannerly gentlemen.''

Devlin threw back his head and roared. His laugh was extraordinary.

"Say, Miss Sturgis," he began, "please don't be sore at me. I didn't know I'd find a girl like you in here. Miss Alexander said you were awfully nice and I thought maybe you'd be doing me a favor one of these days. I took a chance on getting in to see you the way I did. Don't blame the kid.''

"What kid?"

"The office boy. I slipped him a quarter and told him to tell you I was an old friend of yours and wanted to give you a surprise.''

"Upon my word!"

"Well, you see,—we've all got to make our living; you, me and the office boy.''

"There are ways of doing it," said Jeannette acidly.

"I think they're all legitimate.''

"What,—bribing office boys?"

"Well, I didn't bribe him exactly. I deceived him.''
He laughed again. He was Irish, the girl noted, and presumably considered he had a great deal of Irish charm.

"At any rate, I got in to see you.''

"Much good it's done you.''

"I have hopes for the future.''

"I wouldn't cherish them.''

"Ah, well now, Miss Sturgis, don't be cruel!"

"I'm not in the least interested.''

"Won't you tell me who's doing Corey's engraving?"

"I will not."

"I can find out easily enough, and I think I can interest him."

"I think you can't."

"Won't you make an appointment for me to see him?"

"Certainly not!"

"There's other ways I can meet him."

"You're at liberty to find them."

"Aw . . . you're awfully mean. Why don't you give a fellow a chance for his living?"

"You don't deserve it."

"Because I gave the boy a quarter to show me which was your office?"

"Yes, and because you're so . . . so . . . ."

"Fresh,—go on; you were going to say it!"

"Evidently you are aware of it."

"A fellow hasn't a chance to think anything else."

"Well,—you'll have to excuse me. I'm really very busy."

"Can I come again when you've a little more time to spare?"

"I am always busy."

"Can I 'phone?"

"I can't bother with 'phone messages."

Mr. Devlin for a moment was routed.

"Oh, *gosh!*" he said in disgust.

Jeannette was not to be won. She nodded to him, and began to type briskly, the keys of her machine humming. The man stood uncertainly a moment more, shifting from one foot to the other; then he swung himself disconsolately toward the door, and closed it slowly after him. Almost immediately he opened it again and thrust in his head.

"I'm coming back again,—just the same!" he bawled. Jeannette did not look around, and the door clicked shut.

§ 2

The next time he called she was taking dictation from Mr. Corey and was unaware he had come. When she finished with her employer, and picked up the sheaf of letters he had given her, she passed through the connecting door between the two offices, and found Devlin waiting in her room.

"*Really!*" She stopped short and frowned in quick annoyance.

"Well, here I am again!" he said blandly.

"And here's where you go out!" She walked towards the door that led to the outer office and flung it open.

Devlin's face altered, and a slow color began to mount his dark cheeks.

"Aw—say——" he said in hurt tones. The smile was gone; for the moment his face was as serious as her own.

Jeannette did not move. Devlin picked up his hat and gloves.

"My God!" he exclaimed fervently, "you're hard as nails!"

As he went out she suddenly felt sorry for him.

But that was not the last of him. His card appeared the next afternoon. Mr. Corey was again away from the office.

"I'm not in to this person," she said to Jimmy, "and if he bribes you to show him in here, I'll go straight to Mr. Kipps and have you fired."

The next day he telephoned. She hung up the receiver, and told the girl at the switch-board to find out who wanted her before she put through any more calls. The day following brought a letter from him, but as soon as she discovered his signature, she tore it up and threw it in the waste-paper basket. Two minutes later, she carefully recovered its ragged squares and pieced them together.

"My dear Miss Sturgis," it read, "you must overlook my boorish methods. I'll not bother you again, but I beg you will not hold it against me, if I try to make your acquaintance in some more acceptable manner. Yours with good wishes, Martin Devlin."

He wrote a vigorous hand,—strong, distinct, individual.

Jeannette considered the letter a moment, then uttered a contemptuous "Puh!" scooped the fragments into her palm, and returned them to the receptacle for trash.

§ 3

Toward the end of the week, she had a telephone call from Beatrice Alexander. She had not seen the girl for nearly four years but remembered how exceptionally kind she had been to her that first day she went to work, and thought it would be pleasant to meet her again, and talk over old times. They arranged to have luncheon together.

They met at the Hotel St. Denis. Jeannette always went there whenever there was sufficient excuse; she

loved the atmosphere of the old place. Her luncheon
was invariably the same: hot chocolate with whipped
cream, and a club sandwich. It cost just fifty cents.

Beatrice Alexander had changed but little during
the years Jeannette had not seen her, except that now
she wore glasses. A little gold chain dangled from the
tip of one lens, and hooked itself by means of a gold
loop, over an ear. It made her look schoolmarmy, but
she had the same sweet face, the same soft dovelike
eyes, and the whispering voice.

"And you *never* married Mr. Beardsley," she commented. "I heard you were engaged and he certainly
was awfully in love with you."

Jeannette explained about her sister, and how happy
the two were in their little Bronx flat. Her companion
exclaimed about the baby.

She had had two or three places since the old publishing house suspended its selling campaign of the
History. She had been in the business office of the
Fifth Avenue Hotel Company until it closed its doors.
Now The Gibbs Engraving Company employed her;
she'd been there about a year, and liked it all right, but
the constant smell of the strong acids made her a little
sick sometimes. She and Jeannette fell presently to
discussing Martin Devlin.

"Oh, he's all right," Beatrice Alexander said. "He
came there about the same time I did. He's an awful
flirt, I guess, and he gets round a good deal. I don't
know much about him, except that he's always pleasant
and agreeable, never anything but terribly nice to me.
Everybody likes him. He's one of our best solicitors.
I heard from one of the men in your composing room,
who's a kind of cousin of mine, that you were with

the Corey Company and were Mr. Corey's private secretary, and one day I happened to hear Mr. Devlin
talking to Mr. Gibbs,—Mr. Gibbs and his brother own
The Gibbs Engraving Company,—and he said something about how he wished he could land your account
but he didn't know a soul he could approach.   And
then I mentioned I knew you.   That was all there was
to it, only he said you treated him something awful.''

Jeannette rehearsed the interview.

''He struck me as a very fresh young man,'' she
concluded.

''Oh, Mr. Devlin's all right,'' Beatrice Alexander
said again. ''He doesn't mean any harm. He's Irish,
you know,—he was born here and all that,—and he
just wants to be friendly with everyone. I suppose
he was kind of hurt because you were so short with
him.''

''I most certainly was,'' Jeannette said, grimly.

''Well, he's been begging and begging me to call you
up. He wanted to take us both out to lunch, but I
wouldn't agree to that. I told him I'd see you about
it first.''

''I wouldn't consider it,'' Jeannette said, indignantly. ''The idea! What's the matter with him?''

''I imagine,'' Beatrice Alexander said shyly, ''he
likes your style.''

''Well, I don't like *his!* . . . The impertinence!''

They finished their lunch and wandered into Broadway. It was Easter week, and the chimes of Grace
Church were ringing out a hymn.

''Let's not lose touch with each other again,'' said
Beatrice Alexander at parting. ''I'll 'phone you soon,

and next time you'll have to have luncheon with *me*.
I always go to Wanamaker's; they have such lovely
music up there, and the food's splendid.''

§ 4

Jeannette had forgotten Mr. Devlin's existence until
one day as she was typing busily at her desk she suddenly recognized his loud, infectious and unmistakable
laugh in the adjoining office. Mr. Corey had come in
from lunch some ten minutes before, and had brought
a man with him. She had heard their feet, their voices,
and the clap of the closing door as they entered. Now
the laugh startled her. She paused, her fingers suspended above the keys of her typewriter, and listened.
It was Mr. Devlin; there was no mistaking him. She
twisted her lips in a wry smile. He and Mr. Corey
were evidently getting on.

She knew she would be called. When the buzzer
summoned her, she picked up her note-book and pencils, straightened her shoulders in characteristic fashion, and went in.

Devlin rose to her feet as she entered, but she did
not glance at him. Her attention was Mr. Corey's.

''How do you do? How's Miss Sturgis?'' Devlin
was all good-natured friendliness, showing his big
teeth as he grinned at her.

She turned her eyes toward him gravely, gazed at
him with calm deliberation, and briefly inclined her
head.

''Oh, you two know each other? Friends, hey?''
asked Mr. Corey, looking up.

"Well, we're trying to be," laughed Devlin.

Jeannette made no comment. She gazed expectantly at her chief.

"The Gibbs Engraving Company," said Mr. Corey in his brusque businesslike voice, "wants to do our engraving. I'm going to give them a three months' trial. I'd like to have you take a memorandum of what they've quoted us. Mr. Gibbs is to confirm this by letter. Now you said five cents per square inch on line cuts with a minimum of fifty cents . . ."

Jeannette scribbled down the figures.

"Three-color work a dollar a square inch," supplied Devlin.

"Oh, I thought you said you'd give us a flat rate on our color work."

"On the magazine covers, yes, but I can't do that on general color work."

"Well, that's all right." The discussion continued. Presently the girl had all the details.

"Give me a memorandum of that," Corey said, "and send a carbon to Mr. Kipps." He turned to the young man. "We'll talk it over, and let you know just as soon as we hear from you." Devlin rose. The men shook hands as Jeannette passed into her own room. She heard them saying good-bye. Their voices continued murmuring, but she did not listen. Suddenly Mr. Corey opened her door.

"Mr. Devlin wants to speak to you a minute, Miss Sturgis." He nodded to his companion, said "Well, good-bye; hope we can get together on this," and shook hands once more, and left Devlin confronting her.

"Please let me say just one word," he said quickly.

"I met Mr. Corey at the Quoin Club the other day and made a date for lunch. I'm after his business all right, and think I've got it cinched. I don't want you to continue to be sore at me, if my outfit and yours are going to do business together. I'm sorry if I got off on the wrong foot. Please accept my apology and let's be friends."

"I don't think there is any occasion——" began Jeannette icily.

"Aw shucks!" he said interrupting her, "I'm doing the best I can to square myself. I didn't mean to annoy you. I didn't care at first what you thought of me as long as I got in to see Mr. Corey. I confess I thought maybe I could jolly you into arranging a date for me to see him. No,—wait a minute," he urged as the girl frowned, "hear me out. You see I'm being honest about it. I'm telling you frankly what I thought at first, but that was before I even saw you. I had no idea you were the kind of girl you are. It isn't usual to find a person like you in an office. Oh, you think I'm jollying you! I swear I'm not. I just want to ask you to forgive me if I offended you, and be friends."

There was something unusually ingratiating about this man. Jeannette hesitated, and Devlin continued. He pleaded very earnestly; it was impossible not to believe his sincerity.

Jeannette shrugged her shoulders when he paused for a moment. Her hands were automatically arranging the articles on her desk.

"Well," she conceded slowly, "what do you want?"

"For you to say you'll forgive a blundering Irish boobie, and shake hands with him."

He wrung a dry smile from her at that. She held out her hand.

"Oh, very well. It's easier to be friends with you than have you here interfering with my getting at my work."

"That's fine, now." He held her fingers a moment, his whole face beaming. "You've a kind heart, Miss Sturgis, and I sha'n't forget it."

He took himself away with a radiant smile upon his face.

§ 5

It was evident Martin Devlin proposed to be a factor in her life. When he came to the office to see Mr. Kipps or Miss Holland about the engraving,—and the work brought him, or he pretended it brought him, two or three times a week—he never failed to step to Jeannette's door, open it, and give her the benefit of his flashing teeth and handsome eyes as he wished her good-day or asked her how she was. He did not intrude further. His visits were only for a minute or two. Only once when she was looking for a letter in the filing cabinet, he came in and lingered for a chat. He saw she was not typing, therefore ready to talk to him since he was not interrupting her. When she went to lunch with Beatrice Alexander a week or two later at Wanamaker's he joined the two girls by the elevators as they were leaving the lunch-room, pretending, Jeannette noticed, with a great air of surprise, that the meeting was merely a fortuitous circumstance. The subway had a few days before begun to operate. Jeannette had never ridden upon it, so Martin piloted her down the stone steps, boarded the train, and rode with her until they reached Thirty-fourth Street. Beatrice Alexander had said good-bye as they left Wanamaker's.

Devlin had a confident, self-assured way with him. It could not be said he swaggered, but the word suggested him. He was easy, good-natured, laughing, cajoling, irresistibly merry. His good humor was contagious. Men smiled back at him; women looked at him twice. To the subway guard, to the sour-faced little Jew at the newsstand, to the burly cop with whom they collided as they climbed the stairs to the street, he was familiar, patronizing, jocular. He called the Italian subway guard "Garibaldi," the Jewish newsdealer "Isaac," the burly policeman "Sergeant." One glance at him and each was won; it was impossible to resent his familiarity. Everybody liked him; he could say the most outrageous things and give no offense. It was that Irish charm of his, Jeannette decided, back once more at her desk and clicking away at her machine, that made people so lenient with him.

She began to speculate about him a good deal. It was clear he was in hot pursuit of her, and that he intended to give her no peace. He commenced to bring little boxes of candy which he slid on to her desk with a long arm when he opened her office door to say "Hello!" Then flowers put in their appearance: sweet bunches of violets, swathed in oiled paper, their stems wrapped in purple tinfoil, the fragrant ball glistening with brilliant drops of water; there were bunches of baby roses, too, and lilies-of-the-valley, and daffodils. One day she happened to mention she had never read "The Taming of the Shrew," and the following morning there was delivered at her home a complete set of the Temple edition of Shakespeare's plays. She protested, she threatened to throw the flowers out of the window, she begged him with her most earnest smile not to send her anything more. She was talking into deaf ears. The very next day she found on her desk two seats for a Saturday matinée with a note scribbled on the envelope: "For you and your mother next Saturday. Have a good time and think of Martin."

In deep distress she told her mother about him, but Mrs. Sturgis shared none of her concern.

"Well, perhaps the young man is trying to be friends with you in the only way he knows how. I wouldn't be too hasty with him, dearie. You say he's with an engraving company? Is that a good line of work? Does he seem well-off,—plenty of money and all that?"

"Oh, *Mama!*" cried Jeannette, in mild annoyance.

"There's no harm, my dear, in a nice rich young fellow admiring a pretty girl like my daughter. If the young man's well brought up and means what's perfectly right and proper, I don't see what you can object to. You've got to marry one of these days, lovie; you must remember that. There isn't any sense in tying yourself down to a desk for the rest of your life! You've *got* to think about a husband!"

"Well, I don't want *him!*"

"Perhaps not. I'm not saying anything about him. But there's plenty of nice young men in the world, and you mustn't shut your eyes to them. A girl should marry and have a home of her own; that's what God intended. Doctor Fitzgibbons was saying exactly that same thing to me only yesterday. Now this Mr. Devlin, —it's an Irish name, isn't it?——"

"Oh, hush,—for goodness' sakes, Mama! Don't let's talk any more about him. . . . What did Alice have to say to-day?"

"She's really gaining very rapidly now," Mrs. Sturgis said instantly diverted. "She says she's going to let that woman go. She comes every day and does all the dishes and cleans up and it only costs Alice three dollars a week."

"Why, she's crazy," cried Jeannette. "She isn't half strong enough to do her own work, yet. You tell her I'll pay the three dollars till she's all right again. I can't imagine what Roy Beardsley's thinking about!"

§ 6

Martin Devlin begged her to allow him to take her mother and herself to dinner, and "perhaps we'll have time to drop in at a show afterwards," he added. Jeannette declined. She had no wish to become on more intimate terms with him, but he would not take "No" for an answer. He persisted; she grew angry; he persisted just the same. She considered going to Mr. Corey and informing him that this representative of The Gibbs Engraving Company was annoying her, and yet it hardly seemed the thing to do. She spoke of it again to her mother, and Mrs. Sturgis at once was in a flutter of excitement at the prospect of a dinner downtown.

"But why not, dearie?" she argued. "I could wear my lavender velvet, and you've got your new taffeta. . . . I'd like to meet the young man."

After all there were thousands of girls, reflected Jeannette, who were accepting anything and every-

thing from men, wheedling gifts out of them, sometimes even taking their money. Her mother would
get much pleasure out of the event.

When Devlin urged his invitation again, she drew
a long breath, and consented. There seemed no reason
why she should not accept; there was nothing wrong
with him; she liked him; he was agreeable and devoted;
her mother would be delighted.

He called for them on the night of the party in a taxi.
It was an unexpected luxury. He won Mrs. Sturgis at
once. Why, he was perfectly charming, a delightful
young man! What in the world was Jeannette thinking about? She laughed violently at everything he
said, rocking back and forth on the hard leather seat in
the stuffy interior of the cab, convulsed with mirth,
her round little cheeks shaking. He was the most
comical young man she'd ever known!

The taxi took them to a brilliant restaurant, gay with
lights, music and hilarity. Jeannette's blue, high-
necked taffeta and her mother's lavender velvet were
sober costumes amidst the vivid apparel and low-cut
toilettes of the women. But the girl was aware that
no matter what her dress might be, she, herself, was
beautiful. She saw the turning heads, and the eyes
that trailed her as the little group followed the head-
waiter to their table. The table had been reserved,
the dinner ordered. Cocktails appeared, and she sipped
the first she had ever tasted. Her mother was in
gay spirits, and preened herself in these surroundings
like a bird. Devlin seemed to know how to do everything. He was startlingly handsome in his evening
clothes; the white expanse of shirt was immaculate;
there were two tiny gold studs in front, and a black

bow tie tied very snugly at the opening of his collar.
It was no more than conventional semi-formal evening
dress, and yet somehow it impressed Jeannette as
magnificent. She had never noticed how becoming the
costume was to a man before. She realized, as she
glanced at him, he was the first young man she had
ever known, who had taken her out in the evening and
worn evening dress. Roy had been too poor; the
tuxedo he had had at college was shabby; she had
never seen him wear it. She studied Devlin now
critically. His hair was coal black, coarse, a trifle
wavy; he wet it, when he combed it, and it caught
a high light now and then. His eyebrows were heavy
and bushy like his hair, the eyes, themselves, deep-set
but alive with twinkles and laughter. They were ex-
pressive eyes, she thought, capable of subtlest mean-
ings. His nose was straight, his mouth large and red,
and his big even teeth glistened between the vivid lips
with the glitter of fine wet porcelain. He had an oval-
shaped face and a vigorous pointed chin. His skin
was unblemished, but the jaw, chin, and cheeks were
dark blue from his close-shaven beard. It was his
expression, she decided, more than the regularity of
his features, that made him so handsome. In his
evening dress he was extraordinarily good-looking.
She judged him to be twenty-six or seven.

The dinner progressed smoothly. Devlin had evidently taken pains in ordering it, and he gave a pleased
smile when Mrs. Sturgis waxed enthusiastic over some
particular feature, and Jeannette echoed her praise.
There was, as a matter of fact, nothing spectacular
about it: oysters, chicken *sauté sec*,—a specialty of the
restaurant,—a vegetable or two, salad with a red sauce

—Mrs. Sturgis thought it most curious and pronounced it delicious—an ice. To his guests, it seemed the most wonderful dinner they had ever eaten. The girl was impressed; her mother flutteringly excited.

"It's all so *good!*" Mrs. Sturgis kept repeating as if she had made a surprising discovery.

Devlin called for the check, glanced at it, dropped a large bill on the silver tray, and when the change was brought, amounting to two dollars and some cents,— as both Jeannette and her mother noted,—waved it away to the waiter with a negligent gesture. It was lordly; it was magnificent!

Jeannette loved such ways of doing things, she loved the lights and music, the excellent food, the deferential service, the gorgeous restaurant, the beautifully gowned women. She would like to own one rich and sumptuous evening dress like theirs, and to be able to wear it to such a magnificent place as this, and queen it over them all. She knew she could do it; she could dazzle the entire room.

Devlin guided his guests through the revolving glass doors to the street, the taxi-cab starter blew his whistle shrilly, a car rolled up, the door was held open for them to enter, and banged shut. The starter in his gold-braided uniform and shining brass buttons, touched his cap respectfully, and the taxi rolled out into the traffic. Jeannette thrilled to the luxuriousness and extravagance of it all.

It was the same at the theatre. They had aisle seats in the sixth row; the musical comedy was delightful, spectacular, magnificent, in tune with everything else that evening. After the theatre, their escort insisted upon their going to a brilliant café where the music was glorious, and where Jeannette and her mother sipped ginger-ale and Devlin drank beer. Mrs. Sturgis commented half-a-dozen times upon the peel of a lemon, deftly cut into cork-screw shape, and twisted into her glass, which gave the ginger-ale quite a delightful flavor. It was Devlin's idea; she had heard him suggest it to the waiter. He was a very remarkable young man,—very!

They were swept home in another taxi-cab, and he refused to let them thank him for the glorious evening. He hinted he would like to call, and perhaps be asked to dinner. But of course, that was not to be thought of! A grand person like him coming to one of their simple little meals, with Mrs. Sturgis or Jeannette jumping up to wait on the table? That would be perfectly ridiculous! But he might call some time, or perhaps go with them to a Sunday concert. He would be delighted, of course. He held his hat high above his head as he said good-night, and stood at the foot of the steps until they were safely inside.

It had been a memorable evening; they really had had a most wonderful time; Mr. Devlin certainly knew how to do things! Mrs. Sturgis, carefully pinning a sheet about her lavender velvet preparatory to hanging it in the closet, began planning how they could entertain him.

"Is he fond of music, do you know, dearie? I think we could get seats for some Sunday afternoon concert, and then bring him home to tea. It would be much better to ask him here than to go to any of those little tea-places; we could get some crumpets and toast them ourselves, and might buy a few little French pastries. You could see he was dying to be asked."

Jeannette felt vaguely irritated.

"Oh, let's not rush him, Mama."

"Rush him? Who's talking of rushing him, I'd like to know? The young man is a very delightful, presentable gentleman, and he's evidently taken a great fancy to you, and he's even been nice to your poor old mother. I declare, Janny, I can't sometimes make you out! I just was proposing we extend him a little hospitality in return for his extremely lavish entertainment. He's been most kind and considerate, and the least we can do . . ."

Jeannette's mind wandered. It certainly would be wonderful, went her roving thoughts, to have money, and dress gorgeously, and go about to such magnificent restaurants, and then taxi off to the theatre, whenever one wanted to! It would be wonderful, too, to have somebody strong and resourceful always looking out for one's comfort and enjoyment, paying all the bills, never bothering one about money, consulting and gratifying one's slightest whim!

She went to sleep in a haze of golden imaginings. Her mother's voice in the next room planning various schemes, commenting upon Mr. Devlin's attractiveness, grew fainter and fainter, and finally dwindled silent.

§ 7

But the next morning Jeannette vigorously attacked the subject. There had been nothing extraordinary about the past evening. A man in conventional evening dress had taken her mother and herself to dine in a restaurant, and afterwards had driven them in a taxi to the theatre. What was there so remarkable in that? It was being done all the time; the restaurants were packed full of such parties night after night. It had merely *seemed* wonderful to a girl and her mother unused to such entertainment.

Jeannette kept reminding herself of this throughout the ensuing day. She did not propose to have her head turned, as her mother's evidently was, by a little splurge of money. She was not in love with Martin Devlin, she did not care a snap of her finger for him, she would not marry him if he had a million! There was no sense in letting him think she would even consider such an idea. She couldn't help it, if he was in love with her. She had done nothing to encourage him, and she didn't propose to begin. No, the whole thing had better come to an end; it had gone quite far enough; she'd have to call off any silly plans her mother might be making. . . . What! Marry Martin Devlin and give up her job? *Never in the world!*

But Jeannette found she was dealing with a personality very different from that of Roy Beardsley. Mr. Devlin had one idea, one object: the idea was Jeannette, the object matrimony. He besieged her with attentions, he gave her no peace, he hounded her footsteps. Mrs. Sturgis threw herself whole-heartedly upon his side. She was deaf to her daughter's remonstrances; she refused to be discourteous, as she described it, to a young man so attentive and considerate. Mother and daughter actually quarrelled about the matter, refused to speak to each other for a whole day, made up with tears and kisses, but this in no jot altered Mrs. Sturgis' purpose of being Mr. Devlin's friend and advocate.

Jeannette was not to be shaken. She did not desire

Mr. Devlin, she did not want to marry anyone, she had no intention of abandoning her work.

"You *got* to marry me, Jeannette," this purposeful young man said to her one day.

"Never," said Jeannette resolutely.

"Oh, yes, you will," he told her with equal confidence.

"Well, we'll see about that. I don't care for you; I wouldn't marry you if I did; you are only annoying me with your attentions. I would really like you much better if you'd leave me alone."

The very evening this conversation took place she found a beautiful little scarab pin waiting for her when she got home. She mailed it back to him at The Gibbs Engraving Company. The next day came perfume, and a day or two later a large roll of new magazines; he sent her candy, flowers, theatre tickets. She gave the candy away, threw the flowers out of the window, tore up the theatre tickets and sent the torn pasteboards back to him in a letter in which she told him further gifts would only anger her. They kept on coming with undiminished regularity. She wept; her mother scolded her; Devlin called. There was no evading him; he was everywhere.

One day, he grabbed her, took her in his arms, beat down her resistance, strained her to him, and kissed her savagely, hungrily on the mouth. In that instant she capitulated; something broke within her; an overwhelming force rose like a great tide, welled up over her head and submerged her. She wilted in his embrace, succumbed like a crushed lily and longed for him to trample on her.

Love, glorious, intoxicating, passionate, had sprung

to life in her. She resented it; she was helpless
against it. She fought—fought—fought to no purpose. It rode her, rowelled her, harried her. Martin
Devlin had conquered her heart, but her will was
another matter.

§ 8

Jeannette became miserably unhappy. She imagined she had experienced all love's emotions when Roy
Beardsley possessed her thoughts. She laughed now
when she thought of them. She had been little more
than a school girl then, with a school girl's capacity
for love,—a maiden's love, virginal, immature. It was
not to be compared with this flame that seethed within
her now. Oh, God! Her love for Martin Devlin was
an agony! For the first time in her life she knew the
full meaning of fear. She feared this man with a
fear like terror. Ruthlessly he obtruded himself into
her life, ruthlessly he assaulted the securest fastnesses
of it, ruthlessly, she dreaded, he would strike them
down and subdue her will as easily as he had won her
love. He was in her thoughts all day and all night;
she trembled when he was near her; it was torment
when they were apart. Again and again, she returned
to her determination to put him out of her life; he
would only cause her trouble; there was only unhappi-
ness in store for them both. It was useless. Neither
her thoughts nor Devlin had any mercy upon her.
She knew at last what love, real love, was like; it was
a raging fire, white-hot, scorifying, consuming.

His lips never again found hers after that first terrible moment of weakness. Sometimes he caught her
to him and strained her in his arms, but her cheek or

hair or neck received his eager kiss. She resisted
these embraces with all her strength, struggled in his
grasp. She was mortally afraid of him; mortally
afraid of herself. Desire throbbed in all her veins.
She clung desperately to the last redoubt in her de-
fenses behind which every instinct told her safety lay.
She would allow him no avenue of approach; she would
tolerate no moment's weakness in her fortitude.

"Janny, you love me, and, by God, I love you.
You're the finest woman I've ever known, Janny.
When are you going to marry me?" Martin had his
arms about her, but both her hands were pressed
against his breast. He seemed so big and powerful
as he stood holding her; she knew his clean shaven
chin was rough with his beard, firm and cold; he
smelled fragrantly of cigars.

Ah, love! That was one thing,—she had no control
over her heart,—but marriage was another. That was
very different indeed.

"Martin dear,—I *do* love you,—I'm proud I love
you. But I don't want to get married!"

"Why not?"

Jeannette sighed wearily.

"I don't suppose I can ever make you understand.
I like to live my own life; I like to come and go as I
please; I like to have the money I earn myself to spend
the way I like. And besides that, I love my work, I
love being at the office. I've been part of this business
now for three years; I've helped to build it up, I know
every detail; it belongs to me in a way. Does that
sound unreasonable to you?"

"No, not unreasonable exactly. But I don't think
you see it right; you attach too much importance to

it. You'll be just as free and independent as my wife as you are now."

Would she? She wondered. It was of that, that she had her gravest misgivings.

"And then there's Mr. Corey. I wouldn't feel right about leaving him; he depends on me so much."

"Well, for God's sake!" exclaimed Martin. "Do you mean to tell me you would let *that* stand in the way?"

"It's a consideration," said Jeannette honestly. Martin's face settled grimly.

"And then there's Mama," went on the girl. "She's so happy now, living with me. She doesn't have to work so hard any more, and she goes to concerts and visits Alice and does as she pleases. You see, if I married, that would have to come to an end. I don't know what she would do."

"Why, she could do a lot of things," argued Martin. "She might go and live with your sister, for instance, or come with us; she could divide her time between the two of you."

"Alice would love to have her," admitted Jeannette. "Mama's crazy about Etta, and of course it would make it easier for Allie. But I don't think Mama would consent to live with either of her children."

"I've always been a fan for your ma," said Martin, "and that just shows how dead sensible she is. Your sister's husband and I could each send her twenty-five dollars a month, and she could find some place to board easily for that."

"Roy hasn't got any twenty-five dollars."

"We can fix up some arrangement that will be satisfactory all 'round."

"Mama would never consent to give up her teaching. It really means too much to her."

"Well, there you are! You haven't got a real reason on earth for not marrying me to-morrow."

But Jeannette felt she had, though she could find no one to agree with her.

"You're just playing with your happiness, dearie," her mother said to her. "Martin Devlin's a fine young man. You could go a long way before you'd find a better husband. I want to see my dearie-girl in a little home of her own like her sister's."

"Oh, Janny," said Alice, "you don't know what fun, being married is! Why, after you've become a wife, you feel differently about the whole world. Why, I'd marry *anybody* rather than not be married at all! . . . And then, Janny, you haven't got the faintest idea how sweet it is to have a baby of your own. Etta is just the joy of our lives. You ought to see Roy playing with her when he comes home from the office and I am getting her bath ready!"

Jeannette studied her sister's radiant face curiously. There was a mystery here; something she did not understand. This was the girl who had borne her child in agony, who had endured nearly fifteen hours of labor, who had been torn and ripped, and had lain helpless on her back for six long months, fighting her way back to strength and normality, despairing and weakly crying! Yet here she was talking of the joy of having a baby, urging her sister to a like experience!

It was puzzling. How soon mothers forgot! Six months of helplessness already unremembered! It had not passed from Jeannette's recollection. It had been terrible—terrible! . . . And yet she would like to have a baby of her own,—a baby without that fearful ordeal,—a little Martin Devlin. She kissed Etta on the back of her wrinkled fat neck where it was sweetly perspiry and fuzzy with the lint from her blankets.

§ 9

Jeannette was equally sure of two things: she loved Martin with all her soul; she would never consent to give up her position with Mr. Corey and marry him. Martin, her mother, Alice, even Mr. Corey, who soon learned of the situation, could not persuade her.

Corey had a long talk with her about the matter, "I don't know very much about your young man; Gibbs speaks well of him. He tells me he's been with them a little more than a year, and is their star salesman. I think he has more possibilities in him than that. Of course you never can tell. I confess I was impressed when I first met him. Somebody at the Quoin Club had him there as a guest and introduced us, and he talked good business from the start. I don't think much of Gibbs' engraving, but that's no reflection on Devlin. Personally I think you ought to marry. I advised you the same way before. Perhaps you were right in not being too hasty in that instance. I can't know, of course, whether you're seriously interested or not. Your heart has got to tell you that. If you love Devlin well enough and think you'll be happy with him, you ought to marry him. I hate to see you wasting your life down here in this office. You're deserving a better chance. Business is no place for a girl. You ought to be building a home and rearing children of your own. If you make as good a wife as you have a secretary," he ended with a smile, "your husband will have no occasion to find fault with you."

But she could not bring herself to give up her independence. That was what stuck in her throat. She came back to it repeatedly. A little apartment like Alice's to share with Martin, to fix and furnish,—it appealed to her imagination, it had its attractions,—but it would be such a leap in the dark! She was so sure of her happiness living the way she was—why alter it? Yet was there any happiness for her without Martin? She tried to picture it, and her heart misgave her.

Some of the glamor that surrounded him at first had now disappeared. He no longer seemed a scion of wealth, a prince, a lordling, to whistle menials to his beck and call, and to swagger his way in and out of restaurants, leaving a trail of scattered largess in his wake. Familiarity had stripped him of the cloak of splendor with which he first had dazzled her. She liked him all the better without it, for it had only been bluff with him, his way of trying to impress her. She knew him now for an ever merry soul, an amused and amusing companion, possessing rare thoughtfulness, a little vain, a little opinionated, vigorous, direct, domineering, who could, if he so desired, charm an angel Gabriel to softness. He had his faults; she thought she knew them all. He was happy-go-lucky, had small regard for time, appointments, or others' feelings; he was extravagant in all his tastes; and loved pleasure inordinately. But there was a charm about him that made up to her a thousandfold for these trifling shortcomings. He was the handsomest of men, generous and invariably kind-hearted, he could win a smile from

an image, or accomplish the impossible, once his mind
was made up.

It was a satisfaction to learn that he earned only
fifty dollars a week. She had thought him a millionaire
at first. He threw money about with a prodigality
that distressed her. His theatre tickets, his gifts, his
unceasing attentions cost money,—a great deal of
money. She knew his salary did not warrant it. She
was glad he got but fifty a week,—only fifteen more
than she did, herself. Roy was getting forty. Martin
seemed more human to her after she knew the size of
his salary; he was more comprehensible.

And here, once more, was confronting her the matter
of finances were she to marry. She and her mother
together enjoyed an income that was never less than
two hundred dollars a month. She contributed eighty,
as her share towards rent and food, and had still sixty
dollars a month left to spend as she chose, for clothes,
for a gift to Alice, or for delightful adventures with
her mother, lunches and theatres on Saturday afternoons, and the little surprises that were so delightful.
Would she have anything like as much out of the two
hundred dollars Martin earned if she married him?
What part of his weekly pay envelope was he likely
to give her to run their house, and to spend on herself?

It was only fair, since he pressed his suit so vigorously, that this all-important matter should be brought
up and discussed. She did not consider herself merce-
nary. The question of the wife's allowance in marriage seemed a vital one to her. She had tasted independence, and did not consider she should be expected
to relinquish it in marriage. Alice and Roy got along
in amiable fashion on this point. Roy kept five dollars

a week for himself and gave his wife the rest of his pay envelope. Sometimes toward the end of the week he would ask her for fifty cents or a dollar to tide him over until Saturday. That arrangement seemed to Jeannette eminently fair. Roy gave all he could be reasonably expected to, she thought; five dollars a week was about as little as he could get along on for carfare, lunches and tobacco. Of course, his clothing and the pleasures he and his wife shared, came out of what Alice was able to save from week to week,—and she did manage to save a little. But, as Jeannette had often remarked, Alice was different from her. She, Jeannette, had won for herself an economic value to be measured in dollars and cents, and it was not fair to expect her to forego this for a hazy, uncertain condition in which her wishes and wants were only to be gratified at her husband's whim. It was better to have a frank discussion and settle the matter.

Martin shouted a delighted laugh when she expounded this thought.

"Why, my darling," he said, "don't bother your head about it. You can have every cent I make and if that isn't enough, I'll go out and steal for you."

"But seriously, Martin, what do you think a wife should have out of her husband's income? Now, I'm not saying I'll marry you——"

"You darling!"

"No—no,—be sensible, Martin. I want to thresh this out. If I *should* consent to marry you, what would you think would be a fair proportion of what you earn that I could count on as my own?"

"What would you be wanting money for?" Martin asked, amused by her earnestness.

"What would I be wanting money for?" she repeated. "Why, what do you think? . . . For clothes,
for pleasures, to throw away if I liked!"

"Aw, hear her!" he laughed. "Why, my darling,
I'll buy you your clothes and everything your little
heart desires if only you'll say 'yes' to me."

"Martin, I'll never say 'yes' until this is settled,"
she said spiritedly, her eyes with a queer light in them.

Martin was serious for a moment.

"Sweet woman," he said earnestly, "you can have
it all. Divide it any way you like. I don't care in
the least. There's plenty for the two of us."

But Jeannette would consider nothing so indefinite.
She did not want a great deal, but she wanted to feel
sure of something that would be regarded as entirely
her own. With difficulty she persuaded him to talk
about the matter in earnest. They agreed that if his
salary were equally divided, and Jeannette paid all the
table expenses out of her half while he paid the rent
and everything else out of his, that would be an equi-
table arrangement. That satisfied Jeannette; it gave
her something to think about when she considered
marrying him.

But even with this much settled, she was no nearer
making up her mind than she had ever been. Marriage
meant giving up the office, the close affiliations she had
formed there. Propinquity had made her fellow-
workers her friends; she knew them all intimately,
knew something of their private lives, rejoiced or sor-
rowed with them at the inevitable changes of fortune.
When an eminent surgeon from Germany performed a
miraculous operation on Mr. Featherstone's little son
and gave him the use of his legs on which he had never

walked, she shared his father's joy; when Mr. Cavendish married a charming Vassar girl who was the daughter of a wealthy Wall Street banker, she congratulated him with a real pleasure; when Miss Holland's seventeen-year-old nephew secured an appointment at Annapolis and successfully passed the entrance examination, she took keen satisfaction in her friend's delight. She was shocked and saddened when Sandy MacGregor's wife died, and when Mr. Allister was taken ill with pneumonia no one inquired more frequently about him while he struggled desperately to live, or felt more pleasure when it was announced he had turned the corner and would before long be back again at his desk. She was glad when Francis Holme, Walt Chase and Sandy MacGregor each received a substantial gift of the company's common stock at Christmas-time, and was correspondingly sorry that Horatio Stephens and Willis Corey shared equally in the honorarium. When Miss Peckenbaugh asked for a raise in salary, and her request was endorsed by Mr. Allister, she took it upon herself to tell Mr. Corey certain facts about the young lady that had become known to her, and when as a result, the request was refused and Miss Peckenbaugh in anger resigned, she was amused and delighted. At the same time she urged and secured a five-dollar raise per week for old Major Ticknor who had a little blind grandchild he was helping to maintain in a private sanitarium. Young Tommy Livingston in the bindery had impressed her upon a certain occasion with his brightness and ability, and she recommended him warmly to Mr. Corey, and had the satisfaction of seeing him promoted to a desk in Mr. Kipp's department. At her suggestion, window-

boxes filled with flowers were put along the windows
of the press-room that faced the street; she persuaded
the firm to install a lunch-room for the women employees on the eighth floor, and it was her idea that a
regular trained nurse be engaged and established in a
small but complete infirmary within the building.
She induced Mr. Corey to offer a certain rising young
author, whose work had been her discovery and who
was showing steady improvement, an increase in
royalty percentage, and she prevented the publication
of a certain piece of fiction, which Corey had given
her to read, because she considered it vicious, despite
Mr. Allister's strong recommendation. She advised
her chief to instruct Horatio Stephens to order a series
of articles from a woman writer whose work in another
magazine had interested her, and she urged him not
to engage a certain Madame Desseau of Paris, a
designer of women's clothes, as the fashion editor of
The Ladies' Fortune. Jeannette had a hand in almost
every important step that was taken. Mr. Corey respected her judgment, frequently consulted her, and
sometimes followed her advice even when contrary to
his inclinations. He often told her that he believed
her intuition was unerring and the greatest possible
help to him.

§ 10

That particular winter proved an exceptionally
strenuous and exacting one for Mr. Corey. He was
worn out with work and with the ever increasing demands upon him, demands that came more and more
from the outside.

The P. P. Prescott Publishing Company, a house

with a reputation of half a century of high literary output, through mismanagement was in danger of bankruptcy. While the ''P P P'' books were famous the world over, the bank that had financed the concern for years was tired of the arrangement; the tottering house owed the Chandler B. Corey Company nearly a hundred thousand dollars for subscription premiums Francis Holme had sold it, and it was a foregone conclusion that if the Prescott Company failed, there would be no way of collecting the debt. Mr. Corey wanted to take over the Prescott Company entirely,—it could have been bought at the time for practically nothing by assuming its obligations,—but this was one of their chief's bold and brilliant ideas that Mr. Kipps and Mr. Featherstone opposed and, to Jeannette's intense regret, persuaded him against. The result was that instead of absorbing the Prescott Company, and letting the Corey organization administer its various activities, Mr. Corey was forced to become chairman of the board which undertook to put the older publishing house on its feet again, and to do most of the work himself.

In addition to this he was compelled to accept the leadership of a committee appointed by the Publishers' Association to confer with the postal authorities in Washington regarding the rates on second class mail matter which were in danger of being raised. He had been obliged to make several trips to the capital. He was one of the directors of a large paper mill which, in conjunction with some other publishers, he had purchased. He had shown an interest in local politics and had been put on the Republican State Central Committee; he was one of the governors of the Swanee

Valley Golf Club, and executor of the estate of Julius
Zachariah Rosenbaum, a wealthy Jewish capitalist,
whose autobiography he had published during the old
Hebrew's life. No one outside the immediate members of the firm, with the exception of Jeannette, knew
that Rosenbaum had taken sixty thousand subscriptions
to *Corey's Commentary* when the story of his life was
appearing in serial form in that magazine, and when
the book was published he ordered twenty-five thousand
copies, presumably to distribute among his friends.
Poor Rosenbaum! It was doubtful if he had a score,
and when he died there was universal rejoicing
throughout the country that the most grasping of
moneyed barons, who had consistently obstructed the
wheels of progress, was gone. But he left a large slice
of his wealth in charitable endowments, and named
Chandler B. Corey as one of the executors of his will.

These responsibilities weighed heavily upon Mr.
Corey's health and strength. He had been troubled
with indigestion for several months and his general
condition was not good. In addition there were domestic cares. With the increase of their fortunes, Mrs.
Corey had moved herself and her family into a stone
front house on Riverside Drive where she proceeded to
maintain an expensive order of existence. She had
begged hard for this new home, and her husband weakly
had given way. He never seemed able to refuse his
wife anything, Jeannette thought. He could be strong
about other matters, but where Mrs. Corey and his
son, Willis, were concerned he was foolishly irresolute.
Mrs. Corey established herself in great feather in the
new house, hired four servants in addition to a liveried
chauffeur, who drove her Pope-Toledo, and began to

entertain lavishly. Her special victims were authors, particularly visiting ones from England, and if any of them happened to be titled, it was always the occasion for an elaborate affair. Mr. Corey hated these entertainments, and to avoid them frequently went to Washington on the plea of pressing business connected with the postal rates. The new order was exceedingly expensive. Jeannette could not understand why Mr. Corey put up with it.

But his wife's reckless expenditure was a matter of small concern in comparison with his anxiety for his daughter. The unfortunate girl had fallen during a sudden epileptic seizure, and struck her head upon a brass fender at the hearth. She had lain for three months in a semi-conscious condition, and though treatments had partially restored her mind, she was not wholly competent and would never again be able to go about without an attendant. It was a great grief to her father. His troubles had been further augmented at this particular time by Willis, who had been paying marked attention to a married society woman with an unenviable reputation for many affairs with young men. Mr. Corey solved this particular problem by sending Willis on a hunting expedition to South Africa with Eric Ericsson, the Norwegian explorer. Ostensibly the young man went to write articles about the trip for *Corey's Commentary*. It was announced he was to be gone for a year. Jeannette was aware that Mr. Corey had paid Ericsson five thousand dollars to take his son with him; the money had been given, of course, in the form of a contribution to scientific research.

It was small wonder that Corey's physician ordered

a complete rest for him in the early spring of the year. The man was threatened with a nervous breakdown, his doctor told him; the matter of his indigestion must have his serious attention; he must take a vacation, and he must take it immediately. Affairs at the office made it impossible, at the moment, for this vacation to be of any length; even Jeannette realized that it would be hazardous for the company to be left without Mr. Corey's guiding hand on the helm. It was decided that he should go to White Sulphur Springs, play golf as much as he was able, give especial attention to his diet, and keep in touch with the office by mail and telegraph. He would be able, it was hoped, to get a complete change of climate and a proper rest by this arrangement.

"Of course, you'll have to go with me, Miss Sturgis," he said, wheeling round upon her when this conclusion had been reached. "I couldn't do a thing down there without you."

"Why, certainly," the girl answered. As their eyes met a moment, the same thought passed through both minds.

"We'll take your mother along," said Corey in his brisk, direct fashion.

Mrs. Sturgis at once was in a great state of agitation.

"But my pupils, dearie,—my little pupils!" she cried. "What will the darlings do without their lessons?"

"Well, the little darlings can get along without them," Jeannette told her. "When their parents want to take them off to the mountains or the seashore, they just take them, and there's never any question about paying for cancelled lessons. I guess you can do the

same for once in your life. . . . Anyhow, there's no use
arguing about it, Mama. Mr. Corey needs me, and if
you don't go with me, I'll go without you. It's perfectly ridiculous that we have to be chaperoned! He's
like my father! . . . But I thought you'd enjoy the
trip. You know it isn't going to cost either of us a
penny!''

''Why, of course, dearie,—but you kind of spring
this on me. I haven't had a chance to think it over. . . .
Of course, I'd love it.''

§ 11

White Sulphur Springs was beautiful, the weather
perfection; Jeannette enjoyed every hour of her stay.
She had wanted to get off by herself for some time, to
think calmly over what she must do about Martin
Devlin. He had given her one of his hungry kisses
when he said good-bye, and she felt at the moment he
was dearer to her than life itself. He was urging her
with voice, eyes and lips to be his wife. A realization
had come to her that she could temporize with the
situation no longer; she must either agree to marry
him, or in some way bring the intimacy to an end.

Corey played golf mornings and afternoons. Jean-
netted watched his mail, and answered most of it herself, only consulting him when necessary. She would
give him brief memorandums of what his mail contained, and show him the carbons of the letters she had
dispatched, signed with his name, ''per J. S.'' He did
not have to give more than an hour a day to his affairs.

The doctor had warned him about his diet, and had
directed him to take a hydrochloric acid prescription
three times a day. Jeannette watched his food as well

as his mail; she studied the menus in the dining-room and ordered his meals in advance, so that he would be sure to eat the proper food; she made him take his medicine, and persuaded him to try some electric baths that were operated in connection with the hotel. She kept a chart of his weight, and when they met at the breakfast table she would inquire about his night. She saw with satisfaction that he was improving steadily; his face, neck and hands were turning a healthy bronze color, his appetite was excellent, his sleep undisturbed.

At first a problem presented itself in Mrs. Sturgis. The little woman was intensely excited at being so closely associated with Mr. Corey. His presence agitated her; she felt it was her duty to entertain him, to evince an interest in his comings and goings, to maintain a pleasant and polite ripple of conversation at the table or whenever they were together. She believed it was expected of her to show an interest equal to her daughter's in the state of his health, and that she must always inquire how he felt and how he had passed the night. Jeannette knew Mr. Corey hated this kind of fussy solicitude; it annoyed and irritated him. The girl suffered acutely whenever her mother commenced to ply him with her prim inquiries, or when she pretended to be interested in his golf game about which she knew, and her daughter and Mr. Corey knew she knew, not one thing. Jeannette suspected there were moments when Mr. Corey could have strangled her with delight.

There came a distressing hour eventually to mother and daughter. Jeannette had to tell her that Mr. Corey did not like her concern as to his welfare, that he had come down to White Sulphur Springs to rest, and that he must be spared all possible conversation. Mrs. Sturgis wept. She declared she had never been so "insulted" in her life, that she was going to pack her trunk and go home at once.

It was in the midst of this scene that a bell-boy of the hotel brought Jeannette a telegram addressed to Mr. Corey. She tore it open. It was from his wife.

"Dear Chandler, am lonesome without you. Wish to join you for rest of your stay. Wire me if I may come. Can leave at once. Love. RACHAEL."

Jeannette shut her teeth slowly as she read the words. It was most unfortunate. Mrs. Corey would upset her husband, would interfere with his daily routine, clash with him at once over his golf, object to the time he gave to it, find fault with Jeannette's presence, angrily resent her supervision of his health and meals, so that little of the hoped-for good would result from these weeks of rest and recreation. And Mr. Corey would amiably agree to letting her join him!

Jeannette's distress soon persuaded Mrs. Sturgis to forget her own grievances. Once her sympathy for her daughter was aroused, she waxed indignant over Mrs. Corey's selfishness and lack of consideration.

"Why, the woman must be crazy," she said warmly. "He came down here just to get away from her!"

"Oh, I know," murmured Jeannette, "and as sure as I show him her telegram he will tell me to wire her to come at once."

"Well, I wouldn't tell him anything about it," declared Mrs. Sturgis.

They fell to discussing the situation. After long

consultation and several efforts at drafting it, they concocted the following answer:

"Mr. Corey is not well. I think it would be unwise for you to join him just now. He is getting a maximum amount of rest and sleep and anything tending to interfere with these I believe would be unfortunate. Will keep you advised of his condition.
"JEANNETTE STURGIS."

In the middle of the night that followed, Jeannette awoke, and considered what she had done. As she lay awake reviewing the matter, the conviction slowly came to her that she had committed a dreadful blunder. Her mouth grew dry; a cold sweat broke out on her. She got up, went to the window and gazed out upon the flat moonlight that filled the hotel garden below with evil shadows.

Mrs. Corey was certain to be wild! She would be insane with anger! Jeannette could follow the workings of her mind: Was her husband's secretary to presume to tell her what she should do where his welfare was concerned? Was this stenographer at so much a week to take it upon herself to tell her employer's wife she did not think her presence at her husband's side a good thing for him? Was she implying that it would be harmful, distressful for him? Did she have such entire confidence in herself and her judgment that she could send a telegram like that without even consulting him? . . .

Oh, the heavens were about to fall! It was an irreparable mistake! Mr. Corey, himself, would be furious with her! The mental distress she had been anxious to save him, she had, with her own hand,

brought ten times more heavily upon him! She was a
fool,—an utter, inexcusable fool! She was—was—
was——

She did not sleep the rest of the night. She rolled
and tossed in her bed, and walked the floor.

In the morning she went straight to Mr. Corey and
told him what she had done. His seriousness as he
frowned and pulled at his moustache confirmed her
worst fears. He made no comment; asked a few questions; there was nothing more. Jeannette went on
talking volubly, at times incoherently, for the first
time in all the years she had been his secretary, trying
to justify herself. Suddenly a rush of tears blinded
her; she tried to check them; it was useless.

"Well, well, well, Miss Sturgis," Corey said consolingly patting her folded hands. "You mustn't take
it so hard. It's not such a serious matter. You're
making too much of it. I guess I can square it for both
of us."

He drew a sheet of hotel paper toward him and
scribbled a couple of lines with his fountain pen.

"Here," he said, shoving it towards her. "Send her
this telegram and see how it works."

Jeannette read what he had written through blurred
vision.

"Dear Rachael, Miss Sturgis has shown me your
wire of yesterday. I agree with her that it would
be a mistake for you to join me just at present. Am
writing you. Much love.   CHANDLER."

The girl looked up at him with swimming eyes.
Impulsively she caught his hand; his generosity over-

whelmed her; in a moment she had pressed the hand
to her lips.

§ 11

They returned to New York the end of March. Mrs.
Sturgis had been in a flutter of excitement during the
last ten days of their stay; she was madly anxious to
get home to see Alice, who had written she was going
to have another baby. Both her mother and sister were
distressed at the news; they felt it was unfortunate
she was going to have one so soon after her first.
Little Etta was not a year old yet.

On Washington's Birthday, which fell on a Friday
that year, Martin Devlin had come all the way from
New York to see Jeannette. He had brought with him
in his pocket a flawless, claw-set diamond solitaire in
a little plush jeweller's box and had begged Jeannette
to allow him to slip it on her finger. She had found
herself missing him during the weeks of separation
more than she had believed it possible she could miss
anyone; she missed his big hands and his big voice, his
indefatigable solicitude, his joyous laugh, his unwavering love for her. In the months,—it was close to a
year,—that she had known him, she had grown dependent upon these; Martin was part of her life now;
she could not imagine it without him; love had en-
riched the existence of both. But she was no nearer
marrying him than she had ever been. During the
weeks of sunshine, the hours of solitude and thinking
she had enjoyed, it seemed to her that marriage would
be a terrible mistake; she believed she saw her destiny
lying straight ahead; she had chosen a vocation, and

like a nun, who renounces marriage, she too must give up all thought of being a wife. She must pursue her life work unhampered by domesticity. Not forever would she be Mr. Corey's secretary; there were heights beyond she planned to attain. She told herself she had the capacity of being a successful executive; some day she would hold a position like Miss Holland's, have a department of her own. Walt Chase had charge of the Mail Order business; one of these days he would be promoted to something more responsible, and Jeannette intended then to ask Mr. Corey to give her his place. She knew she could do the work,—perhaps even better than Walt Chase. She had plans already to make it larger and to get out special literature designed to arouse women's interest. Walt Chase was getting seventy-five dollars a week now. She would like to be earning that much. She knew what she would do with it: she'd begin to put by a hundred a month, and invest it in good securities; when she grew old or wanted to take a vacation, she would have something saved up. She had only commenced to think of these matters recently, but now the idea fired her. It would be wonderful to have a private income of one's own. And perhaps she might take her mother with her on a little jaunt to Europe! . . . But matrimony? No, marriage was too great a risk, too much of an experiment. She acknowledged she loved Martin Devlin as much as she could ever love any man. Of that she was sure. She was not equally sure she would always be happy with him, that she would like married life itself. Why risk something that might bring her untold sadness?

So Jeannette had argued before Martin arrived to see her and so she had planned to tell him. It was a

familiar conclusion with her, but this time she determined that he should have the truth and she would
convince him that she could never marry him. But
when Martin put his big fingers around her arm and
drew her strongly to him, crushing her in his embrace
while he forced his lips against hers, she wanted to
swoon in his arms and so die. The weakness was but
momentary; she fled from him, won control of herself
again, and the bars were up once more between them.
But she had not been able to bring herself to enunciate
her high resolve; she had refused the ring, yet Martin
had returned to New York with the confident feeling
that some day she would wear it.

Mr. Corey had entirely regained his old buoyancy
during the six weeks' rest. He came back to his desk
with all the dynamic energy which had so impressed
Jeannette when she first became his secretary. She,
too, was glad to be home again, back in her own office,
resuming her daily routine, gathering up the threads
of activity and influence she loved to have within her
grasp, and seeing Martin every day. Alice, with her
round eyes reflecting in their depths that same curious
light Jeannette had noticed when the first baby was
coming, welcomed her mother and sister in the gayest
of spirits. She was having not nearly the same degree
of discomfort, she told them, that she had had while
carrying Etta. She made them come to dinner the
night they arrived in New York; she wanted them to
see the baby, and to show them the sewing machine Roy
was buying for her on the installment plan. Martin
was included in the party. This troubled Jeannette a
little, for it seemed to establish him in the family
circle.

She had returned from White Sulphur Springs on Sunday. On Tuesday, Mr. Corey did not come to the office all day. Jeannette had expected him; he had said nothing to her about being absent; she had no idea where he was. On Wednesday, when he came in, in the middle of the morning, a strained white look upon his face told her at once that something had gone wrong. He rang for her almost immediately, and indicated a chair for her, while he instructed the operator at the telephone switch-board he was not to be disturbed.

"Miss Sturgis," he began, working a troubled thumb and forefinger at the ends of his moustache, "I have some unhappy news for you; it has been unhappy for me, and I fear it will be equally so for you. Mrs. Corey as you know is a high-strung, temperamental woman. You've no doubt observed she had a decidedly suspicious nature. . . ."

Jeannette's heart stood still. In a flash she saw what was coming. A gathering roar began mounting in her ears, every muscle grew tense. She could see Mr. Corey's mouth moving, his lips forming words and she heard his voice, but what he was saying was meaningless to her; she could get no sense out of it. Suddenly he came to the word "divorce." Her whole nature seemed to have been waiting for him to say it; as he pronounced it, she sat bolt upright, and a quick convulsion passed through her. At once her mind was clear and she was able to follow everything he was saying.

". . . wrote her a long letter from the hotel. I was loving and affectionate in it—as affectionate as I knew how to be, for I feared the unfortunate matter of the telegrams would anger her. I think I wrote some eight or nine pages, and I tried to explain that you had been merely actuated by your solicitude for me. In my anxiety to placate her, I spoke very harshly of you, told her that you realized you had overstepped your province, that I had given you a severe reprimand and that you were much chagrined. I explained to her carefully your mother was with us, but she knew that was to be before we left. I assured her of my devotion. I got no answer. I suspected before we reached New York that she was at outs with me, but there have been other occasions when this was so, and I had no doubt that I could soothe her injured feelings. She had always resented your being my secretary; of course, you've known that. I did not dream, however, that she was as angry with me as she evidently is. She has shut herself into her own apartment at home and declines to see me; she is preparing to file against me a suit for absolute divorce, accusing me of improper conduct with you at White Sulphur Springs, claiming that your mother was bribed into conniving——"

"*Oh!*" gasped Jeannette.

"I am telling you these unpleasant details, so that you can fully grasp the situation. You will have to know in any case, and I think it is only fair to you to give you the whole truth from the start. She has gone to Leonard and Harvester and persuaded them to represent her. I don't know what Dick Leonard is thinking about; he has known me for twenty years. Winchell, whom I saw yesterday, has been to interview Leonard, and he informs me that a detective agency was employed to watch us while we were at the hotel, and that affidavits have been obtained from some of the hotel employees which substantiate Mrs. Corey's allegations.''

Mr. Corey smiled wryly.

''I don't want to go on shocking you in this fashion. I just wish to say that Winchell showed me a copy of the plea, and the statements contained in it are as odious as they are false. You and I have been spared nothing.''

Again Mr. Corey paused, and a savage frown gathered on his brow. Jeannette was trembling; she wet her lips and swallowed convulsively.

''The brunt of the attack,'' he resumed after a moment, ''seems to be levelled against you. Leonard told Winchell that Mrs. Corey had no desire to expose me, —that was the word used; she wishes to bring to an immediate termination a relationship which she cannot tolerate; she declines,—so Leonard states,—to remain my wife as long as you are my secretary. As Winchell points out we have no way of determining whether or not she is in earnest. Of course she cannot prove her suit; she can prove nothing; but she sees quite clearly she can blacken your reputation before the world and force you out of this office by the very publicity which is bound to be attached to the case. . . . It makes me angry; it makes me *very* angry. I have been thinking over the situation from every angle, and I would willingly, and, I confess, with a good deal of relish, contest her suit, force her to retract every word she has said against either of us, and assist you in every way I could in suing her for libel. All my life my guiding principle has been justice. I believe in justice; I believe in a square deal, and this is foul, rank and outrageously unfair. If there was any possible way of obtaining justice for you I wouldn't care anything for myself. I would welcome the publicity; certainly I have no cause to dread it. But it would serve you hard. . . . Take our own office here,—how many of those people outside there would believe in your or my innocence, no matter how completely we were vindicated?

"But far more important that the opinion of any one of those out there,—or that of all of them together,—is the effect this unpleasant story would have upon your young man. No doubt he has the same confidence in you that I have, but you will appreciate that no man likes to have for a wife a girl who has been mixed up in a scandal. . . . You see, how it would be? . . . Devlin is a fine fellow; I like him; he will make his mark. You have confided in me that you care for him. . . . Well, Miss Sturgis, I advise you to marry him!—marry him before this ugly story gets bruited abroad. I am convinced it will never be told. I know Mrs. Corey and I know how she will act. As soon as she hears you are married and no longer here, she will withdraw her suit and be anxious to make amends. I have no desire for a divorce. I understand all too well that it will be Mrs. Corey who will suffer if we are separated, not I, and I have the wish to protect her against herself. There are the children to think of, too. This is merely the act of an insane woman,—a woman blinded by jealousy. Outrageously unfair as it is to you, and much as I shall hate to part with you, it seems to be the wisest thing to do. Winchell advises it, and I confess when I think of your own interests and everything that is involved, I agree with him. What do you think?"

Jeannette sat staring at her folded hands. Slowly the tears welled themselves up over her lashes and splashed upon the crisp linen of her shirtwaist. She was not sorrowful; she was only hurt,—hurt and cruelly shocked that anyone could believe the things Mrs. Corey had said of her and this man who was father, friend, and counsellor to her, whom she loved and respected and who, she knew, loved and respected her in return. Their relationship during the four and a half years they had been so intimately associated had been above criticism; it had been perfect, irreproachable. Jeannette felt foully smirched by the base imputation.

"Gracious—goodness!" she said at last upon a quivering breath, her breast rising. Tears trembled on her lashes, but for the instant her eyes blazed.

"Well," Mr. Corey said wearily after a pause, "it's too bad,—isn't it?"

Too bad? Too bad? Ah, yes, it was indeed too bad! Silence filled the book-lined room, the very room she had taken such pains and such delight in furnishing so tastefully. She recalled Mrs. Corey had resented that! She had put some fresh pine boughs in the earthenware pot in the corner yesterday, and the office smelled fragrantly of balsam. The rumble of the presses below sent a fine tremor through the building. Both man and girl stared at the floor. They were thinking the same things; there was no need to voice them; both understood; it was all clear now to each.

He was right. The best thing,—the only thing for her to do was to resign. That would immediately pacify his wife; it would avert the breach and save Corey from an ugly scandal which could only hurt him. And then there was herself to consider, her own good name, her mother and Alice, and there was Martin! Nothing stood in the way now of her giving him the answer for which he eagerly waited. Martin! Ah, there was a refuge for her, there was a haven ready to welcome her! He would take her to himself, protect her, shield her against these slandering tongues!

Suddenly at the thought of him, so merry and strong and confident, of his joy at the promise she was now free to make, the floodgates of her heart opened and, bowing her head upon her fiercely clasped hands, she burst into convulsive sobbing.

CHAPTER III

§ 1

June sunshine streamed in through the open windows in an avalanche of golden light and lay in bright parallelograms on the floor. Jeannette was making the bed. She was in the gayest of spirits and sang as she punched the pillows to rid them of lumpiness, and smoothed them flat. She spread the brilliant cretonne cover, with its gaudy design of pheasants, over the bed, turned it neatly back two feet from the headboard, laid the pillows in place, and folded the cretonne over them, tucking it in gently at the top. The bedcover was not as long as it should have been, and it required nice adjustment to make it lap over the pillows. It was the Wanamaker man's fault, Jeannette always thought, when she reached this point in her morning's housework; she had told him with the utmost pains how she wished the cretonne to go, and it was his mistake that it was not long enough. Short as it was, it could be made to reach by allowing only a scant inch or two at the bottom. She had put the same material at the windows in narrow strips of outside curtaining, and there was a gathered valance across the top. The bedroom was "sweet,"—charming and beautifully appointed like the rest of her domain. Her mother and Alice had "raved" about everything. Martin like it, too, though his wife wished

he could find the same amount of pleasure in their
little home that she did. Martin was like most men:
he did not notice things, never commented upon her
ideas and clever arrangements.

To her the apartment was perfection. It was situated in a building that had just been erected in the
West Eighties, halfway between Broadway and the
Drive. It had five rooms and the rent was fifty dollars a month, more perhaps than they ought to be
paying, but Martin had argued that ten dollars one
way or another did not make any particular difference
and if it suited Jeannette, he was for signing the
lease. So he had put his name to the formidable-
looking legal document, and the young Devlins had
agreed to pay the big rent and to live there for a year.
They could remain in it for life, Jeannette declared,
as far as she was concerned; she could not imagine
ever wanting a more beautiful or a more satisfactory
home.

The apartment contained all the latest improve-
ments: electric lights, steam heat, a house telephone.
The woodwork was chastely white throughout; the
electrolier in the dining-room a plain dull brass; the
fixtures in all the rooms were of the same lusterless
metal; between dining- and living-rooms were glass
doors, the panes set in squares; the bathroom floor was
solid marquetry of small octagonal tiles embedded in
cement, and glossy tiling rose about the walls to the
height of the shoulder; the room glistened with shining nickel and flawless porcelain; the bathtub was
sumptuous and had a shower arrangement with a
rubber sheeting on rings to envelop the bather. Martin
had grinned when his eye took in these details. He

swore in his enthusiasm: by God, he certainly would enjoy a bathroom like that; it certainly would be great. But Jeannette was more intrigued with the kitchen. Here were white-painted cupboards, fragrantly smelling of new wood, and a marvellous pantry full of neat contrivances, drawers, bins and lockers. In one of them Jeannette discovered a little sawdust and a few carpenter's shavings; they spoke eloquently of the newness and cleanliness of everything. There was a shining gas-stove, too, with a roomy oven that had an enamelled door and a bright nickel knob to it. There was even a gas heater connected with the boiler; all one had to do was to touch a match to the burner,— the renting agent explained,—and presto! the flame came up, heated the coil of copper pipe and in a moment,—oh, yes, indeed, much less than a minute!— there was the hot water!

It had seemed so miraculous to Jeannette that she had not believed it would work, but it did, perfectly. No fault was to be found with anything connected with the wonderful establishment.

There had been plenty of money with which to furnish it just as Jeannette pleased. The publishing company had presented her with a check for two hundred and fifty dollars as a wedding gift in appreciation of her faithful services, and Mr. Corey had supplemented this with one of his own for a like amount.

"No,—no,—don't thank me,—please, Miss Sturgis," he had said almost impatiently as he handed it to her. "I feel so badly about your going, and I can never pay you for all you've done for me. This is a poor evidence of my gratitude and esteem. I wish I might make it thousands instead of hundreds."

In addition, he had sent her on the day she was married a tall silver flower vase that must have cost, Jeannette and Martin decided, almost as much as the amount of his check.

Her mother had borrowed five hundred upon the old paid-up policy, asserting that she had done so for Alice, and the older daughter was entitled to a like amount upon getting married. And besides all this, Martin had turned over to his wife on the day the lease had been signed, several hundreds more.

It appeared that a year before, about the very time he had met Jeannette, his mother died. She had lived in Watertown, New York, where Martin was born, and where she had an interest in a small grocery business. Martin's father,—dead for sixteen years,—had been a grocer and had run a "back-room" in connection with his store, where Milwaukee beer had been dispensed but never "hard" liquor. Jeannette did not give her mother these facts when she learned them; it was nobody's business, she contended; everybody when he came to America was a pioneer and began in a humble way. Paul Devlin's old partner, Con Donovan, who had come over from Ballaghaderreen with him in '73, had carried on the business after his demise, and there had been money enough to send Martin to school and to support the boy and Paul's widow. But when his mother had followed his father to the grave, Martin had no longer any interest in groceries, and he gladly accepted the three thousand dollars Con Donovan offered him for his inherited share of the business. It hadn't been enough to do anything with, Martin explained to his wife, so he had just "blown" it. It accounted for the theatre tickets, the presents, the entertainments with which he had backed his wooing. There was nearly a thousand dollars left after the honeymoon to Atlantic City, and Martin had gone to his bank and transferred the whole account to his wife's name upon their return, telling her to go ahead and furnish the new home in any way she fancied.

Jeannette had nearly seventeen hundred dollars in the bank when she began. She had no thought of spending so much, but it melted away in the most surprising fashion. Martin, in a way, was responsible for this: whenever she consulted him, he was always in favor of the more expensive course. She would have been quite satisfied with a two-hundred-and-twenty-dollar dining-room set, but he decided in favor of the one that cost three hundred and fifty. When she said she would be contented with the simple white-painted wooden bed, he had chosen a brass one and ordered the box-spring mattress that had cost nearly a hundred dollars more. He had also persuaded her against her judgment in the matter of the big davenport and the upholstered chairs that went with it for the living-room. Then there had been the matter of the two oil paintings in ornate gold frames upon which they had chanced in Macy's while on a shopping tour. Jeannette had grave doubts about the oils; she did not know whether they were good or bad. Her misgivings in regard to them may have sprung from the fact that they hung in Macy's art gallery; but there could be no questioning the handsomeness and impressiveness of the gold frames.

"Why sure, let's have 'em," Martin said, eying them judicially as he and his wife stood together considering the purchase; "they look like a million dollars, and anything I hate are bare walls! You want to have the place lookin'—oh, you know—artistic and classy."

"The autumn coloring in this one is most lifelike," the eager young salesman ventured. "It seems to me they both have a great deal of depth and quality,— don't you think?—and while, of course, the size has nothing to do with the art, still I really think you ought to take into consideration the fact that this canvas is thirty-six by twenty-seven, and the other one is nearly as large. Now for twenty-five and thirty dollars . . ."

"Sure, let's have 'em," Martin decided in his lordly, arbitrary way, "and if I find out they're no good," he added to the beaming salesman, "I'll come back here and slap Mrs. Macy on the wrist!"

This last was most appreciated, and the very next day, in much excelsior and paper wrappings, the two heavily framed paintings arrived and now hung facing one another in the front room. Jeannette used to study them, finger on lip, wondering if they had merit or were nothing but daubs. They appeared all right; there was nothing to criticize about them as far as she could see, but she knew they would never mean anything to her as long as she remembered they had been bought at Macy's. Her mother warmly shared her husband's enthusiasm.

"Why, dearie, they look perfectly beautiful," she told her daughter, "and they give your home such an air of distinction. I wouldn't worry my head about where they came from, as long as they give you pleasure."

But if Jeannette had misgivings about the pictures,
she had no doubts about anything else her perfect
little home contained. It was complete as far as she
could make it, from the service of plated flat silver her
old associates at the office had clubbed together and
given her, to the carpet sweeper that had a little closet
of its own to stand in along with the extra leaves of the
dining-room table. There were towels, sheets, table
linen, chairs, pictures and rugs. She had indulged
her fancy somewhat in curtaining, had decided on plain
net at the windows with narrow strips of some brightly
colored material on either side. She had picked out
a salmon-tinted, satin-finished drapery at Wanamaker's for the living-room, and gay cretonne for her
bedroom, and she had had these curtains made at
the store.

"I'd be forever doing the work," she had said in
justifying this extravagance to Martin, "and we want
to get settled some time!"

"Sure,—have 'em made," he had agreed genially.

The dining-room had puzzled Jeannette for a long
time, but after the dark blue carpet had been selected
and made into a rug to fit the room, she had found a
blue madras that just matched its tone. It cost a great
deal more than she felt she ought to pay, but she had
bought the twelve yards she needed, nevertheless, and
had determined she could save something by cutting
and hemming the curtains herself; she could take them
out to Alice's and use her sewing-machine.

It was all finished now, Jeannette reflected, pushing
the big brass bed into place against the wall. They
had been a little reckless perhaps, but now they were
ready to settle down, begin to live quietly and to save.

They owed about two hundred dollars at Wanamaker's but would soon manage to pay that off.

She went on calculating expenses as she ran the carpet sweeper about the room. Martin liked a good deal of meat, so she doubted if she could manage the table on less than twelve or maybe, thirteen dollars a week; that would take half of what he gave her on Saturdays. She needed so much for this, so much for that, and she would have to get herself some kind of a silk dress for the hot weather; still she thought she could save five or six dollars a week and Martin ought to be able to do the same; they would have the Wanamaker bill paid in a few months. As she went on running the sweeper under the bed and pushing it gingerly into corners so as not to mar the paint of the baseboards, she reflected that, as a matter of fact, Martin had really no right to expect her to pay anything out of her weekly money on what they owed Wanamaker; every cent of that bill had been for house furnishing, and it had been clearly understood between them that her money was for the table and herself. Still it had been she who had wanted the curtains; she ought to help pay for them.

§ 2

When the bathroom was cleaned, Martin's bath towel spread along the rim of the tub to dry, his dirty shirt and collar put into the laundry basket, his shoes set neatly on the floor of the closet, the ash receiver in the living-room emptied and the cushions on the davenport straightened, Jeannette settled herself in a rocking-chair at the window, her basket of sewing in her lap. She hated sewing; the basket was in tangled

confusion, but it was always that way. Spools and
yarn, papers of needles, pins, buttons, threads, tape,
and scraps of material were all mixed up together in
a fine snarl. She found a certain degree of satisfaction
in its confusion. To-day she had a run in one of her
silk stockings to draw together, and a button to sew
on Martin's coat.

She caught the coat up first and as she held it in
her hands, the song that she had been humming all
morning died upon her lips. She looked at the garment with softening eyes; then she raised its rough
texture to her cheek and kissed it. It smelled of its
owner,—a smell that was fragrance to her,—an odor
scented faintly with cigars but even more redolent of
the man, himself; it was strong, it was masculine, it
was Martin. There was no smell like it in the world or
one half so sweet.

She mused as she searched for a black silk thread,
needle and thimble. When Alice had extolled to her
the wonderful happiness of marriage, how right she
had been! Jeannette pitied all unmarried women now.
There was a Freemasonry among wives, and all spin-
sters, old and young, were debarred from the mystic
circle. She wondered what made the difference. Unmarried women were all buds that had never opened
to the full beauty of the mature flower. They were of
the uninitiated and as long as they remained so would
never attain their full powers. Miss Holland, now,
was a fine woman, efficient, capable, executive, but how
much more able and efficient and remarkable if she had
married! She might be divorced, she might be a
widow. That did not make a difference, it seemed to
Jeannette in the full bloom of her own wifehood; it was

marrying that counted; it was that "Mrs." before a
woman's name, that gave her standing, poise, position
in the world, broadened her sympathies, increased her
capabilities.

She thought her own marriage perfection; she considered herself the happiest, most fortunate of wives;
her pretty home enchanted her, and Martin was the
most satisfactory of adoring husbands. He had his
faults, she presumed, and she, no doubt, had hers, but
there were never woman and man so happy together,
so ideally congenial. She thought of her honeymoon,
—the few days at Atlantic City. She had never learned
to swim, but Martin was an expert. He had looked
stunning in his bathing-suit,—straight, clean-limbed,
with his big chest and shoulders and his slim waist,—
the figure of an athlete, as she indeed discovered him
to be when he struck out into the sea with the freedom
of a seal, flinging the water from his black mop of hair
with a quick head-toss now and then, his arms working
like flails. They had plunged through the breakers
together, and Martin had held her high up as the curling water crashed down upon them. It had been cold
but exhilarating, and a group had gathered on the
boardwalk and down on the beach to watch the two
battling with the waves. Then there had been the
quiet rolling up and down the boardwalk in the big
chair while the tide of Easter visitors sauntered past
them in all their gay clothing. The weather had been
warm, the sunshine glorious. She thought of their
room at the hotel and the intimate times of dressing
and undressing in each other's presence. It had been
emotional, exciting, a little frightening, but there had
been the discovery of perfect comradeship, and all

the other phases of marriage,—pleasant and unpleasant,—had been forgotten. Companionship,—wholehearted, unreserved, constant,—that was the outstanding feature of marriage for Jeannette.

Her mind carried her on to contemplate the future and what it held in store for them. Her marriage with Martin must be a success. There must be no quarrelling, no disagreements, no bickerings. There must never, never be any talk of divorce between them. . . . . Ah, how she hated the word divorce now! She had never given the subject any particular consideration heretofore; it was merely an accepted proceeding by which unhappily married people won back their freedom. But how differently she felt about it to-day! She would die rather than ever consent to a divorce from Martin! She'd forgive him anything! He was a little spoiled, perhaps; he liked to have his own way, and he hated anything unpleasant. It must be her duty to humor and educate him; she must give a little, exact a little. A successful marriage, she believed, depended upon that. A husband and wife must become adjusted to one another. If necessary, she resolved, she would give more than she received. Oh, yes, she would give and give and *give!*

Martin had only one serious fault, and that was he too much liked having a good time. It seemed to her he was never satisfied with anything less than an epicure's dinner; he must have the best all the time. He loved cocktails and wine and good cigars, a "snappy" show, a little bite of something afterwards, a gay place to dine, lively music, lights, color. He wanted "to go places where there was something doing," and he didn't want "to go places where there

was nothing doing." These were familiar expressions
on his lips. His wife told herself she liked a good
time, too; she loved the theatre and to dress well, and
she liked a gay restaurant, good food and music, but
she didn't want them all the time; she wasn't as dependent upon them as Martin was. A husband and
wife, she considered, should not indulge in too much
of that kind of frivolous living, and no later than last
evening she had had a talk with Martin about it.

"Aw,—sure my dear,—you're dead right," he had
assured her. "I know. We must settle down, and stay
at home nights, but we're still having our honeymoon,
and I can't get used to the idea that you're my
wife. It just seems to me we ought to celebrate all the
time."

Martin was always so reasonable, thought Jeannette,
recalling his words. She decided she would have a
specially nice dinner for him that night to show him
how much she appreciated his sweetness. She paused
a moment over the decision, as she recalled that something vague had been said to her mother about coming to dine with them. She knew Martin would prefer to be alone and she wanted to encourage the idea
of his spending the evenings quietly with her. She
would go to see her mother and explain matters; she
would have lunch with her; at Kratzmer's she would
stop and get some salad, and she'd buy some crumpets
at Henri's and take them along with her.

Abruptly, she determined to let the run in her stock-
ing wait. She wound the silk several times about the
button on Martin's coat, pushed the needle through the
fabric twice, and snapped the thread close to the cloth
with an incisive bite of her teeth. Then she carried the

work to her room, hanging Martin's coat on a hanger in the closet.

As she proceeded to dress carefully, she considered each detail of her costume. Her wardrobe was delightfully complete; she had plenty of clothes, a suitable garment for any demand. While an office worker, she had always dressed with certain soberness, an eye to business decorum. But as a married woman, a young matron who lived at the Dexter Court Apartments, she felt she could allow herself more latitude. She ran her eye appraisingly over the file of dresses that hung neatly in her closet; their number gratified her; she was even satisfied with her hats. Now she lifted down her blue broadcloth tailor suit, covered handsomely with braid, and selected a soft white silk shirt-waist that had a V-neck and a pleated ruffled collar; she drew on fine brown silk stockings and fitted her feet into tan Oxfords. Her ankles were trim and shapely. She never had appeared so smartly dressed; her appearance delighted her. But she was in doubt about the hat for the day, and finally selected the Lichtenberg model: a silvered straw, with a flaring brim, trimmed in gray velvet and a curling gray cock's feather. As she pulled her hands into tan gloves and gave a final glance at herself in the long mirror of the bathroom door she decided that was the costume she would wear when she went to the offices of the Chandler B. Corey Company to pay her old friends a visit.

§ 3

Mrs. Sturgis had declared after Jeannette's marriage she preferred to remain in the old apartment where she had been comfortable for so many years. To be sure the rent was thirty dollars a month, but she said she could manage that. She had her music lessons,—four or five hours a day,—and there were other pupils to be had if she needed the income. But it did not appear necessary. Elsa Newman's cousin, Cora Newman, who had been studying with Bellini for two years, had developed a truly remarkable mezzo, and she preferred Mrs. Sturgis to any other accompanist. The very week Jeannette was married Cora Newman had given her first public recital, and Mrs. Sturgis had been at the piano. She had had a very beautiful black dress *made* for the occasion and the affair had been a great success. The critics had praised Miss Newman's voice and the *Tribune* had given a special line to the player: "The singer was sympathetically accompanied at the piano by Mrs. Henrietta Spaulding Sturgis." Now both Elsa and Cora wanted her whenever either of them sang, and there were plans ahead for a concert tour to Quebec and Montreal. If that turned out successfully, they were talking of an up-state trip in the fall through Rochester, Syracuse, as far as Buffalo.

"You know what *I* eat, lovies," Mrs. Sturgis had explained to her daughters when keeping the apartment was being discussed among them, "is microscopic, and it won't cost me five a week. I can always get whatever I need at Kratzmer's and a little tea and toast is often all I want."

"But that's just *it!*" Jeannette had expostulated. "You don't eat enough to keep a bird alive, anyhow, and if you live by yourself, you won't eat *that!*"

Mrs. Sturgis had assured them she would take good care of herself.

"You can't imagine me happy in a boarding-house," she had challenged, "and I wouldn't be able to have a piano there or give lessons!" There had been no answer to this; boarding in one place and renting a studio in another would be even more expensive than keeping the apartment.

§ 4

To-day Jeannette heard the familiar finger exercises as she nearer the top of the long stair-flight of her old home: ta-ta-ta-ta-*de*-da-da-da-da—ta-ta-ta-ta-*de*-da-da-da-da, and as she noiselessly opened the back door kitchenward, her mother's voice from the studio: "*One*-and-two-and-three-and-four-and . . ."

She took off her hat and gloves, laid them on her mother's bed and went to peek in the cupboard; there was a piece of bakery pie and a few eggs. She decided to make an omelette and with the toasted crumpets and tea, a little jar of marmalade and the potato salad she had brought with her, she and her mother would lunch royally. It was ten minutes to twelve; the lesson would soon be over.

They lingered over their repast until nearly two. Mrs. Sturgis had lessons from four to six,—the after-school hours,—but until then she was free. She had had half a notion, she confessed, of going down to Union Square that afternoon to look at some new piano pieces for beginners at Schirmer's. Jeannette told her she would go with her,—she wanted to get an alligator pear for Martin's dinner,—but neither of them appeared inclined to terminate the little luncheon at the kitchen table. They had finished the crumpets, but there was still marmalade left, and Mrs. Sturgis produced some pieces of cold left-over toast with which to finish it.

She was full of news and her affairs. In the first place, Alice and Roy were going to Freeport on Long Island for the summer. They had found a very nice place where they could board for eighteen dollars a week,—oh, yes, both of them and the baby, too,—Roy was going to commute every day, and the Bronx flat was to be closed,—just turn the key in the door and leave it until they were ready to come back. Then there was great talk about the concert tour. Bellini, who had sailed only the day before yesterday for Italy, had thought Miss Elsa and Miss Cora had better study another winter before attempting it, but a most encouraging letter had been received from Montreal, and both the girls were eager to try the experiment. They were in doubt as to whether they should take a violinist with them or not; of course a violinist would be a drawing-card, but they would have his salary and all his expenses to pay, which would cut down the profits—if there were any! Jeannette's mother did not think it was in the least necessary, but if they didn't take one, Miss Elsa had said Mrs. Sturgis had better be prepared to do some solo numbers, and that meant she'd have to do some real hard practising as she hadn't done anything like that for years! She did not know whether to work up the Mendelssohn *Capricioso* or the Chopin *Fantaisie Impromptu;* what did Jeannette think? Of course there was that *Meditation. . . .*

But as her mother rambled on, Jeannette's mind

wandered. Her thoughts were with Martin. She
wondered what he was doing at that moment; with
whom he had lunched; how she could entertain him in
the evenings and keep him from wanting to go out. He
must have some friends whom she could invite to
dinner. There was Beatrice Alexander, of course, and
she had heard him speak pleasantly of Herbert Gibbs,
—the younger of the two Gibbs brothers. He was married, she remembered; his wife had a baby and they
lived somewhere down on Long Island. She herself
would have liked to have asked Miss Holland, but she
was hardly the type that would interest Martin. There
was Tommy Livingston,—but Tommy was really too
young. Her mind rested on Sandy MacGregor! He
was a widower,—his wife had been dead for over a
year,—she knew he would love to come to them, and
Martin was sure to like him. The thought elated her:
Sandy and Beatrice Alexander would make an excellent combination.

She accompanied her mother downtown in gay
spirits, full of determination to put this plan immediately into effect.

§ 5

The dinner-party, when it took place, was not altogether a success; still it was far from being a failure.
Sandy unquestionably had a good time, for he and
Martin took a great liking to each other. Beatrice had
proven the unfortunate element. She had always been
diffident and the eye-glasses hopelessly disfigured her.
Martin liked her because he knew her so well,—one
had to know Beatrice to appreciate her,—but Sandy
had been merely polite and amiable. He enjoyed Mar-

tin and Martin's cocktails, however,—they had one or two before dinner,—and each time they raised their glasses, Sandy said: "Saloon!" which had amused Martin vastly. The dinner itself was delicious,—even Jeannette felt satisfied. The baked onions stuffed with minced ham,—Alice had suggested that and shown her how to do them,—had been enthusiastically praised, the chicken had been tender and the iced pudding, ordered at Henri's, could not have been more delicious.

After dinner they played auction bridge; Martin loved cards in any form and he undertook to teach Jeannette; Sandy was an old hand at the game, but Beatrice Alexander was but a timid player. After three or four rubbers, the men abandoned the cards, which, Jeannette could see, bored them with such partners, and began matching quarters, and Martin had won eighteen dollars. The last match had been for "double or nothing" and Jeannette was hardly able to stifle the quick breath of relief that came to her lips when Martin won. She had always known Sandy to be liberal-handed and he paid his losses good-humoredly, telling Jeannette in a way that made her believe he meant what he said, that he had had a wonderful evening, and would telephone shortly to ask the Devlins to dinner with him. He generously offered to take Beatrice Alexander home, and Jeannette returned from the elevator, where she and Martin had bidden good-night to their departing guests, to the disorder and smoky atmosphere of their little home with the feeling that it had all been worth while.

"My Lord!" Martin said that night as he lay in bed waiting for her to wind the clock, open the window, snap out the lights and join him, "I wish you had a girl out there in the kitchen to help you with all that mess. Damned if I like the idea of my wife doing all those dirty dishes, and having to clean up everything to-morrow. It will take you all day."

"Well," Jeannette answered, "I'll hate it to-morrow myself. But I really don't mind very much. I love the idea of entertaining our friends. But we can't have a girl yet. I've got to do my own work for awhile at any rate. You see, Martin, I was figuring it out . . ."

She had crawled in beside him and at once his arms were about her and she had nestled close to him, her head on his hard shoulder.

"Your friend Sandy's a corker," he said, kissing her hair and ignoring her plan of figures and economy. "I like that guy fine. You can have all that eighteen dollars I won from him."

"Oh, Martin!"

"Sure,—of course."

"I'll put it in the till."

The till was a small round canister intended for tea but converted into a savings bank.

"You'll do nothing of the kind," Martin told her. "You blow it in on yourself, or for something nice for the house."

"But, Mart," she remonstrated, "I want to pay off that Wanamaker's bill! We can't have a girl in the kitchen until we don't owe a cent."

"Aw, don't worry so, Jan. You're always scared we're going to go bust or something. I'll get a raise as soon as summer's over. Gibbs is bound to come through 'cause he knows I'll quit if he don't. I bring in a lot of fine business to that outfit, and all my cus-

tomers are dandy friends of mine. I'll not be working
for him at fifty per much longer.''

"Mart," Jeannette said suddenly, "wouldn't it be
a good plan to have Herbert Gibbs and his wife to
dinner some night and show them how nice we are
and how nice we live and what a good dinner we can
give them? You know it might help; he tells his
brother everything, Beatrice says.''

"Great! Say, that's a bully idea!" Martin was at
once enthusiastic. "Herb would like it fine and so
would Mrs. Herb. I'll get some good old Burgundy
and pour it into him and feed him some Corona-
Coronas and he'll just expand like a night-blooming
cereus.''

And on this happy plan, still with an arm about her,
her head pillowed on his shoulder, they drifted off to
sleep.

§ 6

Some six weeks after her return to New York from
Atlantic City, Jeannette arrayed herself in her braided
broadcloth tailor suit, drew on her tan silk stockings
and tan shoes, set the gray hat at a smart angle upon
her head, added the touch of a fine meshed veil that
brought the curling gray cock's feather close to her
hair, and paid her long-deferred visit to the office.

As she turned in at the familiar portals she was
astonished at the difference between her present feelings and those of old. A year before she had entered
the building with a hurried step, a preoccupied manner, her mind busy as she hastened to her work with
ways of attacking and dispatching it. She had been
conscious then that she was the "president's secre-

tary,'' and had borne herself accordingly as she made
her way through the groups of gossiping girls, aware
they thought her haughty and unapproachable. To-
day, she was Mrs. Martin Devlin,— a matron, smartly
dressed,—come to pay a visit to the publishing house
with the air of a lady who had perhaps arrived to
select a book in the retail department or to enter a
subscription. The dusty office atmosphere was alien
to her now; the bustling, eager clerks, intent upon
their affairs, seemed pettily employed; there was something ridiculous about it all to her. Yet less than three
months ago this had been her world; all the vital
interests of her life had been centered within these
square walls. She still loved it, loved the building, the
cold cement floors, the bare ceilings studded with
sprinkler valves, loved what evidences of her own
handiwork she recognized: the window-boxes, and the
miniature close-clipped trees that stood in the entrance, the name of the house in neat gold lettering on
the street windows.

Ellis, the colored elevator man, was the first to
recognize her; he grinned, flashing his white teeth out
of his black face, chuckling largely.

''Well, it certainly is good to see you; it certainly
is like old times to see you 'round,'' he said, rolling
back the clanging door.

She stepped out upon the familiar fourth floor. It
was the same—no different: the old racket, the old
hum and confusion. A minute or two passed before
she was seen; then there was a general whispering,
machines stopped clicking, heads turned; there were
smiles and nods from all parts of the big room. Mrs.
O'Brien, Mr. Kipps' stenographer, rose and came to

greet her; Miss Sylvester and Miss Kate Smith followed suit. Presently there was a small crowd around her with questions, laughter, little cooing cries of pleasure, a feminine chatter. She caught Mr. Allister's eye as he was leaving Mr. Corey's office.

" 'Pon my word!'' She could not hear him say it, but she saw his lips form the phrase and noted his pleased surprise. He came forward at once, smiling broadly, pushing his way through the women who gave place to him.

"Glad to see you, Miss Sturgis,'' he said beaming. "Only, by Jove, you're not 'Miss Sturgis' any more! . . . 'Devlin,' isn't it? . . . Does Mr. Corey know you're here? He'll be delighted, I know. Wants to see you badly. Two or three matters have come up he'd like to ask you about; nobody 'round here seems to know a thing about them. . . . Come in; he'll be mighty glad to see you.''

He pulled back the swing gate in the counter and walked with her towards Mr. Corey's office.

As Jeannette passed within a few feet of Miss Holland's desk and as their eyes met she mouthed:

"See you in just a minute.''

"Here's an old friend of ours,'' said Mr. Allister, opening Mr. Corey's door.

The white head came up, and immediately a pleased flush spread over the face of the man at the desk.

"Well—well—well,'' he said, getting to his feet and coming to take both her hands. "Miss Sturgis! It's good to see you again.''

"She's not Miss Sturgis any more,'' laughed Mr. Allister.

"That's so—that's so; it's 'Devlin' of course. Well,

Mrs. Devlin, you surely look as though marriage agreed
with you.''

They were all laughing in good spirits. A few moments of inconsequential remarks, and then Allister
withdrew while Mr. Corey made Jeannette sit down.

''Oh, I must have a talk,'' he insisted, ''and hear all
about you.''

The door opened, and young Tommy Livingston
came in with a question on his lips. His eyes lighted
as he recognized the caller.

''My new secretary,'' said Corey smiling.

''Oh, is that *so?*'' Jeannette was pleased; the boy
had always been a protégé of hers. ''Well, Tommy,
this *is* a step up for you!''

''Yes, indeed,'' he said grinning. ''I'm doing the
best I know how. . . .''

''Tommy does very well,'' approved Mr. Corey.

''I didn't know you understood dictation,'' said
Jeannette.

''I don't very well. I've got a stenographer in my
office,—'member Miss Bates?—and I'm going to night
school and learning shorthand; I can run a machine
fairly decently now.''

''Well, isn't that splendid!''

Presently she was alone with Mr. Corey again. He
asked about her, about Martin, about her married life.
She was frank with her answers.

''I shall never thank you enough,'' she said, ''for
persuading me to accept Mr. Devlin. I never would
have married if you hadn't made me, and I never would
have known what I missed. I guess I'd've been here
for the rest of my days.''

She was eager for his news, too.

Yes, he and Mrs. Corey were quite reconciled. She was very sorry she had maligned Jeannette. He was going to England in ten days and was taking her with him. Babs was about the same; she would never be any better; they had an excellent trained nurse for her and she was to spend the rest of the summer at a camp in the Adirondacks. Willis had written a most interesting letter from Johannesburg; he and Ericsson were trekking north through Matabeleland and Bulawayo; Mr. Corey did not expect to hear from him again for three months. Affairs at the office were about as usual; they expected to publish a big novel in the fall by Hobart Haüser; Garritt Farrington Trent had left his former publishers and come over to them; advertising was bad; there was some talk of a printers' strike; *The Ladies Fortune* had been selling excellently on the stands; the pattern business was booming.

There were one or two matters he wanted to ask her about: What was the arrangement with Hardy as to the dramatic rights of *Harnessed?* No record could be found of the agreement. And did she recall from what concern they had bought that last stock of special kraft wrapper? And the folder containing all the correspondence with the Electrical Manufacturing Company had disappeared. What could have become of it? She answered as best she could. When she got up to go, he accompanied her to the door of his office.

"I can't begin to tell you how we all miss you here," he said gravely, "and how much *I* do especially. It's been hard sledding without you. I've thought a hundred times,—oh, a *thousand* times!—of how much you did for me to make the work easier and how much you lifted from my shoulders. I got used to it, I'm afraid, and took a good deal for granted. . . . But I'm glad you're married; that's where you belong: making a home for yourself and leading your own life.''

There was moisture in Jeannette's eyes as she turned away. She loved Chandler Corey, she said to herself; he was a wonderful man; she knew she was the only person in the world who truly appreciated him; and she knew he loved her, too. It was this glimpse of his affection for her that moved her. Theirs had been a rare comradeship, a fine communion, a beautiful relationship. It was ended; it was past and done; they could no longer be together or even find an excuse to see one another without having their actions misinterpreted. It had been the business, the common interest, that had wrought the tie between them, and now that there was no longer any office, the intimacy and companionship was at an end, the bond sundered,—soon they would have but a casual interest in one another!—and she had been closer to him than anyone else in the world, like a daughter, and he a father to her. It was sad; a matter to be mourned; each going a different way, only memories of a splendid coöperation and friendship remaining to remind them of happy years together.

§ 7

Jeannette stopped at Miss Holland's desk and made her promise to take lunch with her at the noon hour when they could have a good talk.

As she left the scene of her former activities, her progress through the aisles between the desks was once again a succession of hand-clasps, congratulations, well-wishes, nods and smiles. It touched her deeply; she had no idea she had been so well liked: everyone there seemed to be her friend.

Miss Holland joined her at half past twelve in the lobby of the Park Avenue Hotel, and they had a delightful luncheon together at one of the little tables edging the balcony about the court. News was exchanged eagerly. Jeannette's was scant, but her companion had endless gossip to retail. Miss Holland's nephew, Jerry Sedgwick, was a midshipman now, and on his summer cruise in Cuban waters aboard a big battleship. She and Mrs. O'Brien had a little apartment down on Waverly Place and managed quite comfortably. The office was getting dreadfully on Miss Holland's nerves; it was so different from what it used to be; in the old days everyone had done the best that was in him or her to make the business a success; no one had cared what the returns were to be; the idea of doing more and better work had been the thought actuating all. Now that the Corey Company had become one of the largest and most prosperous publishing houses in the country, the spirit had changed; everyone thought about "profits." They had conferences of all the heads of departments each week and no one was interested in learning what was going on in the different branches of the business; what commanded their attention was how much "profit" was to be shown. It disgusted Miss Holland; there was no "Get Together Club" any more. Mr. Kipps was becoming more and more critical and fault-finding; he had headaches all the time; Miss Holland believed he was a sick man; he never took any exercise. The pattern business had grown enormously; Mr. Cruikshanks had done wonders with it; they had had to lease a whole big building over on Tenth Avenue to take care of it; *The Ladies' Fortune* had a circulation of nearly half a million; Horatio Stephens had had a very substantial raise, and had grown awfully opinionated and disagreeable.

There was more gossip of lesser significance. Miss Hoggenheimer of the mailing department had gone on the stage, and had a part now in *It Happened in Nordland,* while Miss Gleason had married that big George Robinson of the Press Room, and Tommy Livingston would soon be engaged,—if he wasn't already, —to Mrs. O'Brien's little sister, Agnes, who worked in the Mail Order Department. . . . Oh, yes! and had Jeannette heard what had happened to Van Alstyne? It was terrible! He was in the penitentiary at Atlanta for using the United States mail for fraudulent purposes; he had become involved with some unscrupulous men who advertised worthless stock and the Federal authorities had put them all in jail. . . . And poor Mrs. Inness was dead; she died at her brother's house in Weehawken.

Jeannette devoured these details. She sat absorbed, fascinated, listening to every word that came from her companion's lips; she could not get enough of this chatter about her old associates; she was hungry for every scrap of information, fearful that Miss Holland might neglect to tell her everything.

She walked back with her friend to the office and would not let her go for another ten minutes until she had heard the final details of a violent quarrel between Miss Reubens and Mr. Cavendish.

Miss Holland promised to dine with her and Martin soon, and Jeannette promised in return to come with her husband to dinner with Miss Holland and Mrs. O'Brien in the Waverly Place apartment. They parted with many such assurances.

Jeannette walked all the way home in a daze of memories, thoughts of the old times crowding upon her brain, her interest in business affairs and personal happenings in the Chandler B. Corey Company awake again, stirring with all its former keenness.

§ 8

The dinner to which Mr. and Mrs. Herbert Gibbs were invited and to which after various postponements they ultimately came was a dismal failure from Jeannette's point of view. First of all, she was late with the meal itself, and in hurrying, spattered grease on her gown; the yeast powder biscuits would not rise, and the leg of lamb was underdone, the meat pink when Martin carved it. Then Martin, himself, was nervous and excited, and the cocktails he had with his guest before they sat down went to his head and made him talk and act sillily. Lastly, and most important, the Gibbses were hopeless! Herbert Gibbs was flat-headed and there was no curve at the back of his neck, while the hair grew down under his collar sparse and short; he had an expressionless, stupid face and it was impossible to tell whether he was being bored or amused at the attempt of young Mr. and Mrs. Devlin to entertain him and his wife. Mrs. Gibbs was even less prepossessing. She was a plump German girl, with thin yellow hair done up in a knob on

top of her head which frankly showed her white scalp
through wide gaps. She was irritatingly voluble, had
a piercing sharp nervous laugh, and exclaimed shrilly
about whatever Jeannette said or did. She chatted
unceasingly about her child, little "Herbie," who, it
seemed, was only ten months old but could already
both walk and talk, and she embarrassed Jeannette by
asking in a whisper how soon there was going to be
a little Devlin. There was nothing spontaneous in the
conversation during the whole evening, neither while
they sat at table nor later in the living-room, where
Mr. Gibbs sat stolidly puffing at cigars, sipping the red
Burgundy with which Martin kept his glass filled, and
Mrs. Gibbs rattled on about how they had found their
home at Cohasset Beach on Long Island, and the involved circumstances connected with its eventual purchase. Mercifully they were obliged to take an early
train home on account of "Herbie," but did not depart
until they had warned their young hosts they would
soon be expected to spend a Sunday with them in the
country.

That night, going to bed, Martin and Jeannette had
their first quarrel. It left her shaken and unhappy all
the next day. She ridiculed their guests and Martin
defended them; she declared they were stupid and
common; he, that she didn't know them, that they were
a very good-hearted sort, that she had been cold and
patronizing with Mrs. Gibbs, that her husband had
noticed it, and become awfully "sore"; it would have
been a "damn sight better," Martin concluded storm-
ily, if they had never been asked.

"And after all the trouble I went to!" raged
Jeannette to herself, hugging her side of the bed, re-

bellion strong within her, "cooking all day long, planning everything out, going over to Columbus Avenue twice, getting flowers for the table, working myself dizzy and ruining my organdie, just so he could make a good impression on them and perhaps help himself a little at the office!"

A tear trickled down her nose, and she wiped it off with a finger-tip. She would never give in to him,—never! She would make him beg and beg and beg for her forgiveness! It would be a long, long time. . . . With head aching and trying to choke down a sniffle that threatened to betray her, she fell asleep.

There was an eager reconciliation the next night; promises, vows, assurances, harsh self-accusations, and Martin carried her off after dinner to two dollar seats at the *Broadway*, where Jeannette whispered penitently, hugging his arm in the dark of the theatre, that if the Gibbses *did* ask them to visit them some Sunday, she would go and be her nicest to both.

§ 9

The occasion when Sandy MacGregor had the young Devlins to dine with him in style on the roof garden of the new Astor Hotel was another affair that turned out unfortunately. The lady whom Sandy asked to be fourth in the party,—a Mrs. Fontella,—was not the type with whom Jeannette had been accustomed to associate. She was boldly handsome with great round black eyes, masses of auburn hair, a cavernous red mouth, and a large, prominent bust. She was noisy and coarse, and when she laughed she showed a great deal of gum and rows of glittering gold-filled teeth.

Jeannette froze into her most rigid and uncommunicative self. Just before dessert was served, Martin and Sandy excused themselves from the table and disappeared, leaving her sitting for almost half-an-hour alone with her noisy and conspicuous companion. It was evident when the men returned they had been downstairs to the bar where they had had drinks and had been shaking dice. Jeannette was thoroughly incensed, and although Sandy had seats for the theatre, she complained she was ill and insisted upon going home.

There was another quarrel between her husband and herself that night, but before they went to sleep he won her forgiveness, abused himself for treating her shabbily, told her again and again he was sorry, and promised never to be guilty of neglecting her again.

He could be irresistibly winning when he wanted to be.

CHAPTER IV

§ 1

On the Fourth of July the Gibbses asked Martin and Jeannette to spend the holiday and Sunday with them at Cohasset Beach. Jeannette contemplated the visit in the gayest of spirits. She spent fully two hours carefully packing her own and Martin's suitcases. She had some very smart clothes for such an outing which she had had no opportunity of wearing since the happy honeymoon days at Atlantic City. The idea of appearing in these again at such a well-known summer resort as Cohasset Beach delighted her. She was anxious to be cordial to Mrs. Gibbs for Martin's sake, and meant to dispel any unpleasant impression of herself that either Mr. Gibbs or his wife might have been harboring. To exert herself particularly in her host's direction, "draw him out of his shell"—as Martin expressed it,—and make him like her, was part of her resolution.

Late Friday afternoon she manfully struggled with the two suitcases to the Thirty-fourth Street ferry and met Martin as agreed at the entrance of the waiting-room. They had been anxious to catch an early train from Long Island City, and it had been arranged that Mr. Gibbs and Martin should come to the station directly from the office and meet her at the ferry station.

"My God, Jan!" Martin exclaimed after he had

swung himself off the trolley-car and come running up to where she was waiting. "My God, you look great! Say,—I never saw you look so—so swell!" Mr. Gibbs was pleasantly cordial, though suffering much discomfort from the excessive heat. Sweat trickled down his expressionless face, and continually he removed his straw hat to mop his forehead with a drenched handkerchief.

It was indeed hot, but the vistas up and down the river as the ferry-boat blunted its way toward the Long Island shore were all of cool pinks, palest greens and lavenders in the late summer afternoon, while the sun, setting through a murky haze, cast an enchanted light over the scene. In the train, Mr. Gibbs took himself off to the smoking car, leaving Martin and Jeannette alone. They sat beside a raised window, their hands linked under a fold of her silk dress, and the air that reached them was rich with the scent of the open country. The girl's heart was overflowing with happiness as Martin whispered endearments in her ear: she was a wonder, all right; she looked like a million dollars; gosh! he was proud of her; there was no girl in the world like his wife! The holiday that was beginning for them, and the knowledge that they were not to be separated for two whole days— nearly three!—filled both with great felicity.

Cohasset Beach is a little village of two or three thousand inhabitants on the Sound side of the Island, some twenty-five or thirty miles from New York. The Gibbses lived in an unpretentious, white, peaked-roofed house, with plenty of shade trees about it, and a rather patchy, ill-kept lawn, bordered with straggling rosebeds. There was a lattice-sided porch cov-

ered with a clambering vine. The place was attractive
though shabby; the house sorely in need of paint, the
front steps worn down to the natural color of the
wood, the edges of the treads frayed and splintery.
A sagging hammock hung under scrawny pepper trees,
and a child's toys were scattered about, while close
to the latticed porch was a pile of play sand hauled up
from the neighboring beach.

Jeannette was disappointed. She had pictured the
Gibbses' house more of an establishment. Cohasset
Beach was a fashionable summer resort; the Yacht
Club there was famous; she had thought to find her
hosts living in some style. But she was not to be
daunted; she had come prepared to have a good time
and to make these people like her; she reminded herself
of her determination not to spoil this visit for Martin.

But on encountering Mrs. Gibbs she realized afresh
how little in common she had with her hostess. The
woman was devoid of poise, restraint, or dignity; Jeannette had forgotten her volubility and harsh, unpleasant laugh. Mrs. Gibbs welcomed her guest eagerly,
keeping up a running fire of remarks, loosing her
squeaks of mirth in nervous fashion. She slipped her
arm about Jeannette's waist and before showing her
to her room or giving her a chance to remove her hat,
led her to the nursery to view little Herbie in his crib.
Mr. Gibbs followed for a peep at his son before the child
went off to sleep and he brought Martin with him.
They all hung over the sides of the crib and exclaimed
about the baby, who rolled his solemn, perplexed eyes
from face to face. Jeannette noted he was exactly like
his father: flat-headed, expressionless, with no curve at
the back of his neck, but Martin seemed quite taken

with him and when he tickled him with a finger, the baby opened wide his little red mouth, displayed his toothless red gums and crowed vigorously. Jeannette was sure she detected in the sound the shrillness of his mother's senseless laugh.

The guest room was on the third floor in one gable of the roof, a big room with sloping ceilings; it was equipped with a washstand on which stood a basin and ewer; the bathroom was on the floor below. Hattie, the colored cook, would bring up hot water, Mrs. Gibbs said in her excited way as she left them, urging her guests to make themselves comfortable. Jeannette had carefully packed Martin's dinner clothes, and her own prettiest dinner frock, but there would evidently be no formal dressing in such a household. She stood at an open latticed window that jutted out above the vine-covered porch and looked out over a rippling billow of tree-tops, softly green now in the fading evening light, that tumbled down to the water's edge. The Sound was dotted with little boats riding at anchor and there was one private yacht, gay with lights and fluttering pennants. The lambent heavens in the west touched the shimmering water delicately with pink. She pressed her lips resolutely together, and stared out upon the scene unmoved by its beauty.

"Great,—isn't it?" Martin said, coming to stand beside her and putting his arm about her. "We'll have a home like this of our own, some day,—hey, old girl? And you'll be the boss of the show and be cooking me some of your fine dinners when I come home, and I'll take you out sailing in the yacht on Sundays." He laughed his rich buoyant peal and caught her in his arms.

"Oh, Martin," she breathed tremulously, sinking her face against his shoulder, "I love you so,—I love you so!"

As she had foreseen, there was no change of costume for dinner at the Gibbses' table. The meal itself had as little distinctiveness as the host and hostess: soup and vegetables, a large steak followed by apple pie and the usual accessories. Martin, Mr. Gibbs and his wife drank beer; it appeared that it was imported, and Martin was eloquent in its praise. There were cookies too, which made a special appeal to him; *küchen,* Mrs. Gibbs called them, but Jeannette thought them hard and tasteless. After dinner, the men walked down to the water and back, smoking their cigars, while Jeannette sat and listened to a long tale by Mrs. Gibbs of how she had happened to meet her Herbert, how her parents had objected, how they had tried to separate them, and how love had finally triumphed.

But Jeannette went to sleep that night with a happy prospect for the morrow awaiting her: they were to have lunch at the fashionable yacht club.

§ 2

Disappointment lay in store for her again. At noon, the next day, perplexed by the picnic baskets and shoeboxes of lunch with which they were laden as they left the house, she learned it was the Family Yacht Club and not the imposing Cohasset Beach Yacht Club for which they were headed. Oh, no, Mr. Gibbs explained, only the swell New Yorkers and the rich nabobs who lived down on the "Point" patronized the Cohasset Beach Yacht Club; the dues there were fifty dollars a month; the nice folk in Cohasset all belonged to the Family Yacht Club; she would see herself how pleasant it was there; the steward served hot coffee and everybody brought their own lunches. Jeannette looked straight ahead of her to hide the blur of disappointed tears that for a moment blinded her. Martin was behind with Mrs. Gibbs carrying Herbie in his arms. The resolve to try and be pleasant and make these people like her died hopelessly in the girl's heart. Oh, it was no use! It had been dreadful from the moment they arrived; it would remain dreadful till the end!

The club-house of the Family Yacht Club was a low spreading, wind-blown, sand-battered, gray building that squatted along the shore, separated from the lisping wavelets of the Sound by a strip of white, sandy beach; a long pier ran out into the water and a number of small sail-boats and row-boats were tied to the float at its further end. The pier, the beach, the wide veranda of the clubhouse were all crowded to-day; flags flew or were draped everywhere, and bathers ran up and down along the wet sand or congregated on the raft anchored a hundred yards from shore.

"Whew!" exclaimed Martin when he viewed the scene, "isn't this great!"

His wife threw him a look; it did not seem possible he was serious, but a glimpse of his delighted face showed her he was indeed.

There were no chairs nor benches on which to sit, but the newcomers found a clean space on the sandy shore and prepared to establish themselves there. Jeannette thought of her spotless new white fibre-silk skirt, and in sad resignation sank into place. About them were a dozen or so of similar groups, preparing for the midday meal or already enjoying it. They were all neighbors of the Gibbses, residents of Cohasset Beach, who knew one another intimately, and hailed each new arrival, bandying Christian names. A man some distance away shouted in the direction of the Gibbs party, brandishing a bottle of beer.

"Hey, Gibbsey," he yelled, "hey there! How's the old stick-in-the-mud?"

Mrs. Gibbs shrieked across the stretch of sand at the woman beside him.

"How's the baby?"

"Fine," came the answer. "Mama's got him."

"That's Zeb Kline over there," Mrs. Gibbs informed her husband; "it's the first time he's been out since he was sick. . . . And those folks with Doc French certainly look like his sister-in-law and that cousin of hers, Mrs. Prentiss."

A burst of music and the report of a cannon came distinctly from farther down the shore. Jeannette, craning her neck, could see a large, glistening white building with a red roof, gaily decorated with flags; there were loops of bunting about the railings of its porches.

"That's the Cohasset Beach Yacht Club," said Mr. Gibbs; "the Commodore's just come to anchor; that's his yacht out there; there'll be some fine racing this aft; the Stars are going out."

"Ham or cheese?" Mrs. Gibbs inquired, proffering sandwiches. She was busy with the lunch, snapping strings, opening boxes, squeezing wrapped tissue-paper packages with her fingers, shaking them, hazarding guesses as to their contents.

"I wonder what Hattie's got in here," she kept saying.

"Do have some sauerkraut; I made it myself. I thought maybe you'd like it. Don't you fancy mustard dressing? . . . Well, try the stuffed eggs. Hope you think they're good. The cake's Hattie's; I think her chocolate's splendid. . . . Mr. Devlin, some mustard pickles? Some eggs? . . . Goodness gracious, papa! Look out for Herbie! He'll get himself all sopping!"

"Say, Mr. Gibbs, this beer is great! How do you manage to have it so cold?" Martin asked.

"I bring it down a day or two ahead of time and the steward puts it on the ice for me; just half a dozen bottles, you know; doesn't put him to too much trouble."

"Well, this is a great little Club all right."

"*We* think it's nice. Just a few of us that have children got together and organized it. The Cohasset Beach has a big bar, and there always is a good deal of drinking going on down there. The New Yorkers, you know, come down for a good time. No place for young folk."

"No, you bet your life."

Jeannette, in spite of herself, found she was hungry. The fried chicken in the oiled tissue paper was delicious, and she loved the liverwurst sandwiches. Mrs. Sturgis and her girls had always been extremely fond of liverwurst; Kratzmer kept it, and many a luncheon Jeannette, her mother and sister had made with little else. The hot cup of coffee, that Mrs. Gibbs poured from the tin pot the Club steward brought and set down in the sand, put life into her. The pleasant heat of the day, the sunshine, the life and frolicking in sand

and water, forced enjoyment upon her. But she would
not go in swimming when Martin urged her. One
glance at the crude bath-house with its gray boards
and canvas roof was sufficient to decide her on this
point. She sat stiffly beside Mrs. Gibbs, who had
rocked Herbie to sleep in her arms, and now moved
so her shadow would keep the sun off the child's face,
while she watched Mr. Gibbs and her husband disport
themselves in the water. Martin's swimming always
attracted attention and when he made a beautiful swan
dive from the end of the pier, there was a ripple of
applause. She felt proud of him, proud of his fine
figure, the beauty of his young body, his prowess, his
unaffectedness.

"Who's that young fellow doing all the fancy diving out there?" a man sauntering up asked Mrs. Gibbs.

"S-ssh," breathed that lady, indicating her sleeping
child. "His name's Martin Devlin," she whispered;
"he works for Herbert in the city."

Works for Herbert in the city! Jeannette felt the
blood rush to her face. Works for Herbert! Indeed!
Well, he wouldn't be *working* for Herbert much longer.
She'd have something to say about *that*. The idea!
The impertinence! Giving the impression that her
wonderful Martin was merely an employee of Herbert
Gibbs!

Her husband, wet and dripping, came up to her and
flung himself down panting upon the sand.

"Gee," he said boyishly, "that water's great!
Never had a better swim in my life. It's a shame
you didn't go in, Jan."

He looked at her, sensing something was amiss, but
she smiled at him and pressed his wet, sandy hand.

Late in the afternoon they prepared to go home. As they were about to leave the Club, a man climbing into his automobile offered a lift. Martin and Jeannette begged to be allowed to walk and persuaded their hosts on account of the baby to take advantage of the car. Left to themselves, they commenced a leisurely return.

Along the tree-bordered roads that fringed the shore, other groups in white skirts and flannels were wending their way homeward; flags flew from poles or were draped over doorways; the strains of a waltz drifted seductively from the Cohasset Beach Yacht Club; the blue water of the Sound was dotted with glistening triangles of sails, heeled over and headed in one direction.

"Those are the Stars," Martin exclaimed; "the race is finishing; number seven seems to have it cinched. That steam yacht over there with all the flags is the judges' boat."

They watched for a moment longer. Far out in midstream, one of the Sound steamers was passing; already lights were beginning to twinkle in her cabins.

"Wonderful day," commented Martin, giving his wife's hand, as it rested in the crook of his elbow, a squeeze with his arm. They wandered onward. "I'd love to have a home with you in a place like this, with the sailing and swimming and tennis and all this outdoor fun. It's my idea of living. A fellow Mr. Gibbs introduced me to out on the raft belongs to the Cohasset Beach Club, too. He told me they've got some swell tennis courts over there and he was after me to play with him to-morrow."

"And will you?" Jeannette asked, listlessly.

"Well, I guess I can't. Mr. Gibbs said something about some friends of theirs asking us all to go sailing to-morrow."

"That will be nice," said his wife, still in a lifeless tone, but Martin did not notice.

"By George, I think this is a great place. I was asking Mr. Gibbs about rents, and he tells me we could get a fine little eight-room house for forty a month, and it's only three-quarters of an hour from town."

"And what would you do without your theatres and your shows and your little dinners downtown?" smiled Jeannette.

"Oh—they could go hang!"

The smile upon his wife's face twisted skeptically. She knew Martin better than he knew himself.

"And don't you think the Gibbses 're awful nice folks? They don't put on any airs but 're friendly and simple. They'd take us under their wing and 'd be darned nice neighbors."

Jeannette shut her mouth. It was not the time to shatter his enthusiasm; he was having a good time, imagined these people wonderful; it wouldn't be kind of her to show him now how vulgar and cheap and horrid they and their friends and their little ridiculous Club were. No,—it would only hurt him, and under the influence of the day and the good time, it would lead to a quarrel,—and she was sick of quarrels. She reminded herself she was out of sorts from the long day of boredom and disappointment; it would be madness to say a word now. The time when she could make him see the Gibbses, their house, their friends, their tiresome pleasures and cheap environment as she saw them would come, and she must bide her time.

". . . not so particularly interesting," Martin was saying, "but a darned good sort, and he's got a shrewd business head. I think he likes me first-rate, and I was mighty glad to see you and Mrs. Gibbs pulling together. She told me she thought you were great, said all manner of nice things about how swell you looked. She's not much of a looker, herself, but she certainly has got the right feeling of hospitality. Know what I mean, Jan? She gives you the best she's got, and makes you feel at home and that she's glad you're in her house. I think that's bully. . . . And isn't that kid a corker? Golly, I think he's slick! You know, I carried him all the way down from the house to the Club and he had his arms round my neck the whole way. He made funny little sounds in my ear, you know, as though he was kind of enjoying himself! . . . Gee, he's a great baby!"

That flat-headed, vacant-faced child? . . . Well, Martin was *hopeless!* He must be crazy; there was no use talking to him!

§ 3

In the morning Jeannette vigorously renewed her resolution not to mar her husband's pleasure. For the first time, since her marriage, she felt oddly estranged from him. There was a rent somewhere in the veil through which he had hitherto appeared so handsome, so considerate, so wonderfully perfect, and the glimpse she had of him now through the rift was disconcerting and a little shocking. While they were

dressing, he smoked a cigarette although he well knew
the fumes of it before breakfast made her giddy; at
the table he was unnecessarily noisy, laughed too
loudly, with his mouth wide open and full of muffin,
and after breakfast on the ill-kept lawn, he rolled about
with the Gibbs baby, making a buffoon of himself and
streaking his white trousers with grass green and
dirt. They were to go sailing at ten o'clock,—the
Websters were to call for them,—and it was thought-
less of Martin, and indicated all too clearly his utter
indifference to her feelings. He looked a sight in his
dirtied flannels! . . . But she *would* be sweet! She
would be amiable! She would *not* undo whatever good
had been accomplished. At four o'clock they would
take the train back to the city; there remained less
than seven hours more of this dreadful visit! Martin
had completely captivated Mrs. Gibbs; his enthusiasm
for the baby had been the last compelling touch; she
shrieked at everything he said, thought him "perfectly
killing." Both she and Mr. Gibbs had been cordial
to Jeannette. Grimly, the girl determined she would
hold herself in leash for the few short hours that remained, would smile and smirk and simper and do
whatever they wanted!

But it was the ten-forty train that night which she
and Martin were able to catch back to town. The Websters' yacht had been becalmed, and all day the boat
had rocked upon the slow oily swells of the Sound, the
sail flapping dismally, the ropes creaking and strain-
ing in the blocks. The women had huddled together
in the scant shade of the sail, while the men sprawled
helplessly in the flagellating sun. Herbie had wailed
and whimpered for hours before his mother had been

able to quiet him off to sleep. She had kept repeating
in a sort of justification for his ill temper: "Why, he
wants his bottle; the poor darling wants his bottle;
'course he's cross, he wants his bottle."

At four in the afternoon a motor-boat had come
within hailing distance and generously offered a tow.
Fifteen minutes later they were underway in its wake,
when something suddenly went wrong with the motor-
boat's engine, and both vessels slowly heaved from
side to side on the oily swells. Mrs. Webster frankly became seasick. The men shouted to one another across
the strip of water between the boats, but none of the
suggestions of either party brought results. The
motor-boat being equipped with oars, it was decided
to row for assistance,—a matter of two miles' steady
pull. Martin had wanted to go along and lend a hand,
but Jeannette tugged at his arm and sternly forbade
him to leave her.

Effective aid finally appeared towards eight o'clock
in the evening when the gathering darkness had begun
to make their position really perilous, and an hour
later the party clambered out on the float in front of
the Family Yacht Club, cramped, hungry, but pro-
foundly thankful. By the time Martin and Jeannette
had reached the Gibbses' house and made ready for
their return to town, the ten-forty had been the earliest
train they could catch back to the city. Their hosts
begged them to remain for the night, but Jeannette
was inflexible in insisting upon returning home. She
feared another hour spent at Cohasset Beach would
drive her stark, raving mad.

CHAPTER V

§ 1

WHEN Martin went on his honeymoon to Atlantic City, he had taken his annual two weeks' vacation. During the hot weather of summer, therefore, he and Jeannette were obliged to remain in the sweltering city. But Jeannette did not mind the heat. Adventuring in married life was too utterly absorbing; she loved her new home, and each day found new delight in managing it. She and her husband considered themselves deliriously happy. Nights on which they did not go to the theatre, they roamed the bright upper stretches of Broadway, sauntered along Riverside Drive as far as Grant's Tomb, or meandered into the Park, where electric lights cast a theatrical radiance on trees and shrubbery. On Sundays they made excursions to the beaches, and one week-end they went to Coney Island on Saturday afternoon and stayed the night at the Manhattan Beach Hotel. Jeannette long remembered the glorious planked steak they enjoyed for dinner on that occasion, sitting at a little table by the porch railing, listening to the big military band, while all about them a gay throng chatted and laughed at other tables, and crowds surged up and down the boardwalk as the Atlantic thundered a dull rhythmical bourdon to the stirring music of trumpet and drum.

Her mother departed the first of August for Canada. The concert tour having been finally decided upon,— without the violinist,—every day or so cards arrived from Mrs. Sturgis post-marked "Montreal," "Quebec," "Toronto." The venture could hardly be considered a financial success, she wrote, but she and the girls were having just too wonderful a time! The Canadians were extraordinarily hospitable!

Alice, Roy, and the baby returned from Freeport the last of September; she expected to be confined early in November. The Devlins visited them one Sunday during the last weeks of their stay on Long Island, and Jeannette wondered how her sister could be happy in such an environment. The room the Beardsleys occupied was under the roof and, during the day, like an oven. Etta, Alice told her, woke up sometimes as early as five or five-thirty, and nothing would persuade the child to go to sleep again. As soon as she was awake, she began to fret, and her wails disturbed the other boarders at that hour. Either father or mother would find it necessary to get up, dress, and wheel the child out in her carriage, pushing her around and around the block until she could be brought safely back to the house. On Sundays when breakfast was not until nine o'clock, these hours of the early silent mornings were a long, wearisome, hungry trial. Jeannette thought the food at the boarding-house was markedly meager, and Alice had to admit that as the season was drawing to a close, there were evidences of retrenchment on the part of the landlady, but at first, she assured her sister, the table had been plentiful and good. The effect of all this upon Jeannette had been a determination to order her own life along safer lines. Two or three times Alice

had come up to the city during the summer to spend the
night. On these occasions Roy slept at his own flat
in the Bronx, as there was only a narrow couch available at the Devlins'. To this Martin had been rele-
gated, and the two sisters occupied the bed together.
Alice was very large. It worried Jeannette; she was
once more full of apprehensions. She made up her
mind that for herself she did not want a baby for a
long time, not until she and Martin were out of debt,
and had saved something so that she could be sure of
a certain amount of comfort and care.

Martin's attitude about money distressed her. He
did not seem to take the matter of their finances with
sufficient seriousness. He was ever urging her to
engage a maid to attend to the dish-washing and clean
up after dinner. He hated kitchen work, himself, and
equally hated to have his wife do it. When he finished
his dinner and rose from the table, rolling a cigar about
between his teeth and filling his mouth with good,
strong inhalations of satisfying tobacco smoke, he felt
contented, replete, ready for talk and relaxation. To
have Jeannette disappear into the kitchen and begin
banging around out there with pans and rattling dishes
annoyed him. He could not bring himself to help her;
something in him rebelled at such work. His wife
readily understood how he felt; she sympathized with
him, and did not want him to help her, but she had her
own aversion to letting the dishes stand over night and
having them to do after breakfast the following day.
It took the best part of her morning, and meant she
could never get downtown until afternoon. But Martin was willing to concede nothing; he answered her

arguments by reiterating his advice to her to hire a girl.

"Good God, Jan," he would say in characteristic vigorous fashion, "she would cost you fifteen or twenty dollars a month, and then you could get out as early as you wanted to in the mornings and we could have our evenings together."

It was just that fifteen or twenty dollars a month which Jeannette wanted to save to pay on her bills. She had inherited a sense of frugality; it worried her to be in debt. Martin, on the other hand, was blandly indifferent. He was willing to deny himself very little, his wife often felt, to help her contribute to the "till." They had many arguments about the matter but never reached a conclusion. Their creditors,—they owed a little less than three hundred dollars,—were kept satisfied by a small remittance each month but something more always had to be charged. Jeannette was baffled. She talked it over with Alice. The Beardsleys lived more simply than the Devlins; they did not entertain nor go out to dinner so often nor to the theatre, and they paid only half as much rent. Their whole scale of expenditure was more economical. That was the answer, of course. When Jeannette told Martin they were living beyond their means, he grew angry.

"Damn it," he answered her, "if there is one thing I hate more than another, it's a piker! What do you want to crab about the bills for? Haven't we got everything we want? Aren't we getting along all right? Who's kicking?"

Jeannette heaved a sigh of weariness. Some day before long she would have to persuade him to her way of thinking.

§ 2

Alice's boy was born in October and was christened Ralph Sturgis Beardsley by the Reverend Doctor Fitzgibbons, much to Mrs. Sturgis' tearful satisfaction. Alice had a comparatively easy time with the birth of her second child, but again there was an aftermath which kept her weak and anæmic and necessitated an operation just before Christmas.

It was just before Christmas that Jeannette urged Martin to ask for a raise. Several circumstances encouraged her: she had learned through Miss Holland that Walt Chase was getting eighty-five dollars a week, —a big mail order concern out in Chicago had made him an offer and Mr. Corey had been obliged to raise his salary in order to keep him; Martin had met John Archibald of the Archibald Engraving Company, the largest color engravers in the city, and Mr. Archibald had bought Martin a drink at the bar in the Waldorf and presented him with a cigar; lastly, her husband had landed a new engraving account a few weeks before and had brought in considerable holiday business. Martin heeded her advice and had a talk with Herbert Gibbs, who promised to take the matter up with his brother, Joe, and seemed disposed to recommend the increase. In the wildest of spirits, Martin came home, waltzed his wife around the apartment, kissed her a dozen times, told her again and again she was a wonder, insisted she stop her preparations for dinner, and carried her off to a café downtown where he ordered a pint of champagne and toasted her.

His elation, however, was not fully justified. Martin had asked for a substantial increase and a commission

on all new accounts. It was evident that in discussing
the matter, the brothers had decided this was too much.
They agreed to give him three thousand a year on a
twelve months' contract.

"I always detested that flat-headed pig," Jeannette
exclaimed inelegantly when Martin brought home the
news. "Think of how we tried to entertain him and
that stupid wife of his, and how we went down to visit
them and let them bore us to death! I knew he was
that kind of a creature!"

"Aw, come, come, Jan," Martin remonstrated; "you
want to be fair. Herb did the best he could; it was old
Joe who kicked. Three thousand a year isn't so bad;
that's two hundred and fifty a month. Not so rotten
for a fellow twenty-seven. . . . Now I hope to God
you'll get a girl in here to help run the kitchen."

"Well,—all right," Jeannette conceded, "only
you've got to go on helping me save. I want to pay off
every cent we owe. . . . I suppose I get my half as
usual."

"Sure. I'll be paid now twice a month: first and
fifteenth."

"Let's see; . . . that's a hundred and twenty-five.
I get sixty-two fifty; that's really five dollars more a
week, isn't it?"

"You're a little tight-wad,—do you know that,
darling?"

"No, I'm not," Jeannette defended herself. "I'm
only trying to run things economically and systemati-
cally, and to do that you've *got* to plan ahead. The
trouble with you, Mart, is that you never do!"

The raise led to the appearance of Hilda in the
kitchen. Hilda was a big-boned, good-natured Swedish

girl, willing, but a careless cook, often exasperatingly
stupid. Jeannette paid her fifteen dollars a month, and
established her in the vacant bedroom not hitherto
furnished, which involved an outlay of nearly a hundred dollars.

In spite of the additional income, money continued to
be a problem. Jeannette still felt that she and Martin
were living too extravagantly, and that her husband
did not do his share in helping to retrench. She had
been entirely satisfied in the old days before she married to go to the theatre in gallery or rear balcony
seats, but Martin scorned these locations. When he
went to a show, he said, he wanted to enjoy himself,
and sitting in the cheap seats robbed him of any pleasure whatsoever. It was the same whenever they went
downtown to dinner; he preferred the expensive hotels
and restaurants; when he bought new clothes he went
to a tailor and had the suit made to order; he tipped
everywhere he went far too generously. If there was
any economizing to be done, it was always Jeannette
who must do it, and what made it all the harder was
that he did not thank her for the self-denial. He spent,
—his wife had no way of knowing how much,—a great
deal for drinks, and for the gin and vermuth he brought
home. Once a week, sometimes oftener, he would arrive with a bottle of each, carefully wrapped up in
newspaper, under his arm. Every time they enter-
tained, she knew it meant more gin and more vermuth
for cocktails. Martin was not a tippler. Frequently
several days or a week would go by without his even
suggesting a cocktail. He did not seem to want one,
unless there was company, or he happened to come
home specially tired. Jeannette had never seen him

intoxicated, although on the last day of the year a
number of the men at his office had gathered in the
late afternoon at a neighboring bar, and wished each
other "Happy New Year" over and over. Martin arrived home, glassy-eyed and noisy, wanting her to kiss
and love him. She hated him when he had been drinking; she even loathed the odor of liquor on his breath;
it made it strong and hot like the breath of a panther.
Another expense was his cigars of which he consumed
half-a-dozen a day. She knew they cost money, and
she knew Martin well enough to feel sure that the kind
he liked was not the inexpensive variety.

There was also his card playing to be taken into account. Sandy MacGregor had a circle of friends who
played poker together generally once a week, on Friday nights. At first Jeannette had urged Martin to go
when Sandy had rung him up, asking if he would like
to "sit in." She considered it part of a good wife's
rôle: a man should not be expected to give up masculine
society, or an occasional "good time with the boys"
merely because he was married. She did not entirely
approve of poker, but Martin loved it. Whenever he
won, he woke her up when he came home and announced
it triumphantly; when he lost he said nothing about it,
and she felt she had no right to ask questions. She suspected he did not tell her the truth about the size of
the stakes for which he played, realizing she would
worry, so she never inquired, and if Martin came home
and put seven or eight dollars on her dressing-table,
exultingly telling her that it was half his winnings, she
thanked him with a bright smile and a kiss for his
generous division, even though she was confident he
had won a great deal more.

On the first and fifteenth of the month he gave her sixty-two dollars and fifty cents. She had to apportion the money among the tradespeople, the bills "down-town," and keep enough for Hilda's wages and incidental table expenses for the ensuing fortnight. It left her very little to spend on herself, for clothes and amusements,—far from enough. For years she had been independent, her own mistress, with the disposal of her entire earnings; it was hard for her now to have to economize and compromise and resort to makeshifts because of her husband's indifference and improvidence. It brought back disturbing memories of old days when she and Alice and their mother had had to skimp and struggle in order to eke out the simplest order of existence. It was just what she feared might happen when she had considered marrying.

A month arrived when Jeannette found upon her grocer's bill a charge for gin and vermuth and for half a box of cigars: nine dollars and twenty-five cents! It precipitated an angry quarrel between her husband and herself. Martin had been encroaching in various ways upon her half share of his salary, and she proposed now to put a stop to it. He argued that the cocktails and cigars had been for her friends when invited to dinner; she retorted that neither cocktails nor cigars had had any share in the entertainment she provided, and if he chose to have them on hand and offer them, it was his own affair. She taxed him with the whole score of his extravagance, while Martin chafed and twisted under her sharp criticisms, swore and grew sulky. He hated unpleasantness and tried to evade the issue: he'd pay for the booze and cigars and buy her a hat or anything else she fancied, if she'd only "forget it" and quit "ragging" him. But Jeannette felt that the question of an equal division of their financial responsibility was vital to the success of their marriage, the happiness of both, and she refused to be deflected. He finally stormed himself out of the apartment, viciously banging the door shut behind him. Two days of misery followed for them both, when they met with the exchange of monosyllables only, though their thoughts pursued one another through every hour. Their reconciliation was terrific, each willing to concede everything, eager to make promises and to assure the other of utter contriteness.

From Jeannette's point-of-view matters improved. Twice Martin gave her an extra ten dollars out of his half of his salary.

§ 3

When the year's lease on the apartment neared its end, Martin was not for renewing it. Herbert Gibbs had been talking to him about Cohasset Beach, urging him to move there. Summer was approaching, Gibbs pointed out, with all its good times of swimming and boating, and even in winter, he assured Martin, there was plenty of outdoor sport: skating, tobogganing, even skiing. In particular, his employer counselled, there was a remarkable little house,—a bungalow,— with floors, ceilings and inside trim of oak that had just become vacant through the death of its owner, which could be had for fifty dollars a month. It was a great bargain for the money. Martin was enthusiastic. Gibbs had promised he would be at once elected to the Family Yacht Club, and had described the good times its members had: dances every Saturday night and in

summer, swimming, yachting, picnics. The "bunch,"
he assured the young man, was a "live" one,—the pick
of "good fellows."

Jeannette listened to her husband's glowing recital
with a cold tightening at her heart.

"He says, Jan," Martin told her eagerly, "that
every once in awhile they have masquerade parties
down at the Club, and everybody goes all dressed up,
with masks on, you know, so nobody recognizes you,
and they just have a riot of fun. Then about a dozen
or fifteen of the fellows are going to get sail-boats this
year. There's a ship-yard near there, and the ship-
builder has designed the neatest little sail-boat you
ever saw in your life. He calls it the A-boat, and
they are only going to cost ninety dollars apiece. Just
think of that, Jan: ninety dollars apiece! A sail-boat,
—a little yacht,—for that sum! Gee whillikens! Can
you imagine the fun we'll have? Everybody, you know,
starts the same with a new boat. Gibbs was crazy to
have me order one,—the Club is anxious to give the
ship-builder as big an order as possible so's to get the
price down,—so I fell for it and told him to put me
down. I thought maybe I'd call her the *Albatross?*"

"You—*what?*" asked Jeannette blankly.

"Sure, I told him to put me down. You know, it
made a hit with him; he'd 've been awfully sore if I
hadn't; and it's up to me to keep in with old Gibbsey.
I can sell it if we don't like it. Gibbs put my name up
for membership in the Yacht Club."

"He *did?*" Jeannette said blankly again.

"Well, darling, it's only thirty dollars a year and I
guess that's not going to break us; the initiation fee is
twenty-five,—something like that. Why the Club is

just intended for young married folks like us; there're the dances for the ladies, and the card parties and picnics, and there're the sports for the men. Gee,—I think it will be great! And Gibbsey tells me that by special arrangement this year the Cohasset Beach Yacht Club is going to let us use its tennis courts!"

Jeannette looked into his excited eyes, and a dull exasperation came over her.

"The poor, poor simpleton," she thought. "He thinks he'll like it; Gibbs has filled him full. He'll hate it as I hate it now inside of a fortnight. He never would be contented in such a place; what would he do without his theatres and the gay night life he loves? It's hard enough for us to live as we are,—we have to struggle and struggle to make ends meet,—and here he is mad to try an even more expensive method of living, involving clubs and club dues, yachts and commutation fares! . . . And in such a community with such people! The flat-headed Gibbses and their awful friends picnicking there on the sand that terrible Fourth of July! And Martin proposes I exchange them and their vulgar dreadful society, their masquerades and card parties, for my beautiful little apartment which I've tried to make perfect, which everyone admires, and which is my joy and delight!"

There was a dangerous, fixed smile on her face as she rose from the dinner table where they had been lingering over their black coffee, and rang the little brass bell for Hilda to clear away.

"Well, what do you think, Jan? Don't you believe we'd both come to love the country? Don't you think we'd have a pack of fun down there?"

She eyed him with a cold stare a moment before she answered slowly:

"I won't consider it."

His face fell.

"What's more," she added briefly, "I think you're a fool."

His expression darkened; he glowered at her, hurt to the quick. She ignored him and went about the living-room straightening objects, lowering shades, adjusting lights. All the time she was steeling herself to the wrangle she knew was coming. She would be equal to it; she would give him straight talk; she'd let him have a piece of her mind and make him realize how absurd he was, how utterly insane. Buying yachts and joining clubs! What did he think he was, anyway? A millionaire?

The storm when it broke was the most violent they had yet known; it was even worse than she had anticipated. Martin, usually noisy, cursing, was quick to recover, while she rarely lost control of speech or action. But now the thought of giving up her little home, as he calmly proposed, infuriated her. He had not the faintest conception of how she loved it; he had never done one single thing to improve or beautify it beyond buying those frightful Macy daubs!

For the first time in their quarrels she could not control her tears. Convulsed with sobbing, Martin thought she had capitulated. He waited several minutes in distressed silence and then came to where she lay upon the couch to put his arms about her and draw her to him, but she turned on him with a fury that was shocking. Rebuffed, he stared at her savagely, then snatched his hat and coat and left her with a violent bang of the door.

Jeannette never for one moment thought she could not swing Martin to her wishes. She could not conceive of herself weakening; Martin had always been easy-going, good-natured. But she had forgotten how purposeful he could be when his intent was hot; she had forgotten his perseverance, his patience, his indefatigability when he wooed her; she had forgotten his winningness, his persuasiveness. He brought all these qualities into play now; there was no side-tracking him, no gainsaying him. His mind was locked against the renewal of their lease, and set upon Cohasset Beach. He argued, he cajoled, he pleaded, he coaxed. Never had she known him so irritating or so winning. If she grew cross, he was amiable; if she grew sorrowful, he was consoling and tender; if she advanced arguments that brooked no reply, he was loving and answered her with kisses. But he was determined; nothing swerved him from his purpose.

Once again, Jeannette found no comforting support in anybody. Her mother said she ought to give in to her husband if he was so set upon the plan; it was the wife's place to give way. Alice thought it would be delightful to live in the country, and assured her sister she would come to love it; she and Roy had been talking all winter about moving to some place on Long Island or in New Jersey, but it was hard to find anything really nice for twenty-five dollars a month within commuting distance of the city; they were going to board at Freeport again for the summer and they intended to look around and see what they could find there. It would be ideal for the children. . . . Was there any hope . . . any prospect . . . ?

"No, thank Heaven," Jeannette answered fervently. She had enough to bother her without the complication of a baby just now.

On the anniversary of her wedding day she surrendered. Martin had been so sweet and gentle with her, so anxious to please, so considerate, every impulse within her prompted her to do the thing he wanted. She could see how eager he was for his sail-boat, his new club and the country; he was mad to have them; her heart was full of love for him. She reminded herself that when she had entered into this marriage she had been determined to give more, if need be, than he did, to make their union a success. Here was an opportunity. It meant a great sacrifice for herself; she had no faith in the experiment, but felt sure she would learn to hate all the people and the place, and Martin would soon tire of it and them and share her feelings. But now it was the thing above all else he wanted, and it was her chance to be generous.

She extracted from him two promises, however. It was a foregone conclusion, she told him, that she would not be happy at Cohasset Beach, but if she agreed to go and live there with him, it must be understood between them that she was to be free to come into New York as often as she pleased, to shop or to visit her mother and Alice, or do anything she liked. He must also understand that he was to keep a closer watch upon their finances. With commutation, railroad fares and club dues added to their expenses they would have to practise a much more rigid economy. She wanted to get the table expenditures down to

fifteen dollars a week, and that would be out of the
question if he expected her to entertain. As soon as
they were out of debt and had a little ahead, she would
be more than willing to have him invite people to visit
them.

He promised everything. He was only too anxious
and willing, he said, to agree to all she asked, to show
his deep gratitude.

§ 4

The bungalow at Cohasset Beach, at first sight,
consoled her in some degree for giving up the apartment. The little house was charming, and charmingly
situated. It had been built a few years before by a
rich old lady, an invalid, who had been compelled to
pass her days in a wheel-chair which she operated herself. Because of the chair, the house had been planned
bungalow-fashion, though there was an upstairs of
two small bedrooms and an extra bath, and the doorways between rooms had been made particularly wide
to permit the easy passage of the chair. Inside there
were oak floors throughout, a spacious fireplace, and an
oak-timbered ceiling in a generous-sized living-room,
off which opened two bedrooms and, opposite, the dining-room. There was an acre or so of unkempt ground
about the house with some gnarled old apple trees, in
blossom when Jeannette first saw them, and at the rear
the ground sloped down to a rush-bordered pool in
whose rippleless surface all the colors of the sky, blos-
soming trees and bordering reeds were intensified in
glorious reflection. A white cow stood upon her own
inverted image at the farther side. There was no view
of the Sound,—the bungalow was a good mile from the

water,—but it was picturesquely set, and Jeannette
felt, since she had been forced to abandon the city, she
could not have found a home in the country that suited
her better.

The move from town was accomplished without a
hitch; even Hilda was successfully transplanted. Jeannette set herself determinedly to work to fit herself and
her furniture into the new environment, and was surprised to discover how easily both were accomplished.
Expenses alone distressed her. The vans which
brought down the household effects cost more than she
had expected, and she was obliged to order more furniture and rugs to make the new home attractive. Unfortunately, the bungalow had casement windows and
this necessitated cutting and remaking all her curtains.
Some in addition, too, were needed for the living-room,
and Jeannette had decided that scrim would be both
practical and economical, but the clerk in the store had
shown her a soft, lovely material, stamped with a
design of long green grasses and iris, which he assured her was "sunfast." The pale purple and green
in the goods had appealed to her as so unusually beautiful and effective that she had not been able to resist
getting it. She decided to plant iris about the house in
the long narrow strips of flower-beds, and to carry iris
as a *motif* throughout the place. In a Fifth Avenue
shop there was some china that had a pattern of *fleur-
de-lis* in its center, and her heart was set on some day
acquiring it for her new home.

Martin was immediately elected to the Family Yacht
Club; the Gibbses had him and his wife to dinner and
invited the Websters and another couple to make their
acquaintance; Mrs. Rudolph Drigo and Mrs. Blum, who

were neighbors, called, also Doctor Vinegartner of the Episcopal Church. Alice, Roy, and the children spent a Sunday with her sister and Alice was enthusiastic about everything. She told Roy they would have to find a house of their own at Cohasset Beach without delay. Summer had arrived before Jeannette was half aware of its approach.

The weather turned glorious; the dogwood came and went; the country was full of sweet scents; robins and thrushes sang with open throbbing throats in the apple trees and hopped about in the shade; the frogs shrilled musically at evening in the pool, but Jeannette did not find the happiness for which she hoped. She tried to be content; she sought for joy in her new life and surroundings. She found none. Too many things were wrong. Over and over again she decided it was hopeless.

First of all, there was the Family Yacht Club which Martin loved and she despised. She had known beforehand what it was going to be like, and closer acquaintance proved her premise to have been correct. All-year-round residents of Cohasset Beach made up its membership. There were less than three thousand people in the Long Island village during the winter; it was only in summer that the place became fashionable. Among those who belonged to the little yacht club, Jeannette soon discovered, were Tim Birdsell, the village plumber; Zeb Kline, a contractor, hardly better than a carpenter; Fritz Wiggens, who kept an electrical equipment store on Washington Street; Steve Teschemacher and Adolph Kuntz, who were real estate agents and were interested in a development known as "Cohasset Park"; then there were the local dentist and his wife, the local attorney and his helpmate, and the local doctor, who seemed to be of a better sort than the rest and was fortunately unmarried. The ladies took an active part in the social life of the yacht club and 'Stel Teschemacher, Chairwoman of the Entertainment Committee, went early to call upon the new member's wife to invite her to come to the "Five Hundred Club" meeting on the following Friday afternoon. There was a sprinkling of others who boasted of a slightly more exalted social status: Mrs. Drigo's husband operated a large ice plant in New York City. Mrs. Blum was the wife of the well-known confectioner, and Percy Webster was connected with an advertising agency. If there were more interesting members they kept themselves aloof,—at least Jeannette did not meet them. Once when she was describing to her mother with a good deal of relish the type of people who belonged to this club, and was referring to the list of members in the club's annual booklet, she was surprised to come upon the name of Lester Short and that of a prominent magazine editor well-known to her.

She asked Herbert Gibbs about these people at an early opportunity but elicited nothing more satisfactory from him than: "Oh, they come round occasionally." If such was the case, Jeannette was unable to identify them. She was interested to learn later that Lester Short and his wife had six children and lived about half-a-mile beyond the village in the region known as the "Point."

Martin had no fault to find with his new friends. He was welcomed into their hearts; he charmed them all; he was acclaimed immediately the most popular member, and was appointed by the Commodore, old Jess

Higgenbothen, affable, decrepit and rich, and owner of most of the acres Teschemacher and Kuntz were trying to sell as choice lots in Cohasset Park, to serve on the entertainment committee with 'Stel Teschemacher. Martin was enchanted with the cordiality with which he was accepted; he thought Zeb Kline, Fritz Wiggens, young Doc French "corking good scouts"; Zeb and Fritz were a little rough perhaps but they were regular fellows; Steve Teschemacher was as "funny as a crutch" and his partner, Adolph Kuntz, had about as sharp and shrewd a mind as Martin had ever encountered.

"Why, you ought to hear Adolph talk politics!" he told his wife enthusiastically. "He knows more about what's going on up in Albany right this minute than all the newspapers in New York. You ought to hear him tell some of his experiences in the Republican Party!"

He might be interesting and clever, everything Martin said of him, but to Jeannette he seemed uncouth, ill-bred, a spitter of tobacco juice.

§ 5

When the Yacht Club formally opened its summer season, Jeannette put on her prettiest frock and went with her husband to the dance with which it was inaugurated. It was one of the efforts she made to adapt herself to the village life. She loved to dance. Swimming, sailing, tennis did not appeal to her, but from the dances in the club-house she hoped she might derive a certain amount of genuine pleasure. On the night of the affair, after studying the reflection in her mirror she had decided she had never looked so well; with truth she could say she was a beautiful woman, and in this estimate of herself, she found ample confirmation in Martin's eyes. They hired a hack and drove over to the club.

But for the young wife it proved a dismal experience. The yokels,—the plumber, the electrician, the carpenter, the dentist and real estate agents,—were afraid to approach her,—not that she wanted them to, —and she had been left to the favor of Herbert Gibbs, Doc French, and the old Commodore. The women eyed her covertly, whispered about her and her gown, and made no advances. Herbert Gibbs danced with her once, twice; Martin was three times her partner; Commodore Higgenbothen had passed his "gallivanting" days; Doc French, whom she liked and to whom she would have been glad to be cordial, did not dance at all. The floor was rough and uneven; the music lugubrious; three small boys kept up a fearful racket playing with some folding chairs stacked in a corner. She watched Martin whirling and wheeling about the floor, his face a broad grin, his eyes and teeth flashing, talking, laughing, exchanging an endless banter with other couples, answering here, there and everywhere to calls of "Martin" and "Mart." At half-past ten she could stand no more of it. She knew she was dragging her husband away from a hilarious good time, but she was bored, disgusted with the whole evening and the hoidenish, loud-voiced village folk. She would never make the mistake of going to another of their wretched dances. Martin could go if he wanted to; if he liked to hobnob with such people, he could do so to his heart's content; she wouldn't raise one word of objection, but wild horses wouldn't drag her there again!

In a fortnight, there was another dance at the club, and this time Martin took himself to the party alone, while Jeannette went to bed with a magazine. He woke her up when he came home a little after twelve, and told her he had had a wonderfully good time, and that Lester Short, his wife and their two older children had been present. But Jeannette had no regrets. The Shorts and her husband could enjoy the society of the plumbers and carpenters and their wives if they chose to do so; she felt satisfied that if she had gone she would have been miserable.

§ 6

Besides the Yacht Club there were other things in the new order of existence that proved annoying. Meat and vegetables cost considerably more at Cohasset Beach than in the city, and everything else was proportionally dearer. Jeannette had thought she might save a little on her marketing in the country, and it was discouraging to discover that this was quite impossible. She certainly had not expected to find that prices were actually higher. Then there was not nearly the same variety from which to choose in the stores here as there had been in the groceries and particularly the meat markets of Amsterdam and Columbus Avenues. She and Martin were especially fond of lamb kidneys which she used to buy at the rate of three for five cents in New York. Pulitzer's at Cohasset Beach never seemed to have them. And even more exasperating was the fact that fish could only be had on Thursdays when the fish-man came around blowing his horn.

The neighborhood, too, was a source of discomfort. Jeannette discovered, within a few days after they had moved into the bungalow, that the reason so attractive a house had been for rent at such a figure, with its acre and more of ground, its apple trees and pond and picturesque setting, was that it was situated on the wrong side of town, beyond the railroad tracks, a mile from the water. The desirable, residential section of Cohasset Beach was that in which the Herbert Gibbses lived, on the hill overlooking the Sound. A block from the bungalow, their rear yards abutting upon the railroad tracks, was a row of shabby cottages occupied by laborers, Polacks mostly, who worked in the quarries down on the "Point." Here fences sagged and refuse littered the roadway, dirty children scrambled about and screamed at one another, drying laundry fluttered from clothes-lines, and fat dark women in calicoes and shuffling shoes gossiped from doorstep to doorstep. On Saturday nights there were invariably celebrations among these people at which, from the singing and general racket, it was evident that red wine flowed freely, and the doleful whine of an accordion accompanying hoarse masculine voices rose dismally from sundown until the early morning hours, interrupted by shouts of rollicking laughter. Martin assured his wife that these people were simple creatures, peasants transplanted but a few years from their native soil, celebrating after a week of toil, in a harmless jovial way after the fashion to which, in the old country, they had been accustomed. But Jeannette found it disturbing, not a little frightening, especially on those nights when Martin went off to the Yacht Club and left her alone with only Hilda in the house.

Lastly mosquitoes, germinated in the pond within a hundred yards of her own door, made their appearance in hungry numbers early in July. The pool was practically stagnant,—without visible outlet,—and the neighbor who owned it and who operated a small dairy, refused to oil it as his cows watered there. The bungalow windows were unscreened. Jeannette did not understand how she had failed to notice the fact when she first inspected the premises. The matter had to be remedied immediately, or life would be insupportable. The landlord declined to do anything; Martin thought perhaps they could endure the nuisance until cold weather came, but his wife declared that unthinkable. If the windows were shut with the lights on, the bungalow became insufferably hot and stuffy; if left open, moths, winged bugs, every kind of flying insect of the night together with the pests bred in the stagnant pool, flew in to buzz about the globes and torment those beneath them. Zeb Kline agreed to equip the bungalow with screens,—the frames would have to be fitted to the insides of the windows on account of their being casement,—for sixty-five dollars, and Jeannette, angered by Martin's complacent acceptance of the circumstances, and his indifferent attitude towards that for which she felt him largely responsible, told the carpenter to go ahead.

There were days when in the seclusion of her own bedroom she gave way freely to her tears. She wanted to be happy; she wanted to be a good manager

of her house, a good wife to Martin. Life often seemed
to demand more from her than she was capable of
giving. Concede—concede—concede! It was all con-
cession for her; Martin gave nothing.

§ 7

There came another Fourth of July, one year from
the time of the visit to the Gibbses. Doc French was
a member of the Cohasset Beach Yacht Club as well as
of the Family Yacht Club. There was to be a wonderful party at the former on the evening of the
Fourth; it was the Club's annual show. A dinner was
to be followed by a vaudeville entertainment provided
by a number of talented actors from the Lambs Club,
and after that a dance which would probably last all
night. Doc French invited Martin Devlin and his wife
to be his guests; he was giving a little dinner party
for his sister-in-law, Lou, and her cousin, Mrs. Edith
Prentiss, who were spending the holiday with him.

Jeannette was overjoyed at the prospect. She spent
a day shopping in New York, and bought herself silver
satin slippers, a pair of gray silk stockings to wear
with a silver dress,—part of her trousseau,—which she
had had no occasion to put on since she moved to the
country. It promised to be a delightful affair and
Martin shared her excitement.

It turned out to be all she expected. The spacious
dining-room, the dancing floor, even the awninged
porches were crowded with tables, gay with flowers
and patriotic decorations. There was a beguiling atmosphere of soft lights, color and music, smart and
lovely women, elaborate costumes, attractive men.

Jeannette felt that she herself bloomed with beauty, that she appeared tall, statuesque, superb. People at other tables threw appraising glances and occasionally she saw a lorgnette levelled in her direction. Doc French was admiring and attentive; she liked his sister-in-law and particularly Mrs. Prentiss; the vaudeville show on an improvised stage at one end of the long room was one of the best she had ever witnessed. Some of the actors were head-liners in their profession; with songs and stories, they kept the audience rocking with laughter and stirred it to roars of applause. One of the entertainers particularly drew Jeannette's interest,—a young actor, named Michael Carr. An unusually attractive youth, renowned for his good looks, a matinée idol, he had held the boards on Broadway all winter as the leading attraction in a Viennese opera. Jeannette thought he sang delightfully, and had a most charming personality.

Towards midnight the chairs and tables were cleared away and the dancing began. Doc French did not dance, himself, but he had no difficulty in securing partners for his guests, and Jeannette floated around the gaily decorated ball-room through the soft colors of calcium lights thrown upon the dancers, in an intoxication of pleasure. Men, young and old, seemed anxious to know her and ask her to dance; she was in demand every moment, and in one of these dizzying whirls she was interrupted by Doc French to introduce Michael Carr. The actor had asked to be presented; could he have a dance? The next was promised, but he could have it just the same, she said with shining eyes. She drifted away in his arms presently, a sweet giddiness enveloping her senses, rocking her in sensuous delight.

They glided from the dance and wandered out upon the long pier over the water. The lisping waves lapped the piles and rhythmically beat upon the pebbled shore, the music of the dance reached them plaintively, yachts white and ghostly stood sentinels at their moorings, their cabins pin-pricked with lights, their starboard lanterns glowing green. The night air was caressing, gay voices floated toward them, there was smothered laughter from hidden corners, the heavens were a myriad of golden stars. Quite simply Michael Carr took the slim silver figure in his arms, she melted into his embrace and their lips clung to one another's long and lovingly. It was a night of love, a night for lovers.

The brilliantly lit ball-room, the music drew them back. Jeannette had no sense of guilt; the mood of the hour still wrapped her; for the moment she loved this man whole-heartedly; he was divine, a super-man, a god. No thought of Martin came to distress her. She was supremely content, supremely happy; it was rapture, bliss, enchantment. In her ear he kept whispering:

"You are wonderful, you are beautiful, you are adorable."

Doc French was beckoning to her, but she only smiled amiably at him as she passed and floated on in Michael's arms, bending and undulating with him in perfect symmetry of motion. There was no such thing as time or space; she shut her eyes, and seemed to be floating—floating—floating—— Doc French stopped them with a hand on the actor's arm.

"Sorry to interrupt," he said, "but I fear I must. Your husband, Mrs. Devlin. . . . May I speak to you a moment?"

Carr said, "Oh, I beg pardon," and stepped aside, but Jeannette's thoughts followed him.

"What is it, Doc?"

"Martin had better go home, Mrs. Devlin. He's been downstairs at the bar, and I guess he's had a bit too much. I was going to take him home myself but I didn't know how to get into your house."

"Martin?"

"He's been downstairs at the bar, and I'm afraid the fellows there wouldn't let him get away."

"*Martin?*"

Reality came blindingly upon her with a glare of hideous white light. Her dream shattered. Ugliness obtruded,—things naked and angular, harshness and cold cruelty! She felt as if she were being jerked from enchanted slumber by a rude and horrid hand.

She clutched at her heart as if to tear out the pain that had already stabbed her there.

"Martin!" she breathed again, gasping a little, the blood draining from her face.

"He's all right, Mrs. Devlin,—quite all right, I assure you. Nothing's happened to him—nothing wrong. There's been no accident."

"Accident?" Her eyes widened with sudden fear.

"No—no; it's all right. He's just drunk a little too much, and I thought he'd better go home."

"Oh, surely—right away. Where is he?"

"Well, we've got him out in my car."

"Let's go—let's go then; let's go quickly. I'll get my wraps." She started for the dressing-room.

"Good night," Michael's voice called after her but she did not turn her head.

Doc French led her to the motor car. Martin lay

BREAD 315

huddled in the back, insensate, a long string of saliva trailing from his under lip. A strange man supported him.

A trembling, whispered exclamation escaped Jeannette. Her companion kept on reassuring her.

"There's nothing—nothing the matter," he repeated. "He's had too much to drink, that's all. . . . Get in the front seat with me and I'll drive you straight home and we'll put him to bed."

They bumped over the car-tracks in Washington Street and the dusty uneven ground in front of the station. The dawn was coming up angry and on fire in the east.

Before the bungalow, Jeannette jumped from the motor car and struggled to insert the twisted latch-key in the lock, but her fingers shook so much it took her some time to manage it. Behind her, Doc French and the strange man were lifting Martin from the car. As they wrenched him free he groaned painfully.

Jeannette flew into the house, flung on lights, tore back the gay-figured cretonne cover of the bed. Her underclothes lay upon the chair where she had tossed them when she had been so happily dressing. She gathered these with one swift reach and threw them to the floor of a closet. The stumbling feet were coming; the men were carrying Martin head and feet. With a concerted effort they heaved him upon the bed and he lay there inertly, sprawling, just as he had fallen.

"Can I help you, Mrs. Devlin?" asked the Doctor, dusting off his hands.

"Oh, no,—thank you very much," Jeannette answered in a strained voice.

"Don't you think we'd better undress him? He's pretty heavy for you to manage alone."

Jeannette looked at the helpless figure flung out across the bed, ungainly postured like a child's discarded doll, purple lips parting with each breath, the hair damp and tousled. One of his garters had loosened and dangled now from the wrinkled hose that covered a patent-leather pump.

"No," she said again slowly, "thank you very much for all your kindness, Doc,—but it's my—my job; he belongs to me; I'll take care of him."

§ 8

Three hours later she walked out on the back porch. The heat of the Sunday morning was moist and tropical, giving promise of a scorching day. The bells of the Catholic Church on the "Point" road were ringing sweetly for the children's mass. Her eyes felt burnt out from lack of sleep: two black holes in her head. Hilda was making a small fuss in the kitchen, rattling pans, droning hoarsely to herself. Jeannette stood at the porch railing and looked off across the quiet country, misty with the early heat. Emotions were at war in her heart, and there was pain—pain—pain.

She had not been to bed; she had not even lain down. The silver gown had been put away, her finery discarded, and now she wore the striped velveteen wrapper in which she usually did her morning's work. She had undressed her husband, removed his shoes, drawn off his dress suit, tugging at its arms, rolling him from one side to another to free the clothing. She had washed his face with a cold wet rag and brushed the rumpled hair from his eyes. Then she had put the room in order, opened the casement windows, drawn the shades, closed the door and left him to peace and sleep. The house had needed straightening and to this she had turned her attention, adjusting rugs, pushing chairs into position, emptying ash receivers, carrying away newspapers, arranging magazines and books in neat piles, using broom and dust-pan, wiping the furniture with a dust cloth. Hilda had given her some coffee at eight o'clock and she had drunk it black and crunched some thin slices of buttered toast. Now nothing remained to be done and the thoughts to which she had resolutely shut her mind clamored for admittance to her weary brain. Remorse and reproach, censure and repugnance, disillusionment, humiliation, grief and regret,—they swarmed upon her like so many black flies.

The hours of the morning ticked themselves away. She could not sleep; she could not rest. Over and over her thoughts turned to the incidents of the night, giving her no peace, no surcease. Every little while she would go softly to Martin's door and silently look in upon him; he lay as she had left him. In spite of the opened windows the room reeked of alcohol.

Towards noon she fell asleep on the couch in the living-room, and the afternoon light was waning when she opened her eyes. The sound of water woke her; Martin was running a bath, and when presently she entered the bedroom, she found him shaving. She was shocked at his appearance; his face was dead white, the eyes bloodshot, and his hand trembled as he held the razor, but it was Martin, restored to life and sanity.

They avoided one another's glance, and constraint held them silent. She could see that physically he was weak, his nerves still shattered and that his mind was sick with remorse, and fear of her displeasure. He could not guess she wanted only to take him in her arms, to kiss and comfort him, wanted only to be kind and good to him, to restore him to health and strength again, wanted to utter no word of reproach but to give him all the love she could and so ease the pain and shame within herself.

§ 9

Three weeks later, Doc French drove up in front of the bungalow door in his lumbering motor car. It was late in the afternoon. There had been a heavy thunderstorm about two o'clock but now the sun was glittering on all the dripping trees and drenched shrubbery and the air was fragrant with sweet grassy and woodland smells.

There was to be another dance at the Cohasset Beach Yacht Club the following Saturday night. Doc's sister-in-law and Mrs. Prentiss were coming down for it and would stay with him over the week-end; it happened to be Lou's birthday and he wanted Martin and Jeannette to help celebrate the event at a small dinner he was arranging at the Cohasset Beach club-house before the dance.

Jeannette thanked him and said that, no, she was sorry but she and Martin had another engagement; Doc was very kind to think of them but it would have to be another time.

When her husband came home on the five-twenty, she told him about it.

"Oh, you bet you," he agreed. "No more of that kind of stuff for this young fellow. We're out of our class at that club, Jan."

"I thought," suggested Jeannette, "we might go to the other club that night. There's always a dance there, and it would be our excuse to Doc French. It occurred to me that perhaps after we got to know those people a little better, we might like it."

Martin's face beamed with pleasure.

"Would you? Would you really go?" he asked eagerly. "Say, Jan, that'll be fine. Say, if you only wouldn't be so standoffish and proud, you'd learn to like that gang and they'd learn to like you. They're awfully good-hearted."

"Well, I'll try," said his wife.

CHAPTER VI

§ 1

It was quite an undertaking to go from Cohasset Beach to Freeport, on the opposite side of Long Island. One had to take the steam train to Jamaica and change cars there; the connections were bad; it took the better part of two hours. But Alice had written her sister week after week begging her and Martin to spend a Sunday with them and finally a date had been set. It was the end of the Beardsleys' stay at Freeport, and the visit could not be further postponed if the Devlins were to accomplish it at all. Jeannette was eager to go, but to Martin it meant the loss of his one day in the week of yachting. There were races every Sunday afternoon and since Martin had acquired his little A-boat, there was no joy in life for him equal to the pleasure of sailing it. But it held no joy for Jeannette; she resented the boat and everything connected with it; to her it only meant ninety dollars' worth of extravagance and it took her husband away from her every week-end. He spent Saturday afternoons "tuning up," as he described it, for the race on Sunday. She saw little of him on these days; he was always at the yacht club and would often be half-an-hour to an hour late for dinner. He never had had any sense of time.

o she had patiently urged the expedition to Free-

port and had made him promise weeks in advance that
this particular date should be dedicated to the visit.

The day was a glorious success. Martin was in his
sweetest, merriest mood and no regret over his lost
sport lingered in his heart. There was only a faint
stirring of wind and little indication that it would
freshen, as previous days had been marked by calm;
he was consoled, therefore, in thinking that in all probability there would be no race that afternoon.

Alice, Roy, and the children met them at the Freeport station. They were all going on a picnic over
to the beach it was announced; a launch would take
them to a sandy reef that was their own discovery;
it left a little after eleven; they just had time.

The beach when they reached it was totally deserted.
No one ever came there, Alice explained; it was a narrow, hummocky strip of sand, a mile or more in length
with no habitation on it but a gray weather-beaten
shack falling into ruins. A rickety one-board pier
jutted out into the lagoon that separated this reef from
the island shore and the launch stopped there a moment to let the little party disembark before it went
chug-chugging on its way to Coral Beach farther along
the coast, where a small tent colony was springing
into being. The launch would return for them about
five o'clock.

A sandy tramp of a few hundred yards over the
dunes and sparse gray sea-scrub brought them to the
lunching spot. Here, half covered over with drifting
sand, was a long padlocked pine box. Roy produced
a key and opened it. This was the cache, the Beardsleys explained; they and the children came here every
Sunday and they kept a few things stowed away in

the box. Nobody ever disturbed them. This was their
own little sandy domain, and they referred to it always
as San Salvador. The box disclosed a tall faded,
beach umbrella which was immediately unfurled and
planted upright in the sand; then there was a piece
of clean canvas, some straw cushions, and an iron grill.
The canvas was spread under the umbrella; Roy made
Jeannette seat herself on one of the cushions, and he
propped a board at an angle behind her so that she
might lean back against it and be comfortable; then
she was given Ralph to hold and to feed from his bottle. The others proceeded to busy themselves with
preparations for lunch. Etta was quite able to look
out for herself, Alice assured her sister, and the baby
would be off in ten minutes.

An expedition for driftwood was inaugurated and
presently a large pile of smoothly rounded bleached
sticks, branches and blocks of wood was heaped near
at hand. The lunch consisted of hot cocoa and chops
which were to be grilled, and some round flat bakery
buns to be split in half and toasted. In a few moments
there was a brisk, snapping fire leaping up through
the bars of the grill; a large saucepan and the milk
appeared, the buns impaled on the points of sticks
were set to toasting; at the last moment the chops
were to be put on to broil.

A heavenly felicity stole over Jeannette as she sat
in the shade of the umbrella, the baby in her arms,
watching the scene. The Atlantic thundered in in great
arcs of green water, foamed-crested, which crashed
magnificently in round curling splathers of spray, and
slid swiftly, smoothly, reachingly up the flat beach to
slink back again upon themselves as if deciding these

harmless, picnicking people were not the victims for
which they sought. Seaweed littered the beach in long
whip lashes and bulbous bottles, and seabirds picked
their way about in it, and pecked at sand fleas; gulls
soared in wide circles above their heads, squawking
ugly cries, or skimmed the wave-tops hunting fish.
Far out upon the bosom of the ocean a steamer left
a long scarf of smoke against an azure sky. The salt
air from the sea was scented with the fragrant odor
of the beachwood fire.

Little Ralph lay inertly in Jeannette's arms sucking
greedily at his bottle until the last of it had to be tilted
up against his mouth. At this stage his eyelids began
to drift shut and his head to hang heavily in the crook
of her elbow. He was a cunning child, his aunt
thought, critically studying him. He resembled his
father with a closeness that was ludicrous: a small
replica, with the same small mouth, the same whimsical smile and unruly, tawny hair. His skin was like
satin,—delicately tinted,—and against its faint pink-
ness his long-fringed lashes lay like tiny feathery
fans. His weight against her breast felt pleasant to
her; he seemed so trusting, so certain of protection, as
he lay sleeping thus, a scrap of humanity confident of
the world's love. A sudden tenderness came to the
woman; she bent down and kissed the damp forehead
at the edge of the child's yellow hair.

The entrancing smell of crisply broiling meat and
toasting bread assailed her.

"Uuum—m," she said hungrily, and raising her
head she observed Martin watching her. Puzzled a
moment by the intentness of his gaze, her eyes widened
inquiringly, but he only shook his head at her pleas-

antly and grinned. There was love in his look and it thrilled her as evidence of any affection from him never failed to do.

She gently laid the baby on the strip of canvas, arranged a rumpled little pillow beneath his head, spread a square of netting over him to keep flies from bothering him, weighing down its corners with a few beach pebbles, and joined the others about the fire, where presently they were all munching with gluttonous cries of delight. Never was there better food! Never was there anything so delicious! A bite of grilled chop and a bite of crisp buttery bun! Their appetites were on edge; they grunted in satisfying them. Another cup of hot cocoa, please,—and, yes,—another chop,—just one more,—but this must positively be the last!

As the fire died away, they lay back upon the sand, replete, heavy with food, bathed in pleasant warmth. Etta, stripped of all clothing but a diminutive undershirt, played in the sand and squatted on her heels on the edge of the wave-rips, uttering gurgling cries of fright when her toes were wet. Drowsiness and bodily comfort wrapped the others' senses; a feeling of openness,—sky, land and ocean,—beguiled them; the breakers pounded and swished musically up the beach; sea-birds lifted plaintive cries; the faint breeze was redolent of salt and kelp; the sun's heat warm and caressing.

Jeannette awoke deliciously; Martin was bending over her; he had kissed her, and now he was smiling down at her.

"Come on," he said, "we're all going swimming."

"Oh," protested Jeannette, yawning, with a great stretch of limbs, "must we?"

"Oh, yes, Janny," Alice urged, coming up, "we always go swimming; that's the best part of the fun."

"I didn't bring a bathing suit," objected Jeannette, sleepily.

"I've got an old one of mine for you and Roy borrowed a suit at the boarding-house for Martin."

They dragged her to her feet and as she looked at the emerald waves curling toward her, they suddenly seemed inviting.

In a few moments they were into their bathing suits and ran down to the water together,—the four of them, —holding hands, laughing and shouting. The rushing tide swirled about their knees and leaped up against their thighs.

"Come on!" urged the men, dragging their wives into the frightening turmoil.

A wave engulfed them, quickening their breath, sending their hearts knocking against their throats with its cold sharpness.

"Oh-h-h!" screamed Jeannette, "isn't it *glorious?*"

Martin caught her, lifted her high, as a comber crashed down upon them, burying him in white foam. The water fled past.

Jeannette caught him about the neck and they pressed their lips and wet faces together.

"Mart—Mart!" she cried. "It's just like our honeymoon, isn't it?"

He strained her to him, kissing her dripping hair and cheeks, his arms entwined about her, his face stretched wide with laughter and excitement.

"My God, Jan," he said with almost a groan of feeling, "my God, I love you when you're this way! You're just *wonderful!*"

Her shining eyes were his answer, and he caught her to him again to kiss her fiercely.

A wave suddenly plunged over them. Jeannette felt herself wrenched from his embrace, felt him stumbling on the sand in the big effort he made to keep his footing. Even in that brief frightening moment, when she was totally submerged and they were being dragged apart, she was conscious of the great strength of the man, of arms suddenly taut as steel cables, of fingers and hands that gripped her like grappling hooks of iron and pitted their might against the might of the sea. The tumultuous plunge of water rushed headlong on its course, but Martin stood firm and pulled her to him.

They clung together once more, and laughing like children faced another menacing attack of the ocean.

§ 2

Later as she lay prone upon the hot, hard sand, baking in the sun's delicious heat, her hair spread out behind her on a towel to dry, she watched her husband with Etta in his arms again encountering the waves. The little girl's arms were tight around his neck and she screamed with excitement whenever the water foamed and welled up about them. The child was not frightened; it was remarkable to observe the unusual confidence the little girl had in her uncle. A fine figure of a man, mused his wife; his limbs had the form of sculpture and his body, shining now with the glitter of wet bronze, showed every muscle rippling beneath the skin like writhing snakes. He was indeed a husband to be proud of, a husband any woman might envy her. She must never let his love for her grow less; he must always be *in* love with her, not merely have an affectionate regard for her as most men had for their wives. He was lying on the beach, now, and Etta was covering him with sand, screaming shrilly each time he stirred and cracked the mold she was patting into shape about him.

"You bad, Uncle Martin," came the child's piping voice; "you be a good man and lie still."

He had the child on his back presently and on hands and knees crawled a hundred yards down the beach, sniffing at whatever came into his path and growling fiercely. Etta's shrieks reached them above the roar of the surf. She had a stick now and was belaboring her steed vigorously.

"No, no, Etta, no—no!" called her mother. Martin waved a reassuring hand and pretended to suffer death. "It's wonderful the way Martin has with children," commented Alice; "they seem to take to him naturally."

Everyone did, thought his wife affectionately. He was truly exceptional; children,—boys and girls,—men and women,—everybody felt his irresistible attraction.

A shrill tooting announced the arrival of the launch. There was a mad scramble; no one was dressed. Roy went off to tell the boat to wait while the others hurried into their clothes, gathered plates, forks and other accessories of the lunch into baskets, and flung umbrella, canvas, grill and cushions back into their keep-

ing-place. Everyone was laughing helplessly when
Roy came springing back to tell them to take their time
as the old captain had admitted he was half-an-hour
early.

Fifteen minutes later they clambered aboard the
puffing motor boat, and Martin and Jeannette found
themselves sitting side by side in the stern. His hand
found hers as it lay upon the seat between them and
their fingers linked themselves together; their eyes
shone as they looked at one another.

"Wonderful day, Jan."

"Ah, wonderful indeed," she answered.

§ 3

It was late that night after they were in bed that
Martin said to her:

"Jan, old girl, wouldn't you like to have a baby?
You looked so sweet to-day sitting there under the
umbrella with little Ralph in your arms,—really you
made a beautiful picture: mother and child, you know;
I haven't been able to get it out of my mind since. . . .
I think it would be a lot of fun to have a kid."

Jeannette was silent. She had often thought about
having a child. Martin continued:

"Seems to me, Jan, you'd love a baby after it came.
I know it's a pretty tough experience, and you don't
want one so awfully badly, but Gee Christopher! I
think a baby would be swell; one of our own, you know,
one that belonged to us, that was ours,—and you
would, too. I often look at Herbert Gibbs' kid and
wish to goodness he was mine. Herb's always talking
about him and I know damn well I'd be just as looney

about a son of my own. . . . Now take Roy and Alice, for example: see what fun they get out of their children, and that Etta sure's a heart-breaker! And she's so jolly, too! Did you ever see a pluckier kid than that? You'd like a little daughter like her, wouldn't you, Jan? I think a baby would be a lot of fun, don't you?''

Still she said nothing and he asked his question again, giving her a little squeeze in the circle of his arm.

"I was just thinking about it," she said vaguely. "It means a good deal for a woman."

"That's right, of course. I know it does,—but you wouldn't be scared, would you, Jan?"

"Oh, no, that wouldn't bother me—much," she said slowly. "It's the ties that bind one afterwards that I was thinking of."

"Well-l, you want a baby some time, don't you? You don't want to grow old and be childless, do you?"

"No; certainly not."

"Then what's the good of waiting?"

"A baby's an expense, and we're terribly behind. I think we ought to be out of debt first, don't you?"

"Yes-s,—I guess so."

They went off to sleep at this point, but Martin brought the subject up again a few days later. During the interval, however, Jeannette had made up her mind: they were over five hundred dollars in debt and until that was cleaned up or at least very materially reduced, it would be very foolish indeed for them to consider having a child. If Martin wanted a baby, he must do his share in getting out of debt.

"But Jan, don't you think that a baby would help

us save? I mean if there was one in the house, I don't believe you and I would want to gad so much."

His wife eyed him with a twisted smile and an elevated brow.

"Oh—hell," he said, disgustedly, and went to find a cigar.

CHAPTER VII

§ 1

SEPTEMBER brought an end to the yacht-racing and a few weeks later Martin's beloved A-boat was towed with a number of others a mile or two down the Sound to be housed in winter quarters. Jeannette earnestly hoped that this would mean her husband would spend more time with her at week-ends. He was gone from Monday till Friday all day, and she felt that at least part of his Saturday afternoons and Sundays should be hers. But Martin always wanted to *do* things on these days; he wanted some active form of amusement, some excitement, a "party," as he called it; he was never content to sit at home and read or go for a walk with his wife. He asserted he needed the exercise, and if he missed it between Saturday noon and Sunday night, he was "stale" for the rest of the week. Sometimes Jeannette came into the city by train on a Saturday, met him after the office closed at noon, and together they went to lunch and later to a matinée. Then the alternative presented itself of either remaining in town for dinner and going to another show or of taking a late afternoon train back to Cohasset Beach. Such a program, of course, cost money, but unless Jeannette did this, Martin would go off to the Yacht Club Saturday afternoon, and return there in the evening after dinner to play poker. The

Saturday night dances gave place at the close of the yachting season to "smokers" which only the men attended. A certain group called itself "the gang," and prominent in it were such club lights as Herbert Gibbs, Zeb Kline, Fritz Wiggens, Steve Teschemacher and Doc French. Martin Devlin was warmly hailed as one of them. They played poker every Saturday night and the "session" lasted until an early hour Sunday morning.

Jeannette came to hate these men; she resented their taking her husband from her; she begrudged his gambling when he could not afford to lose. When she protested, the only answer from him was a testy: "Quit your crabbing." He almost invariably won and divided his winnings with her, or at least divided what purported to be his winnings. His wife despised herself for taking the money; it made her want him to win, though she wished to be indifferent to his card-playing, since she did not approve of it. She tried to justify her acceptance of the money on the ground that it went to pay off some of their bills. But sometimes she bought a small piece of finery for herself with it. She was becoming very shabby in appearance. She reminded herself almost daily that she had not bought any new clothes since she was married, and the bride's wardrobe, though ample, was now worn and much depleted.

§ 2

It was towards the end of summer, when already there was a brisk touch of fall in the air, that Roy Beardsley fell ill with typhoid and for three weeks

was a desperately sick man. Martin, who had various
talks with the physician, told Jeannette that there
was small hope of his recovery; certain phases of the
case made it appear very grave.

Jeannette took Etta and Ralph to say with her in
the country and Mrs. Sturgis moved out to the flat in
the Bronx to help Alice fight for Roy's life. Jeannette,
from the first, believed he was going to die; destiny, it
seemed to her, had ordained it. For the first time in
many years she got down on her knees in her bedroom
and prayed. She realized more clearly than anyone
else in the family what a tragedy Roy's death would be
to them all,—to helpless Alice and his helpless children,
to her little mother, to Martin, to herself. She did not
know what would become of Alice and her babies!
How would they live? She and Martin would have to
shoulder the responsibility, and they had difficulty in
making ends meet as it was! Where would Martin get
fifty or even twenty-five dollars a month to send Alice?
And how could Alice and the children manage on so
small a sum? Roy, she knew, had a three thousand
dollar life insurance policy,—hardly more than enough
to bury him decently! Alice could not go to work; she
had not the faintest notion of how to earn a living. She
was clever with her needle, but that was all. It was
impossible to imagine her a seamstress! But she
would either have to go into that work and let Jeannette keep the children, or she would have to live with
her mother, while Mrs. Sturgis and Martin,—between
them,—would have to contribute what they were able
to their support! It was a terrible prospect in any
case. Jeannette was ridden with fear of the catastrophe. How different it would be, she reminded her-

self, were she in Alice's situation,—she with her profession and her experience in business! She had nothing to fear on that score; she could always take care of herself. Poor Alice!—poor little brown bird!—there would be nothing for her to do; she could not support *herself*, not to mention her two children! Jeannette remembered that once she had begged to be allowed to follow her sister's example and go to work, and she recalled how she and her mother had vigorously opposed her. She wondered now if that had been right. Perhaps every woman ought to have a profession or at least a recognized means of earning her livelihood. How secure Alice would feel now in that case if Roy died! Grief-stricken, yes, but with the comforting knowledge that neither she nor her children need be dependent on anyone!

All day long as Jeannette watched Etta and Ralph playing under the apple trees, which had begun to shed their yellow leaves and the scant weazened fruit from their scraggy branches, she thought of Roy's possible death and her sister's plight. Any one of the family group could be spared better than he! Yes, even Alice! . . . Oh, it would be a calamity,—a dreadful, horrible calamity if Roy died! . . . Twenty times a day she closed her eyes and thought a prayer.

She enjoyed having the children with her. Etta was an affectionate, ebullient child, always ready with hugs and kisses; little Ralph placidly viewed the world with reposeful solemnity, made no demands, was amiably satisfied with any arrangement his elders or even his big sister thought wise, and in his gentleness was extraordinarily appealing.

Late in the afternoons, Jeannette would dress them

in clean rompers, pull on their sweaters and set them
out on the lower step of the front stoop to wait for
Martin. There they would sit for sometimes an hour,
or even longer, watching for him and at the first
glimpse, Etta would run screaming to meet him with
arms flung wide, Ralph following as best he could.
Martin was particularly in love with the boy, and he
would hold the baby in his lap for long periods, neither
of them making a sound; or the child would grasp his
finger and toddle beside him, see-sawing from one
slightly bowed leg to another, to inspect the pool and
perhaps capture a frog.

Only a miracle would stay Death's hand, the doctor
had said, but the miracle happened; very slowly the
tide began to turn and inch by inch the flood of life
came back to the wasted body of Roy Beardsley. Jeannette shed tears of gratitude when it was definitely
asserted he would get well. She left the children in
Hilda's care and went to the city to rejoice with her
mother and sister. They clung together the way they
used to do before either of the girls was married, wept
and sniffled and kissed one another again and again.
Roy's blue eyes seemed enormously large and dark
when his sister-in-law saw him; his lip was drawn
tight across his teeth and these protruded like the fangs
of a famished dog. His cheeks were sunk in great
hollows beneath his cheek-bones, and his hands were
the hands of the starved. He was a living skeleton,
but his great eyes acknowledged her presence and her
smile, and there was a faint twitching of the tight-
drawn lip. Although she had been prepared, she could
not keep from betraying the shock his altered appearance gave her; he was indeed ghastly.

The averted tragedy sobered them all. Roy would be many weeks getting back his health and he must take particular care of himself during the approaching winter, the doctor cautioned. No one ever whispered the word "tuberculosis" but each knew it was that which Roy must guard against. If it could be managed, he ought to be taken to a warmer climate, the physician advised, and he must make no effort, but rest, drink milk and eat nourishing food for a long time until he had entirely regained his strength. His father eagerly wrote him to come to California; Jeannette and Martin asked to keep the children; everyone urged Alice to take her husband to the Golden State. So just before the first snow of the year, she and Roy departed westward, waving good-bye through the iron grill at the station to the little group behind it, who waved vigorously in return until "All aboard" was shouted, the porter helped Alice up into the vestibule and the train began slowly to move.

§ 3

The winter was hard. It was unusually cold and snow lay heavy in great mounds along the edges of the village streets, and beaten trails of it meandered through the frozen fields. Soot from the trains blackened the white drifts and the road-beds were rutted in sharp ridges, and gray ice, that crackled and shivered like glass underfoot, formed in the hollows. The leafless trees spread their branches in black nakedness against the bleak sky and the wind blew chilly across the bare countryside from the icy waters of the Sound.

Yet Jeannette knew her first happiness at Cohasset

Beach. Her days were full of the care of her small niece and nephew. They were endearing mites, exacting, but warmly affectionate. She had had no experience in bringing up children but her mother came down to stay with her for a while, and Mrs. Drigo, who lived a hundred yards or so down the street, and had four healthy youngsters of her own, gave counsel in emergencies. Jeannette devoted herself to her task. She attacked the problem much as she would have met some untoward circumstance in business. She considered herself efficient, set great store by efficiency, and proposed to apply it to the care of her sister's children. She devised a system and adhered to it.

In the cold mornings when the children woke, they might look at their picture-books until she came in to dress them. They must not make any noise and Martin must not go in to play with them or even open their door to say "Hello" when he got up early to fix the furnace. They had their "poggy" and milk at eight and immediately thereafter were bundled into their woolly leggings, sweaters, hooded caps and mittens and sent out to play in the snow. They were to amuse themselves until eleven, when, furred and properly shod, their aunt appeared to take them with her to market, wheeling Ralph in his go-cart, while Etta trailed along beside them. Upon returning, the children had their luncheon, always a good full meal of baked potato, cut-up meat and vegetables, and a little dessert. Jeannette believed small children should have light suppers, and that their "dinner" should come at midday. After they had eaten, it was nap-time, and this was the blessed interval of relaxation for herself. Her charges must stay in bed until three o'clock, when they were

re-dressed in their woolly leggings, sweaters and caps,
and permitted to go out again to play in the snow. For
the rest of her life, bits of watery ice stuck to the fine
hairs of woollen garments always brought back to
Jeannette with poignant emotion the memory of these
days. When the children stamped into the house at the
end of their play, their skins hard and coldly fresh,
their breaths puffs of vapor, their cheeks crimson, the
little sweaters and leggings would be encrusted with
hard, icy snow. Jeannette would have a log fire going,
and she would undress them before its crackling blaze
and hang their damp outer garments on the fire screen
to dry. The little naked figures dancing in the warm
room in the flickering firelight was always a delightful
sight to her. They were their merriest at this hour
and said their cutest things with which she remembered later to regale Martin. Upstairs the oil heater
would be warming the bathroom which Hilda had made
ready and presently there would come a mad dash
into the dining-room and up the cold stairway to the
grateful temperature of the little room. And here
began a great splashing with shrieks and admonitions,
and here Jeannette dried their sweet little bodies and
slipped them into their cotton flannel double-gowns.
Then downstairs once more before the replenished log
fire to sit on either side of her and empty their warmed
bowls of crackers and milk and listen to the story she
either read or told them until Martin came in to find
them so. Then followed kisses and hugs all round and
immediately thereafter the children were dispatched
to bed with a final warning from their aunt that there
must positively be no talking.

Thus it was day after day, always the same, relent-

lessly the same, undeviating monotony. Martin
always praised Jeannette, her mother praised her,
even the neighbors praised her. Alice wrote loving
messages of deep gratitude. She responded to the
general approval, delighted in the applause. The
thought that she was proving herself equal to this
unfamiliar rôle, that she was doing her job efficiently,
comforted and inspired her. Revelling in her righteous
duty, she threw herself passionately into its perfect
execution. She gave it all her energy, thought and
time. She told her husband and mother with much
emphasis that Etta and Ralph were far better behaved
now than they ever had been with their own father and
mother.

"It's routine, I tell you," she would say. "Children
respond to routine and this business of deviating from
a strict schedule is demoralizing. A little firmness is
all that is necessary in making children good. They
really are very adaptable. I confess I was surprised.
They learn so quickly! The minute Etta and Ralph
saw when they first came that I wouldn't stand for
any foolishness, they were as meek as lambs. . . .
I declare! Alice is so soft and easy-going with them,
I hate to think of their being spoilt when they go back."

It was another surprise to Jeannette to discover
how little the presence of the children in the house
disturbed Martin. She had thought he would grow
restless after a time and that they would be certain
to annoy him. She had been sure he would soon object
to ties which would chain her to the house. Martin
loved children—loved them particularly well for a
man, perhaps—but he was often unreasonable where
her time and movements were concerned, and had

always rebelled at restraint. Now he mildly accepted
the new element in their lives without protest and as
time passed continued amiable. If she could not
go out with him or accept an invitation, he did not
reproach or even urge her, but praised her for her
devotion, and often stayed at home to keep her company. Saturday nights, however, when the "gang"
gathered at the Yacht Club, he went off to join them,
but since the children were with her, Jeannette did
not mind being alone in the house.

"Come home early," she would say to him. "It's
such fun to have you in the house on Sundays and the
children love it. I hate to have you wake up tired and
hollow-eyed, and you know, Martin, when you get only
two or three hours' sleep you are sometimes a little
cross and the children notice it."

"You're dead right," he would agree with her
readily. "I'll tell the boys I've got to quit at midnight. They can begin the rounds then; there's no
sense in our sitting up until three or four o'clock in
the morning."

And often he kept his word.

§ 4

Alice and Roy had planned to stay six months in
California, but in April Jeannette received a letter
from her sister with the news that they had decided
to return the first of May; Roy was in fine shape,—
he was even fat!—they both were mad to see their
children.

The letter left Jeannette feeling strangely blank.
What was she to do without Etta and Ralph? She

had talked a great deal about the fearful responsibility, the exacting care these youngsters involved and what a relief it would be to her when their mother came home to take them off her hands. She had aired these views to her own mother and to Mrs. Drigo, Mrs. Gibbs, and particularly to Martin. Yet now that Alice was coming a month, even six weeks sooner than she intended, she had none of the expected elation. A sadness settled upon her. She wondered how she would occupy herself when the babies were gone.

"What do you suppose Roy intends to do?" she asked Martin one day. "He hasn't got a job. I don't see how he's going to manage for Alice and the children. . . . He might leave them with us for awhile. . . . No,—I suppose Alice will want them back immediately! . . . It will be some time before he gets settled."

"Oh, he'll find something to do, right away," Martin answered her cheerfully.

That was one of Martin's irritating qualities, reflected his wife. He was always so optimistic, so confident, never appreciating how serious things sometimes were. Roy and Alice were facing a grave situation; it might be desperate. Martin refused to regard it as important.

"I wonder if Mr. Corey would take him back at the office?" Jeannette hazarded. Very probably he would. It was a brilliant idea and, acting upon it at once, she went the following day to see her old employer.

The visit to the publishing house was strangely disquieting. She was struck by the number of new faces, the many changes. The counter which formerly defined the waiting-room on the fourth floor had been removed and now the space, walled in by partitions, was converted into a retail book store with shelves lined with new books and display tables. A gray-haired woman inquired her name with a polite, indifferent smile, and when she brought back word that Mr. Corey would see Mrs. Devlin, undertook to show Jeannette the way to his office!

There were changes behind the partitions as well. It was amazing the differences two years had wrought. There was none of the flutter of interest her appearance had caused at her previous visit. One or two of her old friends came up to shake her hand and to ask about her, while a few others nodded and smiled. She did not see Miss Holland anywhere, and Mr. Allister of whom she caught a glimpse in a distant corner accorded her a casual wave of the hand. She was forgotten already, she, who had once enjoyed so much respect, even affection, who had been the president's secretary, had been known to have his ear and often to have been his adviser! Miss Whaley, whom she remembered as having been connected with the Mailing Department, she met face to face on her way to Mr. Corey's office, but the girl had even forgotten her name!

But there was nothing wanting in her old chief's reception. Mr. Corey rose from his desk the instant she entered his room, and reached for both her hands. He was the same warm, cordial friend, eager to hear everything about her. How was she getting on? How was that good-looking husband of hers? Where were they living? He reproached her for not having been in to see him, appeared genuinely hurt that she had neglected him so long. He had changed, too, Jean-

nette noticed; his face sagged a little and he no longer
bore himself with his old erectness. She observed he
still dyed his mustache; a little of the dyestuff was
smeared upon his cheek.

News of himself and his family was not particularly
cheerful. Babs was in a private sanitarium at Nyack;
Mrs. Corey was badly crippled with rheumatism,—a
virulent arthritis,—and, in the care of a trained nurse,
had gone to Germany to try to get rid of it; Willis
had picked up an African malarial fever while he had
been exploring, and although he was home again, re-
current attacks of it kept him in poor health. Jeannette noted a gentleness in Mr. Corey's voice as he
spoke of his son; he blamed himself for Willis' condition; that African trip on which he had sent him was
responsible for the boy's broken constitution. As for
business, things were in bad shape, too. The public
did not seem to be buying books any more; they
weren't interested; *The Ladies' Fortune* was doing
pretty well, but the increased cost of production
knocked the profits out of everything; the office was
demoralized, the "folks" did not seem to coöperate as
they had done in the old days; he, himself, found daily
reasons to regret the hour when Jeannette had ceased
to be his secretary; he hadn't had any sort of efficient
help since she left; recent secretaries all had proven
a constant source of annoyance to him. Tommy Livingston had got married and asked for one raise after
another until Mr. Corey was obliged to let him go;
he believed he was doing very well for himself in the
news photograph business; Mr. Corey finally had had
to take Mrs. O'Brien away from Mr. Kipps, but even
she was far from competent. There were other details

about the business that awoke the old interest in Jeannette. Something in this office atmosphere fired the girl; it brought buoyancy to her pulse, it stimulated her, it put life into her veins. How happy she had been here! Never so contented, she said to herself.

She hastened to tell Mr. Corey the object of her visit, and he promised to find a place somewhere in the organization for Roy.

"I have only a hazy recollection of the young man," he said, "but I'll do whatever you want me to, on your account, Miss Sturgis."

Jeannette smiled. She would always be "Miss Sturgis" to Mr. Corey. She liked it that way; her married name meant nothing to him, never would. She thanked him warmly and promised to come to see him again.

As she made her way out through the crowded aisles of the general office, amid the familiar rattle of typewriters and hum of work, past old faces and new, her heart tugged in her breast. She was still part of it; some of herself was implanted eternally here in this tide of work, in the busy, preoccupied clerks, in the hustle and bustle, in the smell of ink and paste and pencil dust, in the very walls of the building.

§ 5

The good news she had to tell Roy of the job she had secured for him warmed her heart. There was no time to write, but she treasured it to herself and imagined a dozen times a day, as he and Alice were speeding homeward, how she would break it to him.

Martin was unable to be present when they arrived

at the Grand Central Station, but Mrs. Sturgis, Jeannette and the two children were there waiting for them
to emerge from the long column of passengers that
streamed in a hurrying throng from the Chicago train.
There were screams of joy and wet lashes as the parents' arms caught, hugged and kissed the children
again and again. Mrs. Sturgis had a cold luncheon
prepared at home, and with bags and children, the
four adults bundled themselves into a taxi and drove
to Ninety-second Street, laughing excitedly, interrupting one another with inconsequences after the manner
of all arriving travellers.

Roy indeed had put on weight; the emaciated look
had entirely disappeared. His plumpness altered
his expression materially and his sister-in-law was
not quite sure she liked it. There could be no
question about his splendid health. His face was
round and there were actually folds in his neck where
it bulged a trifle above his collar. Alice looked prettier
than ever and as Jeannette studied her, she realized
how much she had missed her sister during the past
few months and how much she loved her. Yet when
the children climbed into their mother's lap and tried
awkwardly to twine their short arms about her neck,
Etta announcing shrilly that she loved her "bestest
in all the world," Jeannette experienced a cruel pang
of jealousy. Now Alice would immediately begin to
spoil them and undo all her good work! . . . It was
going to be very hard,—very hard, indeed.

She was anxious to tell her good news. Roy must
be worrying about the future and it was not fair to
keep him in the dark. But when she told him triumphantly, he and his wife only looked at one another

with a significant smile. They had good news of their own: they were going back to California and meant to take the children with them; they intended to live out there for a year or two in a place called "Mill Valley," just across the bay from San Francisco, with Roy's father. Dr. Beardsley was a dear old white-headed man,—the dearest on earth, Alice declared,—and he was rector of a little church in Mill Valley and lived in the most adorable redwood shake house up on the side of a mountain just above the village. The house was a roomy old place and Dr. Beardsley had talked and talked to them about coming to California and making their home with him for two or three years until Roy had gained a start, for it appeared that Roy wanted to write,—he had always wanted to write,—and while he had been convalescing out in California under the big redwoods, he had written a book,—not a big one,—but a story about an old family dog the Beardsleys had once owned, and he had sent it to a magazine and they had paid three hundred dollars for the serial rights and there was a very good chance that some publisher would bring it out in book form! The money was not very much of course, but it was unquestionably encouraging and Dr. Beardsley felt that he and Alice ought to combine forces and give Roy a chance at the profession he hungered to follow. He had never had an opportunity to show what he could do with his pen, and it was not fair to have him give up this ambition merely because he had a wife and two children on his hands. Dr. Beardsley had three or four thousand dollars in the bank and he declared he had no particular need of the money and was ready to invest it in his son's career as a promising speculation in which he,

himself, had faith. He believed, he had said, he would
get a good return on his money! He had urged Alice
and Roy to come with their two children and make
their home with him for a while, live the simplest kind
of life,—living was extraordinarily cheap in Mill
Valley; Mama wouldn't believe how cheap after New
York!—and wait until Roy was on his feet with a well-
established market for his work.

"So we talked it over and said we would," concluded
Alice with her soft brown eyes shining confidently at
her husband, "only it's going to be awful hard to leave
you Mama, and Sis."

Mrs. Sturgis promptly grew tearful.

"No—no, dearie," she said between watery sniffles
and efforts to check herself, "I don't know *why* I'm
crying! It's quite right and proper for you and Roy
to accept his father's kind offer. There's no question
in my mind he'll be a great writer, and I think you're
very wise, and it will be lovely and healthy for the
children and I approve of the whole idea thoroughly,
only—only California seems so terribly far away!"
A burst of tears accompanied the last. Jeannette felt
irritated. Her mother would soon be reconciled to
Alice and the children being in California,—but in
her own heart there was already an ache she knew
would not leave it for many months.

§ 6

The end of May, when the dogwood was again powdering the new-leafed woods with its white featheri-
ness, when the Yacht Club had formally opened its
season, and Martin had towed his adored A-boat out

of winter storage, had pulled it with a row-boat the two-and-a-half miles to its summer moorings, Alice, Roy and the children departed, and Jeannette faced an empty home with what seemed to her an empty life.

It was inevitable she should reach out for distraction. During the spring, Doc French had married Mrs. Edith Prentiss, a rich widow, whom Jeannette had liked from their first meeting. The new Mrs. French was her senior by only a year or two, and much the same type: tall and dark with beautiful brows and skin and masses of glistening black hair. She had a great deal of poise, and dash, and dressed handsomely. At the opening of the season for the Cohasset Beach Yacht Club, when there was a dinner and dance, the Devlins were Doctor and Mrs. French's guests and had a particularly good time. Jeannette bought herself a new dress for the occasion. She would not have been able to go otherwise, she told Martin, as she had absolutely nothing to wear! All the pretty clothes that had formed her trousseau were completely gone now; she did not have a single decent evening frock left!

The affair led to the young Devlins being asked to a Sunday luncheon on board the new Commodore's sumptuous yacht and this had been another happy event. Martin had been in high feather, and had proven himself unusually amusing and entertaining. The Commodore's wife had singled him out for attention; the Commodore, himself, and Doc French had urged him to allow his name to be put up for membership in the Yacht Club.

It was a great temptation for both the young husband and wife, but it was out of the question for them

to belong to two yacht clubs, and Martin resolutely
refused to resign from the Family. No, he said, there
were too many "good scouts" in the little club, and
he wouldn't and couldn't "throw them down." Jeannette did not urge it, although it was hard to decline
the invitation to join the Cohasset Beach Club. Yet
she felt that membership in it was beyond their means
and would lead to other extravagances, while specially
was she afraid of the free drinking that went on there.
Martin had a mercurial temperament; one drink excited him; more made him noisy and silly; he was not
the type that could stand it. Better the Family Yacht
Club as the lesser of the two evils. She would have
been satisfied if he never entered either.

She voiced her complaint to her mother, with a good
deal of vexation:

"It makes me so mad! Martin *won't* economize,
won't help me save and insists upon being a member of
that cheap little one-horse organization with its cheap
common members, spending his time and money in a
place he knows I detest and where I never set my feet
that I don't regret it. And if he would only help me
get out of debt and would behave himself when there
was liquor around, we might be able to join the
Cohasset Beach and associate with nice, decent people
of our own class and enjoy some kind of social life.
It's unfair—rottenly unfair! I've been struggling all
winter taking care of my sister's babies, and of course
it's been expensive and we haven't been able to put by
a cent. I've done my level best to economize; I haven't
bought myself so much as a pair of shoes since last
year, . . . and look at me!"

She held out her foot and showed her mother where

the stitching along the sole had parted. Mrs. Sturgis shook her head distressfully, and made "tut-tutting" noises with her tongue.

"And what does he expect me to do?" Jeannette went on, her voice rising as her sense of injustice grew upon her. "Here's Doc French and his wife, Edith,— she's really a stunning girl, Mama, and I like her so much!—anxious to be nice to me, wanting me to go with them to the smart Yacht Club all the time, asking me to their house for dinner and cards, or to go motoring with them in their beautiful new car, and Commodore and Mrs. Adams inviting me to luncheon on *The Sea Gull,* and I haven't a decent stitch to my back! If I complain to Martin, he says I'm 'crabbing' or tells me to get what I need and charge it! And that's just madness, Mama,—you know that. He denies himself nothing and expects me to do all the self-sacrificing. I declare I'm sorely tempted sometimes to take him at his word, to go ahead just as I like, get whatever I need and let him meet the bills as best he can. That's what most wives would do! I've never known such humiliation since I went to that Armenian dance with Dikron Najarian. In all the time I was supporting myself, I was never so shabbily dressed as I am right this minute! It does seem to me that Martin could manage better. I know *I* did when I was earning my own money and financing my own problems. Martin makes just about what you and I used to have when we were living together, and you know perfectly well, Mama, we had money to *throw away* then. Why we used to go to the theatre and everything! I haven't been inside a theatre in—in—well, since last September and that's nearly a year! *I* don't know what he

does with his money! He swears he doesn't gamble
any more, but he's always broke and I have the hardest
time getting my sixty-two fifty out of him on the first
and the fifteenth. He tried to borrow some of it back
from me last month! I tell you, he didn't get it! He
never takes me into his confidence about money matters and he never comes and gives what's coming to
me out of his pay envelope of his own accord! I
always have to *ask* him for it! Think of it, Mama,
having to *ask* him to give me what's my right! I never
had to go to Mr. Corey and *ask* him for my salary on
Saturday mornings, and I work ten thousand times
harder for Martin Devlin than I ever did for Mr.
Corey! . . . I was no shrinking violet when Martin
married me! I was a self-supporting, self-respecting
business woman and when we married we made a
bargain, and I intend he shall live up to it. I don't
propose he's going to welch on me merely because I'm
a woman. He's got to give me just as much consideration as he would a man with whom he's made a
contract. Our marriage was an honorable agreement
with certain specified provisions, and if he doesn't live
up to them, neither shall I!''

"Oh, Janny, Janny!" cried her mother in alarm;
"don't talk so reckless, dearie! What on earth do
you mean?"

"Walk out on him!" flashed Jeannette. "I'll go
back to my job and run my own life the way it suits
me!"

§ 7

Martin spent every Saturday afternoon at the Family Yacht Club, "tuning up" his boat. He loved to

tinker about her, adjusting this, tightening that; he
was never finished with her; there was always something still remaining to be done. He and Zeb Kline
sailed the *Albatross* together in the races; they constituted her crew.

As soon as Martin reached Cohasset Beach from the
city on the last day of the week, he hurried directly
from the station to the yacht club. He kept his outing
clothes,—they consisted of little more than a shirt, a
pair of duck pants and "sneakers,"—in a locker at the
club. By two o'clock he was squatting in the cockpit
of the teetering little boat, busy with wrench, knife,
or rag, thoroughly happy. If there was sufficient wind
later in the afternoon, he and Zeb might take a short
sail up the Sound, round the red buoy, and home
again, or over two legs of the course. The afternoon
was all too short; it was six,—seven, before a realization of the passing time came to him. He wanted a
quick swim then before re-dressing himself, and if
someone did not give him a lift, there was the long
hike homeward.

He would be sure to find one of three situations when
he opened the door of the bungalow upon reaching
home: Jeannette would be there, coldly unresponsive,
resentful of his tardiness; she would be dressing for
a dance at the Cohasset Beach Yacht Club in frivolous
mood, or she would have already departed to dine with
Doc and Edith French, having left word with Hilda
for him to follow if he cared to. He came to accept
these circumstances. He did not particularly like them
but he did not know how to go about changing them.
To dress and join his wife was generally too much
effort after his long afternoon on the water. He either

found his own amusements or else, thoroughly weary, went to bed.

At an early hour on Sunday he was usually astir and often left the house while Jeannette was still asleep, or else they breakfasted together about nine o'clock and made polite inquiries as to one another's plans for the day. Every Sunday afternoon during the summer there was a race and Martin would not have missed one for any consideration. As soon as he could leave the house, he was off to the club and Jeannette did not see him again until he came stumbling home late in the evening, sunburnt and thoroughly exhausted.

One Saturday night it was nearly eight o'clock when the flickering acetylene lamps of Steve Teschemacher's big brass-fitted motor car swept into the circular driveway before the Devlins' home, and Martin got out, called "Good-night and many thanks!" and opened the door of his house. Dishevelled, his hair blown, his shirt open at the throat, carrying his cravat and collar, he walked in upon a dinner party his wife was giving. The four people at his table were all in immaculate evening dress. He recognized Doc French and Edith, but the remaining person in the quartette was a man he had never seen before.

"Mr. Kenyon, my dear," said Jeannette, introducing him. "Our little party was quite impromptu. I didn't know how to get you. I telephoned the club twice but Wilbur said you were out on the water."

Doc French welcomed him, clapping him on the back.

"Get a move on, Mart," he said, jovially, "your cocktail's getting cold."

Martin hurried. The blankness passed that had

come to him as, unprepared, he arrived upon the scene. His good-nature asserted itself; he was always ready for a good time. In fifteen minutes he was entertaining his wife's guests with an Irish story, told with inimitable brogue, and had them all roaring with laughter.

Kenyon he did not fancy. The man was too perfectly dressed, his white silk vest had a double row of gold buttons and fitted his slim waist too snugly; the movements of his hands were too graceful, too studied; his heavily lashed eyes squinted shut when he laughed, and the eyes, themselves, were glittering and glassy.

Martin went with the party to the Cohasset Beach Yacht Club for the dance to which they were bound. Since he had declined to become a member he felt he ought not to go at all to the club, but Doc French on this particular night would not listen to him, and carried him off with the others. There were the usual drinks, the usual gay crowd, the usual music and the usual dance; Martin, pleasantly exhilarated, had his usual good time. He saw his wife here and there upon the dancing floor during the evening, and thought her unusually vivacious and pretty, but it was not until three or four days later that a casual happening brought back to him a disquieting recollection that each time he had caught a glimpse of her that night, her partner had been Kenyon.

The incident that stirred this memory was the chance discovery of two cigarette stubs in a little glass ash tray on the mantel above the fireplace. Jeannette did not smoke. She explained readily that Gerald Kenyon had been to tea the previous afternoon. But Martin was not satisfied. Kenyon was a type of rich man's son,—idler and trifler,—whom Martin thought he recognized; Jeannette had said nothing about having had him to tea and the circumstance was too unusual for her to have forgotten to mention it; now he recalled the matter of the dance.

One of their old angry quarrels followed. It left both shaken and repentant, and in the reconciliation that followed, much of their early warm love and confidence in one another returned. Many differences were settled, many concessions and promises were made, and better harmony existed between them thereafter than they had known for a long time.

§ 8

It was then that Jeannette seriously considered having a baby. Martin was anxious for a child, and she knew how happy one would make him, how grateful and tender he was sure to be to her. She dreaded the ordeal more than most women; she was fearful of the agony that awaited her at the end of the long, dreary, helpless nine months; Alice's hard labor, and the following weakness from complications that had kept her practically bedridden for half-a-year, had made a grave impression on Jeannette's mind. She shuddered at the idea of being torn, at being manhandled by doctors, at being pulled and mauled and treated like an animal. It represented degradation to her, but she was prepared to go through with it. She wanted a child; she wanted one as much as Martin did; she wanted more than one. Her husband had accused her once of not loving children, but after the devotion she had lavished upon Etta and Ralph during the long months of the past winter, she felt she had convinced him that such a reproach was wholly unjustified. Far

more than the agony of childbirth, Jeannette appre-
hended the fetters that maternity would forge about
her feet. Once a mother she knew her liberty was over.
She would be bound then by the infant at her breast, by
ties of duty and maternal instinct, and above all by
love. She hated the thought of restriction; she hated
the thought of giving up her independence; she rebelled at inhibitions which would prevent her from
going her own way, living her own life, being her own
mistress.

Once again the question of money obtruded itself.
What did the years ahead hold in store for her as
Martin's wife? How would she fare at her husband's
hands when she was thirty, forty, fifty? The infatua-
tion of the bride for the man she had married, was
gone now; she saw him in a cold, critical light. She
loved him; she loved him truly and honestly; she loved
him more than she had ever thought to love any man.
Never was she so happy as when they two were alone
together and in sympathy. She liked often to recall
the happy day they had spent with Alice and Roy on
the sand reefs off Freeport. Martin had been so sweet,
and splendid and dear that day! No woman could love
a man more than she did, then; he had been everything
that stirred her admiration. But that was a year ago
and he wasn't the same; he and she had drifted apart.
Perhaps it was as much her fault as his; perhaps their
grievances against one another were no more than
those of any average couple. She realized that both
were strong-willed and opinionated; it was inevitable
that they should sometimes clash. But if Martin dif-
fered with her, he could pursue his own way independent of his wife, while she must wait upon his

pleasure. She did not—could not trust Martin with the old confidence he had once inspired. Perhaps that was the experience of all wives. Most women put up with it, *had* to put up with it, made the best of conditions, lay with what equanimity they could in the bed they had chosen in the first flush of love. But with her,—and always with this thought ever since she had been a wife, Jeannette had breathed a prayer of gratitude,—there was a way out! The girls that had married blindly out of their father's and mother's house had no alternative if their marriages proved unsatisfactory but to endure them or seek divorce. But she and all other women who had achieved a livelihood of their own in the world of business, who had won for themselves an economic value that could be measured in dollars and cents, could go back to work! They did not have to appeal to the law, the disreputable divorce courts, to free them from an intolerable alliance, or compel a reluctant man to support them with alimony gouged from his unwilling pocketbook!

Ever since she had become Martin's bride, Jeannette realized she had hugged this thought to herself and always found consolation in it. It had even been in her mind when she considered marriage; she had said to herself in those uncertain days, that if the experiment did not prove satisfactory, there was a stenographer's job waiting for her somewhere in the world. Now this knowledge that she could be independent again if she chose had a vital bearing on the question of her having a child. Once a mother, the door of escape from a situation which might some day become intolerable would be forever closed. She could not leave a baby as she could leave a husband.

Should she risk it? Should she take the plunge, leave the safe return to shore behind her and strike out into unknown waters, placing faith in her husband's devotion and his ability to take care of her? Ah, if she could only be sure! If she could only be convinced of Martin's dependability! She did not care a snap of her finger for Gerald Kenyon, Edith French or the Cohasset Beach Yacht Club or anything! All she wanted was that Martin should be good to her, should protect and provide for her with as much thought and care as she had given herself when she had been a wage-earner and her own mistress! If Martin would stand back of her, she would welcome a baby, she would bear him half-a-dozen,—all that her strength was equal to! She would banish her fear of the ordeal!

She told him so passionately. She showed him the reasonableness and righteousness of her stand, and he admitted the truth of what she said. He promised to do anything she wanted.

"You're dead right, Jan," he said with a gravity that went straight to her heart, "I see your point. I'll do the best I can. And golly! won't it be great when there's a kid in the family,—you know,—a kid that's our own? Why, you were never so happy or so pretty, and you never were so good to me and I never loved you more than when Etta and Ralph were toddling round here."

But she would agree to nothing until he had demonstrated to her that he had changed and was as much in earnest about the matter as she proposed to be.

"Mart, you've got to show me; you've got to convince me you've turned over a new leaf. I want to

be satisfied that I am always going to be glad I'm your
wife before I anchor myself to you for the rest of my
life. Now we're in debt. While I've been out of
sympathy with you, I've done some charging in town,
—new clothes I had to have in order to go about with
Edith French. If we have a baby it's going to cost
money, and we've *got* to be out of debt first,—don't
you think so? You can reëstablish my faith in you by
showing me now how you can help me save. If we cut
down and put our minds to it, we can save a thousand
dollars by the first of the year. Now I'll let Hilda go
and do my own work, if you'll resign from the Family
Yacht Club!"

It was a challenge and Martin's startled eyes found
hers.

"And sell my A-boat?" he asked blankly.

"And sell your A-boat," Jeannette repeated firmly.

"Well-l, my God,—that's kind of tough," he said
slowly. "But all right,—if you say so, I'll get out,
I'll sell it and quit."

"Do you really mean it, Mart?"

"Yes, I'll—I'll resign. . . . Only, Jan, can't I finish
the season? Zeb and I've got a swell chance for the
cup and all the A-boats have been invited over to
Larchmont for their annual regatta, and Zeb knows
that course, and we're all going to be towed over the
day before. . . ."

He was like a little boy pleading for a toy. She
could not find it in her heart to refuse him.

"Very well," she conceded slowly, "only as soon as
the season's over you'll positively resign?"

"Sure. I'll tell the fellows to-morrow that it's my
last year, and I'll quit after the final race."

§ 9

June, July and August passed, Labor Day came and
went, the yachting season closed with gala festivities,
special boat races, a big dance at each of the clubs,
and one day Martin announced that Zeb had paid him
sixty dollars for the *Albatross,* and that he had sent
in his letter of resignation to the board of directors.
It was then that Jeannette told Hilda she would be
obliged to let her go. She had grown fond of the girl
and was sorry to lose her, but in the face of this evidence of her husband's good faith, she felt she must
begin to carry out her part of their bargain.

Apart from this, there were other considerations
which made her welcome this new régime of curtail-
ment and self-denial. She was not satisfied with the
recent order of her life; her conscience troubled her;
there had been certain evenings during the past summer, memories of which were not altogether pleasant.

Hardly a week had gone by without Doc and Edith
French inviting her to go with them to a dance at the
Cohasset Beach Yacht Club or on a jaunt to some road-
house on Long Island, and Gerald Kenyon invariably
had been along. He had made love to her, flattering
love to her, and she had been diverted. She liked him;
he danced well, he was rich and a prodigal host, he
was agreeably attentive. She would have early sent
him to the right-about had it not been he proved a
convenient escort. Martin was rarely on hand to
accompany her; Gerald was eager to go with her anywhere she wished. She suffered his attentions, reminding herself that it was only for a few weeks,—just
until the end of the summer,—and it was her last fling

at gaiety. She would rid herself of him by September
and prepare her household and her life for the time of
retrenchment. Nothing of serious significance had
happened on any of these merry evenings; Martin
could not have found fault with her; Gerald had never
so much as kissed her cheek, but the atmosphere that
had prevailed was disturbing to Jeannette. Gerald
often imbibed too freely, but he was never offensive.
He and the Frenches sometimes grew noisy and there
was a good deal of loose talk. A drink or two had a
marked effect on Edith, and Jeannette wondered sometimes at the things she said and did. Not that her
words and actions were in themselves particularly
shocking, but coming from a woman of her graciousness and refinement they sounded rough. Jeannette
was ready, now, to be quit of these intimates. Their
society was not healthy, and in her soul she was conscious she did not belong in it. Her innate sense of
rectitude took offense at such behavior.

Thus it was that she turned to the period of self-
denial with willingness, even zeal. She threw herself
whole-heartedly into the program of her new existence.
She wanted to clean her soul as well as her life.

She was happy in the changed order of her days;
she liked doing her own work since it meant penance
for her as well as saving; she liked to think she was
preparing herself for her child. She figured out
how long it would take them to be out of debt: less
than a year if they saved only fifty dollars a month.

"Now, Martin," she reminded her husband, "I'm
not going through with this unless you stand back
of me. You've got to save penny for penny with me,
and you've got to show me you're deadly in earnest."

She said this because he did not seem as enthusiastic,
now, as he had been when the plan was first discussed.
The eagerness was missing, and he was rather sour
about it. She knew he grieved over the sale of his
boat, and it was bitter hard for him to give up his club.
But this time she was determined. She had renounced
her frivolous, expensive friends; he must renounce
his; she proposed to get along without the luxury of a
servant, he must deny himself, too.

"Well, damn it!" he growled at her implied reproach, "ain't I doing everything you want? The
boat's gone, and I've sent my letter in to the club!
What more do you want me to do?"

"Martin! that's no way to speak to your wife!
You're not doing it for *me!*"

She sighed in discouragement. He had a long way
to go.

His efforts to divert himself about the house on
Saturday afternoons and Sundays were pathetic. He
started vigorously to spade up a bit of ground which
he declared would make an admirable vegetable bed
in the spring. The spading lasted half a day and all
winter Jeannette saw the snow-covered shovel sticking
upright in the ground where he had left it. He was
bored by inactivity. Books did not interest him; he
scorned the solitaire she suggested and in which she
herself could find amusement; likewise he grew impatient at walks in the woods now full of autumn tints.
Jeannette tried her best to entertain him. Several
times she asked the Drigos over for auction bridge
but Mrs. Drigo and her husband quarrelled so much
when the cards ran against them, that Martin declared
he did not care to play with them. Jeannette tried

"Rum" but that, too, bored him; there was no pleasure in the game, he told her, without stakes and one couldn't gamble with one's wife. At the end of her resources, she shrugged her shoulders and let him seek out his own amusements as best he could. His attitude nettled her. He ought to face the new life, she felt, with the same fortitude, conscientiousness and willingness that she displayed. She told him so with a good deal of rancor one day: he was acting like a spoiled boy; he wasn't being a good sport about it. He only glowered at her in reply and stalked out of the house.

She had her own suspicions where he went, but she did not reproach him. In her heart she was sorry for him; his empty evenings and his week-ends hung heavy on his hands. She hoped he would get used to the idea and by and by be moved to follow her example.

But as the weeks and then the months began to go by, and she saw that it was only she who was making the sacrifices,—cleaning, cooking, washing dishes, denying herself clothes and even trips to the city to see her mother,—a dull anger kindled within her. This burst into flame when she learned by chance that Martin was still a member of the Yacht Club. 'Stel Teschemacher telephoned her one day to remind her to be sure and come to a bridge tournament the ladies of the club had arranged for the following Wednesday afternoon. Jeannette explained with some relish that she feared she was not eligible to participate since her husband was no longer a member of the club, but 'Stel Teschemacher assured her that such was not the case.

"Oh, no, you're mistaken, Mrs. Devlin. He's still a member and a very valued one. The Directors refused absolutely to accept your husband's resignation; they just positively made him reconsider it. . . . Why, we couldn't get along without Mr. Devlin! He's just the life of the club!''

Jeannette said nothing to Martin. She was bitter, feeling he had tricked her, was not playing fair. She decided she would go to New York and pour out her grievance in a stormy recital to her mother. It would relieve her mind. On the train she met Edith French and when the city was reached, her friend triumphantly carried her off to lunch at the Waldorf.

§ 10

Not very long after this, she learned that Martin had been playing poker, and had lost. He had had a bad streak of luck and was obliged to confess to her he did not have enough money to pay the rent without making a levy upon her share of his salary; she must count on only forty dollars when his next pay-day fell due.

At that her resentment burst forth. She had denied herself consistently since the first of September. With her own hands she had made the little Christmas presents she had sent Alice and the children, and even what she had given her mother, in order to save a few dollars, and here was Martin gambling away at the card table money that was hers!

"You're no more fit to be a father than a husband," she told him, her anger blazing. "You expect me to bear a child to a man like you! You're no better than a common thief!"

"Aw, cut that out, Jan," he answered, a dull crimson reddening his neck; "I'll admit I'm in wrong and

that you've got every right to be sore at me, but what's
the use in accusing me of being dishonest?"

"Dishonest?—dishonest?" she repeated furiously,
her hands clenched. "Half of every dollar you earn
belongs to me,—and don't you forget it! It's mine
by right of being your wife; it's mine by right of your
definite promise when I married you that we should
share and share alike. I made a financial sacrifice
then because I thought you and I were going to build
a house and rear a family. I used to earn a hundred
and forty dollars a month,—let me tell you,—and
every cent of it I spent as I chose and for what I chose.
I've never seen that much or anything like that much,
since I married you. Don't fool yourself you *give*
me a penny! You work in your office and I work here
and we both earn your salary. When you take my
money and gamble with it and lose it, you're doing
exactly the same as if you put your hand in Herbert
Gibbs's cash drawer and helped yourself! It's just
plain thievery!"

Martin was on his feet, his face congested.

"If you were a man, I'd knock your damned head
off."

"If I were a man," retorted his wife, "you'd be
afraid to!"

§ 11

It was in this mood of fury, with her grievance seeth-
ing within her, that she gladly agreed to accompany
Edith French on a day of shopping in the city. Edith
telephoned she had been invited by a certain famous
Fifth Avenue importer to witness, at a private showing, the opening of some sealed trunks just received

from Paris containing the new spring models. She wanted Jeannette to go with her, and the two women arranged to leave for town on an early morning train.

It was a cold, glittering winter's day when the crispness in the air set the blood tingling; snow was piled in the street and there was a general scraping of iron shovels on stone and cement. Edith and Jeannette feasted their eyes on the new styles as they eagerly discussed clothes and fashions. Edith, stimulated by her privileged glimpses, bought herself a new hat, which Jeannette declared to be the most beautiful thing she had ever seen in her life! Edith, it seemed to her companion, was free to purchase anything that took her fancy. If a garment or bauble attracted her, she got it without hesitation. Jeannette's heart was sick with longing. She watched her companion enviously. In a reckless moment, urged by her friend to whom she had confided at luncheon the tale of Martin's perfidy, and who had been gratifyingly sympathetic, she selected and charged a long woolly, loose tan coat that had a deep collar of skunk. The coat had been "on sale" and Edith had been so full of admiration for the way Jeannette looked in it, that she offered to buy it and give it to her as a present. To this Jeannette would not agree, but later, wrapped in its soft ampleness and with a glowing satisfaction that it was the most becoming garment she had ever owned, she did not press an objection when Edith proposed to telephone Gerald Kenyon and ask him to take them to tea. At five o'clock sitting against the crimson upholstered wall-seats of a glittering café, sipping her hot tea and nibbling her thin, buttered toast, listening to the music and the pleasant chatter of her companions, conscious of Gerald Kenyon's admiring eyes, Jeannette decided that it was the first happy moment she had known in months, and that if Martin chose to go his way, she had ample justification to go hers.

A madness descended upon her. She was near to tears most of the time but went dry-eyed upon her way, shutting her ears to the voice of conscience, refusing to allow her better nature to assert itself. On and on she stumbled into the forest of imprudence, allowing herself to give no heed to the gathering shadows, taking no thought of how she should ever find her way out of the gloom when the hour came for her to turn back,—for, of course, she must some time turn back!

Little by little she was beguiled into doing the things she had foresworn. She allowed Edith to persuade her into going almost daily with her to the city; she spent here and there the dollars she had so hardly saved; she began heedlessly to charge again: shoes, silk stockings, a smart French veil, gloves. The two friends fell into the habit of lunching or taking tea with Gerald Kenyon and sometimes going to a matinée with him, and the day came—as he had carefully planned it should come,—when Jeannette lunched with him alone. And over the small table at which they sat so intimately, still in the grip of the insanity that fogged her sense of righteousness and values, she confided to his eager, understanding ears the story of her husband's selfishness, and listened to his persuasive voice as he offered to help her out of her difficulties.

"Why, listen here, Jeannette," he said, bending toward her earnestly across the littered luncheon cloth, "I can make five thousand dollars for you over night. There's no sense in your troubling yourself about money matters. If you're in debt, I can show you a way that will pull you out of the hole and give you all the spending money you need! The old man, you know, is in steel. He's on the inside and there's nothing that goes on down in Wall Street that he doesn't know. He gave me a tip the other day: a sure-fire tip. Did you ever hear of Colusium Copper? Well, it's one of the subsidiary companies of the United States Steel Corporation, and its stock's going right up. The old man telephoned me to come down and see him, and he says to me: 'Gerald, put what you can lay your hands on on Colusium Copper; it's due to go to seventy-five and you want to get out about seventy-two or three.' It was fifty-eight then; it's about sixty-six to-day. Why, look here,—it went up a couple of points yesterday." He showed her the figures convincingly in a newspaper he drew from his pocket. "Now you just let me buy a few of those shares for you this afternoon before the market closes, and I'll hand you a check for five hundred to-morrow when you meet me for lunch. You don't have to put up the money; I can fix that for you; I'll just telephone my brokers you want to buy a few shares and that I'll O.K. the deal. It's a sure-fire proposition, Jeannette. You won't be risking a cent."

He was very earnest, very persuasive; his voice was gentle and so kindly. Five hundred dollars! thought the girl; it would wipe out all those little purchases here and there that she had had charged to her account about which Martin knew nothing!

Gerald was a *dear!* He was really a most generous, warm-hearted friend! It was wonderful of him to take such an interest in her trifling financial problems.

And the next day he showed her the check: $515.60 beautifully made out,—W. G. Guthrie & Company, Stock Brokers,—and it was drawn in her name. Her fingers trembled a little as she took the stiff bank paper in her hands.

"You see what I told you!" Gerald said with a triumphant smile. "Why, say, I could have made it five thousand just as easy if you had only said the word. The old man knows when anything like this is coming off in the Street. You have to laugh at the way the public runs in and lets the big guns fleece them. The big fellows stick up the bait and the poor fools rush after it and then chop—chop go the axes! . . . Any time, Jeannette, you want a bit of change just let me know and I can fix it for you. I'll just give the old man a ring and ask him what's good. . . . Now, for Heaven's sake don't get the idea that what I'm able to do for you on a little flier down in Wall Street is anything in the nature of a present or anythink like that. I'm just slipping you a little piece of inside information,—savvy, dearie?"

The endearment was unfortunate. It suddenly reminded Jeannette of her mother and she remembered she had not been to see her in weeks. Besides, it was the first time Gerald had addressed her with any such familiarity.

"I don't think I'd better take this," she said abruptly, tossing the folded check at him. She leaned back in her chair and drew her hands close to her breast.

He picked it up, tapped his fingers gently with it and began to argue. He argued long and eloquently: the money did not belong to him, it was hers, it represented the profits of her own little deal, he hadn't a right to a cent of it, it was impossible for him to touch it. But now no word from him could reach Jeannette. Fear was awake in her; she began to be very frightened; her panic grew. Suddenly she wanted to get up from the table and run into the street. She wanted to go to her mother; she wanted her mother badly. She felt she must get out of the restaurant, must get into the air, must get away from that table and this man at any price. She was like one who stands with her back to a precipice and, turning around, finds herself within a few inches of its edge, a chasm yawning at her feet. Fright made her giddy, her mouth was dry, her throat closed convulsively.

"If I can only stand it for ten minutes more," she said to herself, gripping tight her folded hands beneath the table, "and keep my head and not let him suspect! . . . I must go on and pretend. . . . Just ten minutes more."

She managed it badly. The experienced eye of her companion guessed all that was passing in her mind, and he cursed himself for having been too precipitous. The wary hare that he had been at such pains to coax to his side for so many months had taken flight at the first lift of his finger. He would have to begin all over again, and this time proceed more leisurely. For the present, he knew his cue was to withdraw.

He let her make her escape without remonstrance.

He asked if she would not allow him as a friend to mail her the check, and when with more vehemence than she meant to display, she refused, he tore the paper neatly into bits and let the fragments flutter from his finger-tips to the table.

"Well,—it's too bad," he said with a shrug that eloquently expressed his hurt. "Sorry. My only object was to try and help a bit."

He left her at the door of the restaurant with a graceful lift of his hat, saying he hoped to see her soon again. It was lost upon the girl. She hurried to a telephone booth in a drug store at hand and tried to reach the apartment on Ninety-second Street, but there was no answer. She thought of Martin but there was the uncomfortable confession she would have to make to him of her recent extravagances. Her recklessness, she realized, had robbed her of the righteousness of her quarrel with him; reproach he could meet with reproach.

She longed then for her sister,—her quiet, brown-eyed sister,—who had never judged her harshly in her life, but Alice was in far-away California. There was nobody, nobody in the world to whom she could turn for comfort, for sympathy and counsel, and then coming toward her with a pleased and smiling recognition in his face she saw Mr. Corey. She fluttered to him with almost a sob, and put both her hands in his; as he greeted her affectionately she wanted desperately to lay her head against his shoulder and give way to the fury of tears that fought now to find escape. In that moment, everyone seemed to have failed her,—mother, sister, husband,—but this stanch, loyal, rock-solid friend who believed in her, who knew only the best of her, whose faith in her was unbounded, who knew her as she really was.

He was talking but she listened not to his words but to her own heart that told her here was the haven for which she sought, here was the counsellor, the friend who would help her without cavil or reproach.

"Tell me about yourself," he was saying. "You promised you'd come in to see me once in awhile,—and that brother-in-law of yours? I thought we were going to find a job for him? What happened?"

Jeannette attempted to explain: Roy was trying to become an author, his first story was appearing as a serial and he and his wife and babies were in California. As she spoke of Alice, her voice suddenly grew husky and when she tried to clear her throat, the hot prick of tears sprang to her eyes, and she was obliged to stop and press her lips together. Mr. Corey's brows met sharply.

"What's the matter? You're in trouble?" He waited for her to speak but she could only shake her head helplessly and blink her swimming eyes.

"Come in here with me," he said in the old authoritative voice she still loved to obey. They turned from the crowded street where they were being jostled, into the drug store she had just quitted. It was crowded in here, too, with a swarm of elbowing people before the soda fountain. Corey guided the girl to the rear and they stopped by a deserted counter.

"Now what is it? Tell me about it," he said shortly. "Can I help you?"

She tried again to answer him but she was still

too shaken; at any effort to speak her tears threatened.

"Please," she managed, gulping.

He left her, went to the soda counter and returned with a glass of water. She drank it gratefully; the cold drink steadied her.

"I've just been acting foolishly," she said at last, dabbing her eyes with a corner of her handkerchief. "It's all my fault, I guess."

By degrees he pried her story from her: Martin had been treating her badly; he had been very unfair to her; their marriage was a hopeless failure; she couldn't make it a success alone; she had struggled and struggled and she didn't believe it was any use; he was fearfully extravagant and she had to do all the saving to keep them out of debt; she had done without a servant just so they could get a little ahead, but try as she would, they kept falling behind, and Martin didn't care. . . .

She had no intention of misrepresenting her case to Mr. Corey, but hungered for his sympathy, for his justification and approval, for his censure of her husband.

He heard her with furrowed brows, his keen eyes watching her face, and when she fell silent, he waited a long moment.

"Life's hard on young people," he said at length with a deep breath and a dubious shake of his head. "It's hard enough for them to get adjusted to one another without having to worry over money matters. I'm sorry your marriage has not turned out well. I feel particularly badly because I urged you into it. Devlin seemed a likely fellow to me."

They both considered the matter, studying the floor. Jeannette felt as she stood there her life was breaking to pieces.

"If you're in debt," said Mr. Corey at length, "and it's merely a question of money to tide you over present difficulties; you must let me lend you what you need."

"Oh, no, thank you," she said quickly.

"Oh, yes, but you must," he insisted.

With firmness she declined. She wasn't begging; she just had had one man try to give her money; she couldn't accept financial assistance from anyone. No, it was her own problem,—she could work it out herself without anyone's help.

"Very well, then," he suggested, "come back and work for me awhile. I've an abominable person as secretary now; I intended to fire her anyhow, and it will give me tremendous satisfaction to do so at once, for I never needed efficient help more desperately than now."

The words of polite thanks on Jeannette's lips died. She raised her eyes and fixed them on the face of the man before her, a light breaking slowly in them.

"You mean . . . ?" she began. Her face was like radiant dawn.

"I mean exactly what I say: come back for as long as you wish. Stay until you've earned what you need, and be free to go when you're ready: three months, six months, whenever you like. . . . It will be good to see you back even for a short time at your old desk."

Her intent gaze leaped from pupil to pupil of his smiling, earnest eyes. Her thoughts raced: there was Martin; he would say "No" of course; he wouldn't consider letting her do this; he'd be furious, but Martin would have to be won over, and if not . . . well then . . . there was her mother and her own old room waiting for her in the apartment on Ninety-second Street!

"Well?" said Mr. Corey amused, at the glowing color in her face.

"Mrs. Corey?" Jeannette faltered.

"She's in Germany and a very sick woman. It's rheumatism, you know, and she's been crippled a long time. I doubt anyhow if she'd care."

Somewhere up above like pigeons fluttering forth from heaven's dome came happiness winging down upon the girl.

"Oh, yes,—if you'll have me,—indeed I'll come back. . . . I'll be there Monday morning! . . . Oh, it will be *wonderful!*"

END OF BOOK II

BOOK III

BREAD

CHAPTER I

§ 1

THE cat was crying to get in. Jeannette, deep in
slumber, was irritated by persistent mewings. Every
once in awhile the outside screen door at the back of
the apartment shut with a small clap as the animal,
sinking its claws into the wire mesh, tried to pull it
open. The noise awoke Jeannette finally and she sat
up with a start.

It was morning. Gray light filled the room. She
peered at the alarm clock, blinking her eyes, and saw
there were still twenty minutes before she had to get
up. In the next room, the sound of a closing window
announced that Beatrice Alexander was already
astir.

"She's put Mitzi out," thought Jeannette, drawing the bed clothes over an exposed shoulder. "I
wish she'd remember to leave the door ajar."

Presently Beatrice's steps passed in the hall and
in another moment the annoyance ceased. Jeannette
dropped gratefully back to sleep. But it seemed she
had hardly lost consciousness when the whirring clock
bell aroused her again. Though still drowsy, she immediately got up; she never permitted herself to re-

main in bed after the moment arrived for rising; in-
dulgence of this kind was weakness of character, and
she despised weakness in herself or in others. As
she dressed, she heard Beatrice in the kitchen busy
with breakfast preparations. From the window a
glimpse of the street showed the sun's first rays striking obliquely through the haze of early morning.

The apartment in Waverly Place had now been her
home for seven years; she and Beatrice Alexander
had taken it together a month after her mother's
death, and life for the two women as time rolled on
had become undeviating in its routine. There was
small variation in their days.

It was Beatrice's business to prepare breakfast.
She rose at seven; Jeannette half-an-hour later. The
meal was always the same: fruit, boiled eggs, four
pieces of toast, and a substitute for coffee,—cubes of
a prepared vegetable material dissolved in hot water.
Beatrice set the table daintily, with a small Japanese
lunch cloth and a yellow bowl filled with bright red
apples in its center. Knives, forks and spoons were
nicely arranged and she never neglected to put tum-
blers of drinking water beside the triangularly folded,
fringed napkins, and finger-bowls at each place with
a bit of peel sliced from the bottoms of the grape-
fruits or oranges which began the breakfast. Beatrice
was a fastidious person, Jeannette often thought
gratefully; she liked "things nice."

While her friend was busy in kitchen and dining-
room, Jeannette dressed with her usual scrupulous
carefulness. She gave but meager attention to household affairs; these were Beatrice's province; it was
Beatrice who did the ordering, paid the bills and man-

aged the small establishment. Jeannette's companion was much like Alice and these duties came naturally to her. Besides, during the years Mrs. Sturgis and her daughter had lived together, it had been her mother who attended to such matters; Jeannette had grown accustomed to leaving household details to someone else. She took pains to explain this to Beatrice when they discussed the project of an apartment together and the latter had assured her it would be quite satisfactory. There had never been the slightest friction between the two women; Beatrice Alexander, with her soft, whispery voice and shy manner, was one of the sweetest-tempered persons in the world.

The years had dealt not unkindly with Jeannette. At forty-three, she was still a handsome woman,—no longer graceful and willowy, perhaps,—but erect, aggressive, substantial-looking. There was a solidarity about her now; her arms were big and round, her shoulders broad and plump, her bosom well-developed; she was thirty pounds heavier, and walked with a sturdy tread. There was gray in her hair, too, and a certain settled expression about her mouth that proclaimed middle age, but she was a fine looking woman with clear eyes and skin, an impressive carriage, and much that was commanding in poise. She dressed smartly and was always meticulously neat. Every morning she donned a fresh shirtwaist, crisply laundered. It was a matter of concern to her that this should set so snugly and correctly where it joined the plain dark tailored skirt that closely fitted her back, the effect should be of the skirt holding the blouse trimly in place. When she had completed her toilet, she was the embodiment of trigness and trimness, from her dark lusterless hair with its streaks of gray, which she now wore in a smooth sweep encircling her head like a bird's unruffled wing, to her tan-booted feet in sheer brown silk stockings. She always had taken a great deal of pains in the matter of attire, and her hats, shoes and garments were of the latest approved styles and the best materials, and came from the most exclusive shops in New York. She still observed the strictest simplicity in the matter of clothes when she dressed for the office.

She surveyed herself now in the mirror with approval, and as she noted her fine tall figure, the breadth of her shoulders, the round, neat, firm waist line, her calm, strong face,—shrewd, capable, resourceful,—she could understand the awe and respect with which the girls in her department regarded her. A hint of a smile touched her resolute lips as she thought that to them she must appear a super-woman, a sort of queen, the fount of all wisdom, justice and power. She liked the idea.

She flung back the covers to let her bed air during the day, and righted the flagrant disorder in her room with a few effective movements. As she opened her closet door or bureau drawers, the scrupulous neatness of their contents pleased her; the row of dresses in the closet suggested the orderliness of a company of soldiers; her shoes and slippers, each pair equipped punctiliously with boot-trees, ranged themselves on a shelf in effective array, her lingerie was carefully be-ribboned, folded in piles, and a scent of sachet arose from its lacy whiteness.

As she busied herself she came upon a muss of face powder that had been spilled upon the glass top of her bureau. A small sound of annoyance escaped her. She crossed the hall to the bathroom, returned with the moistened end of a soiled towel, resurrected from the laundry basket, and wiped up the offending litter vigorously.

About to quit the room she paused a moment with her hand on the door-knob for a final inspection, and turned back to make sure the lower bureau drawer was locked and that she had put the key in its hiding place under the rug; she raised the window an inch higher; a white thread on the floor attracted her eye and she picked it up with thumb and finger to deposit in the waste-basket before she joined Beatrice Alexander in the dining-room. A glance at her wrist watch assured her she was on time to the minute.

"Morning, Beat," she said saluting her companion. "What was the matter with Mitzi this morning?"

"I let her out early; she was clawing the carpet and growling. She wouldn't stop, so I just had to get up and put her out."

"Strange," commented Jeannette, eyeing the cat who blinked at her comfortably from beside an empty soup plate that had held her bread and milk. She began to talk baby talk to the pet:

"Mitzi-witzi! Yes, oo was,—oo went out to see a feller,—ess oo did . . ."

The two women sat down to the breakfast table together. Jeannette spread her *World* out before her; Beatrice propped the *Times* against a water pitcher. They picked at their fruit, raised egg spoons to their lips delicately, broke off bits of toast and inserted them in their mouths, sipped their coffee with little fingers extended. Silence reigned except for the small noises of cup and spoon, and the crackle of newspapers.

"I *do* think France ought to be more lenient with Germany," Beatrice remarked at length, adjusting her eyeglasses.

"I'd make her pay to the last mark she's got," asserted Jeannette. She folded back her newspaper carefully to another page.

"They had quite an accident in the subway," Beatrice observed.

"So I see. . . . Does seem to me the papers are awfully hard on the Interborough. I should think they ought to be permitted to charge an eight-cent fare; everything else is going up in price."

"Do you suppose that Hennessy woman will get off?" asked Beatrice after an interval.

"Well, I'd like to see her."

"Senator Knowles died, they think, from drinking whiskey that had wood alcohol in it."

"Served him right. I wish they all would."

§ 2

At twenty minutes past eight, Jeannette put on her hat carefully before the mirror, drew about her shoulders her tipped fox scarf, jerked her hands vigorously into stout tan gloves, and proceeded down the two flights of stairs to the street. As she descended she noted with customary pleasure the effect of the cream-painted woodwork in the halls, the width of the stairs, and the flood of light from the skylight above the stair-well which effectively illuminated the interior of the house. She and Beatrice had indeed been fortunate in

finding a home in such a pleasant, well-arranged building. It was the same apartment Miss Holland and
Mrs. O'Brien had occupied for so many years, until
the latter married again, and the former went to live
with her nephew, Jerry,—who was a Commander now,
had a wife and babies, and was stationed at the Brooklyn Navy Yard. The trend of Jeannette's thoughts
reminded her she had not been to see Miss Holland
for nearly two months; she resolved upon a visit in
the immediate future.

The street was filled with morning sunshine as Jeannette stepped out upon the stone flagging of the lower
hall, closed the inner door behind her, and felt in her
purse with gloved fingers for the key to the mail-box.

She found two letters for herself: one from Alice
saying that Etta was going to town on Saturday,
would love to lunch with Aunt Jeannette and be eternally grateful to her if she'd help her pick out the
dress; the other was a circular from Wanamaker's. It
was the latter rather than the former communication
that started the train of thought which occupied Jeannette's mind as she firmly stepped along the Avenue.
Her walk to the office took twenty-three minutes and
as she passed Fourteenth Street she noted by a clock
in front of a jeweller's store that she was a minute
ahead of time. The Wanamaker circular set forth the
advantages of a sale of women's suits, yet it was not
the attractive prices nor the smart models that occasioned Jeannette's thoughts. The envelope containing the circular was addressed to "Mrs. Martin Devlin." No one called her by that name any more.
When she went back to work as Mr. Corey's secretary,
she had been welcomed as "Miss Sturgis." "Miss

Sturgis'' had meant something in the affairs of the
Chandler B. Corey Company; no significance was attached to ''Mrs. Devlin.'' It seemed wiser to drop
her married name,—and after the break with Martin,
she had no desire to keep it.

Odd to have been a man's wife, to have belonged
to someone! It would be hard to think of herself as
a ''Mrs.'' again, to call herself ''Mrs. Martin Devlin.''
How many years ago had it been? Fifteen? Sixteen?
Something like that. Had there really ever been an
interval of four years in her life when she had been a
married woman? It seemed to her she had always
been part of the Chandler B. Corey Company,—or the
Corey Publishing Company as it now was called,—
part of it without a break since those days of long ago
when it had occupied three floors in a clumsy old office
building and had looked out, with Schirmer's Music
Store and Tiffany's, upon Union Square. What a
slim, tall, ignorant, ill-equipped young thing she had
been that day she went eagerly to meet Roy at the office and had watched Miss Reubens looking at photographs in the reception room! Jeannette smiled now
at the memory of herself. It strained the imagination
to believe that the present Miss Sturgis of the Mail
Order Department had been that awkward girl so long
ago.

The years—the years! The changes they had
wrought! Jeannette thought of her last painful interview with Martin and the shadow of a frown came
to her brow. She had gone over every detail of it a
million times. It had indeed been harrowing. Poor
Martin! He had pleaded so hard for her to come back
to him, he had offered to do anything she wanted, but

it was too late then; she couldn't make him see it. She reminded him again and again that he had talked just the same way when he begged her to marry him; she had doubtfully agreed then, had consented to give their union a trial, and it had turned out a failure,—a hopeless failure. No, she didn't blame him; she told him so over and over and admitted it was as much her fault as his; she was no more fitted to be a wife than he a husband; many people were constituted that way; they weren't suited to married life. She pointed out to him that unless a marriage was happy, it was a mistake, and neither he nor she had been happy as man and wife. Why, she had never been for one minute as happy married to Martin Devlin as she had been since she became her own mistress again! She loved her independence, she told him, too much to surrender it to any man. And he? Well, it had been clearly demonstrated that he liked the society of men and enjoyed outdoor sports more than he did being a husband. She tried hard not to reproach him, had even said she saw no reason why they, two, could not go on being friends, occasionally seeing one another, but at that point Martin got angry,—a sort of madness seemed to take hold of him and he had said all sorts of terrible things to her, even called her names,—unforgettable ones. It had ended in a dreadful scene, a terrible scene,—dreadful and terrible because in spite of the fury and bitterness that gripped them, they knew love still remained. Jeannette would never forget the storm of tears, the abject grief that had come to her at their parting. Love Martin though she did, she realized she loved her re-won independence more, and she would not,—*could* not return to him. Mr. Corey

had taken her in; she had promised to work for him
for a while at least, and it was utterly impossible for
her to tell him, after he had discharged his other secretary, that she was going back to her husband again. If
Martin had only given her a year or two she might
have been willing to be his wife once more, and she had
told him as much, but Martin refused to listen; he had
thrown down his challenge and forced her then and
there to choose between her job and himself. There was
nothing else for her to do; she had made her decision,
and Martin had gone his way. She had never regretted it, she said to herself now; she was far better
off to-day, far happier and more contented than she
ever would have been as Mrs. Martin Devlin. As his
wife she would have had ties and known sickness; she
and he would have quarrelled and there would have
been everlasting recriminations; she would have lost
her looks, and her clothes would have become shabby;
she would have grown familiar with poverty and have
had to fight for herself and family the way Alice did,—
poor, deserving, hardworking Alice, with her five children and unsuccessful husband! No doubt she, Jeannette, had missed much in life, but hers had been the
safe course, the prudent and sure one. She was now
in charge of the Mail Order Department of the Corey
Publishing Company, she was earning fifty dollars a
week, had five Liberty bonds all paid for, and was beholden to no one. . . . Of Martin she had not heard
for years. On a visit to Alice at Cohasset Beach,
she had one Sunday encountered 'Stel Teschemacher
and that lady had informed her that Zeb Kline, while
on a brief visit to Philadelphia, had seen Martin, and
Martin had an agency for a motor-car there and was

doing quite well. Jeannette would have liked to hear more, but she did not care to have 'Stel Teschemacher suspect she was interested.

It was 'Stel's husband who sold the Beardsleys their home at Cohasset Beach. The purchase had followed the death of Roy's father and the return of Roy and his family to New York. Dr. Beardsley had not lived long enough to make a writer's career for his son possible. His death had sadly broken up the small home in Mill Valley, and Roy and Alice had deemed it wiser to put the little money the clergyman left them into a home of their own than spend it in paying rent, butchers' and grocers' bills on the chance that Roy's pen might some day earn a livelihood sufficient for their needs. He had been only moderately successful as an author. His dog story had been published and he had placed several short stories but these had been few and far between and then little Frank had come to add his chubby countenance to the family circle and his parents decided a writer's career was too precarious for a man with a family. A job on a newspaper or magazine would insure a steady income. So with grief over their bereavement and disappointment in their hearts for the abandoned profession, Roy and his wife returned to New York and then in quick succession had come the finding of his position on the *Quart-z-Arts Review* which carried with it a moderate salary, the purchase of the house at Cohasset Beach, and in time the arrival of the small Jeannette, —'Nettie she was called to distinguish her from her aunt,—and Baby Roy, who was seven years old now and had recently asserted his manhood by resenting the identifying adjective by which he had been known

since birth. Jeannette paused a moment in her retro-
spective thoughts to calculate: Twenty-two years!
Yes,—Alice and Roy had been married twenty-two
years! They were an old married couple now.

§ 3

She realized abruptly she had reached the office.
Men and women, up and down the street, were con-
verging in their courses toward the doors of the publishing company. The great concrete block of eight
stories, crowded now to the limit of its capacity, with
the thundering presses on the lower floors, had often
seemed to her a monster that sucked in through its tiny
mouth each morning a small army of workers, mulled
them about all day between its ruminating jaws, fed on
their juices and spewed them forth at evening to go
their ways and gather new strength during the night
to feed its hungry maw again upon the morrow.

Though the picture was grim and repellent, she
cherished no hostility toward the institution that employed her. With the exception of the four-year in-
terlude of adventuring in matrimony, she had been an
employee of the self-same concern since she was
eighteen; for nearly twenty years her name had appeared upon its pay-roll; in November she could make
that very boast. More than any building in the world
this block of steel and concrete was bound up with her
destiny; she had spent most of the days of her life
within it; she had seen its beginnings, had watched it
spring into being, had had a hand in altering and
adapting it to the needs of business, had observed its
almost barren floors slowly fill year after year with

human activity until now the use of every square foot
of space was a matter of debate; she was one of the
half dozen still gleaning a livelihood within its walls
to-day who could speak of a time before its existence
had even been conceived.

Most of those early associates on Union Square
were gone now,—dead or following other lines of endeavor. Old Kipps still pottered about in the manufacturing department, Mr. Cavendish white-haired,
gray-moustached and rosy, still edited *Corey's Commentary;* Miss Travers, her merry face now lined
with many criss-crossed wrinkles, had succeeded Mr.
Olmstead and while not accorded the title of Auditor,
which he had enjoyed, was known as the Cashier. Then
there was Sidney Frank Allister, who, while he did
not date back to the Union Square days, was still to
be reckoned among those early associated with the
fortunes of the publishing company, and now very
much identified with them since he had become President and sat in the seat of Chandler B. Corey.

For Mr. Corey was dead. He had died the year
Jeannette lost her mother and had followed his son,
Willis, to the grave after a few months. Mrs. Corey
had left him a widower many years before. There remained only his daughter, Babs, in an Adirondack
sanitarium for the insane, to inherit his wealth and
fifty-one per cent of the stock of the business he had
created. He died a rich man and his will provided
that his wordly possessions should be divided equally
between his two children, their heirs and assigns, and
of these last there were none, for Willis had never married and Babs could not. Jeannette often used to
muse upon the futility of human ambition when she

thought of the man she had served so long as secretary. She knew it had been the great desire of his
life to found a publishing house that should become
identified with the growth of American literature and
pass on down the years in the hands of the Corey
family, father and son succeeding one another after
the fashion of some of the great English houses.

One day while sitting in his office intent upon affairs of business, his head dropped forward and
banged on the hard surface of his desk before him,
and he was dead. His heart had suddenly grown
tired of its work. Even before he was laid away at
Woodlawn, there had begun the mad scramble for the
control of stock which would elect his successor. Jeannette never learned how Mr. Allister succeeded in obtaining it, but Mr. Featherstone had shortly been
eliminated entirely from the affairs of the company
and it was whispered that Mr. Kipps had played a
double game. However that may have been, Sidney
Frank Allister was by far the best man to fill Corey's
place, in Jeannette's opinion. He was not so shrewd
nor so far-seeing, but he had certain literary
qualifications which fitted him for the position. Mr.
Featherstone, Jeannette had early come to regard as
a blustering blow-hard, while Mr. Kipps was hardly
grammatical in speech or in letters, and had grown
into a fussy old man. Francis Holm or Walt Chase
might have proven themselves even better material,
but three years prior to Mr. Corey's death, both these
young men had broken away from the old organization; Holm had launched forth into the publishing business for himself, and Walt Chase had gone to Sears,
Roebuck & Co. in Chicago at a salary, it was ru-

mored, of ten thousand a year, and Jeannette had succeeded him as head of the Mail Order Department.

Much as she had enjoyed being secretary to Mr.
Corey, she was forced to realize as the years rolled
by, that the position held no future for her. She would
always be the president's secretary as long as Mr.
Corey lived but against the congenial work and easy
rôle her ambition had protested. Recollections of
early resolutions she had made on entering the business world returned to disturb her complacency. She
remembered vowing then she would go to the very top
and some day become herself an executive instead of
a secretary. She saw no reason why she should not
follow in Walt Chase's footsteps and be worth ten
thousand a year, if not to the Corey Company then to
some other. She had great confidence in herself, felt
especially qualified to do mail order work, and was sure
she could increase sales and manage the department
better than Walt Chase. It was a pet idea of hers that
women, not men, bought books by mail, and she was
confident that attacks directed at women, written from
a feminine standpoint, would show results. When the
offer from Chicago came and Chase announced he was
going, she determined suddenly to seize the opportunity and asked Mr. Corey for Chase's place; she had
played secretary long enough, she told him,—she
wanted her chance at bigger work.

There had been a great deal of demurring and discussion before she was allowed to try her hand. Mr.
Kipps and Mr. Featherstone had vigorously opposed
the plan, arguing that while Miss Sturgis had proven
herself an incomparable secretary, there was no indication she would be equally successful in charge of

the Mail Order Department. Walt Chase had built up a steady sale for the company's publications, and had been doing many thousands of dollars' worth of business a year. Mr. Kipps and Mr. Featherstone shared the opinion that a woman was not competent to manage affairs involving so much money,—they were too large for the feminine mind to grasp. They contended, too, that she had had no experience in mail order affairs, and that a young man, named Owens, who had been Chase's assistant for over a year, was his logical successor, and had been led to expect the promotion; it was doubtful, they said, whether he and Mr. Sparks, and old Mr. Harris and the one or two other men who had been under Walt Chase would consent to remain if a woman was placed in charge of them; this particular branch of the business had become exceedingly profitable and it was pointed out to Mr. Corey that he was in great danger of demoralizing it by permitting a girl to assume its management.

Jeannette had stood firm and resolutely pressed her request in the face of opposition which she considered stupid and which angered her. Mr. Corey finally agreed to give her a trial although it was clear he had his misgivings. But during the nine years in which Jeannette had filled the coveted position, she had amply demonstrated to everyone's satisfaction her faith in herself to be warranted, and this in spite of the fact that Owens and Sparks had promptly resigned as predicted by Mr. Featherstone and Mr. Kipps, and for a time the work had been demoralized indeed.

Yet she triumphed, as she knew she would, and the ideas she had long cherished for conducting mail order campaigns had borne fruit. Last year she had the satisfaction of stating in her annual report that the business of her department had doubled in size since she had taken it in charge. It had been a long struggle fraught with interference and constant criticism of her methods. It had been particularly hard at first when Mr. Kipps supervised everything she did and vetoed some of her pet projects. He had hampered her in every way he could, not because he had any personal feeling against her but because she was a woman and he had no faith in a woman's judgment. That was the way he had always treated Miss Holland; but now since Miss Holland had resigned and gone to live with her nephew in Brooklyn, he was willing at any minute to wax eloquent in praise of her extraordinary ability: ah, yes,—yes, indeed,—Miss Holland was a remarkable woman,—fitted in every way for business,— brain like a man's,—wonderfully clear-sighted, excellent judgment; they didn't "make" many women like Miss Holland,—she was the exception, one in a million!

Jeannette had to contend against such prejudice for the first year or two, but eventually she overcame it. Mr. Corey helped her whenever possible. She strove to keep the affairs of her department to herself and when forced to seek higher authority, made a practice of going directly to the President who had been the first to be convinced of her ability. As time went on, Kipps and the other members of the firm inclined to question her gradually allowed her to go her way. It had taken nearly a decade to win their confidence but there was satisfaction in the thought that at last it was hers, the victory was complete. Of course old Mr. Kipps would always purse his lips and frown dubiously about anything she proposed for he would never be completely convinced of her ability until she followed in Miss Holland's footsteps, but Kipps was stooped and aged now and little attention was paid to what he said or did. The Board of Directors was satisfied with the generalship of Miss Sturgis whose monthly reports of sales and profits confirmed their confidence. When some other department reported a loss, or when business in general was poor, the Mail Order Department could be depended upon to show a consoling profit.

§ 4

One section of the sixth floor was Jeannette's domain. She had tried for years to have her department walled off by partitions but the best she had been able to obtain for herself and her girls was a line of screens and bookcases. She had twenty-four clerks under her now, although the number fluctuated, particularly during October when the fall campaign was in progress. Then her force often swelled to over a hundred and the extra help was quartered temporarily in neighboring vacant lofts and offices, rented for a few weeks. She then had her lieutenants to superintend the work, which for the most part consisted merely of folding and inserting circulars in envelopes, sealing and stamping.

Her department was well organized; the work had been so systematized that it now moved with perfect smoothness. Old Sam Harris,—who represented all that was left of Walt Chase's régime,—supervised the card catalogues; Miss Stenicke was in charge of the girls; the "inquiries" were checked and answered by

Mrs. M'Ardle, while orders were entered and forwarded to the stock room for filling by little Miss Lacy. Jeannette devoted herself to the preparation of copy for letters, circulars and advertisement. This was the most important part of the work, and she believed her time and brains could not be better employed. She kept huge scrap-books in which she pasted circulars and letters issued by other mail order houses and spent hours poring over them.

§ 5

Her desk stood on a low platform and from this vantage-point she could overlook her department as a school teacher surveys her schoolroom. She prided herself she could tell at a glance what any particular girl ought to be doing; if ever in doubt she promptly summoned Mrs. M'Ardle to her desk and inquired. All the girls respected and admired her; they knew her to be fair-dealing and straightforward, though swift in censure where merited. She liked to have them think of her in this way and cultivated the idea.

"You're conscientious and you try hard," she would say in admonishing some unfortunate bungler. "I want to be just to you. In conducting the affairs of this department, I want to be as lenient as I can. I strive to forget personalities and think only of my assistants,—or perhaps I had better say 'associates,' —as co-helpers in a big machine, each one functioning to the best of her ability at her particular piece of work. I've explained my ideas to Mr. Allister repeatedly. I want the girls in the Mail Order Department to be every one her own boss, to come and go as she pleases, and feel responsible—not to me but to the work. . . . I want to be a 'big sister' to every girl under me. I'm placed here to help, advise and direct, not to scold. But if you fail to perform properly the work assigned you, if you're clumsy and careless and haphazard in your methods, then it is my duty to call the fact to your attention. . . . I want to be fair to everyone; I have no favorites. . . ."

The lecture might continue at some length particularly if Miss Stenicke, Mrs. M'Ardle or little Miss Lacy was within earshot.

For a long time this Mail Order branch of the business of which she was the head had called forth Jeannette's great pride. She had felt it was all hers,—her work. But of late, she had been stirred less and less. After all what had been accomplished? For nearly ten years she had bent her energies to making this phase of the activities of the Corey Publishing Company aboundingly successful. There no longer remained any question as to whether or not she had achieved her purpose. A year or two ago a recalcitrant spirit among her girls had immediately aroused in her a determination to break it; the discovery of an error at once had challenged her to trace it to its source; the questioning of her authority or trespassing upon her prerogatives had stirred her upon the instant to battle. One of the keenest pleasures of her days had been to draft laws that should govern her girls and to see that these were enforced. She had begun to detect in herself within the last year or two an increasing indifference to all such things,—she did not care as she once had cared. She was no longer hampered or troubled by those "downstairs"; her assistants and her girls gave her small occasion for supervision; the work of the department ran on well-oiled wheels. With opposition eliminated, the task of organization perfected, the maximum volume of business attained, there remained nothing to fire her spirit or brain, to stimulate fresh effort. And she was distressed by a suspicion that more and more persistently obtruded itself upon her consciousness that perhaps she was getting old, that the indifference to what went on about her and to her work was merely a sign of approaching age!

She rebelled at the idea; she put it from her vigorously; she refused to entertain it. Why, she was only forty-three! She was in the heyday of her powers. Her judgment, her mind, her capacities were never so keen as now. She was equal to far more exacting, more difficult work. Disturbed by this fear, she decided to look about her for fresh fields of endeavor. There was no higher position in the Corey Publishing Company open to her; more important places were all filled by members of the firm, and it was not likely that any one of them would step aside and give her a chance at his work. No,—though proud of her long years of service and her record with the publishing company, —she decided that neither was of sufficient importance to keep her indefinitely on its pay-roll until she was ready to follow in Miss Holland's footsteps. She let it be known in mail order circles that she was looking for a job.

Of Walt Chase she continued to think enviously. She had heard he was now one of the big men in Sears Roebuck & Company, a fact that exasperated her, because she felt herself to be cleverer than he, more able in every respect. He was getting ten thousand—twelve thousand—fifteen thousand,—whatever it was,—a year and climbing the ladder of success rung after rung, while she was doing the work he had left behind him at the Corey Publishing Company in a far more efficient, economical, and profitable way and was being paid fifty dollars a week!

One day she learned of a vacancy in the American Suit & Cloak Company, where they were looking for someone familiar with mail order work. She wrote and applied for the position. A conference with the General Manager followed. It developed he was in search of a man,—a woman, it was feared, was not qualified to do the work,—but the Manager admitted he knew Miss Sturgis by reputation and would be glad to make a place for her in his organization if she was dissatisfied where she was,—and he could promise her,—well, he could pay her thirty-five dollars a week. Jeannette declined and eased her mind by writing a coldly worded letter of thanks and regret; the General Manager of the American Suit & Cloak Company must have a poor opinion of her sense of values, if he expected her to resign from a position where she was the head of a department and receiving fifty dollars a week to accept an underling's place at a smaller salary! But fifty dollars a week from the Corey Publishing Company was far below what she was worth, Jeannette considered. It infuriated her to think that while Mr. Allister and those "downstairs" were glib with their commendation of her work, there was never any talk of expressing this appreciation by a raise in salary.

§ 6

Her first business in the mornings upon reaching
her desk was to fasten a sheet of paper about each
of her wrists and pin another to the front of her shirtwaist as a protection against dirt. It was almost impossible to go through half a day and keep one's linen
clean without these shields. Dust from the street filtered in through the windows, that must be kept open
at the top for ventilation and occasionally little feathery balls of soot made their appearance. Contact with
office furniture always held the risk of a smudge. Jeannette had her desk and chair thoroughly wiped off by
one of her girls before she reached the office in the
morning and again when she went to lunch but in an
hour or two after these protective measures, she would
begin to feel grit under the tips of her fingers and
observe a fine gray layer on the surfaces of white
paper.

She usually arrived five or ten minutes before nine
o'clock at which hour the business of the day was supposed to begin. Never late herself, she had trained
her girls to be equally punctual. It was a matter of
pride with her that in the Mail Order Department
work began promptly on the stroke of the hour. There
was no formality about the way it commenced. Without sign or sound from Jeannette the girls set about
their various duties with simultaneous accord, the
noise of chatter and laughter died away, there was a
general scraping of chair legs on the cement floor, and
the buzz of typewriters, like the chirping of marsh
frogs, began slowly to gather volume.

First Jeannette turned her attention to her "Incom-

ing" basket, neatly stacked the clipped correspondence, memorandums and communications before her,
and, armed with a thick blue pencil, began their disposal, marking certain letters and papers a vigorous
"No" or "O.K.-J.S."—pinning a sheet of scratch pad
to others and scribbling thereon a brief direction or
query. Most of the pile before her disappeared into
her "Outgoing" basket, but in an upper corner of her
desk was a folder inscribed: "Mr. Allister," and into
this she would occasionally slip a letter or memorandum. Its contents would go to him by boy later in the
day; once in a while she carried some important matter to him herself but she troubled him as little as
possible. She tried to keep the affairs of her department to herself; the less she attracted the attention of
the Directors, the less they were likely to ask for reports or feel called upon to supervise or investigate
her work; she preferred to let the monthly statements
of sales speak for her.

By ten o'clock the "Incoming" basket would be
empty, and she could begin the preparation of copy for
an advertisement, a circular letter, or the arrangement
of a leaflet setting forth the features of a new set of
books. This was the work she loved best to do, knowing she was unusually good at it; there were daily evidences her copy "pulled," that the touches she gave
her advertisements were productive of sales. No one
"downstairs" appreciated how clever she was, though
there were the reports of sales to attest to her ability.

She often wished there was more of this particular
kind of ad-writing and circular-preparing to be done,
but the books of the Corey Publishing Company sold by
mail, year after year, varied little in type: These were

a standard dictionary, a Home Library of Living Literature, a set of handbooks for Garden and Kitchen, and then there were the dressmaking books issued in connection with the pattern department: "How to Sew," "How to Knit," "How to Embroider." In addition to the circularizing for these was that for subscriptions to the magazines, offered in conjunction with some particular premium.

When a special letter had to be prepared, Jeannette preferred to write it at home or come back to the office at night when she could be alone and undisturbed. There was continual interruption during the day; she rarely enjoyed five minutes of consecutive thought. One source of distraction and a great annoyance was having personally to initial every request for supplies, no matter how trifling. This was one of Mr. Kipps' schemes. He had made it a rule that heads of departments must O.K. all such requisitions. A paper of pins, a pot of paste, a pad of paper could not be issued by the stock clerk to any of her girls without Jeannette's initials being affixed to the request. All day long she was interrupted by: "C'n I have a pencil, Miss Sturgis?" "Please O.K. my slip for some paper, Miss Sturgis." " 'Xcuse me for interruptin' you, Miss Sturgis, but I need some pen points." Mr. Kipps' idea was to prevent waste, but Jeannette frequently realized with exasperation that her time was of a great deal more value to the company than pencils, pens or paper, and there was a far greater waste in interrupting a line of constructive thinking than in trying to conserve the supplies of the stock room.

The telephone at her desk was continually at her ear: the composing room wanted the cut for Job 648;

the engraver didn't have the "Ben Day" she had specified; Mr. Sanders, Mr. Kipps' assistant, wished to know if she could use a Five-and-a-quarter envelope just as well as a Number Six; she had requisitioned five thousand two-cent stamps and they had not been delivered; she needed a hundred thousand more "Dictionary" circulars, and would like Stamper & Bachellor to submit her some "m.f. laid, 24 by 36" in various tints; the stencil machine was out of order and she wanted to borrow one from the mailing department.

One thing followed another all day long.

"If we insert that return postal, we can't mail this attack under two-cent postage."

"Hello, Miss Sturgis,—say, *Events* can only give us a half page; will you prepare new copy for the smaller space? They're waiting to go to press."

"Miss Sturgis, we're running short on '*How to Knit.*'"

"Miss Sturgis, we'll have to get in some extra girls if you want those letters signed by hand."

"Miss Sturgis, do you want these mimeographed or printed?"

"Miss Sturgis, Mr. Allister'd like to see you."

"Miss Sturgis, c'n I have some pins?"

At a quarter past twelve she went to lunch. She made a point of going promptly. There was a time, some years back, when she had fallen into the habit of letting her lunch hour lapse over into the afternoon, allowing the demands upon her further and further to postpone it, and it had been two o'clock, sometimes three before she went out. As a result, indigestion and headaches commenced seriously to trouble her, and the doctor advised a regular hour for lunch. At

twelve-fifteen, therefore, she compelled herself to drop
whatever she had in hand and leave the office; one of
the girls was instructed to call her attention to the
time.

She always went to the Clover Tea Room for her
luncheon. This was a little basement restaurant operated by two elderly sisters. It was prettily appointed with yellow lights, yellow candles, yellow embroidered table doilies and yellow painted furniture.
Jeannette had her own special table daily reserved for
her. Lunch cost sixty-five cents and consisted generally of a small fruit cocktail, a chop, a little fish, or an
individual meat pie, with an accompanying dab of
vegetable, and a dessert.

She was accustomed to enter the Tea Room at
twelve-twenty almost to the minute: a tall, fine-figured,
handsome woman in her dark tailor-made, her modish
hat and fur scarf. She would proceed directly to her
table, exchanging a smile and a word of greeting with
the elder Miss Hanlon as she passed her desk. Un-
buttoning her gloves and drawing them from her
hands, she would study the handwritten menu:

Minnie would presently come for her order.

"Morning, Miss Sturgis; what's it to-day? Stew
looks good."

"Good morning, Minnie. Well, if you say so, I'll
have the stew. And don't forget to bring lemon with
my tea."

The Tea Room would be but partially filled when
Jeannette entered, but as she waited for her lunch
other people began to arrive. Ah, here was Miss
Hogan of Lyman & Howell, and here was that pretty
Miss Thompson of Altman's; Mr. Crothers of the

Stationers' Supply was late,—no, here he was; Mrs.
Diggs had that funny looking hat on again; this person was a stranger and that couple, busily talking,
were quite evidently shoppers. A gray-haired woman
in the corner appeared at the Tea Room several times
of late; Jeannette decided she must ask Miss Hanlon
who she was, and find out where she was employed.

At quarter to one or perhaps ten minutes before the
hour, Jeannette would pour a little drinking water
from her tumbler over her finger-tips into her empty
dessert saucer, moisten her lips, wipe them on the little
yellow napkin, and draw on her gloves nicely. She
always left ten cents for Minnie and paid her check at
Miss Hanlon's desk on her way out. Usually she had
the better part of half-an-hour before it was time to
return to the office. Between the Tea Room and the
corner of the Avenue, she almost invariably encountered Miss Travers, the Cashier, who likewise patronized the little restaurant. They would nod and smile
at one another as they passed but neither had time to
pause for words. Jeannette frequently had a small
errand to perform: gloves to get at the cleaners', her
shoes polished, a bit of shopping, a book to exchange
at the library. When there was nothing specially
pressing, she would pay a visit to a bustling Fifth
Avenue store, where she would make her way through
crowds of jostling women, and inspect counters, ex-
amining, even pricing the merchandise that attracted
her. In the long years she had been an office-worker,
she had spent many a luncheon hour in this fashion;
she never grew tried of such visits, nor of acquainting
herself with the new fads, novelties and latest styles
in feminine apparel.

Just one hour after she had left it, she would be
back at her desk, readjusting her paper cuffs, and re-
pinning the sheet at her breast. At once the demands
upon her would recommence:

"Miss Sturgis, while you were out, engravers
'phoned and said they can't find that cut."

"Miss Sturgis, Mr. Kipps wants to know how many
copies of *Garden and Kitchen* we sold up to November first last."

"Miss Sturgis, Miss Hilliker went home sick."

"Miss Sturgis, will you sign my requisition for a box
of clips?"

"Miss Sturgis, c'n I have a pencil?"

Thus it would continue for the rest of the day. The
afternoon light would shine bleak and garish through
the fireproofed windows with their meshed wire embedded in the glass, the dust would settle on desks and
papers, the thundering presses on the lower floors
would send fine vibrations through the building,
typewriters would maintain a clicking droning,
a buzz of small noises would harass the ear, there
would be a continual flash of paper and of white hands
at the folders' tables, while pervading everything
would be the thick sweet smell of ink emanating from
stacks of new print matter fresh from the press-room.

Five o'clock always surprised Jeannette. Her work
absorbed her; if she threw a hasty glance at the neat
small mahogany-cased clock on her desk, it was to
ascertain if there was time enough to complete one
more task that day, or to begin preparations for a
new one. The ringing gong that sounded "quitting
time" invariably startled her into a blank sensation
of discouragement. She would wish at that moment

for another hour to finish the matter in hand,—just
a little longer and she would have it out of the way!
The commotion among the girls which instantly followed the gong never failed to annoy her. In less
than five minutes,—save for Mrs. M'Ardle, little Miss
Lacy, Miss Steinicke, and old man Harris,—her department would be empty. These assistants remained
a little later to clean up the day's work and prepare
for the morrow's. In another quarter of an hour,
they too would begin to bang desk drawers shut, and
prepare to depart. Presently Jeannette would be
alone. She usually was the last to leave. It was then
that a feeling of fatigue, a weariness of soul, a distaste of life would begin to assert themselves. Reaction from the racing events of morning and afternoon
would close down upon her and of a sudden her work,
her days, her whole life, would seem drab, colorless,
profitless. What did it matter if a few more copies of
the Dictionary were sold, what difference did it make
if the new attack was a success, whether or not little
Miss Lacy was inclined to be careless, or that Mr.
Kipps had attempted to interfere with her again? Of
what importance was the Mail Order Department of
the Corey Publishing Company anyway? Or the concern itself? Mr. Corey had worked hard all his life
and then had died and left it behind him! What good
had it ever done him? This racketing building represented such trivial enterprise after all! It seemed
ridiculously trifling. . . . She would get to her feet
with a great sigh of apathy, disgust for her work and
life rising strong within her. Frequently with a sweep
of an impatient hand she would scoop the papers be-

fore her into the top drawer of her desk, or thrust them back into her "Incoming" basket. They could wait until the morrow; to-night they bored her; she wanted to get away; to shut them out of her mind! . . . Ah, it was all so petty! No one would thank her for working after hours! She was sick to death of it!

She would adjust her hat with her usual care before the mirror in the dressing-room, tucking her hair neatly beneath its brim, don fur and gloves, and proceed to the elevator.

On the way out she might encounter Mr. Kipps or Mr. Allister.

"Good-evening, Miss Sturgis."

"Good-evening, Mr. Allister."

The street would be blue with gathering dusk, and crowded with dark hurrying figures homeward bound. Lights here and there streamed from office windows, dabs of brilliant yellow in the purple scene. Motor trucks and delivery wagons backed to the curb were being piled with crates and packages by hustling, calling men and boys. The tide of workers let loose from desk and counter set strongly in conflicting currents. Long lines of traffic filled the congested thoroughfare and waited for the signal to move forward. A dull clamor, a pulsing bass note, a sound of feet, voices, motor horns, a banging and bawling, a thumping and hubbub, clatter and rumble, throbbed persistently. There was a sense of hurry and dispatch in the air. No one had any time to waste; it was the hour of home-going, the end of the day's toil, the feeding time of the great army of workers.

§ 7

Dinner had still to be prepared by the time Jeannette reached the apartment in Waverly Place. Beatrice, who was employed by a manufacturer of soaps and toilet waters a few blocks from where she lived, was usually in the kitchen when her friend arrived. Beatrice did the marketing at her lunch hour, or in going to and from her office. Mrs. Welch, who lived downstairs, obligingly took in packages and kept an eye on Mitzi, well qualified, however, to look after herself. The cat mysteriously disappeared during the day to present herself bright-eyed, hungry and affectionate the instant Jeannette's or Beatrice's steps sounded in the hall.

The dinners the two working women shared were usually simple. Very seldom they ate meat. Eggs in any form were popular and the evening meal,—nine times out of ten,—began with a canned soup served in cups. From the delicatessen on Sixth Avenue a variety of canned food was obtainable. Jeannette and Beatrice were particularly fond of canned chicken *á la King,* which had merely to be heated, seasoned and poured over toast. Sometimes they made their dinner of soup, a can of asparagus tips, tea and crullers. The asparagus tips made frequent appearances. Beatrice kept in the ice-box a little jar of mayonnaise, which she usually whipped together on Sundays. Macaroni salad was another prime favorite, and there were also tuna fish, creamed or made into a salad, and fish balls whenever they could be obtained.

Once in a while on a Sunday or on one of those rare occasions when company was expected Beatrice

struggled with meat and potatoes for a three-course
meal, but in these ventures she received small encouragement from Jeannette. The latter was forever pro-
claiming she ''despised'' to cook and was therefore
averse to betraying any interest in plans for an elaborate meal; the odor of meat cooking in the house
smelled the place up horribly, she declared.

Punctiliously, however, she performed her share of
the work in cleaning up after dinner. She dried the
dishes, gathered the small luncheon cloth by its four
corners and gave it a quick shake out of a rear window,
put away the silverware, and restored to the sideboard
drawer the two fringed napkins in their red lacquer
rings, rearranged the table and pushed back the chairs
against the wall. Beatrice meanwhile would be busy
fussing in the kitchen, washing the one or two pans
she had used, the tea-pot and few dishes, feeding Mitzi
the remnants of the can of soup and perhaps a bit of
fish or a little fried liver. By half past seven dinner
would be a thing of the past and the little home in
order again.

Jeannette made it a practice to spend the ensuing
hour or two in the seclusion of her own room. In many
ways, this was the happiest time of the day for her.
She was alone finally and could count upon being unhurried and undisturbed. First she made her bed with
care: the undersheet must be stretched tight and tucked
well under the mattress, there must be no wrinkles
and the covers must be folded in loosely at the bottom;
she affected a baby pillow which twice a week must be
slipped into a fresh embroidered case. Five minutes
followed with the carpet sweeper; the room was tidied,
—everything put in its right place. When all was

done, she would feel free to turn her attention to herself. If there was mending, she next disposed of it; distasteful though sewing had always been to her, she had grown dexterous with her needle. She spent fifteen minutes manicuring her nails, and an equal time brushing her hair and rubbing a tonic into her scalp. The gray was very thick over the right temple and Beatrice had urged her to have it "touched up" but Jeannette rather liked it as it was; she considered it added a distinguished touch. There were other intimate offices she performed at this hour with great thoroughness, her vigorousness increasing as time carried her into middle age. Twice a week, sometimes oftener, she took a hot bath about nine o'clock. Great preparations were attached to this performance, and she indulged herself in perfumed bath salts, perfumed soap, and delicately scented powder. When Mehitable brought home the "wash" on Friday nights, Jeannette devoted half-an-hour to running pink satin ribbons through her chemises and brassières. The ribbons she carefully steamed herself once a month and pressed with the electric iron in the kitchen. But those nights on which she did not bathe, when her room was in order and her toilette completed, she would don a kimona, and, with hair hanging in pig-tails down her back, her feet in Japanese wicker sandals, shuffle her way to the front room, with a book under her arm, to join Beatrice for perhaps an hour's chat or reading before finally retiring. Neither she nor her companion ever went to the movies, and seldom to the theatre. Saturday afternoons Jeannette spent in tours of shrewd and calculated shopping, and on Sundays she went to Cohasset Beach to spend the day with Alice and the children.

JEANNETTE, on her way to Cohasset Beach, let her Sunday newspaper drift indifferently into her lap, and turned her attention to the October landscape through the car window. The train was filled with Sunday visitors like herself, bound for friends and relatives in the suburbs. They would enjoy a hearty meal around a crowded table at one o'clock, would inspect the local country club for a view of the links or the golfers in their "sports" clothes, indulge, perhaps, in a motor trip to gain further aspects of the autumnal foliage, or, complaining of having over-eaten and demurring at any effort, establish themselves at the card table to while away the rest of the afternoon at bridge. At five o'clock the swarm that had filtered into the country all morning through the Pennsylvania Station would decide with one accord to return to the city, the cars would be jammed and every seat taken long before the westbound trains reached Cohasset Beach. It was always a noisy crowd with crying, tired babies wriggling in parents' laps, golfers arguing about their scores and the adjustment of their bets, silly girls convulsed at one another's confidences or lifting shrill pipes of mirth at the hoarse whispered comments from slouching male escorts, returning ball teams of youthful enthusiasts who banged each other over the head and vented their high spirits in rough jibes or horse-play.

Sunday travel was a bore, thought Jeannette in mild vexation. Even the outbound trains during the morning, which were never more than comfortably filled, stopped at every station along the line, no matter how insignificant. It took ten minutes longer to get to Cohasset Beach on Sundays than on any other day of the week; the express trains that left the city late in the afternoons from Monday to Saturday landed Roy home in nineteen minutes. It used to take a weary forty-five, Jeannette remembered, when the East River had first to be crossed by ferry and the rest of the way travelled in the old racketing, shabby, plush-seated, puffing steam trains from Long Island City.

She fell to musing as she idly watched the country flying past. She recalled the time when she and Martin had paid their first visit to Cohasset Beach as guests of the Herbert Gibbses and had gone picnicking on the shore at the Family Yacht Club. The Gibbses owned a handsome home on the Point to-day, and the little Yacht Club had been merged into the Cohasset Beach Yacht Club, which, since the fire that had laid it in ashy ruins, was now housed in a large, imposing edifice of brick and stone. The town itself,—then hardly more than a summer resort for "rich New Yorkers," a few hundred houses scattered carelessly over some wooded hills,—had grown within the last dozen years into a flourishing community with banks, brick business blocks, and fireproof schools, with paved streets, and rows upon rows of white painted houses with green shutters and fan-shaped transoms above

panelled colonial doorways. The woods were gone; the
sycamores and gnarled old apple trees had given place
to spindling elms set at orderly intervals on either
side the carefully graded streets and to formal little
gardens and close-cropped patches of lawn. The dilapidated wooden station had been supplanted by a
substantial concrete affair, surrounded with cement
pavements, and provided with comfortable, steam-
heated waiting-rooms. The whirring electric trains
swept on to other thriving villages further down the
Island, and paused, coming or going, but a minute
or two at the older town which had once been the ter-
minal. There were now blocks and blocks of these
trimly-built, neatly-equipped houses at Cohasset
Beach, each with its garden, its curving cement walks
and contiguous garage, and Messrs. Adolph Kuntz and
Stephen Teschemacher had built stone mansions for
themselves in the center of Cohasset Beach Park, to-
day the "court" end of town.

Alice and Roy lived in humbler quarters: the old
frame house Fritz Wiggens and his paralytic mother
had once occupied. It was yellow and gabled, rusty
and blistered, and spread itself out in ungainly fashion over a none-too-large bit of ground. It had, by no
means, been a poor investment, although the building
had needed a steady stream of repairs since the
Beardsleys acquired it. Roy had been offered three
times what he paid for it on account of its desirable
location overlooking the waters of the Sound. Every
now and then he and Alice discussed selling the place
but invariably reached the same conclusion: Rents
were prohibitive and no other house half as satisfactory could be purchased for the money without assum-

ing a mortgage, an additional financial burden not to be considered; their problem was to devise ways of reducing expenses rather than increasing them.

§ 2

Jeannette had decided to walk to her sister's house, but on the platform as she descended from the train she unexpectedly encountered Zeb Kline and his wife, awaiting the arrival of Sunday guests. Zeb had married Nick Birdsell's daughter and gone into partnership with his father-in-law; Birdsell & Kline, General Contractors, had built most of the new houses in Cohasset Beach, and now Zeb had a fine stucco one of his own, and his wife drove about in her limousine and kept a chauffeur.

At the time Jeannette and Martin separated, the former had been aware that the sympathy of the community was with her genial, amusing, good-looking husband. The townsfolk considered she had treated him "shamefully"; only Edith French and the Doc were acquainted with the true facts of the case and had defended her, but the Doc and his wife had moved away within a year after Jeannette returned to work, and she had lost touch with them. Word reached her that they had settled in St. Louis, that the Doc had had his right hand amputated as the result of an infection from an operation, and that he was running a drug store there. Later Jeannette heard that Edith had left him and married an actor.

Suspecting a hostile attitude among these friends and acquaintances of her married years, Jeannette had

kept herself carefully aloof from all of them when
Roy and Alice selected Cohasset Beach for their home.
She would avert her eyes when passing any of them
on the street, or would bow with but a brief, unsmil-
ing inclination of the head when forced to acknowledge
recognition.

Now, as she came face to face with Zeb Kline and
his wife, Zeb, a trifle flustered, lifted his cap and
greeted her by name, and Jeannette, also taken unawares, responded with more cordiality than she felt.
She was somewhat perturbed by the incident and was
conscious of Kitty Birdsell Kline's appraising eye following her as she made her way across the station
platform.

It was this trifling occurrence that induced her to
alter her intention and ride to Alice's. Mrs. Kline
might be admiring her,—her clothes and carriage,—
or she might be sneering. In either case, the scrutiny was unwelcome, and, straightening her shoulders,
Jeannette directed her steps toward one of the shabby,
waiting Fords, and climbed in. She had no intention
of letting the Klines sweep by her in their limousine
while she trudged along the sidewalk.

Established in her taxi and rattling over the familiar
route to her sister's home, a pleasant thought of Zeb
came to her. After all, he was the best of that rough
and common group; he had always been polite to her,
honest and straightforward; she remembered how kind
he had been about the construction of the screens for
the bungalow's windows, hurrying their making and
charging her practically no more than they had cost.
She wondered if he had been to Philadelphia recently

or had heard anything more of Martin. If she should chance to meet Zeb in the street some day, she debated whether or not she should ask him for news.

Baby Roy, clad in his Sunday corduroy "knickers" and a white shirt, which Jeannette knew well had been put upon him clean that morning, was sprawled on the cement steps of the Beardsleys' home as her vehicle stopped before it. The cleanly appearance had departed from Baby Roy's shirt, the trousers had become divorced from it, his collar was rumpled, and the bow tie, which his aunt suspected Etta's hurried fingers had tied before church, was bedraggled and askew over one shoulder. He lay on his back, his head upon the hard stone, his fair hair in tousled confusion, gazing straight upward into the sky, his arms waving aimlessly above him. He made no move at the sound of the motor-car and only stirred when Jeannette reached the steps.

"Hello, Aunt Jan," he drawled in his curious, indolent voice.

"Well, I declare," said Jeannette, surveying him with puzzled amusement, "will you kindly tell me what you're doing there? What are you looking at? What do you think you see?"

Baby Roy smiled foolishly, and with open mouth, twisted his jaw slowly from side to side.

"Aw,—I was just thinking," he answered in awkard embarrassment. He got to his feet and put his arms around his aunt's neck as she stooped to kiss him.

His cheek was soft and warm, and he smelled of dirt and sunburn.

"You're a sight," she told him; "your mother will

be wild. Why don't you try to keep yourself clean one day a week at least?"

"Ma won't care," the youngster observed, "and Et won't say nothin'."

"Pronounce your 'g's, Baby Roy,—say 'noth-*ing*.' Why will Etta say nothing?"

" 'Cause she's got her feller."

"Who? That pimply-faced Eckles boy?"

The child nodded and then irrelevantly added:

"Nettie's got appendicitis."

"Good gracious!" exclaimed Jeannette. "Where did she get that?"

Further information was not forthcoming. The woman's mind flew to the possible complications such a calamity would precipitate as she opened her bag and felt among its contents for the nickel package of lemon drops she had purchased at the Pennsylvania Station while waiting for her train. She shook three of the candies out into Baby Roy's dirt-streaked palm, and was admonishing the recipient that they were to be eaten one by one, when there was a clatter of hard shoes on the porch and a boy of thirteen catapulted out of the house.

"Dibs on the funny paper!" he yelled.

Jeannette eyed him with assumed disapproval.

"There's no necessity for such a racket, Frank; it's Sunday, remember, and your sister's sick and everything."

She proceeded at once, however, to unfold her newspaper and to hand him the comic section.

"I brought you one out of the *American*, too." Frank seized the papers and grunted his thanks.

"How is Nettie?" inquired his aunt.

She had to repeat her question for the boy's attention was already absorbed by the colored pictures.

"Oh, she's all right, I guess," he answered carelessly.

"Is she really sick?"

"I dunno."

Reproof was on Jeannette's lips but she checked herself. Frank was her favorite among her sister's children; he was the only one of them, she was at pains to declare frequently, who had any "gumption." The rest were like their easy-going, amiable parents. Frank had some of her own energy; he was like her in many ways. It was clear he was destined to be the mainstay of his father's and mother's old age. He was sure to get on, make money, be successful no matter in what direction he turned his energies. A fine, clever boy, she considered him, with some "get-up-and-get" in his composition.

She left the two brothers seated side by side on the steps, poring over the "comics." Their voices followed her as she entered the house.

"Go on, read it to me;—go on, read it to me. Don't be a dirty stinker."

"Aw, shut up, can't yer? Wait till I get through first."

Jeannette met Alice in the hallway and her first question was of the sick child. Alice kissed her with affection and hugged her warmly.

"I don't think anything's the matter," she said reassuringly. "Nothing in the world but an old-fashioned stomach-ache; something she's eaten,—that's all. I thought it wiser to keep her in bed for to-day,— give her insides a good rest."

"Why, Baby Roy said it was appendicitis!"

"Oh, nonsense! The child isn't any more sick than I am!"

"Well, it gave me quite a turn."

"Of course!" agreed Alice.

Jeannette eyed her sister a moment in suspicion. Allie's vehement rejection of the idea that anything might be seriously the matter suggested Christian Science. Jeannette had heard Mrs. Eddy's teachings discussed more or less frequently of late by her sister and brother-in-law. She suspected they both leaned toward that faith but lacked courage to come out openly and declare themselves. She wondered how far these idiotic principles had laid hold of them, and now, with a searching glance, she asked:

"Has error crept in?"

Alice blushed readily and laughed.

"I don't know anything about that. If she's any worse to-morrow, I'll send for the doctor.

"I should hope so," Jeannette approved warmly.

"Etta's delighted with her dress," Alice said with an abruptness that suggested a desire to change the subject. "You were a dear to help her out."

"It was nothing at all,—less than five dollars. It seemed a shame not to get something that was becoming, and there's real value in that garment."

"Oh, yes, indeed. I could see that."

Great thumping, banging and scraping were going on somewhere down below.

"Roy and Ralph are cleaning the furnace," explained Alice in answer to her sister's puzzled look. "It hasn't been fired,—oh, I don't think since last March. . . . Come upstairs and lay your things on

Etta's bed. I've got Nettie in mine; it's so much pleasanter in our room.''

The two women mounted the creaking stairs. In the front room a little girl was propped up in bed with several pillows; she was cutting out pictures from magazines and the bed clothes and carpet were littered with scraps and slips of paper; a thin, plaid shawl was about her shoulders, fastened clumsily across her chest with a large safety-pin. She was not a particularly pretty child; her face was too long and too pale, but her hair, soft and rippling, had the warm brown color that had distinguished her mother's, and her eyes were of the same hue.

''Look, Moth', I put a new hat on this lady and she looks a lot nicer.'' The child held up a wavering silhouette for inspection. ''Oh, hello, Aunt Janny,'' she cried as her aunt appeared in her mother's wake; ''was that you in the taxi?''

There was a note of real pleasure, Jeannette felt, in the little girl's greeting, and she put some feeling into her kiss as she bent down to embrace her.

''I brought you some lemon drops, Nettie, but since you're upset perhaps you'd better not have them.''

''Oh, I'm quite all right,'' said the little girl brightly. ''I'm not the least bit sick.''

Here was the cloven hoof of Christian Science again, thought her aunt darkly; the child had been coached, no doubt! It was a great pity if that rigmarole was going to be taken up by Alice and Roy to make them all miserable!

''Well, I think I wouldn't eat candy till to-morrow,'' advised Jeannette. ''What I think you need is a good dose of castor-oil,'' she added firmly with a glance at her sister. "But here,—I have something here, I know you'll like much better," she went on, searching in her bag. She brought to light a gold-colored, metal pencil about three inches long with a tiny ring at one end, and gave it to the child.

"Oh, thank you, Aunt Janny,—thank you awfully," cried the invalid, immediately beginning to experiment with the cap which, in turning, shortened or lengthened the lead.

"Where's Etta?"

"Gone to church," Alice replied.

"Heavens! . . . What for?" Jeannette turned inquiring eyes upon the girl's mother. It was not that she lacked sympathy with any religious observance on her niece's part, but church-going for Etta was unusual. The younger children were sent dutifully to Sunday school but the rest of the family were rather casual about attending divine services. Alice smiled significantly in answer to the query, elevated a shoulder, and indulged in a slight head-shake.

"I suppose that means a boy again," Jeannette said, interpreting the look and gesture. "Doesn't she see enough of them afternoons and evenings? I declare, Alice, I don't know what you're going to do with that girl. Yesterday afternoon, all she could talk about was the movies, and she even stopped me in front of a photographer's show-case to ask me if I didn't think a man in it was perfectly stunning! . . . He was old enough to be her father!"

"Well, all the girls are like that nowadays."

"It was decidedly different when we were that age."

"Oh, indeed it was," agreed Etta's mother. "I was thinking only yesterday how we used——"

"You made a great mistake," interrupted Jeannette, "in letting her bob her hair. It's affected her whole character. She was never quite so frivolous before."

"That was her father's doing," said Alice mildly.

"Oh, well,—he'd let her do anything she wanted! She has but to ask! . . . What do you intend to do with her? Let her run round this way indefinitely? I'd make her take up sewing or cooking or learn some language."

"Etta can sew quite nicely," said her mother loyally, "and she's a good cook. She wants to go to work,—you know that. She thinks you'd have no difficulty in getting her a position at the office."

"Well, perhaps I would, and perhaps I wouldn't. But I don't approve of the idea! She'd much better go to Columbia or Hunter College."

"But, Janny dear, we've been all over that, time and time again. That costs money. It would take several hundred a year to send Etta to college, and we haven't got it. Roy thinks it's much more important that Ralph should follow up his engineering at some university."

Jeannette tapped her pursed lips with a meditative finger.

"When's he ready?"

"This is his last year in High School."

"It would be wiser to send him to business college."

"Roy's heart is set on Princeton, but if we can't afford that,—and I don't see how we possibly can!— then Columbia. He could commute, you know."

Voices and the sound of feet on the porch announced

arrivals. Jeannette drew aside a limp window curtain
and gazed down at the front steps.

"It's that pimply Eckles youth," she announced.

"His dog has nine puppies and he's promised one to
me," came from the bed.

"I hope Etta doesn't ask him to stay to dinner,"
Alice remarked, "it'll make Kate furious."

"No, he's going. . . . I must take off my things."

Etta running upstairs a moment or two later found
her aunt before the mirror in her room, powdering
her nose.

"Oh, darling!" The girl rushed at her and flung
her arms about her enthusiastically.

"Careful,—careful, dearie,—I've just fixed myself." Jeannette held Etta's arms to the girl's sides
and implanted a brief kiss on her forehead. The
enthusiasm of her niece was in nowise crushed.

"Didn't we have fun yesterday, Aunt Jan? Oh, I
just *love* going shopping with you! You know *everything!*"

Jeannette smiled complacently. She was a dear
child, this! So responsive and appreciative!

Suddenly she glanced at her sharply, whipped a
handkerchief from the bureau, and before unsuspect-
ing Etta could guess what she was about, gave the
girl's lip a quick rub. There was a tell-tale smudge
of red on the white linen. Jeannette held forth the
evidence accusingly and her niece began to laugh,
hanging her head like a little girl half her years.

"I tell you, Etta, it doesn't become you! Your lips
are red enough without putting any of that Jap paste
on them! When you rouge them, it makes you look

cheap and common. . . . I don't care *what* the other girls do!"

She surveyed the girl critically: a handsome child with a lovely mop of dark brown hair that clung in rich clusters of natural curls about her neck and ears; her eyes were unusually large and of a deep, velvety duskiness, though there was a perpetual merry light in them, and her mouth, too, had a ready smile; her teeth were glistening white, but her complexion was bad, given to eruptions and blotches.

"And I wish," continued Jeannette, "you'd stop eating candy and ice-cream sodas, and leave cake and pastry alone. Your skin would clear out in no time. It's a shame a girl as pretty as you has to spoil her looks by injudicious eating."

"Isn't it the limit?" agreed Etta. Her face clouded and she went close to the mirror to study her reflection narrowly.

"I never knew it to fail!" she said in disgust. "Wednesday night, Marjorie Bowen's giving a bridge party, and she's invited a boy I'm just dying to meet! And there's a blossom coming right here on my chin! I always break out if there's anything special doing!"

"Well, I tell you!" exclaimed her aunt. "You wouldn't have those things if you'd diet with a little care. Massaging won't help a bit; you've got to remember to stop eating sweets. . . . Who's the new beau you're 'dying to meet'?"

"Oh, he's a high-roller,—lives down on the Point,—drives a Stutz and everything! The girls are all mad about him. He's been at Manlius for the last two or three years, and now he's freshman at Yale. . . . Name's Herbert Gibbs!"

"Goodness gracious!" ejaculated her aunt.

"What's the matter?"

"Well, . . . nothing . . ."

"Oh, tell me please, Aunt Jan!—Please tell me!"

"Don't be foolish! I knew his father, that's all, and I once saw your 'high-roller' in his crib when he was less than a year old. . . . Isn't he rather expressionless and flat-headed?"

"No; I think he's perfectly stunning. He wears the best-looking clothes and he's an awful sport!"

"Well, you'd never expect it, if you'd known his father," her aunt said dryly.

There was an ascending tramp of feet on the stairs, and Roy with his eldest son appeared, dishevelled and sooty.

"That was a dirty job, all right," declared Roy after he had greeted his sister-in-law and kissed her with the tips of his lips for fear of contaminating her. "I don't think she's been cleaned for years. We shovelled out a ton of soot. Ralph did all the hard work."

He seemed a little ridiculous, a little pathetic to Jeannette, as he stood before her with his smirched and blackened face, and his tight, wan smile, the upper lip drawn taut across his row of even teeth. His stuck-up hair was still unruly, and had begun to recede at the temples and to thin on top; his face was lined with tiny wrinkles and he wore spectacles with bifocal lenses and metal rims,—an insignificant man, industrious, conscientious, weighed down with the cares and responsibilities of a large family. Life had dealt hardly with him, and somehow, remembering the boy with the whimsical smile who had once made such earnest love to herself in the flush of youth, Jeannette

could not but regard the result as tragic. She was
fond of Roy, nevertheless; he was always amiable,
always good-tempered and cheerful, but she wondered
at this moment as she took stock of him what sort
of a man he would have become if she, and not Alice,
had married him. Different, no doubt, for she would
have pushed him into material success; she would not
have been as easy-going with him as Alice; he had
wanted to write; well, if she had been his wife, he
would probably have turned out to be a very successful
author for he had ability.

Roy's oldest son, Ralph, was in many ways like his
father. He had the same sweet, obliging nature and
was even gentler. His voice had the quality of Baby
Roy's: indolent, drawling, dragging, and he spoke
with a leisureliness that was often irritating. He was
slight of build, narrow-chested and stoop-shouldered,
a student by disposition, forever burrowing into a book
or frowning over a magazine article. Jeannette would
have considered this highly commendable had Ralph
ever shown any evidence of having gleaned something
from his reading, or displayed any knowledge as a result of it. What he read seemed to pass through his
mind like water through a sieve.

She had brought down an advanced copy of the
forthcoming issue of *Corey's Commentary* for him,
and he accepted this now, with an appreciative word.

She always made a point of bringing presents to
her sister's children whenever she visited them; she
liked the reputation of never coming empty-handed.
The gifts, themselves, might be trifling,—indeed she
thought it becoming that they should be,—but she
strove to make them sufficiently appropriate to indi-

cate considerable thoughtfulness in their selection.
She regarded herself as very generous where her nieces
and nephews were concerned. Yesterday she had
enabled Etta to buy a more expensive dress than was
possible with the money her mother had given her, and
last week she had sent Frank a fine sweater from a sale
of boys' sweaters she happened upon in a department
store. Of all her sister's children, Frank baffled her.
He treated her casually, almost with indifference.
While the other children swarmed about her with
effusive gratitude and affection, whenever she gave
them anything, Frank either grunted his thanks or
failed to express them at all. She loved him by far the
best, and was continually making him presents or defending him from criticism. Her partiality was so
noticeable she was mildly teased about it by the rest of
the family; but it drew no recognition from the boy.
His aunt, eyeing him with great yearning in her heart,
would often wonder how she could bribe him to put his
stout, rough arms about her neck and kiss her once with
warmth and tenderness. She was never able to stir
him to the faintest betrayal of sentiment.

Her benevolence toward her sister's family frequently went further than presents for the children.
At Christmas-time she was munificent to them all, and
she never forgot one of their birthdays. Once a year
she took Nettie, Frank and Baby Roy to the Hippo-
drome, and on the occasional Saturdays that Alice or
Etta came to the city, she always had them to lunch
with her, accompanied them on their shopping trips,
and contributed, here and there, to their small purchases. Not infrequently when she knew Alice was
worrying unduly about some vexatious account, she

would press a neatly folded bill into her hand. She
liked the power that money gave her where they were
concerned; she delighted in their gratitude and deference to her opinions; she was an important factor in
their lives and she enjoyed the part.

§ 3

At one o'clock dinner was announced. There was
little ceremony about the Beardsleys' meals; the important business was to be fed. Kate, the cook and
waitress,—a big-bosomed, wide-hipped Irish woman,
with the strength of a horse and the disposition of a
bear,—had scant regard for the preferences of any
one member of the family she served. Her attention
was concentrated upon her work; indeed, it required
a considerable amount of clear-thinking and planning
to dispatch it at all, and she brooked no interference. Roy, Alice, and the children were frankly
afraid of her; even Jeannette admitted a wholesome
respect.

"Oh, Kate's in an awful tantrum!" the whisper
would go around the house and the family would de-
port itself with due regard to Kate's mood.

She piled the food on the table, rattled the bell and
departed kitchenward, leaving the Beardsleys to as-
semble as promptly or as tardily as they chose. There
never were but two courses to a meal: meat and dessert. Kate had no time to bother with soup or salad.
Her cooking was good, however, and there were always
great dishes of potatoes and other vegetables as well
as a large plate of muffins or some other kind of hot
bread. Jeannette firmly asserted that Kate's meat

pie with its brown crisp crust could not be surpassed in any kitchen.

To-day there were but seven at table as Nettie remained upstairs in bed. She would have crackers and milk later, her mother announced.

"Milk toast," Jeannette suggested. But Alice shook her head and made a motion in the direction of the kitchen.

"She doesn't like anyone fussing out there," she whispered, "and I don't like to ask her to do it herself; it's extra work no matter how trivial. The Graham crackers will do just as well; Nettie's quite fond of them."

It was a cheerful scene, this gathering at the table of Roy, his wife, and their children. Tongues wagged constantly; there was happy laughter and loud talk, much clatter of china and clinking of silverware. Roy stood up to carve and he served generously; plates were passed from hand to hand around the table to Alice who sat opposite him and she added heaping spoonfuls of creamed cauliflower or string beans, and mashed potatoes. The pile of food set down in front of each seemed, by its quantity, unappetizing to Jeannette, but the others evidently did not share her feeling, for they cleaned their plates, while Frank and Baby Roy almost always asked for more. The remarks that flew about the board had small relevancy, but she found them interesting, liked to lean back in her chair, with wrists folded one across the other in her lap, and listen comfortably.

"Mr. Kuntz tells me he's sold the Carleton place; the Hirshstines bought it," Roy might observe.

"Oh, golly,—those kikes!"

"Frank, you mustn't speak that way; Mrs. Hirsh-stine's a nice woman, and Abe Hirshstine's very public-spirited."

"They may be Jews all right, but I wouldn't con-sider them 'kikes'; there's a lot of difference." Ralph's drawl often had that irritating quality his aunt disliked.

"Well, *she's* certainly a dumb-bell, if there ever was one." Jeannette would infer this was of the daughter.

"That's because Buddy Eckles's after her!"

Etta with curling lip would dismiss this without comment.

"He likes to drive her Marmon,—that's what *he's* after."

"She spoke about taking us all over to Long Beach, Saturday, and Buddy's going to drive."

"Hot dog!"

"You can't go, smarty!"

"*Why?*—Why can't I go?"

"'Cause you've got to go to the dentist's."

"Aw,—cusses!"

"Do you think I'd better have the storm windows put up to-morrow, Roy, when that man comes to fix the radiators?"

"I wouldn't hurry about it; it isn't November first yet."

"I know, but it keeps the house so much warmer, and I was thinking about Nettie. . . ."

"Ralph and I can do it when you need them."

"We get Barthelmess at the Plaza Friday and Saturday!"

"Oh, c'n I go, Moth'?"

"We'll see; perhaps your father will take you."

"Do you let the children go to the movies much, Alice?"

"Depends on the picture. Barthelmess is always clean and good."

"Friday I'll be late coming home, and Saturday night I'm afraid I'll have to go to the Civic Improvement meeting."

"Bet I'm gypped!"

"Don't worry, Baby Roy; I'll let you go by yourself, Saturday afternoon, if you're a good boy."

"Pulitzer's closing out his meat market; going to handle nothing but groceries from now on."

"Well, I guess he's made money. He's a good citizen, all right. He subscribed two hundred and fifty for the district nurse."

"Did you get on to my classy hair part, Aunt Jan? All the women-getters at school do their hair this way now."

"Really, Frank! Your language . . . ! I don't know where or how you pick up such phrases."

"Don't be too critical, Alice. He attaches no significance to them. You know what boys are."

There was an endless stream of such talk, Roy and his wife frequently maintaining one conversation between ends of the table, while their children carried on another across it.

Kate crammed the soiled dishes on the oval, black, tin tray, piled them high, and grasping the tray with strong arms, bore it to the kitchen, kicking the swing door violently open as she passed through.

Dessert made its appearance, usually a deep apple pie, a chocolate pudding or a mound of flavored jelly in which slices of banana careened at various angles.

Kate refused flatly to bother with ice-cream. Once in a while she condescended to make a layer cake.

During the meal it was customary for the telephone to ring several times. Instantly at each summons, Etta would be upon her feet and make a quick dash for the instrument. Long conversations would ensue in which Etta's voice would drift down to the dining-room.

"Well, I didn't . . . Well, you tell him I didn't . . . Well, you tell him I didn't say anything of the kind. . . . I never did. . . . He's just crazy. . . . I never said anything of the kind. . . . Well, you tell him I didn't . . ."

"Etta!" her father would call presently. The voice would continue unfalteringly, and Roy at intervals would repeat her name until finally the long-winded parley would be brought to an end.

By two o'clock on this particular day the meal was over, and there was a general breaking-up of the group. Alice went out into the kitchen to prepare Nettie's tray. Frank vanished in pursuit of his own affairs, which usually took him to the house of "Chinee" Langlon, whose parents were wealthy and had lavished everything they could think of on their one son, including an elaborate wireless outfit. Buddy Eckles arrived a few minutes past the hour, planting himself on the front steps, and waited ostensibly for Etta to go walking with him. Jeannette had her own ideas as to where they actually went. She suspected they made their way without delay to the home of some girl friend, whose parents were absent or had lax ideas about the Sabbath, and there, having carefully pulled down the window-shades, out of deference

to the possible prejudices of passers-by, they rolled
back the rugs, turned on the Victrola, and with other
couples as frivolous as themselves, danced until within
a minute or two of the time when it was necessary to
return to their respective families. Ralph disappeared up into his den,—a wretched, ill-lighted,
cramped chamber he had built himself in the attic.
He kept the door of this apartment carefully locked
at all times, and when within, by the light of a kero-
sene lamp, read what his aunt earnestly hoped was
entirely edifying literature, and where, she was thoroughly persuaded, he indulged secretly in cigarettes.
Baby Roy wandered amiably and uncomplainingly
about, listening to his elders' conversation, or took
himself off into the scraggy garden where he hid in
strange nooks and told himself stories in a droning
voice which always ended in frightening him. Jeannette regarded him the strangest of her sister's children; she frankly declared she did not understand him
and thought Alice outrageously lenient where he was
concerned.

§ 4

To-day's visit was an unusually happy one for Jeannette. Nettie drifted off to sleep while her mother
and aunt established themselves in shabby grass-
rockers on the side-porch and had a long, comfortable
talk. The day had turned unexpectedly warm and
there was a reviving touch of dead summer in the air.
In a neighbor's garden, chrysanthemums and cosmos
were still in bloom, and the brilliant colors made the
Beardsleys' own unkempt little yard appear gay and
luxuriant. A mechanical piano tinkled pleasantly

somewhere, and every now and then there came the
vibrant hum of a passing motor-car. Kate marched
past her mistress and her mistress's sister presently,
clad in sober town clothes and wearing one of Jeannette's discarded hats which the giver thought, at the
moment, became her nicely. Kate was off for the rest
of the day, and Alice with Etta's help would manage
the cold supper for the family at half-past six. A
stillness on this midafternoon settled about the house
usually teeming exuberantly with life. Through an
open window near at hand, the women on the porch
could hear an occasional rustle of papers as Roy,
prone upon the leather-covered couch in the living-
room, read the Sunday news.

Alice drew a deep sigh of weary comfort.

"I ought to get at my sewing, I suppose, but I don't
like bringing it out on the porch Sunday; people *can*
see you from the street. . . . It's so pleasant out here,
I hate to go in."

"Sit awhile," encouraged Jeannette. "You're always worrying yourself about something, Alice."

"I have to. Frank's stockings have *got* to be darned
or he can't go to school to-morrow; Baby Roy's cap is
torn and I noticed his school suit needs cleaning."

"You ought to make Etta do these things."

"Etta does enough," her mother defended her;
"she's only young once, you know, and Sunday ought
to be as much of a holiday for her as it is for other
young folks. . . . And there're some letters I must
write, one to Nettie's teacher for Frank to take to
school with him in the morning. . . . Mercy! there's
never any let-up to it. I've got to go over this month's
bills with Roy some time to-day and decide what we're

going to do about them. You know, I just *won't* bother him about money matters when he comes home all tired out at night, and I have to wait until Sunday."

"How are you off this month? Any worse than usual?"

"Roy's premium falls due. I've got the money all right, but some of the monthly bills will have to wait. . . . You know, Jan, I'm sick to death of this ever-constant worry about money; I've had it all my life, ever since I was a little girl. I wish to goodness I could earn something on the side. When the children were little, I couldn't spare the time, but that isn't a consideration now. Etta could perfectly well take care of the house, and I could devote several hours a day to some kind of work that would bring in money. I thought I'd knit a few sweaters and see if I could induce some shop in the city to handle them; it would only cost me the wool. If I'd learned typing, I think I could get some copying to do. You know it makes me ashamed to realize how little I could earn if I was obliged to get out and seek my living. I'd be worth about ten dollars a week. That would be what they'd call my 'economic value.' . . ."

" 'Economic value!' " cried Jeannette. "What do you mean? The mother of five children has an economic value of ten dollars a week! Why, Alice, you talk like a crazy woman!"

"I may be worth a great deal more than that to the nation, but that's all I'd be worth to a business man."

"The Government ought to give you an annual income the rest of your life for every child you bring into the world; that would represent your economic value!"

"Well, there's no likelihood of their doing it," laughed Alice. "I wish I had a definite way of earning money,—I mean a profession like a stenographer or a nurse. I've always claimed, Janny, that every woman, married or single, ought to learn a trade or profession. You have no idea how I envy you, sometimes. You're independent, you're beholden to no one, you're utterly free of all these cares and responsibilities that harass me from morning to night."

Jeannette shook her head emphatically.

"You don't know, Alice," she said. "If you envy me my life, I envy you a hundred times more. I envy you these very cares and responsibilities of which you complain; I envy you your husband and your children and all those things that go to make a home. . . . Oh, I think sometimes, I was a blithering *fool* to have left Martin!"

His name had not crossed her lips for months, and for a little time there was silence on the porch.

"Do you ever hear from him?" asked Alice in a lower key.

"No. I understand he's in Philadelphia in the automobile business. You know as much about him as I do."

"And he's never married?"

"We've never been divorced."

Again there was an interval of silence.

"Would you go back to him, Jan?"

Jeannette stared out into the warm sunshine, and her rocker ceased its slow movement.

"I've thought about it," she admitted. "I'd like a home. I'm so tired of the office. There's nothing to

work for in the business any more. I've got as far
as they'll let me go; there's no future for me.''

"Why don't you write him?" Alice suggested,
watching her sister's serious face. "He may be as
lonely as you are.''

"It's fourteen years,'' mused Jeannette. "We've
both changed. He may be very different.''

"He may still be thinking of you and blaming himself for having treated you so unkindly. . . . Why
don't you write him and just say you'd be glad to
know how he's getting on?"

"I don't know his address.''

"Well, that could be found out easily enough.''

There was a sound within, and Roy came stumbling
out on the porch to stretch himself, luxuriously.

"Whew!'' he said, enjoying a great yawn. "I
nearly went to sleep in there.''

"Why didn't you? A nap would have done you
good.''

"I don't like to miss a single minute of my one day
at home. It's too pleasant out here.''

Alice began to fidget, clearing her throat nervously.

"Do you feel like going over some bills with me,
Roy?" she ventured with obvious reluctance.

"Sure,'' he agreed good-naturedly.

He sat down on the steps, while his wife went in-
doors and presently returned with a sheaf of bills,
a pad and pencil. She established herself next to him.

"Now you see, Roy,'' she began, "in the first place,
there's the two hundred and forty that's due on the
fifth. I've got one hundred and fifty saved up, and
that means I must take ninety out of next week's

salary. It's going to leave me precious little, and there's your commutation for next month that's got to come out right away. I figure we owe about,—well, it's not over six hundred; I'm not counting Frank's teeth nor Gimbel's; they can wait. But here's the first of the month coming and Pulitzer, you know, won't let you charge unless you pay up by the tenth. Now I was thinking . . ."

The voices went on murmuring, and Jeannette mused. Here it was again: the eternal war against want, the fight for existence, the battle for bread. There was never any end to it; it was perpetual, incessant, unending. In all the houses within the range of her vision, in all the trim, orderly, little dwellings that made up Cohasset Beach, in all the thousands and thousands of homes that dotted Long Island, in the millions that were scattered over the United States, and over the world, this struggle was going on. It was easy in some; it was bitter hard in others. Alice, who was among the most readily satisfied and uncomplaining of women, had protested against the everlasting drudgery, a moment ago! . . . Well, she, Jeannette, had solved that particular problem for herself pretty much to her satisfaction. It was many years since she had had to worry about a bill; her income more than covered her expenses; she had saved and was going on saving; she had nearly enough money in the bank to buy another bond. In a few years she would have ten thousand dollars securely invested. Then, she would resign from the Corey Publishing Company,—they would pay her something, part salary, as long as she lived, the way they did Miss Holland,— and perhaps she would travel, or perhaps make her

home with Roy and Alice. They would not want her
particularly, but theirs might be the only place to
which she could go; she knew their loyalty and affection would make them urge her to come to them. . . .
And there was Frank! She would like to do something for that boy: pay his way through college or
make him some kind of a handsome present that would
render him eternally grateful to her. But she supposed he would be getting married as soon as he was
grown up and would have no eyes nor time for anybody except the fluffy-haired doll he would select for
a wife! . . . Love was a funny thing! . . . Her mind
drifted to Martin,—Martin, with his youth, his charm,
his good looks, his winning personality. Ah, he was
a man of whom any woman might be proud! Well,
she *had* been proud of him; she had always admired
him; he had always had a particular appeal for her.
. . . It was the selfsame thing that was agitating Roy
and Alice to-day, that had caused her disagreement
with Martin,—this struggle for money, for the means
to pay bills, for the wherewithal to buy bread! . . .
Ah,—and they had had enough, more than enough,
if Martin only had been reasonable! . . . Undoubtedly he was very successful now; an agency for a
motor-car in Philadelphia indicated success; he was,
in all likelihood, a rich man. She wondered what
would have happened to him and to her if she had
stuck to him! . . .

Her mind wandered into strange speculations. She
had once viewed the streets of Philadelphia from a
car window on her way to Washington. She thought
of the city as blocks and blocks of small brick houses,
with pointed roofs, standing close together, row after

row, each with a little square bit of lawn beside brown stone front steps. She imagined herself and Martin in one of these; she was keeping house again, and she had a cook and perhaps a maid, and of course she would have an automobile, since Martin had the agency for one. Her life was full of friendships; she was able to dress beautifully; Martin's associates admired her, thought her handsome, regal; she took a keen interest in her children's schooling,—for, of course, there would be children,—a twelve-year-old Frank, and perhaps a younger Frank, as well, and one daughter, a girl different from either Etta or Nettie, a tall girl with a fine carriage, gracious, dignified, beautiful. How she would enjoy dressing her, and how proud Martin would be of his children, and of herself,—her poise and beauty, her fine clothes and the way she wore them, her graciousness to his friends and her capable management of his home. . . .

"No man ever had a better wife than I have; no man was ever prouder of his wife and children; no man was ever more grateful. You're a wonder, dear, —have always been a wonder! Other men envy me,— envy me your beauty and your goodness and your devotion. Everything I've amounted to in this life I owe to you; you've made me what I am; you've made our home what it is! My friends look at you and think how lucky I've been. I look back on all the hard years we've been together, on all the tough times we've had and somehow pulled through, and I know it's to you, and not to me, the credit belongs. Oh, yes, it does! You've made my home for me, you've given me my children, you've taken the burden of everything on your shoulders, you've carried us both along and made our venture as man and wife, as father and mother, successful. I owe everything in the world to you, and to me you're the loveliest and dearest woman in the world . . .''

It was Roy's voice that she heard in the hush of the warm Sunday afternoon, and it blended with the queer thoughts of the woman who sat so still in her rocker as to be thought asleep.

"No—no, Roy," Alice interrupted him. "We've done it together. Money doesn't count with me,— really it doesn't. Sometimes I protest a bit when I think of what the children have to do without, but there is nothing that can take the place of the love we all share. We're a little group, a little clan that's always clung together, and I'd rather be cold and hungry and see the children shabby and needy than have one less of them, or have discord amongst us. You and I have had our trials and our disagreements, but we've always loved each other and loved the children. . . .''

Alice was crying now, softly crying with her head against her husband's shoulder and his arm about her, and the hot prick of tears came to Jeannette's eyes and a burning trickle ran down the side of her nose. She dropped her forehead into her hand and shielded her face with her palm.

"We'll weather this difficulty as we've weathered many another," Roy said consolingly. "I'll go into the insurance company's office to-morrow and fix it up with them; we'll pay them half on the fifth, and I'm sure they'll give me thirty days on the balance. Then you can settle what's most pressing and give the others a little on account. . . . Why say,—we've faced worse times than this! Do you remember that Christmas when Ralph was only three and we'd been out trying to find the kids some cheap presents and I lost that ten-dollar bill out of my pocket? And do you remember when I was so rotten sick with pneumonia and the doctor thought I was going to get T.B.? And do you remember the time when Baby Roy was coming and you fell downstairs and broke your collar-bone? . . . I tell you, Alice, we've *lived*, you and I! We haven't had very much to do it on, but we've *lived!*''

"You're such a comfort, Roy. You're always so sweet about everything and you always put heart into me. You're wonderful!"

"It's *you* that are the wonder, Alice,—the most wonderful wife a man ever had!"

Their heads turned toward one another in mutual inclination and their lips met lovingly. They sat on for awhile in silence, Alice's head once more against her husband's shoulder, their hands linked, the man's arm about his wife.

There came a faint sound from somewhere in the house.

"That's Nettie," Alice said, immediately arousing herself and getting to her feet. "I'll go up. The child's slept quite a while; it's almost four o'clock."

She crossed the porch with careful tread not to disturb her sister, and in another minute her voice and her daughter's, alternately, floated down from an upstairs window. Roy produced a pipe from his coat pocket, and proceeded to empty, fill and light it with attentive deliberation. When he had it briskly going, he rose and leisurely crossed the strip of lawn to his neighbor's yard, vaulted the low wire fence, and was lost in a moment beyond the cosmos and chrysanthemums.

Jeannette remained as she was, head in hand, thinking, thinking. The tears had dried upon her face, her eyes were staring, and there was an empty hunger in her heart that she recognized at last had been there for a long, long time.

CHAPTER III

§ 1

"Etta! Is that you?"

"Yes,—it's me, Aunt Jan."

"Say 'it's I,' dear. What brings you to the city, Sunday?"

"I stayed in town last night. There was a dance at Marjorie Bowen's cousin's house and Moth' said I could go. We had a perfectly divine time! Her aunt chaperoned us and I slept with Marj. I thought maybe you'd be going down to Cohasset Beach this morning, and we'd go together. So I got up, left the girls in bed, had my breakfast, and took a 'bus to come down to see you. I want to talk to you about something."

"But, dear,—I wasn't going to the country to-day. I promised an old friend of mine who lives at the Navy Yard in Brooklyn, I'd go to see her this afternoon."

Etta's face fell and she frowned disconsolately at the carpet. Her aunt suspected something was troubling her.

"Couldn't you tell me what's on your mind, now?"

"Oh, it wasn't anything particular; I wanted to ask your advice, and I thought we'd have a talk as we went down in the train."

A bright light suddenly came into the girl's face.

"Is it Miss Holland you're going to see, Aunt
Janny? Won't you let me go with you? Remember
I met her that day she was here to lunch? She's
perfectly *sweet!* I'd just love to visit the Navy
Yard!"

"Well, I don't think you'll find many ensigns or
lieutenants hanging about on Sunday."

"Oh, but it would be lots of fun, just the same! I'll
'phone Moth' I'm with you and take a late train this
aft! Please say yes, Aunt Janny,—please say yes!"

The girl was jumping up and down in eagerness.

"Well-l," her aunt said with an amused but doubtful smile, "I don't see what you'd get out of it, particularly."

"I'd just love the trip, and I'd like being with you,
Aunt Janny,—really I would!"

Jeannette narrowed her lids and eyed her skeptically. She was pleased, nevertheless. Her niece's excessive ebullition and high spirits never failed to divert
her; she liked the child's company; the girl had a
great respect for her worldly judgment, much more
than she had for her mother's or father's, and the
older woman found it an engaging business to expound
her theories of life and her views of affairs to the
younger one.

"I'm not going until after lunch," she said, still
with a vague hesitancy in her manner.

"I don't mind waiting a bit."

"Can you amuse yourself until noon? I have some
office work to do that will take me about an hour. Miss
Alexander's gone to church but she'll be back directly."

"Could I make some egg muffins? We could have

'em for lunch, an' they're awfully nice and I'm really good at them.''

Jeannette noted the child's palpitant eagerness again with mild amusement.

"I think that would be lovely," she consented, her fine eyes twinkling. "But don't get things out there in a mess; Miss Alexander won't like it if she comes home and finds everything upset."

"I'll be ever and ever so careful," agreed Etta, already skipping toward the kitchen.

Jeannette took herself back to the cold front room, seldom used by either herself or Beatrice, and brought her thoughts once more to the construction of the half-finished circular letter which must be ready for the composing room early Monday morning.

She heard Beatrice come in presently, and an hour later, as she was completing the last revision of her work, Etta appeared breathlessly to announce lunch.

The egg muffins were excellent and received enthusiastic praise. Jeannette ate them with the heated canned tamales, and sipped her tea, one eye on the clock, for she was anxious to make an early start if Etta was to catch, at any seemly hour, a train back to Cohasset Beach.

It was after two before she and her niece found themselves seated in the thundering subway.

"Well, now, tell me your troubles, my dear," Jeannette began; "I want to hear all about them."

But Etta had to be coaxed before she would become communicative.

"Oh, it's *this!*" she finally burst out, striking her skirt with disdainful fingers. "It's my clothes, Aunt Jan! I was horribly ashamed last night. There wasn't a girl there at Marjorie's cousin's party who wasn't a lot better dressed than I! I felt *awful* and was so embarrassed! One of the girls' older sister was there and I saw her taking an inventory of everything I had on! I just wanted to sink through the floor! Moth' does everything she possibly can to see that I look decent, and I know better than anyone else what she does without so that I can have things! But I don't want that! I don't want Moth' and Dad denying themselves on my account. I want to be able to take care of myself and buy my own clothes, earn my own living and be independent! . . . Aunt Jan, won't you get me a job at your office? Won't you back me up with Moth' and Dad, and urge them to let me go to work? I don't want to stay at home and just help Moth' here and there with the housework and do nothing else but go to the movies and dance jazz! They call me a 'flapper,' and I suppose I am one,—but what else is there for me to be? I hate it, Aunt Jan,—I *hate being a flapper!* I want to be something different and better; I want to make my own way in the world and not be obliged to stick round home until a man with enough money comes along and asks me to marry!''

It was the old familiar cry, the cry of youth calling for self-expression, the cry of budding life eager for experience, the cry of young womanhood demanding independence, emancipation.

The words rang familiarly in the older woman's ears, and she smiled sadly with a sorry head-shake.

''Why, what's the matter, Aunt Jan?'' asked the girl after a troubled scrutiny of her companion's face. ''Don't you think I have a right to earn my own living if I want to?'' She renewed her arguments with characteristic vehemence. There was nothing new in them for Jeannette; she had voiced them all herself twenty-five years ago. A memory of her patient, hard-working little mother came to her, and she saw her once again with the comforter over her knees, the knitted red shawl pinned across her shoulders, thin of hair, with trembling pendent cheeks, bending over the canvas-covered ledger, figuring—figuring—figuring. And she saw herself, the impatient eighteen-year-old, striking her faded velvet dress with angry fingers, protesting against the humiliation her shabby attire occasioned her, asking to be allowed to work, to earn the money that would permit her to dress as other girls dressed, and be her own mistress, self-supporting. How well, she, Jeannette, could now sympathize with that earnest, tearful, little mother!

She looked at Etta and, in her mind, saw her anxiously taking dictation from some frowning business man, saw her white flying fingers busy at some switchboard disentangling telephone cords, pictured her perched on a tall stool, bending over a great tome, making careful entries, saw her folding circulars, writing cards, filing letters, giving her youth, her eagerness and beauty to the grim treadmill of business life, and her heart filled with pain.

''. . . and there's no reason on earth,'' Etta was saying, ''why I shouldn't help out at home. Dad and Moth' have given all their lives to us children; they've denied themselves and denied themselves just so we can have clothes for our backs, enough to eat and go to school! It isn't fair. It's time I helped. I could go to business college, take a course, and in three

months, I could learn to be a stenographer and earn
fifteen or twenty dollars a week. . . ."

"Hush, child,—hush! You don't know what you're
talking about!" Jeannette broke in, suddenly stirred
to speech. "I threw away my life, talking just that
kind of nonsense. To learn to earn her own living
is a dangerous thing for a young girl."

"Why, how do you mean, Aunt Jan?"

"Its effect is poison; it's like a drug, a disease! I've
paid bitterly for my financial independence. I sacri-
ficed everything that was precious to me because I
wanted to be self-supporting. Etta dear, life is a hard
game for women at best, but waiting within the shelter
of her own home for the man she'll some day come to
love and who will love her is the best and wisest course
for a girl to follow."

"But I hate the kind of life I'm living! There's
nothing ahead of me but marriage, unless I go to
work! You wouldn't want me to marry just because I
was bored at home,—and I've known lots of girls to
do that! I never meet any attractive men,—only High
School kids and rah-rah boys out of college. Wouldn't
I have a much better chance to meet a finer class of
young men around business offices,—I mean serious-
minded, ambitious young men? It seems to me I'd
have much more opportunity to meet a man I'd ad-
mire, and who might want me to marry him if I went
to work than I ever will waiting stupidly at home."

"It doesn't make any difference where you meet
him, whether it is in business or at a High School
dance," Jeannette answered. "He's bound to find
you, and you him. . . . I hate to see you go to work.
You pay a fearful penalty in doing so. It makes you

regard marriage lightly, and prejudices you against having children——"

"Oh, I shall want children!" exclaimed Etta, promptly. She proceeded to outline just what were her requirements in a husband, and to give her views on the subject of having children. Her aunt was somewhat disconcerted to discover that she had these matters, as far as they concerned herself, entirely settled in her own mind. "Oh, yes, indeed," Etta repeated, "I shall want children. Perhaps not such a lot of them as Moth' and Dad have. They would have had a much easier time of it, if they'd had only one or two. Instead of always being poor and having to struggle, they could have lived in considerable comfort, and now there would be no question about their being able to send me to Bryn Mawr or Vassar. I think two children are enough for any couple. Now, my idea, Aunt Janny,——"

"Oh, for Heaven's sakes, Etta!" Jeannette interrupted with impatience; "you don't know what you're talking about! What does your education or Ralph's education amount to in comparison with the lives of Frank, Nettie, and Baby Roy? You'll have a great deal more worth-while education pounded into you by having brothers and sisters and by having to help your mother take care of them, than you would ever get at Bryn Mawr. More than that, just living in the same house with them, being brought up with them and learning to deny yourself, now and then, for their sake has taught you unselfishness, forbearance that will make you a far better wife and mother than ten years' of college education! . . . Your father and mother with you children about them, with the hard problems you present, with the ever-pressing question of ways and means before them, with the solving of these problems,—for there is always a solution,—are among the most enviable people in the world. There was a time when I used to feel sorry for your mother, but now I look at her with only admiration and jealousy. You think of her as poor! Well, I think of her as rich! And I attribute much of the happiness she has had out of life to the fact that she never went into business. . . . Stay out of it, Etta my dear, whatever you do! It's an unnatural environment for a girl, and in it her mind and soul as surely become contaminated as if she deliberately went to live in a smallpox camp. . . . Look at me, my dear! I've given twenty years of my life to business and what have I to show for it? Nothing but a very lonely and selfish old age!''

"Oh, Aunt Jan!" cried the girl, shocked into protesting. "How can you say such things! Why I think you're one of the handsomest, happiest, most enviable, smartest-dressed women in the world!"

Jeannette laughed.

"Well, I didn't mean to deliver a 'curtain' lecture! I just hated the thought of your following in my footsteps. It makes me actually shudder even to think of it. But I didn't mean to get started the way I did——

"Here," she suddenly cried, gathering her things together and hurriedly getting to her feet, "this is the Bridge! We have to get off here and change cars."

§ 2

The house just inside the high iron fence of the Navy Yard in which Commander Jerome Sedgwick lived was a three-story, square, dirty cream-painted cement affair, which bore his name in a small, neat sign on the third step of the front stairs. Across the street from it, children racketed upon a city play-ground, and in its rear some green-painted hot-houses leaned haphazardly against one another, their backs turned upon a quadrangle where several orderly tennis courts were located. Jeannette had visited Miss Holland here many times, and one summer a few years ago, had spent her two weeks' vacation keeping her old friend company, while the nephew, Jerry, was enjoying a month's leave with his family, fishing among the Maine lakes.

A little girl of five, just tall enough to reach the knob, opened the door a few inches and stared up unsmilingly at the visitors.

"How do you do, Sarah?" said Jeannette, recognizing the child. "Is your mama at home?"

Sarah continued to stare stolidly a moment, then turned and disappeared, leaving the door hardly more than ajar. Jeannette and Etta could hear the sound of her shrill, piping voice, and her small running feet within.

Mrs. Sedgwick came rustling to greet the callers promptly, and in her wake limped Miss Holland.

"Oh, you *dear!*" exclaimed the latter, catching sight of Jeannette. "I'm so glad you came; I've been hungering for a sight of you for weeks." She kissed her friend warmly on both cheeks. Etta was presented.

"The child begged to be allowed to come," explained her aunt. "She wanted a glimpse of the Yard."

"Why, certainly," exclaimed Mrs. Sedgwick cordially. "I'm delighted you brought her. Jerry unfor-

tunately isn't home but I have to take Sarah and
Junior out shortly, and I'll be charmed to show your
niece about, and leave you two to gossip by your-
selves.''

Miss Holland, her thin, knuckly, white hand on Jeannette's forearm, drew her into the sitting-room.

"Take off your things down here, my dear; I can't
climb stairs very well on account of my knees, and no
one's coming in.''

"How *is* your rheumatism?'' inquired Jeannette.

" 'Bout the same; it keeps me rather helpless, and
the doctor is actually starving me to death. What with
the things he says I can't eat and the things I don't
like, my menus are rather limited.''

The two women settled themselves before the small,
glowing coal fire in an old-fashioned grate, and began
talking in low tones. Mrs. Sedgwick excused herself
to make the children ready to go out, while Etta stood
at the window, gazing with absorbed interest at any
evidence of Navy life that came within the range of
her vision.

" 'Xcuse me, Miss Holland,'' she interrupted presently with her usual breathlessness, "do you happen
to know, or did you ever hear Commander Sedgwick
mention a young ensign named White?''

Miss Holland looked doubtful.

"My friend, Marjorie Bowen, knew him, or knew
his sister, I think, while he was at Annapolis.''

"Well, I'm afraid . . .'' began Miss Holland.

Etta proceeded hastily to another observation.

"There was a destroyer in Cohasset Bay last summer,—anchored right off the Yacht Club,—and I saw
two of the officers on shore one day. . . . I don't know

what their names were, of course, but during the war
I knew several of the boys in the reserves. Asa
Pulitzer was a boatswain's mate; . . . I think that's
what he was.''

Jeannette turned an indulgent smile upon Miss Holland.

"Asa Pulitzer is the local grocer's son."

"Well, I don't care if he is!" protested Etta. "He
made good——''

Mrs. Sedgwick rustled downstairs at this moment,
making a timely entrance. She carried Etta off, with
assurance of returning in time for tea.

"Well-l," said Jeannette comfortably, as the pleasant hour of companionship and confidences began.
"You don't *look* as if you'd been ill!"

"Not ill exactly; it's this wretched rheumatism that
will not get better."

Miss Holland's tone was not complaining; indeed
she always spoke with remarkable placidity. Jeannette regarded her with all her old admiration. There
was an unusual aristocratic quality about Miss Holland that never failed to stir her. She was white-
haired, now, fragile and thin looking, and there was
an uncertainty about her movements, but she still bore
herself with distinction,—a gentlewoman to her finger-
tips. Even more than the air of gentility that surrounded her, Jeannette esteemed the shrewd brain,
nimble wit and judgment of this woman. It seemed
a sad and sorry thing to her that so splendid a personality, so fine an intellect should have had so little
opportunity for self-expression in the world, and that
at sixty, Miss Holland should be no more than what
she seemed: an old maid, growing yearly more and

more crippled, passing what days remained to her with her nephew and her nephew's family, somewhat of a problem, somewhat in the way! Of course they loved her; Jeannette knew that Commander Sedgwick was devoted to his aunt and treated her with as much respect and affection as ever son did his mother, but, after all, on the brink of old age, Miss Holland's course was run, and how little she had to show for all her years of toil and faithfulness! She had spent her life at an underling's desk and given her wisdom and her strength to a business that had paid her barely enough to support herself and make it possible for her to give her nephew his profession!

"Miss Holland," Jeannette asked impulsively, "what did the Corey Company pay you towards the end of your employment there?"

"Fifty dollars a week for the last five years I was with them."

"And altogether, you were there?"

"Twenty-five years. . . . Why do you ask?"

"I was thinking how little they appreciated you."

"Mr. Kipps told me," Miss Holland said with a reminiscent smile, "that it would never do to pay women employees more than fifty a week; they wouldn't know what to do with the money."

"He didn't!"

"Oh, yes! He claimed it would demoralize them. He used to say they would be sure to throw it away on 'fripperies.' 'Fripperies,' you remember, was a great word of his."

"It still is!"

"Mr. Kipps' attitude is typical, I think, of the average employer of women. This is a man-made world, as perhaps you've noticed, my dear. Did you ever stop to consider the injustice to which working women are subjected? Do you realize there are about twelve million working women on pay-rolls in the United States, that twenty dollars a week is a very high wage for any one of them to receive, and six million of them, or half of the entire number, earn between ten and twelve a week? . . . I happen to have the statistics issued by the woman's bureau of the Department of Labor."

Miss Holland pushed herself up erect from her chair, and her face showed the pain the effort cost her.

"Can't I get it for you?" offered Jeannette hastily.

"No—no; thanks very much; it's right here. I can put my hand on it in just a minute." From a desk near at hand she produced a government report.

"I came across this the other day, and I saved it because it proves what I have always felt about the unfairness with which women are treated in business. They may perform equal work with men but very few of them are paid as well. The average annual earning power of the male industrial worker now is at the rate of a thousand dollars a year; that of the woman industrial worker five to six hundred. Among office workers the disparity is much greater. When I was getting fifty dollars a week as Mr. Kipps' chief assistant, there was a youth helping me who was being paid sixty."

"I know," agreed Jeannette. "When Tommy Livingston followed me as Mr. Corey's secretary, he did not do the work half as competently as I had done,—Mr. Corey often told me so,—and yet he was paid more at the very start, and asked for and received one raise

and efficient work in such positions as you filled and as I fill to-day, they are paid fifty dollars a week!''

"I answered him," Miss Holland went on, after an appreciative nod, "that neither could the men he employed be considered as fixtures. I reminded him of Van Alstyne, Max Oppenheim, Humphrey Stubbs, Walt Chase, Tommy Livingston and Francis Holm. There are a hundred others. How many boys starting in to business, do you suppose, stick for the balance of their lives with the concern for which they first began to work?''

"Not many.''

"Few indeed! It's to keep and hold these same boys and young men that the large corporations to-day are offering to sell them stock at advantageous rates.''

"Of course, it is the girls living at home," observed Jeannette, "partially supported by their fathers and mothers or some relative, willing to work for small salaries to buy themselves a few extra clothes and a measure of amusement, that are keeping down the salaries paid to women entirely dependent on their earnings.''

"During the war," observed Miss Holland, "a hundred thousand women were employed by the railroads to perform the work which the men formerly did before they went into the army. Women cleaned locomotives, tended stock-rooms of repair shops, sold tickets, took charge of signal stations, worked as carpenters, machinists, and electricians; women took the places of men in the steel mills, in the munition plants, in the foundries and even in coal mines. The National War Labor Board, headed by William H. Taft, undertook to protect the women workers, and laid down the principle that women doing the work formerly performed by men should receive the same pay. In other words, the pay was to be fixed by the job and not by the sex of the employe. Employers throughout the nation followed the ruling of the Labor Board.''

"But that was a war-time measure," said Jeannette, "and we all did things, then, that were altruistic and patriotic."

"If women had the physical strength of men," Miss Holland asserted, "and could defend their principles by force, there would be a speedy end of injustices. Why do male waiters in our restaurants get higher wages than waitresses? Certainly they don't work any harder, or give better service. Suppose all the women workers in New York City formed unions, and struck for what they decided adequate pay, a uniform scale of salaries, and could use the same methods that men would use in preventing women who had not joined the ranks from taking their places! Think what would happen! The work in every office, every bank, every corporation in this city would come promptly to a standstill; the strike would last forty-eight, seventy-two hours, and then the demands of the women would be conceded. . . . You want to remember one thing, my dear: *women never banded together since history began, and asked anything that was unfair or unjust!*"

"I was having a very interesting talk with my niece as we were coming here," broke in Jeannette; "Etta wants to go to work, wants a position as stenographer in some office, not only to earn extra money with which to help out at home, but to acquire an interest in life that will fill her days. There are a hundred thousand young girls like her in this city to-day. Consider what effect a job would have on an immature character like Etta's! I've been all through the bitter mill, and I speak from experience. Financial independence is a dangerous thing for such young girls. It makes them regard marriage with indifference. There is many a girl who has declined to marry a young man to whom she undoubtedly would have made a good wife merely because his income, which would have to do for both of them, was no more, or perhaps only a little more, than what she was earning herself.''

Jeannette's lips closed firmly a moment and she stared out of the window at the bleak prospect of the Yard's quadrangle bordered by closed and silent brick warehouses.

''But suppose the girl office-worker decides to give matrimony a trial,'' she continued, ''as I did, her mind has been distorted by having known what it means to be financially her own mistress. Instead of bringing to her job of wifehood the resolute determination to make a success of it, from the first she is critical, and on the constant lookout for hardships in her new life, comparing them with the freedom of her old. I should have made Martin a much better wife, Miss Holland, if I had brought to my problem of being his partner the passionate determination that was mine in wanting to make good as Mr. Corey's secretary. I always hugged to myself the thought that if the time came when I wouldn't like Martin any more or like being a wife, I could go back to my job,—and that is exactly what this thought led me to do. Making any marriage a success is the hardest work I know about both for

men and women, and there should be no avenue of
easy escape from it for either of them. I'd never
have left Martin, I'd have endured his unkindness and
lack of consideration,—or at least what seemed his
unkindness and lack of consideration to me then,—if
there hadn't been an easy way out for me, and we'd
have gone on together and made a home for ourselves
and our children. All I had to do was to walk out of
Martin's house and go back to my job. That's what
every wife who has once been a self-supporting wage-
earner says to herself from the day she marries. She
doesn't even have the trouble of getting a divorce to
deter her. . . . It's wrong, I tell you, Miss Holland!
It's all *wrong!* The more I live, the more I am convinced that women have no place in business. No,—
please let me finish,'' she said earnestly as her friend
started to interrupt. ''There's one other angle to this
question: the girl who has once tasted independence
but who decides to give matrimony a trial may go so
far as to consent to be a wife, but she stops at becoming a mother! She dreads children. And why? Because she realizes that once a baby is at her breast,
she's bound hand and foot to her husband and her
home. She can't leave her child with the nonchalance
she can her husband. In the homes of women who
have achieved economic independence before they
marry, you will find few children, and in the majority
of cases, none at all. I know a score of girls, at one
time in office jobs, who quit them to be married, but
have drawn the line at babies.

''It seems to me this is of national significance. The
country is being deprived of homes and children because of this great invasion of women into business

during the last twenty or thirty years. When I went to work twenty-four years ago, it was the exception for nice girls to go into offices. I remember how my mother fretted over my wanting to do it and how bitterly she opposed me. Now, every girl, rich or poor, desires a year or two of business life. Women are devised by Nature to be home-builders and mothers. Anything tending to deflect them from fulfilling their destiny is contrary to Nature and is doomed to failure or to have bound up in it its own punishment. When women compete with men in fields in which they do not belong, they are acting against Nature, and as surely as one gets hurt by leaning too far out of a window, so surely do such women pay a penalty for their deeds. Man was condemned in Genesis to 'work by the sweat of his brow'; there is nothing said about women having to work; she was given her own punishment. And here is an obvious fact, Miss Holland: No man likes to work under a woman boss. When I took charge of the Mail Order Department, three men who had been with Walt Chase resigned rather than work under me. I didn't blame them. It was as repugnant to me to give them orders as it was for them to take them.

"Now that is a biological obstruction in the way of woman's progress in business that you cannot get away from, and which you cannot lay to man's door. Men don't like to work for women, and women don't like to have men assistants, and since man is intended by God and Nature to be the worker, and woman is ordained to bear children, I say again that women have no place in business."

"But Miss Sturgis, Miss Sturgis!" cried Miss Holland. "Do you mean to tell me that women have not the right to earn their own living? Do you mean to tell me that you and I and all the women in the world must always look to some man to support us? Do you mean to tell me that widows with children to take care of, and women whose husbands are incapacitated or who desert them or who turn out to be drunkards or brutes, and women who are adrift in the world, and perhaps have never married because they've never been wooed, haven't a right to turn their brains to account and earn their livelihoods?"

"Well, it might be a good plan to limit the women workers to just the classes you mention," Jeannette answered. "Certainly I won't concede to you that every eighteen-year-old flapper like my niece or your sweet young college-graduate has the right to plunge into business and unfit herself for wifehood and motherhood, driving at the same time some needy soul of her own sex out of employment. Comeliness, a fair complexion have much to do with securing a job for a woman and with helping her to retain it. The plain girl or, more particularly, the middle-aged woman with two children to support, whose beauty has long since deserted her, has small chance against the pink-skinned eighteen-year-old with the bobbed hair and the roguish eye who may only have one-tenth of her ability. No employer ever hires a good-looking young man in preference to a homely one whose years of experience and ability are known. The more faded a woman becomes, the less she is wanted about an office. Looks play an important part in the rôle of the business woman. She should be judged, I think, not by her appeal to the eye, but by her industry. This is one more reason why

I believe women under thirty should be debarred from going to work. If women workers were limited, confined to thousands, let us say, instead of millions, then those privileged to work could earn a proper living wage, and dictate the terms under which they should be employed. There are certain professions and callings to which women are recognizably better suited than men; nursing and dressmaking are but two of them. If the supply of women for these vocations were limited, the demand would soon fix an adequate wage.

"It has occurred to me many times," persevered Jeannette, "that it would perhaps solve the problem,—or help solve it,—if certain professions and certain kinds of work were restricted by law to women. I've been told that in Japan only those who are blind may be embalmers of the dead. It restricts this vocation to a class of unfortunates which otherwise would have great difficulty in earning its living, and as a consequence there are no blind mendicants in Japan. I would advocate legislation in this country that would restrict certain occupations solely to women, and then I would limit the women who were eligible to fill them to widows or to those who could prove they must support themselves."

"There is little doubt that becoming wage-earners tends to keep women out of matrimony," Miss Holland said thoughtfully. "I know it did with me. There was a young professor of archæology from Wesleyan who wanted me very earnestly to marry him, and I should have liked to have done so, but I was working then, and had taken Jerry to live with me,—he was only eight,—and the professor's salary was not large enough for the three of us."

"And think what a wonderful wife you would have made!"

"I don't know about that," smiled Miss Holland, "but I was interested in his work and I should have enjoyed helping him."

"Exactly!" cried Jeannette. "I have no doubt you would have helped him very materially, whereas you gave your wits and your life in helping Mr. Kipps over the rough parts of his business days for a consideration of fifty dollars a week!"

"He could have found somebody else who could have helped him just as well."

"But that doesn't make it any fairer," insisted Jeannette. "What have you got to show for your twenty-five years of helping Mr. Kipps? . . . This!" She spread out her hands significantly.

"Well, I have my old age provided for," said Miss Holland, with an indulgent smile. "I get my check for half-salary from the office regularly the first of every month. I suppose I'll continue to get that until my rheumatism or my heart carries me off."

"But is that any reward for twenty-five years of slavery and drudgery? How many thousand and tens of thousands of dollars have your brains saved the Corey Publishing Company?"

"That isn't all of it. You must remember I have Jerry."

§ 3

Yes, she had Jerry, said Jeannette to herself, lying awake that night for long aching hours of whirling thoughts after she was in bed. Miss Holland's old age was rich in the love this nephew, his wife and children bore her.

And it came to the sleepless woman in the bed that it was not the love Miss Holland received that mattered; it was what she gave and had given that made her life, in spite of old age, rheumatism and growing helplessness, glorious with complete and satisfying happiness.

CHAPTER IV

§ 1

"DENT—Department—Derrick—Desmond—Deutsch —Deveraux—Deverley—De Vinne—Devlin . . ."

There it was: "Martin Devlin, Motor Cars,—North Broad Street." Jeannette's polished finger-nail rested beneath the name and her lips formed the words without a sound. She closed the Philadelphia Directory, turned from the telephone desk in the big New York hotel, and walked slowly out into the bright autumn glare of the street.

Thanksgiving was next week; there would be no difficulty in securing leave at the office to be absent from Wednesday night until Monday morning.

"I'd just like to see," she kept repeating to herself. "There'd be no harm in *seeing* what kind of a place he has. I could learn so much just walking by."

An odd excitement took possession of her. She saw herself in the train, she saw herself in a large, comfortable room at the Bellevue-Stratford, saw herself in her smartest costume, sauntering up Broad Street.

"I've a good mind to do it," she whispered. "It could do no possible harm. I'd just like to see."

She was unable to reach any definite conclusion, but she inspected her wardrobe carefully, deciding exactly what she would wear if she went to Philadelphia, and then did a very reckless thing: she bought herself a

sumptuous garment, a short outer jacket of broadtail
and kolinsky, a regal mantle fit for a millionaire's wife.
A giddy madness seemed to settle upon her after this;
her savings in the bank,—the savings which were to
buy another bond,—were almost wiped out, and she
deliberately drew a check for what remained. Some
power outside of herself seemed to take charge of her
actions; she moved from one step to another as if
hypnotized; she spoke to Mr. Allister about two extra
days at Thanksgiving, she bought her ticket and chair-
car reservation at the Pennsylvania Station, she wrote
the Bellevue-Stratford to hold one of their best outside rooms for her, she explained with simulated care-
lessness to Beatrice Alexander that there was a Book-
Dealers' Convention in Philadelphia which the firm
had requested her to attend, and the four o'clock train
on the afternoon of the holiday found her bound for
the Quaker city.

As she sat stiffly upright in her luxurious armchair,
staring out upon the dreary New Jersey marshes,
panic suddenly came upon her.

What was she doing? Was she *crazy?* Was Miss
Sturgis of the Mail Order Department this woman, so
elegantly clad, speeding toward Philadelphia? And
on what mad errand? After years of careful living,
after years of prudent saving, was it actually she,
Jeannette Sturgis, who had recklessly flung to the four
winds the bank account of which she had been so
proud? Oh, she must be mad, indeed!

She grasped the arms of her chair and instinctively
glanced from one end to the other of the palatial car.
She was seized with a violent impulse to get off.
There was Manhattan Transfer; she could take a

train back to the city from there. Determinedly, she gazed out upon the empty, cold-looking platform when the train reached the station, but she made no move, and as the wheels commenced to rumble beneath her once more, she sank back resignedly into her seat, and a measure of calmness returned.

She was not committing herself merely by going to Philadelphia and walking past Martin's place of business! Suppose she *did* meet him! Suppose they actually encountered one another, face to face! What then? There was nothing compromising in that! She could explain her presence in Philadelphia in a thousand ways should he be interested. She blessed the judgment that had prompted her to confide in no one; Beatrice believed she was attending a Book-Dealers' Convention, Alice that she was having her Thanksgiving dinner with Miss Holland.

§ 2

As she left the overheated parlor car at Broad Street Station her composure was thoroughly restored. There was a tingling nimbleness in the air; the clear, November day was bright with metallic sunshine. Jeannette tipped the "red-cap" for carrying her bags, climbed into a taxi-cab and with a casual air that seemed to spring from familiarity with such proceedings, directed to be driven to her hotel.

The cold bare streets, deserted on account of the holiday, the brilliant foyer of the Bellevue, the urbane room-clerk, the gilded elevator cage, the large high-ceilinged bedroom with its trim, orderly furniture, its double-bed, glistening with white linen, its discreet engravings of Watteau ladies in the gardens of Versailles, followed in quick succession. Then she was standing at the window looking down into the wide, dismal gray street far below, and the departing bell-boy softly closed the door behind him.

She was here; she was in Philadelphia; she would have that to remember always. If nothing else happened, she could never forget she had come this far. . . . Somewhere in the city was Martin; he was preparing to eat his Thanksgiving Dinner; it was a quarter past six, he was probably dressing! . . . Suppose he elected to eat the meal with friends in the main dining-room of her hotel! Her throat tightened convulsively and her fingers twitched. Well, she would be equal to facing him if he saw her; she would not be frightened into abandoning the course that was natural for her to follow. If it had been actually the case that she was here in Philadelphia to attend a Book-Dealers' Convention, she would put on her black satin dinner frock and go down to dinner with her book; she did not propose to allow herself to do differently. . . . It would be ridiculous to eat her Thanksgiving dinner up-stairs in her rooms!

She bathed, she did her hair with unusual success, she powdered her neck and arms, she donned the black satin with the square neck and jet trimming, and with her book beneath her arm, mesh bag in her hand, descended to the dining-room at half past seven. There was an instant's terror as she stood in the curtained doorway of the brilliantly-lit dining-room. There rushed upon her impressions of flowers, music, the odor of food, a wave of heat, the flash of napery, the gleam of cutlery, faces, faces everywhere,—heads turning,—eyes following,—whispers,—a hush as she made her way in the wake of the obsequious head-waiter.

Steeling her nerves, measuring every movement, she seated herself with deliberation, deliberately set her bag and book at her right hand, deliberately turned her attention to the menu, deliberately raised her eyes, and gazed about the room as she deliberately ordered.

But there was nothing! There was nobody! No one was looking at her; no one had noticed her entrance! The music was wailing in waltz measure, the diners were talking and laughing, attendants hurrying to and fro. He was not there; there was no one faintly resembling him in the room.

She cleared her throat and raised a tumbler of water to her lips, but as she did so, her teeth chattered an instant against the thin glass.

§ 3

Philadelphia awoke the next day with the bustle of business. Feet clip-clipped on the pavements, taxies chugged and honked, trucks bumped and rattled, street-cars rumbled and clanged their bells. Life, teeming, bustling, rushing, burst from every corner and doorway.

Mechanically Jeannette moved through her early morning routine; she dressed, breakfasted, read her newspapers; she drew upon her shoulders the handsome fur jacket, as, gloved, hatted and gaitered, she stepped out on the street.

"Taxi, lady?" No, she preferred to walk. Her number was only a few squares away.

An intent and hurrying tide of pedestrians set against her, congested traffic choked the street. She was an interested observer, and made but a leisurely progress, stopping at the shop windows, studying their displays. Nothing unusual in any of them attracted her; New York was more up-to-the minute in fads and fancies; the merchants there were more enterprising; they knew what was what; these Philadelphia shop-keepers merely aped their ways and followed their leads. There was no city in the world, she thought with pride, where merchandising was such a fine art and where novelties so quickly caught on as in New York. She wondered why people lived in Philadelphia when they could just as well live in New York. She passed a theatre and read the announcement on the bill-board; the play had been in New York six months ago!

She captured her wandering thoughts and looked about her, wondering how far she had walked.

"Vine Garden?"

"The next cross-street, Madam."

Her pulses stirred and unconsciously she quickened her pace. She was presently in the neighborhood of the number she sought. It ought to be right here. . . . She edged her way towards the curb and gazed up at the façades of stores and buildings. Strange,—there was nothing here that resembled an automobile agency! That building was a piano store, and in the next sewing machines were sold. . . . Suddenly the name leaped at her in a window's reflection. It was across the street! She wheeled about and there it was: Martin Devlin—Motor Cars. The name was in flowing script, the letters rounded and bright with gold, and the sign tilted out slightly over the sidewalk. Her heart plunged and stood still. That was her husband's place of business! There it was: Martin Devlin— Motor Cars!

The appearance of the agency impressed her. Across its front were four large plate-glass windows, two on each side of the entrance. On these also appeared Martin's name in the same style of flowing script, and beneath, in Roman type, the name of the automobile he handled. The show-room was spacious and softly illuminated with reflected light from alabaster bowls hung from the ceiling by brass chains. There were a half dozen models of the motor car, ranged within, three on a side, their noses pointing toward one another obliquely. The high polish of nickel and varnish, here and there, reflected the bright electric radiance above. The place had the air of elegance.

Curious, but with galloping pulses, Jeannette picked her way across the street, and slowly strolled past. Through the plate-glass windows she could see two young men standing, their arms folded, talking. Neither was Martin. She turned and retraced her steps, swiftly inspecting. Every moment her confidence increased. She noted the walls of the show-room were of cream-tinted terra-cotta brick, the floor of smooth cement with rich rugs defining the aisles; in the rear was a balcony where she could see yellow electric lights burning over desks, and make out the faces and figures of two or three girls. That was where the offices were located, no doubt, where Martin would have his desk.

Was he in? Would she risk a meeting? Did she have nerve enough to go inside and say: "Miss Sturgis would like to see Mr. Devlin!" . . . It was extraordinary, amazing! . . . How utterly overcome he would be! . . . To have his wife, whom he hadn't seen for fourteen years, walk in upon him that way! . . . It wasn't fair to him, after all. She had better go back to the hotel and write him,—or perhaps it would be better to telephone.

Emotions, impulses, strange and contradictory, pulled her one way and another. The apprehension, the misgivings of yesterday were absent now. There was no longer any question in her mind as to whether or not she wanted to see Martin; she knew she wanted to see him very much; in fact, her mind was made up, she must see him. It would be a thrilling experience, after so many years. . . . When they parted, it had not been because they had ceased to be fond of one another. They had liked,—yes, even loved each other, at the very moment of separation. . . . How was it to be managed? How could she arrange to meet him with propriety? Her appearance, she was aware, would make an impression upon him; that effect would be lost in writing or telephoning. . . . Perhaps she had better go back to the hotel and think it over, but then she might never again find the courage which was hers at that moment. . . . She must do something; she could not stand there indefinitely gazing through the window at the motor cars inside! The young men within, she observed, had noticed her.

With heart that hammered at her throat, she stepped

to the heavy door; it swung back at her touch. There was a pleasant warmth within. One of the young men came hurrying forward, rubbing his hands, one over the other, bowing politely, a beaming smile upon his face.

"Good morning, Madam. Interested in the *Parrott?*"

Jeannette swept the show-room with a quick look before answering. There was no one there remotely like Martin.

"I was thinking about one," she admitted.

"Most happy to arrange a demonstration at any time. . . . What model did you fancy?"

Jeannette moved about the cars, peering into the interiors of their tonneaus, commenting upon the upholstery and finish, pretending an attention to the young salesman's glib explanations.

"Shift here is automatic . . . cylinders . . . compression . . . hundred-and-eighteen-inch wheel-base, . . . equipment just as you see it, . . . rear tire extra, of course, . . . lovely car for a lady to drive . . . rides like a gazelle . . . just like a gazelle . . . . you wouldn't know you were moving . . . Lovely engine, isn't it, Madam? . . . A child could easily take it apart."

Jeannette nodded and appeared interested. All the time she was thinking: "I wonder if he's up there— I wonder if he's up there."

"Mr. Devlin . . . ?" she hazarded.

"Oh, you know Mr. Devlin?" The possibility seemed to fill the salesman with rare pleasure; it was a discovery, unexpected, delightful.

"I—I used to know him years ago," Jeannette faltered.

"He's a splendid man, isn't he?" glowed the youth. "Wonderful personality,—a regular 'good fellow.' He's made quite a record with the *Parrott*, you know. Unfortunately he's out just now, but he's expected. I'm sure he'll be glad to know you called, and I'll be very pleased to tell him. You didn't mention . . . May I ask the name?"

Jeannette hesitated. This was not the way she would have him hear of her.

"No,—I'll call again; I'll come in later. I'm—I'm stopping at the Bellevue; it isn't far."

"Couldn't I arrange a demonstration for you this afternoon? At any hour you say. I'd like to show you the way the *Parrott* rides,—just like a gazelle. I'll have our driver come with the limousine, or perhaps you'd prefer the landaulet model. . . . You might like to pay some calls this afternoon; it would give you a chance to test the *Parrott* and see how you like it. . . . Ah, here's Mr. Devlin!"

The heavy glass front door opened. Jeannette felt the cold air from the street. She gave a quick glance as she turned her back, her heart plunging. It was Martin all right, but what a changed and different Martin! So much older, so much larger than she remembered him! He wore a Derby hat and had a cigar.

The salesman had left her side and was communicating her presence to his employer. Jeannette stood with both hands pressed tightly against her heart and fought for self-possession.

She heard Martin speak. That voice . . . ! That voice . . . ! It suffocated her. An avalanche of memories and forgotten emotions swept down upon her. . . . He was coming! She even recognized his step!

" 'Morning, Madam,"—there was the old briskness, and alertness in his tone!—"what can I——"

She straightened herself and turned regally.

"Good morning, Martin," she said smiling. Her color was high, she was trembling, her pulses racing.

There was a quick jerk of his head,—a well-remembered mannerism,—and a lightning survey of her features.

"Good God! . . . *Jan!*"

Emotions played in his face, his eyes darted about her, his color faded and flamed darkly. His confusion gave her composure. He was handsome still, smooth-shaven and clean; his cheeks were fuller, a trifle florid, he had a well-defined double-chin, his black, thick hair was streaked with wiry, white threads; he had grown stouter, had acquired a girth, but his fatness was robust and healthy. He had gained in presence, in firmness of feature, in polish,—a man of business and affairs, energetic, a leader.

"Are you surprised to see me, Martin?"

"Well, of course, . . . well, . . . I should say!"

She was conscious that her beauty and stateliness, her costume, her fashionableness overwhelmed him.

"I'll be . . . I'll be damned!" he enunciated. "Excuse me, Jan,—but I'll be . . . I'll be damned!"

An amused sound escaped Jeannette. She was smiling broadly; she felt she had the situation well in hand.

"I'm sorry I startled you, Martin. I happened to be passing and I saw your name and thought I'd drop in. . . . How've you been after all these years?"

"Oh,—all right, I guess. Sure, I've been fine. . . . And you? I guess there's no need of asking."

"I've been quite well. I'm never sick. I came down to Philadelphia to attend a Book-Dealers' Convention. . . . I'm stopping at the Bellevue."

"Well—er, you going to be in town long?"

"Oh,—two or three days. I'm going back to New York Sunday, I guess. I think I can get away by that time. . . . This is a fine car you handle; its lines are really very beautiful."

"It's a good car, all right. I had a big year this year,—and last year, too."

"Well, that's good; I'm glad to hear it. . . . I never heard of the *Parrott* before."

"You *didn't?* . . . Well, we think we advertise a good deal. It ranks up among the best. . . . Are you —are you married or anything like that?"

Jeannette laughed richly.

"Not since an experience I had some fourteen years ago that didn't take!"

Martin echoed her amusement. He was regaining his ease; she could see he was beginning to enjoy himself.

"You know I took my maiden name when I went back to work; everybody knew me there as 'Miss Sturgis'; it seemed easier."

"Yes, I see," Martin agreed.

"I'm still with the old company."

"What,—the same old publishing outfit?"

"Yes; I'm in charge of the Mail Order Department now. . . . We do quite a business."

"Is that so? And how do you like it?"

"Oh, I like it all right. They think a lot of me there,

and I do about as I please. . . . I'm thinking of resigning though; one of these days, pretty soon, I'll quit. It gets on your nerves after awhile, you know."

"Yes, I guess it does."

A momentary embarrassment came upon them.

"Well, it was pleasant to catch a glimpse of you, again, Martin. If you're ever in New York, ring me up. You know the office——"

"Well, say,—I don't like to have you go away like this! I'd like to see something of you while you're in town,—and talk over old times. There's a lot of things I'll bet we'd find interesting to tell one another."

"I shouldn't wonder," she said lightly.

"I got a business engagement for lunch unfortunately"; he scowled in troubled fashion. "I can't very well get out of it. . . . You're at the Bellevue? . . . Well, how about dinner? Couldn't we get together for dinner?"

"Why, I guess so. Yes,—that would be lovely," said Jeannette with an air of careful consideration.

"I'll bring my wife; Ruthie will be glad to meet you. You knew I married again, didn't you?"

Jeannette's expression did not alter by the quiver of an eyelash; she continued to regard Martin with smiling eyes.

"No, I hadn't heard. . . . I didn't suppose. . . . So you married, again?"

"Yes, I married a widow,—a widow with two kids: girl and a boy,—splendid youngsters. . . . Say, you *got* to see those kids; they're Jim-dandies!"

"That's . . . that's fine."

"And I think you'll like Ruthie, too, Jan. She

isn't your style exactly, but she's all right. There's no side to Ruthie. I think you'll like her; she's a fine little woman and a great little mother. You'll like her, I'll bet a hat.''

"I'm sure I shall.''

"Then it's all right for to-night? Ruthie'll join me downtown and we'll come over to the hotel, and the three of us will have a great little dinner together and chew the rag about old times. . . . Say, d'you ever see that old ragamuffin, Zeb Kline?''

"Oh, yes, indeed. I saw him two or three weeks ago. He's quite successful, now, you know; he's made a great deal of money; married Nick Birdsell's daughter.''

"Is *that* so! Well, is *that* so! He was a card all right, a great old scout. . . . And d'you ever see any of the rest of the old gang: Adolph Kuntz, an' Fritz Wiggens, an' Steve Teschemacher an' old Gibbsy?''

"Oh, yes, occasionally.''

"Say, what's old Gibbsy doing? He was a wormy little rat, all right, wasn't he?''

"He's got a very fine place, now, down on the Point, —quite an estate.''

"Well, wouldn't you know it! He'd be just the kind of a little tightwad that would build himself a swell house! . . . And what happened to old Doc French?''

Jeannette's countenance changed and she shook her head.

"Don't bother to tell me now. Save it up for to-night. We'll have a great talk-fest. . . . Ruthie and I will show up at the hotel,—what time? Let's

make it early so we can have all evening. Six-thirty?
How's that?''

Jeannette smiled assent.

"We'll be there at six-thirty, and say, Jan, you
know this is going to be my party all right—all right.''

He accompanied her to the door, knocking the Derby
hat nervously against his knee, his cigar gone out.

"Then we'll see you to-night, Jan. Six-thirty, hey?
. . . Gee, I'm glad you dropped in! We'll have a
great little old talk-fest.''

"To-night, then.''

"Sure. At the Bellevue. We'll be there. Six-
thirty.''

§ 4

Married? Married? It couldn't be possible! Why,
they had never been divorced! . . . How could he be
married again?

A great weariness came over Jeannette. It was disgusting! What had he wanted to get married again
for? Pugh! It was most disappointing. . . . Another
woman! . . . She had never imagined anything like
this. . . . Was he living with her without a ceremony?
Probably. She must be a cheap sort of creature.
. . . But it didn't make any difference whether she
was legally his wife or not; it was the same thing.
The fact remained he had taken up with someone else.
No doubt she was known as "Mrs. Devlin.''

Jeannette went back to the hotel and upstairs to
her room, laid aside her beautiful fur jacket, her hat,
took off her dress, put on her kimona. Her mind, like
a squirrel in a cage, went around and around over the

same ground. How *could* he be married? Why, they had never been divorced!

The prospect of the evening suddenly palled upon her. Even though he *had* married, a dinner and chat alone with Martin would have had some piquancy; it would have been quite exciting and amusing to have recalled old friends, old memories. But there would be no spontaneity in their talk with another woman beside them, a bored and critical listener! It would be dreadful! An intolerable situation! . . . She thought of a hurried return to New York, a telephone to Martin that she had been unexpectedly called home. Yet that seemed undignified; he would be sure to guess her reason, or if he did not, "Ruthie" could be depended upon to enlighten him. She shook her head in distaste. She was committed to this unpalatable program, now; she would be obliged to see it through, —but oh, how she was going to hate it! How she was going to despise every moment of it!

She considered the other woman, trying to imagine what she would be like . . . Well, Ruthie might be comfortably established in her place, but she should have no ground for believing she was envied!

A reflection of herself at this moment in the mirror forced a smile from Jeannette's lips as she detected upon her face a look of haughty condescension. She had been fancying the encounter with Ruthie and had unconsciously assumed the expression that would suit that moment. . . . Well, Ruthie would have the benefit of that withering, imperious glance; she would realize the minute she saw Jeannette Sturgis that here was a woman that would brook no patronizing airs from her, and in the course of the evening she would

have it pointed out to her, in a manner which would
leave no room for misunderstanding, that it was she,
Jeannette, who had left Martin; hers had never been
the rôle of the deserted wife; as far as "leavings"
were concerned, Ruthie had them and welcome! . . .
Ah! She *hated* her!

The telephone trilled. Jeannette's heart plunged
as she heard Martin's voice.

"Hello, Jan! Say,—I 'phoned Ruthie and she says
for me to bring you out to our house to-night; she
says it will be much pleasanter there and we can talk
a whole lot better. I rang her up and explained about
our having dinner with you at the Bellevue, but she
insists that you come on out to our house. She said
by all manner of means to bring you. She said she'd
'phone you, herself, but I said I didn't think that was
necessary."

"Why-y,—I'm afraid——"

"You know we live out at Jenkintown; it's an awful
pretty suburb. I'd like you to see it and I'm crazy to
have you see the kids. They'll still be up by the time
we get there. I'll call for you a little after six and
drive you out."

Jeannette's mind worked rapidly. There was
nothing for her to do but to accept, and to accept
graciously.

"That will be lovely, Mart. As you say it will be
much nicer in the country. I shall really like to see
your home and to meet—" she cleared her throat,—
"Mrs. Devlin."

"Well, that'll be fine, Jan,—that will be great. Say,
you couldn't make that five-thirty just as well, could
you? You see the office closes at five, and I'll just

have to bum 'round here doing nothing until it's time
to call for you,—and then besides you'll have a little
light left so you c'n see something of the country, and
I want to tell you, Jan, Jenkintown's a swell little
suburb.''

''Why, yes, Martin. Five-thirty will be perfectly all
right for me.''

''That's fine then; I call for you at five-thirty.''

She hung up the receiver and bent forward so that
her brow rested lightly against the mouthpiece of the
instrument, her eyes closed, and after a moment she
squeezed them tight shut. . . . Ah, what pain! . . .
What heart stabs! . . . The prick of tears stung her
eye-balls like needle points.

§ 5

She powdered her shoulders and did her hair; she
red-lipped her mouth; she hooked the black satin dress
about her; she hung her generous string of artificial
pearls around her neck and screwed the large artificial
pearl ear-rings upon her ears. At five o'clock she was
ready, and for the ensuing thirty minutes she studied
her reflection in the glass, turning first to one side,
then to the other, noting various effects. She wore
no hat, but to-night her hair, with its distinguished
touch of white, was dressed high, and thrust into its
thick coil at the back of her head were three large
brilliant, rhinestone combs.

Promptly at the half-hour, Martin was announced,
and slipping on the marvellous jacket, rolling the fur
luxuriously against her neck, Jeannette descended in
the elevator and met him in the foyer. The glance he

gave her satisfied her; she knew Martin; he had not
changed. There remained only Ruthie, and in that
instant it came to Jeannette a cold, disdainful manner would put herself, bound and helpless, at Ruthie's
mercy. They were two shrewd and clever women,—
she assumed Ruthie would be shrewd and clever,—
meeting one another under strange and difficult circumstances; any hint of condescension, any suggestion of a patronizing air, and Ruthie would be laughing
at her. No, the part for her to play was one of all
sweetness and amiability; graciousness was her only
salvation.

Martin guided her out of the hotel, his fingers at
her elbow. A limousine swept up to the door. It was
a *Parrott,* and there was a liveried chauffeur at the
wheel.

"Get right in, Jan."

He stooped through the doorway and sank heavily
against the upholstered cushions beside her. The
"starter" touched his cap, and banged the door.
Memories swept back upon Jeannette, memories of
another motor-car, a taxi-cab, and another "starter"
who had banged shut an automobile door upon the
two of them, and of a night pulsing with high emotions,
hopes and young love. Her little excited mother with
her pendent, trembling cheeks, dressed in her lavender velvet, had been with them on that other night,
and she had sat beside her daughter where Martin
now was sitting, and Martin had occupied the small
collapsible seat opposite, and had balanced himself
there with his knees uncomfortably hunched up, to
keep his feet out of the way!

". . . what we call the *Parrott* Convertible; it's

just out this year," Martin was explaining. "You see with a little manipulation of the glass windows and seats you can turn it from a limousine into a Sedan and drive it yourself."

"How clever!" she said. "You know, Martin, it delights me to think of your being so successful. It was coming to you. You were born to be a good salesman, and I'm glad you've gotten into a line of business where your talents count for something. You were entirely out of your element with that Engraving Company; they didn't begin to appreciate you."

"They didn't, did they? That younger Gibbs,— Herbert Gibbs,—he was certainly a little rat, if there ever was one. You know I had a terrible row with him after—after . . ."

"And I'm glad, too," proceeded Jeannette hastily, "that you've married again and 've got your son and daughter. You were always crazy about children. Remember how you used to rave about Alice's Etta and Ralph when they were babies?"

"You bet you. How are——?"

"And then you were much too fine and too good for that Cohasset Beach crowd——"

"They were a bunch of good scouts, all right."

"Weren't they?" Jeannette said veering quickly. "Every one of them has made good. Steve Teschemacher's quite wealthy."

"Tell me about him,—tell me about 'em all. Say, do you ever go down to Cohasset Beach any more?"

"Oh, yes; frequently. Alice and Roy bought there, you know."

"The deuce they did! You don't mean to say so?

Well, say, Jan, who's living in the bungalow? . . .
Say, Janny, I often think . . ."

They were busy in reminiscences, interrupting one
another, laughing, ejaculating, now and then arrested
by a memory that was not altogether mirth-provoking
and unexpectedly stirred them. At times Martin
swayed in his seat and pounded his knee.

"By God!" he would shout gleefully, "by God, I'd
forgotten that!—by God, that was a hot one, all right!
Say,—that had gone completely out of my mind.
You're a wonder for remembering little things, Jan!
. . . By golly!"

The car rolled smoothly out over the paved high-
way that circled through the hills. Large, handsome
houses with lights shining here and there from windows, and surrounded by tall, gaunt, leafless trees,
alternated on either side of the road and fled past.
Their own vehicle was but one link in a long chain of
nimble bugs with glowing antennæ which crawled hard
upon one another along the winding course.

There came an abrupt turn, the motor car swung
up a steep driveway, slid on to crunching gravel, and
stopped.

"Here we are!" exclaimed Martin. The chauffeur
leaped from his seat and attentively opened the car
door.

A large frame house of gracious lines, with exterior
stone chimneys, many windows, and a precipitous
lawn that swept down to the roadway a hundred feet
or more below.

"We get a splendid view of the valley here," said
Martin, coming to stand beside Jeannette as she
looked out across the country. The landscape was

shrouded in dusk, pricked with a myriad of lights;
there was a jagged silhouette of distant tree-tops and
beyond a pale, mother-of-pearl sky touched faintly
with dying pink.

They turned to the house and as Martin stooped to
insert his latch-key there was the quick run of small
feet within, the door was flung open and a little girl
hurled herself upon him with a violent silent hug.

"Well, well," said Martin, "how's my darling?"
He kissed her with equal vigor, his hat knocked at an
angle upon his head.

"This is 'Tinker,'" he said, smiling at Jeannette.
"Everybody calls her 'Tinker,' but her real name's
'Elizabeth.' Where's your brother, Tinker?"

An answering clatter and rush came from an interior
region, and a small boy flung himself upon the man.

"And this is Joe, Janny. He has a nickname, too;
sometimes we call him 'Josephus,'—don't we, old blun-
derbuss?"

There was another vigorous embrace.

The two children regarded Jeannette with shy but
friendly glances. The little girl was about nine, the
boy two or three years younger. Tinker was brown
of skin and brown of eye; her hair was short and
tawny and swept off her face in an old-fashioned way,
held back by an encircling comb that reached from
one temple to the other. She was freckled and had an
alert, engaging expression, while her brown eyes were
sharp as shoe buttons, and twinkled between long
tawny eyelashes. Simply, she approached Jeannette
and held up her brown arms as she offered her lips.
The boy was diminutive and wiry with furtive glance
and grinning mouth that displayed a gaping hole left

by two missing front teeth. He hung his head as he held out his small hand, but as Jeannette took it, he darted a quick upward look into her face and gave her a friendly elfish grin.

Jeannette was moved, captivated at once by the charm of both.

"They're darlings!" came involuntarily from her, and then there was the sound of descending feet upon the stairs and Jeannette straightened herself from the crouching position in which she had greeted the children to face their mother.

"A pretty woman—and sweet—younger than I expected," went Jeannette's thoughts; "nothing to fear here."

Ruthie was in truth a pretty woman, pretty without being either beautiful or handsome. Her expression was bright, alert, eager, her manner friendly and effusive. She resembled her small son.

"This is Ruthie, Jeannette——" began Martin.

"How do you do?" said Ruthie, hurrying forward, leaving no doubt of her cordiality. "It was very nice of you to come to us to-night."

"Not at all," Jeannette responded with her best smile. "It was nice of you to want me."

"I was anxious to know you," said Ruthie.

She could afford to be gracious thought Jeannette. She had everything: the home, the children, money, position,—she had Martin! . . . Was it possible they were really married? Or did Ruthie merely *think* she was his wife?

Jeannette was piloted upstairs to a large, pleasant bedroom. The chairs, the tables, the bureau and chiffonier, the twin beds were all of bright bird's-eye maple; rose hangings were at the windows, rose silk comforters were neatly folded at the foot of each bed, rose shades on the wall lights diffused a soft rosy radiance. The dressing-table glittered with silver toilet articles, and Jeannette noticed they were all monogramed ''R.T.D.'' Flanking them were large silver-framed photographs, one of Martin,—a handsome, fierce-looking Martin in evening dress,—the other of the two children, Tinker with her arm about her brother. Domesticity radiated everywhere.

''I never looked better,'' Jeannette thought consolingly as she caught a full-length reflection of herself in the long mirror impanelled in the bathroom door. Her hair pleased her; her high color was most becoming; she knew herself to be beautiful. She went downstairs, serene and confident, sure of being able to carry off the evening with lightness and ease.

''I thought it would be quieter and perhaps a little pleasanter without the children at table,'' said Ruthie brightly as Jeannette joined her, ''so I arranged to give them an early supper, and now Martin's been scolding me. He thinks you'll be disappointed.''

''Oh, it doesn't matter,'' Jeannette murmured.

''Martin's almost unreasonable about them; he wants them all the time,'' continued Ruthie. ''I tell him if he had them on his hands all day, perhaps he wouldn't be quite so enthusiastic!'' She laughed an amused little laugh like the twittering of a bird. ''He couldn't be fonder of them if they were his own,'' she added.

There was a moment's pause.

"You see, I'd lost my first husband before I met Martin," Ruthie continued thoughtfully. "My first marriage wasn't very successful."

She *did* think she was married then!

"You were divorced?" asked Jeannette. If there was a barb to the question it failed in effect.

"No; Mr. Mason was killed. He was—was rather intemperate, and there was an accident. I met Martin some time afterwards and he was wonderful to me."

"You've known him long?"

"Let me see. About seven years. Joe was only a baby, and we were living in Scranton. Martin and I married about a year after my husband's death. I was having a very hard time of it; Mr. Mason carried but very little life insurance and I took up manicuring; I had to; there was no other way for us to get along."

She smiled at the last.

He was sorry for her, thought Jeannette; that was the way of it.

"That had been your—your profession formerly?" Jeannette asked with an innocent air.

"No, I had to learn it," Ruthie said, unruffled. "I had to do something. I only did private work, you know." She cast a quick glance at Jeannette's face. "Martin and I didn't meet in a barber shop!" she added with a bright laugh.

Jeannette could think of nothing to say to this, so she nodded, and gazed into the red coals of the grate-fire before which the two women were standing.

"Here he is!" Ruthie said, suddenly.

Martin's step could be heard approaching and in a moment he entered the living-room. Jeannette noticed he had changed into dinner clothes.

"Well, Jan, it's mighty darned nice to see you here," he said advancing, rubbing his hands. He appeared well-groomed, was freshly shaved, his clothes fitted him to perfection, his thick neck and swarthy skin seemed clean and wholesome.

"Have a little cocktail?" he suggested. "I've got a cracker-jack bootlegger that brings me the stuff direct from New York,—real old Gordon! If this damned governor of ours has his way, we're not likely to get any more of it. This prohibition stuff makes me sick, doesn't it you?"

"It doesn't bother me, Martin," Jeannette answered lightly. "I never drink anything."

"Well, how about having a little cocktail to-night? Just by way of celebration? Huh? What d'you say?"

"No-o, thank you, Martin; not to-night. I really never touch it, but don't let me stop you two."

"Ruthie doesn't drink either. She's a plumb tee-totaler,—believes in it! What do you know about that?"

Martin laughed good-naturedly. His mirth had the old-time extraordinary infectious quality.

"Don't bother about mixing a cocktail to-night, Martin dear," Ruthie said in a persuasive voice. "It takes you so long with the ice and everything, and dinner's late, now."

"I'll have a little of the straight stuff, then," he said, still rubbing his hands in high good humor.

They went together into the dining-room through the double glass doors, curtained in shirred folds of pink silk. The table was glittering with polished silverware and sparkling glass; in the center was a low fern in a metal fern-dish. Martin unlocked a door in the sideboard, took out a whisky bottle, held it up a moment to the light to inspect the measure of its contents, and poured himself an inch into a tumbler.

"D' you remember that guy who used always to say 'Saloon' when he was taking a drink?" asked Martin, grinning at Jeannette. "He was a card all right? . . . Well, 'saloon!' "

He drained the drink in two gulps, followed it with a draught of water, and sat down, smacking his lips.

A maid appeared, bearing a tureen of soup, and presently passed cheese straws. Jeannette observed her spotless white bibbed apron and black dress, and she took note of the fine sprays of celery and olives in side dishes on the table, twinkling with ice. The dinner proceeded comfortably,—well-served, well-cooked, stereotyped: a roast of beef, with potatoes browned in the pan, canned French peas, a salad of chopped apples and nuts, a dessert of cake and ice-cream. She recalled with a sharp twinge the "company" dinners she had struggled so hard to prepare for Martin and his friends, and the effort she had made to serve him things he liked so as to make him want to stay at home. . . Ah, she had tried, she reminded herself, she had really tried hard to be a good wife to him! . . . It was all so much easier for Ruthie; she had her cook, her waitress, and there was even the chauffeur. So easy to sit still and merely tell them what to do! . . . And Martin? . . . Well, he had matured, he had settled down, was more seasoned, more reasonable, more disciplined. . . . She noticed for the first time a jagged white scar on his right temple; it had not been there when she had known him!

Throughout dinner he was in the gayest of spirits;

Ruthie turned bright alert eyes from one face to the other; Jeannette felt the last vestige of constraint slip from her. The talk was all of Tinker and Josephus, of the good schools of Jenkintown, of motor cars and the future of the automobile industry, of traffic laws and Philadelphia and things in general. Every once in awhile a chance remark would sound a personal note, but the three with one accord would veer away from it and pursue another topic. There was no telling where rocks of disaster might be hidden.

But after dinner, when Martin stood before the sucking coal fire in the living-room, stirring his coffee, a fresh cigar tilted up in the corner of his mouth, his head twisted to one side to avoid the smoke, it was evident the moment had arrived when he wanted to hear news of his old friends and start recalling old times. Tinker and her brother presented themselves to say good-night and their mother made them an excuse for leaving her husband and her guest together.

"She's far smarter than one would ever suspect from that affected bright expression," thought Jeannette smiling at the children as they tumbled themselves out of the room.

Ruthie did not reappear until nearly ten o'clock, and then came in with many apologies for having been detained. Martin, by that time, had heard all the news, had heard of Roy and Alice, of poor unfortunate Doc French, of 'Dolph Kuntz, and Fritz and Steve, and even of some of the changes in the publishing company which interested him. He was far from satisfied, however, and wanted to go over it all once more.

"Say, do you remember that night, Jan, you and I and that Scotch friend of yours and that awful fright he took along with him had dinner up on the Astor roof? What became of that guy?''

And——

''D'you 'member that time we got stuck out in the Sound aboard the Websters' yacht? . . . Say, do they have any more racing down there? . . . What's become of all the little A-boats?''

But Jeannette knew the time for leave-taking had come. She rose smiling.

''I'm sorry, Martin; I shall have to say goodnight. I really must be going. My day's very full to-morrow.''

He was loud in protest, a little unnecessarily loud, Jeannette thought. She tried to dissuade him from accompanying her back to the hotel, but he insisted.

''I wouldn't *think* of you riding back all by yourself, Jan! That wouldn't do at all. The car's right here; the man's waiting. He'll run me in and run me out again in less than an hour; I'll be home again in no time.''

Ruthie urged, too.

''Oh, yes,'' she insisted brightly. ''You must let Martin take you back to town; it won't hurt him a bit, and you two have such a lot to talk over together about old times and everything.''

The little woman's face was wreathed with smiles; she was confident, solicitous. She was sure of herself; sure of Martin; her concern had every semblance of sincerity. Jeannette felt baffled, vaguely irritated.

The two women said good-night to one another with appropriate phrases and amiability. Ruthie stood in the shining arch of the doorway as the motor car swept up to the steps, crunching on the fine gravel of the drive, and Jeannette and Martin got in. She even managed a little wave of the hand as its door slammed and the car started.

Jeannette hated her. It was impossible to guess what thoughts were behind that alert expression of innocent pleasure.

"You've come on in the world, Martin," she observed.

"Yes, I've made a little money, but I'm going to make more,—a good deal more. You know, I often think of the old man and the old woman up there in Watertown settling down forty, or I guess it's fifty, years ago, to running that little grocery business of theirs, and I can't help wishing sometimes they were round to see how good I've made. They'd get an eyefull, all right! But I've worked for my success, Jan,—that is, I've worked hard the last five years. You know I was down and out for awhile?"

"Were you? I didn't know that. How did that happen?"

Martin cleared his throat and twisted a little in his seat so as to talk more directly at her.

"I was pretty badly cut-up, Jan, when you ran out on me!"

"Were you?"

"You bet I was, and I began hitting her up there for awhile; I let things go to the devil and I was boozing a good deal. There were two or three years there when I wasn't much better than a bum."

"Martin!"

"Well, I was sore at the world,—and sore, I guess, at you. Yes, pretty damn sore. You know, Jan, I didn't think you treated me quite right, and then I blamed myself an awful lot for the way I treated you.''

"It was too bad,'' Jeannette said slowly. "I think maybe we were both wrong. We were very young and inexperienced, Mart.''

"Yes, that's right. We pulled the wrong way.''

"I'm sorry you took it so badly. I didn't feel extra good about it myself. I've often wished since. . . .''

"Oh, there's no use going over the old ground now. It's all over and done with, but I was mighty fond of you, Janny.''

"Don't, Martin.''

"You bet I was. I took it pretty hard when you left me; I didn't care what happened to me.''

"I'm sorry. It wasn't easy for me either. If you'd only come back,—or sent word . . .''

"You don't understand, Jan. I was down and out then. I had nothing to offer you. I'd punched Gibbsy's face and I'd lost my job and I was driving a truck,—that is, when I was working at all.''

"Martin!''

"Oh, what's the use of going back over old times!'' he said with sudden harshness. "You've changed and I've changed. I'm married now,—got a home and family,—and I'm happy, Jan. Ruthie's a good little woman.''

"When did you marry, Mart?''

"In—let's see!—in 1917; just before we got into the war. I got a job as a salesman in an automobile agency in Scranton. Tinker and her mother were living next door to my boarding house; it was Tinker that caught my eye first; she and I used to have great times together; I was crazy about that kid, and then I met Ruthie.''

"And after that you were married?"

"Well, not right away. I had to get free first. You were awfully decent about not contesting the suit, Jan, but then I was pretty sure you wouldn't."

"And was there a suit?"

"Why, sure. I got a decree in New York. They gave it to me. You never showed up."

"I don't remember," said Jeannette vaguely.

"You were served with a summons; we had the testimony of the process server! You let the case go by default."

"Did I? . . . I can't . . . I don't seem to remember. What were the grounds? I thought in New York State you had to prove——"

Martin leaned forward in his seat and stared at her through the dimness in the car, trying to see her face.

"Say, what *is* this?" he asked. "Are you trying to kid me,—rub it in, or something like that?"

"No, Martin," she answered earnestly. "I don't know what you're talking about. I never supposed we'd been divorced."

"Good God! Did you think we were still married?"

"Why, certainly."

The man dropped back against the upholstery with a short explosion of breath.

"Tell me about it, Martin."

"You make it damned hard, Jan. If you're trying to rub it in, you're certainly doing a nifty job."

"No, Martin, truly. I'm quite honest."

He was silent and Jeannette had to plead again for enlightenment.

"I don't understand this," he said, troubled.

"But tell me. I want to know."

"Well, you know I was damned sore at you," he began at length. "I wanted to get married; Ruthie, Tinker and the baby needed me. She was up against it and was having a tough time trying to make ends meet. I wanted to help out but she wouldn't let me and the only thing for it was to get married. So I went to a lawyer there in Scranton and asked him if he'd fix it so I could get a divorce from you. He got in touch with a firm in New York and they dug up all that rot about you and Corey——"

"Oh, my God!" gasped Jeannette in a whisper.

"Oh, I knew it was the bunk; you'd told me the story and I knew you'd given me the straight dope. But there was the evidence and the sworn affidavits of the hotel employees that Corey's wife had secured. It made enough of a case. I'm damned ashamed of it now, Jan. I wish to God, I'd never done it, but I was sore, remember, and I wanted to get married to Ruthie."

There was painful silence in the swaying car. Jeannette sat very still, two fingers of each hand pressed against either cheek.

"I was pretty certain you'd let it go by default," Martin went on after awhile in a distressed voice. "It was no case you'd want to contest, and I thought you probably wanted your freedom as much as I did. . . . I thought surely you'd married long ago."

Silence reigned again, Jeannette struggling with herself, Martin concerned at her voicelessness.

"By God, Jan, I thought you knew all about it,— I swear to God I did! The process server stated in court he'd handed you the summons, and saw you pick it up; I heard him say it with my own ears. The referee warned him about perjury, thought he smelled collusion, or something of that sort; he ragged me something fierce. . . . It was rotten the way it turned out, for the case came up right after your friend Corey died, and I felt pretty mean blackening a man's character when he wasn't more 'an cold in his grave, 'specially as I knew it was a frame-up.''

A pent-up breath escaped Jeannette like a moan. A scene flashed before her mind: a dark street,—the street just in front of the office—it was late and the crowd of clerks and workers was pouring out of the doorway, hurrying homeward with gravity in their hearts and the news on their lips that Chandler B. Corey, the president of the company, had that day dropped dead at his desk. And among these sobered men and women walked herself, shocked and shaken, trying to realize that the best friend she had in the world was gone, and would never be at hand again to advise her nor be interested in what befell her. As she stepped into the street a man in a slouch hat confronted her, demanding to know if she was Mrs. Martin Devlin, thrust a folded paper at her, and disappeared. She remembered drawing back, frightened and affronted, and after the man had made off, rescuing the paper from the sidewalk at her feet where it had fallen. It was dark in the street,—too dark to read. She recalled holding the paper up to decipher what was printed on the first page, and then, indifferent, her heart and mind heavy with the tragedy of the day, had thrust it into her muff and sorrowfully made her way homeward. Days later, when she re-

membered the incident and searched her muff, the
paper had disappeared. It had fallen out; it was gone;
and she dismissed the matter from her mind.

Now she realized the folded paper had been the
summons bidding her come to court to defend herself
against calumny, and to show reason why Martin Devlin should not be free to take unto himself another
wife!

Suddenly something very precious died within her
dismally. The excitement of the night dwindled and
departed; the piquancy of her adventure drooped and
faded; her interest in a situation that had up to that
minute stirred pulse and imagination, shrivelled and
evaporated. She was weary and bored; she felt disgusted and sick; she wanted to be quit of the whole
affair, of smiling, alert, complacent Ruthie, of the
homely, clumsy children, of this sleek, fat, selfish man
beside her! . . . Ah, she had been a fool ever to think
. . . ever to imagine . . . A woman of her position,
sensible, capable, independent,—stout, settled, middle-
aged and gray! . . . Oh, it was detestable,—it was
humiliating,—*insufferable!*

They were at the hotel.

"You don't want to let what I told you bother you,
Jan. I never stopped to think how you'd feel about
it. And you want to remember that those things never
get out; they're all kept strictly Q.T. It happened six
or seven years ago and there isn't a soul—Here, I'm
coming in with you."

"You needn't bother, Martin."

"That's all right. I'll see you inside."

They moved through the revolving glass doors and
mounted the steps into the brilliant lobby.

"Well, it's been great to see you, and I surely have enjoyed talking over old times. By God, it's been a great evening."

"Yes, indeed. It's been very amusing."

"I'm awfully glad you looked me up. . . . And say, Jan, you like Ruthie, don't you? Don't you think she's a nice little woman? Not your style exactly,—no side, or anything like that,—but she's a damned agreeable little person, hey? . . . You're not sore at me now, are you, for that rotten trick I played on you? I'd never have done it if it had been up to me. It was the lawyers, you know. They dug up the story and put it over. I'd never have done it,—I swear to God, Jan, I wouldn't! I'm—I'm sorry as the devil, now; by God, I am!"

"Let's not talk about it, Martin; it's all past and forgotten."

"Well, that's damned white of you, Jan,—damned white! I always said you were a sensible woman."

Jeannette turned and held out her hand.

"Aw, say," Martin protested, "aren't you going in to the café with me and have some ginger ale or something? I hate to say good-night so soon. There's a lot of things I want to ask you. I'd like to keep this evening going forever."

But Jeannette's one desire was to end it. She wanted her room, to have the door shut and locked behind her, to be alone.

"I'm sorry, Martin——"

"Just a small glass of ginger ale?" he pleaded.

"Thank you, no, Martin; I think I'd better go up."

"Well, am I not to see you again? You're not going until Sunday, are you?"

"I shall be busy to-morrow; I'm engaged all day."

"How about to-morrow night?"

"I'm not free then either."

A frown settled on the man's face.

"Damn it . . ." he began disgustedly. She continued to smile pleasantly but offered no suggestion.

"Well, I'll see you in New York some time soon," he asserted finally; "I have to go up there once in awhile."

"Yes, do that," Jeannette said without enthusiasm.

"I'll 'phone you? I'll give you a ring at the office."

"Yes, do that," she repeated.

"Well, then, I guess I'd better say good-night."

"Good-night, Martin."

She turned toward the elevators, giving him a nod and a brief smile over her shoulder. As the gate of the cage slid shut, she caught another glimpse of him, standing where she had left him, perplexed, frowning, disconsolate,—staring after her.

§ 6

The train was crowded. Jeannette had chosen one at midday, thinking to have her lunch in the dining-car and so beguile away part of the tedium of the trip. It was Saturday; she had decided to return home at once rather than wait until Sunday; there was nothing to hold her in Philadelphia and she was anxious to get back to the little apartment in Waverly Place. Many other travellers had apparently conceived the same idea of having the noon meal on the way, and Jeannette discovered there were no seats left in the chair-car, so she was obliged to share one in a day coach with a short, plump lady with a prominent bust and short fat arms who sat up very straight beside her and wheezed audibly at every breath. Jeannette's heavy suit-case was stowed in front of her, and pressed uncomfortably against her knees, while there was no place for her hat-box except in the aisle where it was stumbled over and cursed by every passing passenger. There were cinders embedded in the plush covering of the seat, the car was badly ventilated and smelled of warm, crowded humanity. At Trenton, feeling dirty and dishevelled, she made a swaying progress toward the dining-car only to find twenty people ahead of her. Disheartened, she returned to her seat, concluding to wait until she reached the city before she lunched. Perhaps she would go directly home and persuade Beatrice to make her some tea and toast.

The day was leaden, the country forlorn and dreary; the trees stood bare and black upon bare and blackened ground; the houses seemed cold, desolate and grimy. It began to rain as the train slowed down through smoky Newark, and long diagonal streaks of water slashed the dirty window-panes. Waiting travellers on platforms huddled under station sheds or bent their heads and umbrellas against the sharp wind and driving drops as they struggled toward the cars. The train grew steadily more crowded; people stood in the aisles, swayed and were pitched against those in the seats. Jeannette's head began to ache dully and at every knock or kick her offending hat-box received she winced as though struck. In the tube beneath the Hudson River, the train came to a standstill and there was a long wait; women grew nervous, and

a man said in a loud, laughing voice to a neighbor:
"Say, Bill, it'd be some pickings, all right, if the
river came in on us while we were stuck here."

"Oh, Jesus Mary!" gasped the woman next to Jeannette, and for some minutes the wheeze of her breathing rose to a higher key.

Finally, with much whirring, jerking and dancing of
lights, the train rolled into the Pennsylvania Station.

"I'll go home and get into bed, and Beatrice will
bring me some tea and toast," Jeannette whispered to
herself, cramped and weary, fighting the pain in her
head that grew steadily worse. She stumbled into a
taxicab and went bumping and racketing down Seventh
Avenue. The rain was now coming down in a forest
of lances, and was driven in through the three-inch
opening at the top of one of the windows. Jeannette
tried to close it; her attempt was pitiful. The taxi
skidded violently into Eighth Street and she was
thrown to her knees, her hat jammed against the opposite side of the car.

"That's all right, lady; nothin' happened!" yelled
the driver.

"In five minutes!" breathed Jeannette, one hand
pressed hard against her breast.

Ah, here she was! Here she was, at last!

Her fingers shook as she fumbled with the key to the
street door.

"Thank you, so much," she said to the taxi-driver
who brought her bags up to the landing. She handed
him his fare. "Keep the change; I can manage the
rest."

Inside, she grasped her luggage with either hand,
and resolutely mounted the two long flights of stairs,

forcing herself to go to the top without pausing. She was panting, then, her head splitting.

She tried the apartment door; it was locked.

"Beatrice! Beatrice!" she called, rapping impatiently upon the panels.

A faint mewing came to her ears. There was no other answer.

"Oh, God,—she's out!" Her cry was almost a sob. Of course! it was still the Thanksgiving vacation; Beatrice would be with her cousins in Plainfield; she wouldn't be home until Sunday night!

Jeannette fumbled for her door-key. There was little light and she was obliged to kneel before she could find the hole in the lock. With a gasp she finally threw open the door and stumbled into the flat. It was cold, unaired, deserted. Mitzi, tail on end, welcomed her with shrill, complaining cries.

"Oh, you baby you," Jeannette said aloud, blinking through her own distress and eyeing the cat. "You've been shut up in here since the day before yesterday and you're just about starving."

Mitzi confirmed this with a wail. Jeannette scooped the animal up with a long arm and carried her into the kitchen. It was cold and bleak in here, too, smelling foully of Mitzi's incarceration.

A groan was wrung from Jeannette's lips.

In the ice-box she found only a bowl half full of pickled beets, a plate of butter, two rather shrivelled bananas, and a few pieces of dried toast. She clapped the kettle on the stove, lighted the gas, and stood caressing the cat until the water had warmed; then she moistened the toast and set it in a soup plate on the floor.

"Here, you poor critter, eat that until I get you something decent." Mitzi leaped at the meal, jerking the food into her mouth, growling gluttonously.

Jeannette put her fingers to her head and watched the performance, breathing hard.

"I must," she said aloud. "It won't kill me."

She went into her own room, laid aside her fur coat, put on an old mackintosh and felt hat, once more went out into the rain, and presently dragged herself up the stairs again with a bottle of milk and a bag of provisions.

Her temples throbbing and little streaks of pain darting through her eyeballs, she moved resolutely through the next few minutes. While the kettle was heating, she got herself into her kimona, and braided her hair. Then she returned to the kitchen, mixed a large bowl of bread and milk for the cat, and dutifully made herself tea which she drank, munching between sips some saltine crackers warmed in the oven.

Peace gradually descended upon her. Mitzi, replete and satisfied, licked milk-stained whiskers, and eyed her comfortably from the floor. The pain in Jeannette's head was less violent, but she was very cold.

"I'll get a hot-water bottle and go to bed," she said. "I think I'll go crazy if I keep on this way."

She proceeded to her room, made her bed, then commenced to unpack her bags and put away her things. When she was about finished, she came upon the fur coat where she had left it on a chair. She picked it up and stared at it, observing its brilliant silk lining, its smooth, plushy surface, the soft texture of its fur collar. Suddenly she flung it from her into a far corner on the floor, and for a moment stood a tragic figure with clenched hands, flashing eyes and heaving breast.

There was a diversion,—a sound close at hand that startled her. Mitzi had jumped on the bed, and was gazing up at her with head twisted to one side, glassy eyes fixed inquiringly upon her face, long tail alert, the tip waving gently. The cat opened her mouth and mewed plaintively. Jeannette relaxed, gathered the animal into her arms, and slowly sank down upon the bed. Mitzi, nestling comfortably against her, began to purr rhythmically. A slow trembling came to the woman, and her fingers shook as they stroked Mitzi's back. She fought desperately to check the gathering tempest within her, and for a moment struggled with firm pressed lips and shut teeth, as the tears welled up into her eyes, rolled down her cheeks, and splashed upon her hand. Then suddenly the floodgates of her heart burst, grief overwhelmed her, and she sank sideways on the bed, carrying the cat to her neck, cuddling and stroking it, while burying her face against the soft fur, and passionately sobbing:

"Oh, Mitzi—Mitzi! I love you so—I love you so!"

THE END